Teaching and Reading *New Adult* Literature in High School and College

An introduction to the rapidly growing category of New Adult (NA) literature, this text provides a roadmap to understanding and introducing NA
books to young people in high school, college, libraries, and other settings.
As a window into the experiences and unique challenges that young and new
adults encounter, New Adult literature intersects with but is distinct from
Young Adult literature.

This rich resource provides a framework, methods, and plentiful reading
recommendations by genre, theme, and discipline on New Adult literature. Starting with a definition of New Adult literature, Kane demonstrates
how the inclusion of NA literature helps support and encourage a love
of reading. Chapters address important topics that are relevant to young
people, including post-high school life, early careers, relationships, activism,
and social change. Each chapter features text sets, instructional strategies,
writing prompts, and activities to invite and encourage young people to be
reflective and engaged in responding to thought-provoking texts. A welcome
text for professors of literacy and literature instruction, first-year college
instructors, researchers, librarians, and educators, this book provides new
ways to assist students as they embark upon the next stage of their lives and
is essential reading for courses on teaching literature.

Sharon Kane is Professor of Education at the State University of New York
at Oswego, USA.

Teaching and Reading *New Adult* Literature in High School and College

SHARON KANE

Routledge
Taylor & Francis Group

NEW YORK AND LONDON

I dedicate this book to my sons, Patrick and Christopher.

Contents

New Adult Literature: Coming of Age, Again and Again

1

Introduction and Definition(s)

What's in a name? What's in a label? Both names and labels can identify, describe, define, expand, clarify, limit, help, and hurt. It's appropriate that this book starts with an examination of the term *New Adult literature*. Where did it come from? Is it necessary? Is everyone thrilled with it?

New Adult (NA) literature is a recently emerged category that intersects with and branches off from Young Adult (YA) literature. It is aimed at an audience ranging roughly from ages 17 to 26. That represents a time in life when people encounter a multitude of changes and complex landscapes involving varying levels of independence and interdependence. NA literature reflects those first steps—and next steps—in terms of education, relationships, civic responsibility, spirituality, political activity, jobs, and other arenas. It is concerned with issues of identity in its many facets.

"I am independent." When, and under what conditions or circumstances, can we say that? Of course, we realize there are stages toward independence, as well as markers. The kindergartener hopping onto the school bus has made it in a way her toddler brother has not. There are graduation ceremonies celebrating the completion of preschool, elementary school, middle school, high school, college, and beyond. Each is a commencement, representing the beginning of something new as well as the end of what has been. These transitions involve mixed feelings. We might feel comfortable and content in a setting, and may have worked hard to get to that point, and then they tell us it's time to move on, venture into new territory.

DOI: 10.4324/9781003221685-1

That is what NA literature is all about—navigating new territory and becoming somewhat new in the process. It can be seen as a second step in the coming-of-age process. Author David Yoon explains, "Here's the thing about coming-of-age stories: they are not just for young adults. They are not just about young adults, either. We are always becoming.... Each age is a bridge crossing this Rubicon or that" (2019).

We have always struggled when it comes to labeling literature, and rightfully so. A few decades ago, YA literature was not recognized as a category. After authors including Judy Blume, Robert Cormier, Madeleine L'Engle, Robert Lipsyte, Paul Zindel, and S.E. Hinton gave teens books written for—and featuring—them, librarians and publishing companies recognized it as distinct, though overlapping at both ends. These books did not fit what was normally thought of as children's literature; that much was for sure. But what to call it? In the eighties and nineties, there were discussions about whether to refer to the new category as adolescent literature or YA literature. Even today, I can go to branch libraries within my county public library system and find sections labeled "Young Adult" or "Teen." And the boundaries in terms of the age range keep stretching. In 2013, Michael Cart pondered, "Traditionally the term young adult has referred to those ages 12–18, but given the burgeoning "adultescent" phenomenon, it may now be time to extend that age group" (p. 5). Noting the "second decade of adolescence," he describes twenty-somethings who "...continue to be heavily invested in teen popular culture...Like Peter Pan, they simply won't grow up" (p. 5). Cart published the helpful resource *Michael Cart's 200 Adult Books for Teens* in 2013. He interviewed publishers to get their view on the phenomenon of NA literature, finding that some consider NA to be only a subset of romance, or to be escapist. But he notes that "crossover" books have been with us for a long time, citing YALSA's Alex Awards, given annually to ten books published in the adult marketing world that have appeal for teens (Cart, 2016).

When we try to define literature categories by determining what age groups they appeal to, we can run into difficulty. I converse with three women in their eighties whose favorite genre is YA fiction. Teachers and parents see evidence of students in middle grades "reading up," preferring to interact with characters who are older than they are, and in places they have yet to go. I'll be talking about books that were published for children and explaining why they are also appropriate for much older readers, and I'll be showing how we can use books marketed for adults in ways that make them relevant for readers we might not yet see as fully adult.

When we try to categorize books by the age of the main characters, we again find ourselves in a messy situation. Marcus Zusak's *The Book Thief* (2005) features Liesel, who is around ten, but the book is not intended for 10-year-olds; the story is narrated by Death, and the events occur in 1939 Nazi Germany. The title characters of *Leonard and Hungry Paul*, by Rónán Hession (2020), are in their thirties, but have not yet checked off the milestones we usually associate with adulthood, such as moving out of their childhood homes to live independently. Stellar books are ones that we can read at various points in our lives, experiencing them differently each time.

Is New Adult Literature Actually New?

In one sense, I'd say no to the above question. I think back to my own reading as a young person. Series especially helped to show how characters grow up. I loved L.M. Montgomery's *Anne of Green Gables* (2008), and went on to read all the sequels, following Anne into her teaching years. The same happened with Louisa May Alcott's *Little Women* books. Jo is fully adult in *Jo's Boys* (1994). And think of the classics that bring characters from childhood to adulthood: *Great Expectations* (Dickens, 2009), *A Tree Grows in Brooklyn* (Smith, 1998), *Tess of the D'Urbervilles* (Hardy, 2003). James Joyce's autobiographical novel *Portrait of the Artist as a Young Man* (1996) seems to have all the characteristics of today's NA literature.

What *is* relatively new is the label itself. It began with a contest promoted by St. Martin's Press in 2009. Also, publishers have increasingly been printing books that were originally self-published. The popularity of books featuring characters between 17 and mid-20s has increased. Some people are actually against the label, calling it a marketing ploy, and a totally unnecessary classification; some prefer the term "crossover books." Others use NA as a descriptor, but only in terms of fiction. Some think only of romance, but nothing says we *have* to use these limited, and limiting, boundaries. Cart (2016) quotes Francesca Lia Block, author of the Weetzie Bat series, as foreshadowing the NA phenomenon:

> "I feel I've been writing New Adult for twenty-five years .... I'm very interested in the years between adolescence and full adulthood as this time marks an important threshold in human development.... For me it's more a case of naming a category that already exists in my oeuvre and my heart."
>
> (p. 145)

I believe we are at an exciting time when we can help shape what NA literature becomes; we can help construct the construct. Just as YA literature went through growing pains on its way to becoming a recognized, valued category, NA literature is on the verge of becoming independent, similar to the point at which NA characters, and NA readers, find themselves. I teach a course called "New Adult Literature" for incoming college students, and they are perfectly comfortable with the designation of literature meant for them. *New Adult* is a construct, which I will use as loosely and fluidly as possible, for the benefit of readers. It can encompass virtually all genres, including realistic fiction, historical fiction, science fiction, biography, memoir, and poetry.

What about the *quality* of NA literature? I don't worry about that. There is no category where all the literature is excellent, or all the books are trashy. There will always be beach reads and books that qualify for the medals given for literary quality. And what one person considers fluff, another might find life changing. So much depends on the reader. Depending on our purposes, we can concentrate on guiding our students to the beautiful writing and the insightful stories. We can teach students to be discerning, to critique and evaluate books, and to read with a critical perspective. We can discuss books with them, offering our own responses, comparisons, and applications.

Gender Issues

At first glance, it may seem that NA literature is directed primarily at female readers. Some have compared it to advanced *chick-lit*. So, our job will be to bring some balance, to seek out and promote books that appeal to readers regardless of gender, and to include in our libraries books that might even be seen as generally appealing more to men than women. This has always been a tricky subject. When I ask my college students whether there is such a thing as "boys' books" and "girls' books," they think the right answer is no, of course not. Books should be gender-neutral. Some young women will mention loving *Batman* comics, or *Hatchet* (Paulsen, 1987), or *Lord of the Flies* (Golding, 1954). A male might confess to sneaking his sister's books out of her room and secretly reading them for enjoyment and for help in understanding how girls think, what girls want; or maybe reading the Twilight series by Stephenie Meyer because…well, just because. Yet we don't have to go further than looking at book covers to realize that, at least in the eyes of marketers, there is indeed a perceived difference between what male and female readers prefer.

I explain to my students that we need to do many things simultan-eously, as well as over time. We need to help readers see that they can enjoy books with main characters who are not the same sex they are, or who iden-tify as transgender or nonbinary. We needn't apologize when assigning Tim O'Brien's *The Things They Carried* (1990), Walter Dean Myers' *Sunrise over Fallujah* (2009), or Rainbow Rowell's *Fangirl* (2013) for whole-class reading. We can supply excellent books about sports, or war, or romance, with male, female, and gender-neutral or gender-queer characters. There are legal thrillers, detective mysteries, and fantasies starring men, women, and nonbinary heroes. You will find book talks for novels and memoirs that will contextualize and investigate gender identity. We can also respect readers' preferences; if someone wants to tarry for a while in the light romance department, or on battlefields, or among fictional urban gangs, we can trust that they will not remain there forever; or they may analyze, review, and critique the handling of the topics in sophisticated ways, whether the focus is on gender or other aspects of the texts.

Coming-of-Age: In Stages, More than Once

When do people stop identifying themselves as children and start saying they are adults? And when are they perceived as adults by others? It depends. In a 2007 commencement speech at Stuyvesant High School, Conan O'Brien told the graduates:

> At this point many of you have ideas of what you want to do with your lives, but for many of you those ideas will change. And that's because you think you know who you are right now, but you don't. Trust me. When I look back at eighteen-year-old Conan, it's a ridicu-lous sight. …But life and the choices I've made have changed me in a thousand ways. And none of it would have happened if I had rigidly 'kept my eye on the prize' or decided, with great determination, to "follow my dream." I didn't have the slightest idea what my dream was when I was eighteen. It had to find me.
>
> (pp. 303–304)

In *Dreams from my Father*, Barack Obama (2021) says that, even after college, "I was operating mainly on impulse, like a salmon swimming blindly upstream" (p. 122).

Similarly, in fictional literature, some characters at 18 think they know who they are, but find out through the course of events that there are some surprises left. Others recognize that they are still lost, though they might be trying to hide that from others, acting confident. And some recognize later that they were not where they had thought they were in terms of identity.

In *The Paradox of Vertical Flight*, by Emil Ostrovski (2014) (who was a New Adult himself at the time he wrote the novel), Jack is an 18-year-old philosopher who is on a strange road trip with his newborn son, the baby's mother, and his best friend. He hears Jess refer to Tommy as a man in uniform. He reflects:

> It's strange to hear Jess call Tommy a man…Of all the times I've called Tommy "man," I've never really meant it, never really thought of him as one. We've always been boys. Boys will be boys will be boys…When do you stop thinking of your best friend as a boy? Of yourself as a boy?"
>
> (p. 119)

In *The Rosie Project*, by Graeme Simsion (2013), Don is turning 40 and is attempting to "re-form" himself. He reflects, "At eighteen, just before I left home to go to university, statistically approaching a quarter of my life…I had very little understanding of who I was. It had taken me until tonight, approximately halfway, to see myself reasonably clearly" (p. 276).

Ryan Dean West is a character in Andrew Smith's *Winger* (2013) who has thought a lot about chronological age. Because he is academically gifted, he has skipped a couple of grades, making him two years younger than his classmates. During his junior year, when he is asked by the girl he loves to share a wish, here's how he responds:

> I drew two overlapping circles: A Venn diagram…. I put my finger in one of the circles. "These are all the boys here at Pine Mountain. We're all almost totally the same. We dress the same, we all pretty much like the same stuff, we all play sports, and every one of us thinks you, Annie Altman, are totally hot" …. I put my finger in the narrow crescent of the other circle, the outside part. "And here's Ryan Dean West. Well, at least it's the one tiny part of Ryan Dean West that makes him stand out as being so different, the only thing that everyone notices about him. The number fourteen. And you think that makes me so different, like I'm a little kid. But the thing is, everyone has that little part that's outside the overlap of everyone else. And a lot of people zero in on that one little thing they can't

get over. Like for Joey, 'cause he's gay, I guess. Some people are better than others about not getting that outside-the-overlap part so noticed, but not me. So that's my wish."

(pp. 132–133)

One thing is certain: chronological age is not the only way, and not even the best way, to determine adulthood. I'll mention many books throughout the chapters where a young person has to take on adult responsibilities, sometimes because of circumstances taking away the responsible adults, sometimes because the teens are more mature, healthy, or moral than the adults with whom they are interacting. Yet, readers will recognize that some characters, such as 29-year-old Eleanor in *Eleanor Oliphant Is Completely Fine* (Honeyman, 2017), seem to behave in ways that seem less mature than what we might consider typical for their chronological age.

Introducing Myself and Recognizing my Readers

I am a teacher, and for the past three decades I've been especially interested in YA literature. I've watched it come of age, and I've watched students and family members as they've experienced YA literature as teenagers and beyond. I laughed when Krisi, who as an undergraduate and graduate student had taken four courses with me, told me after an interview for a high school teaching position that the principal had asked her what she read other than YA literature, and she had responded, "Why would I need to read anything else?"

So, it's obvious that I am not in the target range for NA literature. The authors are not writing primarily for me. That's OK. I find my own way in. Sometimes, I read paying close attention to the parents and other adults in the stories. And luckily, I have always had young people in my life; if there comes a time when this is not true, I will at least have the pleasure of meeting new young people as new books get published. I'm reminded of a sentence in *The Storied Life of A.J. Fikry*, by Gabrielle Zevin (2014). Referring to a character who had grown up in a bookstore, raised by the store's owner, the text tells us, "It had not been a lonely childhood, though many of her intimates had been somewhat less than real" (p. 216).

I realize that I can't assume that you, my readers, will neatly fit any category; nor will you all be reading this text for the same purposes. Some of you will be in the target audience for NA literature, hence having a lot of credibility. Some of you will be reading this for a college course. Certain parts will pertain more than others. Some of you will be librarians, parents, teachers, and you will be bringing yourselves to the text—looking for ways to engage high school and college students, those in your care or realm of your job description. I am talking to all of you. Feel free to skip the parts that don't apply to you right now. Keep an open mind. It's not going to hurt to read a teaching/responding strategy or assignment. You might enjoy thinking about it, imagining your answers—or you could surprise yourself by ending up completing one of them!

You might be an aspiring teacher or librarian, or a veteran educator, or a parent of teens, or a New Adult yourself. Whatever descriptions fit, I invite and encourage you to use this book in the way that works best for you. Sometimes I will be talking directly to you, and other times it will seem like what I'm talking about is more for one of the audiences of which you are not a member. When you become aware of that, try to figure out what the best course of action is—skip that part? Maybe. Put yourself temporarily in the shoes of another type of reader, perhaps a friend or family member? Possibly. Put the book down and run to the nearest library to look for the NA titles that appeal to you? Try things out, and do what works for you.

Rationale for Reading and Teaching with New Adult Literature

Reasons for exploring NA literature could be divided into two large, overlapping categories. The first is that reading is an absolutely wonderful way to spend one's time, and offers a myriad of personal benefits, including pleasure. We almost wouldn't need to go beyond that. Kelly Gallagher and Penny Kittle, both high school teachers as well as writers, state, "We believe in the value of reading and writing for their own sake, and we know there is a wide range of novels that will create an urgency to read" (2018, p. 11). Whole books have been written about the wonder of reading literature, showing how it can be good for the body, mind, and soul. Francine Prose introduces her book *What to Read and Why* (2018) this way:

> A book is a kind of refuge to which we can go for the assurance that, as long as we are reading, we can leave the cares and worries of our everyday lives behind us and enter, however briefly, another reality, populated by other lives, a world distant in time and place from our

own, or else reflective of the present moment in ways that may help us see that moment more clearly.

(p. xiii)

A second major reason for including the teaching of NA literature in high school and college courses is that wide and deep reading of relevant literature can lead to increased skill, knowledge, and academic achievement, and those are goals instructors work toward (e.g., Torppa et al., 2019). A 2019 Position Statement on Independent Reading by the National Council of Teachers of English notes the numerous and varied purposes reading serves. "Reading promotes knowledge acquisition and vicarious journeys, encouraging exploration of multiple experiences, plot lines, points of view, and interpretations that enhance the knowledge bases of readers, tying together meaning through their personal and cultural lenses" (unpaged).

There have also been recent calls for increased attention to reading at the college level. The Conference on College Composition and Communication (CCCC) issued a Position Statement in 2021 that:

> …affirms the need to develop accessible and effective reading pedagogies in college writing classrooms so that students can engage more deeply in all of their courses and develop the reading abilities that will be essential to their success in college, in their careers, and for their participation in a democratic society. This statement assumes that, like instruction in writing, instruction in reading is most ethical and effective when it engages students' diverse experiences, needs, and capacities and when it works from an asset-based (rather than a deficit-based) theory of learning.
>
> (2021, unpaged)

Introducing college students to NA literature and working with it in ways that recognize an asset-based foundation; and matching books with students in a way that respects their diverse experiences, capacities, and interests can not only increase their stamina, which they will need as they encounter the heavy reading load that comes with courses in every discipline, but also instill confidence and build background knowledge.

Wilner in *Rethinking Reading in College: A Cross-Curricular Approach* (2020) offers substantial evidence that few college instructors actually teach students the reading skills needed to understand and work with the discipline-specific texts they assign. She asks us to challenge the assumption that college students arrive prepared to read college-level texts, and explains four ways of reading: rhetorical, meta, disciplinary, and critical; these are essential for students to understand and become adept at. She asks, "How then, might college instructors address the needs of students throughout the four years by cultivating, in their design of assignments, the habits of mind that foster rhetorical reading not just in English classes but in all disciplines?" (p. 17). In each chapter, I show strategies, prompts, and activities using NA literature that foster the ways of reading Wilner recommends, ways that invite and encourage readers to be active, self-aware, and responsive as they grapple with thought-provoking texts that are relevant to them as well as to various subject areas.

Many colleges invest heavily in programs whose purpose is to help first-year students succeed academically, emotionally, and socially. Beth Black, an undergraduate engagement librarian at the Ohio State University, reminds us that students do not stop needing support after their freshman year. Calling the following year of higher education the most overlooked year, she notes, "Typical second-year students experience transitions academically, in relationships, and in personal identity" (p. 5). She goes on to explain why second-year programs involving librarians and faculty matter. For our purposes, we can recognize that college sophomores are New Adults, and so could benefit from relevant literature meant especially for them.

Civic, College, and Career Readiness: Where and How Does NA Literature Fit in?

There has been great concern about the number of students entering two-year and four-year colleges who do not have the skills and knowledge to succeed. Colleges have offered an increasing number of remedial or preparatory courses, often noncredit bearing, to narrow the gap between what students are able to do and what they need to do to be successful in courses that will count toward their majors and graduation from college. There have been and continue to be many initiatives to remedy this situation. A central purpose of this book is to show how NA literature can be used to increase and enhance readiness for prospective, incoming, and current college students, including underserved or underrepresented populations. Readiness will be addressed in its broadest sense, consisting of both academic skills and aspects such as maturity, responsibility, self-discipline, creativity, emotional development, and ability to empathize with and work with others.

Much research has demonstrated the value of student engagement and wide, voluminous reading in terms of raising achievement levels in literacy (e.g., Ivey, 2014). I hope this book will spur students to read many works of fiction and nonfiction within the category of NA literature. They could participate in classroom or online book discussion groups. As they write reactions and respond to those of others, they will think deeply; evaluate and generate ideas; read critically; and write clearly and persuasively in ways that are authentic, relevant, engaging, cross-disciplinary, and lasting. The book will provide prompts that will encourage and stimulate a high level of thinking.

A key to engagement and achievement is providing students with relevant texts they will be interested in. My scholarly work and my teaching have been deeply influenced by the work of Rosalie Fink. She interviewed twelve adults who were highly successful in their work, including a physicist, a biochemist, and a company CEO. All of them had dyslexia and had had significant problems with reading throughout their school years. While she expected to find that they had avoided reading and discovered ways to bypass it or compensate with other strategies for learning, she found the opposite. "To my surprise, I found that these dyslexics were avid readers...they rarely circumvented reading. On the contrary, they sought out books" (Fink, 1995/1996, p. 272). The pattern Fink discovered was that all of her subjects had been passionate in some personal interest. The areas of interest included religion, math, business, science, history, and biography. What mattered was that they read voraciously to find out more.

My own experience with students has confirmed what I learned from this study and Fink's subsequent research. One of the most unusual places I have witnessed the joy of reading was in a high school in-school suspension room. Our School of Education has a Professional Development School partnership with the school, and I was the PDS liaison, so I stopped in the room frequently to talk with the students and with Mr. S., who was in charge. One of his nonnegotiable rules was that every student had to be doing schoolwork or reading for pleasure, and his room was filled with YA literature. Every time I walked in, there were different books on display, and new books that had arrived from various sources were piling up. Mr. S. read, too, and was able to get the right books in the hands of the students because he listened to them to discover their interests. (Librarians refer to this as Readers' Advisory.) One day he introduced me to a student, telling me that Carmen had deliberately left her gym clothes home so that she would have to spend the class period in the in-school suspension room, where she could finish her novel.

Krashen (2013) shows that discussion of good books and reading itself will lead to more reading, which will lead to achievement. We don't have to wait for policies to change in order to have classrooms and libraries where students want to be to talk about books and figure out what they can read next.

Muhammad (2020) promotes a way of teaching based on the roots of literacy learning in Black communities of the nineteenth century. She offers a layered equity framework that includes the goals relating to the development of identity, skills, and intellect, as well as criticality, which is "… the capacity to read, write, and think in ways of understanding power, privilege, social justice, and oppression… (p. 120). She believes that teaching criticality "…humanizes instruction and makes it more compassionate" (p. 117).

I have kept in mind the four tenets of Muhammad's approach for cultivating the genius that is present in students and teachers as I selected NA titles and found or created the strategies and prompts that accompany them. You will find much attention to aspects of identity; you'll see fictional characters who strive to become better in terms of intellect, knowledge, and skills that will help them be the healthy, productive, and happy adults they strive to become. There are also nonfiction texts dealing with these same issues. Criticality will be perhaps most evident in Chapter 6 on activism, but is really everywhere, infused in chapters about preparing for and going to college; career exploration and choices; and relationships. I want avid readers of NA literature who recognize the genius in themselves and others.

So now, I offer my recommendation of numerous NA titles that have the capacity to intrigue readers in their late teens and their twenties. This literature can serve as a means to both pleasure reading and to the acquisition of skills that will serve readers well as they prepare for and enter the worlds of college, career, and civic engagement. At the same time, it can address issues related to relationships and the social and emotional challenges that go hand in hand with these responsibilities connected with new responsibilities.

Organization of this Book

In each of the middle chapters, I will include the following sections:

- Some information and discussion of issues relating to the chapter's topics;
- Sample text sets (explained below);
- Numerous book talks that teachers and librarians can use or adapt as they recommend books to high school or college students;
- Instructional strategies or activities for teaching with NA books; and
- "Thinking and Writing Prompts" for responding to and working with NA books. Some prompts will come at the end of particular book talks, while others that call for thoughts about multiple books and ask readers to combine literary exploration with their own experiences will come later in the chapter.

The final chapter includes a sample syllabus for a course on NA Literature based on a course I taught to college freshmen.

TEXT SETS

Each chapter of this book will have one or more text sets, grouping some NA literature together by theme, concept, or purpose. A curated text set can consist of books combined with articles, websites, blogs, art, songs, films, artifacts, podcasts, maps, and other genres and formats. Because this book focuses on literature, the text sets I offer will consist of books fitting our NA category. It should not be difficult for you, perhaps with the help of students, to search for related, current texts that can extend what is here to make it more multimodal. Ways of formatting text sets vary, according to curricular needs and students' interests. A core text could be in the center, with options supplementing it; or an essential question could be the focal point, with all the texts helping readers to grapple with complex problems and formulate their own opinions. I will present some text sets in narrative form, while simply listing related titles at other times, indicating with an asterisk those for which I have written book talks.

There are great benefits of using a range of texts on a particular topic that represent a variety of stances, helping students to realize the complexity of issues and the variety of ways situations can play out and individuals and groups can deal with them. Cappiello and Dawes (2021) explain that text sets can both build prior knowledge and enhance comprehension. "It's an approach to student-centered teaching that allows you to cover what you need to cover while engaging students in perspective-taking and sense making" (p. 6). Students learn to think critically when they compare, contrast, and synthesize information and perspectives over a range of connected texts. Here are three sample text sets.

Characters Facing Mortality

Our first text set will be devoted to the topic of death at an early age, which denies people the ability to even *have* the experience of "New Adulthood" as defined by the literary category we will be pursuing. I wish there was not such a category in life for literature to reflect, but many writers have dealt with the topic, and many readers have benefited.

I'll begin with *Ways to Live Forever*, by Sally Nicholls (2008). We learn on the first page that our 11-year-old narrator Sam is dying of leukemia. Why am I including this in a book about NA literature? Because I say that if an *author* is in the target NA age range, the book can count. Sally Nicholls wrote this debut novel when she was 25. I find that inspirational, and I believe many college-aged aspiring writers will, too. In case you don't buy that rationale, I also think that Sam, probably largely because he has been forced to think about his impending journey to eternity, shows more maturity in some ways than most people leaving their teen years and entering that nebulous stage, "adulthood." And speaking of adults, you can read this book paying close attention to Sam's parents and teachers. I use the character of Sam's father in my classes when I talk about the concept of character development. He goes through intense grieving as he watches his son's health failing, finding that he is powerless to protect his child. His behavior changes drastically over the course of the book's action.

There are several examples of high-quality NA literature with characters who are facing the reality that their lives will not extend beyond their teens. Readers can compare the ways these young people deal with their illnesses and relate to family and friends; decide what values are the most important; and ultimately define themselves by their decisions, words, and actions. In Wendy Wunder's *The Probability of Miracles* (2011), Cam understands that her prognosis is dim and that Harvard (to which she has been accepted) is not in her future; but she goes along with her mother's plan to leave their Florida home and their jobs at Disney World to go to Promise, Maine, a town that offers the hope of a miracle cure. She does find things there, including love.

D.Q., in Francisco X. Stork's *The Last Summer of the Death Warriors* (2010), is angry because of the brain cancer that is stealing his life, as well as angry at his mother, who is forcing him to have more treatment that he knows is futile. But he is a philosopher, and puts his energies into creating a manifesto that defines the rules for living with purpose. He offers Pancho, the revenge-filled 17-year-old who accompanies him to Albuquerque for the treatment, some new values to consider; perhaps more importantly, he offers friendship.

In *The Fault in Our Stars*, by John Green (2012), we meet two teens dealing with cancer. They meet in a support group. How exactly do they support each other? There are several answers. They exchange favorite books. They take a trip. They fall in love. They face questions together about the meaning of life, especially about life that gets taken away seemingly before they can accomplish anything worthwhile. They choose to live life fully and exuberantly. Readers will also want to check out the nonfiction book *This Star Won't Go Out: The Life and Words of Esther Grace Earl* (Earl, 2014). John Green wrote the foreword, telling of how knowing Esther inspired his novel.

Deadline, by Chris Crutcher (2009), is, unlike the previous three novels, a story that does NOT involve a road trip. Faced with a diagnosis that gives him a year to live, senior Ben Wolf chooses to tell no one, and to take risks to ensure that he packs as much life as he can into the time he has. He can't solve the problems of the world, but he can tackle some issues within his community. He takes a stand and pushes to have a street in his Idaho town (filled with white residents) named after Malcolm X. Can a dying kid really accomplish that? Maybe it depends on whether that kid is Ben Wolf.

In Julie Murphy's *Side Effects May Vary* (2014), Alice is diagnosed with leukemia, and given the impossibly tough prognosis of having only about three months to live. She creates a "Just Dying to Do" list. After she carries out some of her wishes that are harmful to others, figuring she won't be around to have to deal with the consequences, she encounters new challenges when she goes into remission.

Lenni is a 17-year-old with a terminal illness. She finds a way to add another eighty-three years of experience to her life. You can read a book talk for *The One Hundred Years of Lenni and Margo*, by Marianne Cronin (2021), later in this chapter.

Adulting

Ponder these two quotes for a moment to get you thinking about the next topic: "How do we go about turning into the people we are meant to be?" (Lucy Grealy, *Autobiography of a Face*, p. xxii); and "Although of course you end up becoming yourself" (David Foster Wallace, in Lipsky, p. 52).

The word *adult* has not always been used as a verb. The verb form began to be seen on social media sites around 2008, and its use has grown exponentially since then. It relates to the often mundane tasks and responsibilities that go along with the more exciting aspects of growing up: earning money, paying bills, housecleaning, and so forth. People can playfully adapt the definition to serve their purposes. Here's how BuzzFeed explains it in the Introduction to their cookbook *Tasty Adulting* (2020), which has its own book talk later in this Text Set:

> Adulting is stepping up to the plate when it matters. But adulting is also phoning it in when you need to. Adulting is enjoying the freedom that comes with independence, and adulting is learning that actions have consequences. Adulting is treating yourself in flush times, nourishing yourself in lean times, and eating cake for breakfast because you can. Adulting is about having fun,

living thoughtfully, taking responsibility, making bad decisions, throwing caution to the wind, practicing self-care, and being iconic.

(p. 7)

The majority of the novels in the coming chapters feature characters negotiating aspects of adulting. So here I've chosen a sample of nonfiction, how-to books on the topic to get you started thinking about the various paths to full, or at least approaching adulthood.

Andrew, M. (2018). *Am I There Yet?: The Loop-de-Loop, Zigzagging Journey to Adulthood*. New York: Clarkson Potter/Publishers.
Part memoir, part guidebook; part text, part illustrations; combination of humor and wisdom. Readers will enjoy traveling with Mari throughout the world, and throughout her 20s. She tells of new experiences, new clothes, new jobs, new boyfriends, new appreciation for herself, others, and life itself. Mari describes her book as a scrapbook of her journey to adulthood (recognizing that she is not yet at a final destination) and talks directly to readers, hoping her book "… will bring you comfort if you, too, are on a less-than direct journey through life" (p. 9). Her drawings and labels often use contrast, such as "Searching for Yourself vs. Creating Yourself" (p. 17); and comparison, like "Navigating a Foreign Place" and "Navigating Young Adulthood." (pp. 62–63).

Mari offers tips for traveling, for building healthy relationships, for living alone, for healing after grief, and for forgiving. She doesn't expect anyone to follow her route or aspire to be exactly like her. The book is always encouraging, totally positive even when speaking of difficulties, failures, and challenges. Readers may want to follow Mari's example and begin their own journal, or "Museum of my Life" (p. 178) or timeline called "What Makes Me Me?" (p. 188). Almost certainly, they will feel like they have a new friend in Mari, one who has shared herself as an artist and a seeker.

BuzzFeed, Inc. (2020). *Tasty Adulting: All your Faves, All Grown Up*. New York: Clarkson Potter/Publishers.
The audience for this cookbook is described on the back cover: "*Tasty Adulting* is made specifically for the young (and young at

heart) cooks who are just getting their footing as grown-ups." After giving a list, pictures, and tips about needed items for a well-stocked kitchen and pantry, chapters filled with recipes that will work for breakfasts, snacks, desserts, etc. follow. The accompanying photos are colorful and appealing. Inserts offer some "Life Skills" such as the scoop and swoop plating move for serving vegetables with sauce; toasting nuts or seeds on the stove; cooking pasta *al dente*; cleaning an iron skillet; cracking eggs and separating yolks from white; squeezing lemons; and quick ways to pickle almost anything.

Which of the seventy-five recipes to try first? Adults and near-adults of all ages can decide for themselves. In a section called "How to Navigate this Book," the authors assure us that we can dive in deep to try out fish, or play with healthy vegetarian options. We can aim for cozy foods or company foods; nutritious breakfasts or impressive desserts. The authors reassure young readers that they will be taught how to "… drag some of your childhood favorites into adulthood with you. Literally, we adulted them" (p. 11). Tasty!

Fielding, L.E. (2019). *Mastering Adulthood: Go beyond Adulting to Become an Emotional Grown-up.* Oakland, CA: New Harbinger Publications.

"Are You Ready to Solve the Great Mystery of You?" (p. 8). If so, Fielding's book is ready to offer exercises meant to guide the reader on an adventure of self-exploration. Throughout the text that is filled with advice, skills, rationales, stories, and examples, she asks questions in gray areas labeled "PAUSE," such as "Do you already have an idea of some of your own habits that may make you feel better in the short term but are not so helpful in moving you toward your long-term goals?" She requests that readers write their responses in a journal designated for the project of mastering adulthood.

Fielding devotes a lot of time and space to the topic of emotions, explaining their purposes, which include communicating to others, motivating actions, and signaling deep needs. She encourages leaning into discomfort rather than masking it or fleeing from it; letting go of judgment; and learning to discern "… when to practice acceptance and when to push for change" (p. 70). Exercises offer ways to identify patterns in one's relationships, as well as values that indicate overarching directions for how to live a life of integrity. The book covers topics relating to commitment, self-compassion, nutrition, sleep, exercise, motivation, mindful listening, and more.

Readers who practice what this book preaches may indeed feel like they can control the course their adulthood will take, and might consciously use the map provided to pursue paths leading to emotional wellbeing and habits that will serve them and others well.

Lythcott-Haims, J. (2021). *Your Turn: How to Be an Adult*. New York: Henry Holt and Company.

Do young people making the transition from adolescence to adulthood really need a 469-page handbook giving lists, helpful hints, roadmaps, explanations, and all sorts of lessons from how to manage money to how to be kind to oneself and others? Not all. Some may prefer to trust themselves, figure things out through experience, or follow in the steps of role models. Some will peruse this book, read headings, and choose sections that match their present needs or interests. But for those who are in the perfect place and mood for listening to guidance, this book will be a treasure that may be long remembered, and returned to as needed.

Major topics covered include understanding and rejecting perfectionism; making ethical decisions and developing character and positive values; forming mutually supporting relationships at work and beyond; self-care and coping with stress, grief, and trauma; and growth, resilience, and perseverance. Along with each chapter's advice are scenarios demonstrating the principles in the actions and situations of real people.

Lythcott-Haims, who identifies as a Black, biracial, queer person, uses her experience as a college dean in addition to other jobs and areas of expertise to relate to readers and invite them to interact with the text (and her). She asks direct questions to get things started:

> Who are you? What are you good at, and what do you love and value? What kind of work would sit at the intersection of those things? Where do you find belonging? What kinds of people do you want to invite into your life? Can you give yourself permission to be that person, and then chart a path that's most right for you?

> (p. 130)

Morgan, G. (2020). *Undecided: Navigating Life and Learning after High School, 2nd edition.* Minneapolis, MN: Zest Books.

The author speaks directly to her target audience—students nearing the end of high school—and provides multiple checklists, quizzes, charts, and writing prompts that allow the text to be interactive. While there is a chapter on higher education with lots of practical information about two-year and four-year colleges, she does not make college the default option. Rather, she lets readers know that there are many options if they feel that they are not ready for college or that their interests and passions lie elsewhere. She encourages looking into trade schools, distance learning, and studying abroad. There is a whole section on military service, civil service, and foreign service. Another section explores jobs, careers, internships, and starting a business. Yet other chapters deal with travel, community service, grassroots activism, and other productive ways to grow and mature during a gap year.

Morgan is positive and encouraging throughout, offering stories of various routes famous people took to where they are now, and providing resources for further exploration. She concludes:

> Live boldly and loudly and without fear…. You may face financial and technological roadblocks, you may be cheated and afraid and heartbroken, and you will have to work extremely hard. But I know you have the capacity to rise above hardship and find real joy. And purpose. These are the antidote to anxiety and despair, and they are worth taking risks to gain.

> (p. 275)

Reeves, L. (2018). *…And then You Die of Dysentery: Lessons in Adulting from The Oregon Trail.* New York: Houghton Mifflin Harcourt.

"You never forget the first time you die. For me, it was at the age of 7, when I was hit with a terrible case of dysentery" (unpaged). The opening sentences of this combination advice book and homage to the computer game Oregon Trail will intrigue readers and alert them to the humor that will accompany the lessons regarding handling adult responsibilities. The author transforms the thousands of childhood hours spent playing the game into lessons she could apply to her everyday life, "Like how watching the pioneers migrate from Missouri to Oregon for a better life motivated me to move from Alaska to New York City" (unpaged). Reeves deftly merges pixelated images and directions from the game with textspeak and references to today's social media-connected world. Sarcasm can be detected in both the first line about the game ("You can be anything you want—as long as it's a banker, farmer, or teacher") and the subsequent lines reflecting an opinion about current situations ("Remember, bankers have no useful skills, only money. Those one percenters will just try to *buy* their way to Oregon").

Today's gamers might use this book as a mentor text as they apply lessons learned from their favorite video games to ways they are beginning to handle the adult responsibilities they are encountering, no matter what their stage or age. Might as well add some fun to adulting.

Rose, A. (2017). *Almost Adulting: All you Need to Know to Get It Together (Sort of)*. New York: Harper.

The author ("person of the internet" according to the front cover) published this book when she was in her early twenties. But first, she was an actress and creator of a YouTube channel that was quite a hit. No pressure—Arden doesn't want you to compare yourself to others who seem to have their lives together. She assures you that everyone else in high school "… is having a mild existential crisis at the same time, so it results in a messy sludge of teenagehood that will leave you begging to be thirty" (p. 194).

Arden now wishes that she had not been so hard on herself and had not let other people get to her. She offers advice in this book that may help readers traveling on the road to adulthood to do so with more confidence, wisdom, and humor. Chapters include "My Mom Isn't Going to Grocery Shop for Me Anymore?"; "Creating the Perfect Apartment without Wads of Cash or Buckets of Tears"; and "It's Okay to Feel Sad. Or Happy. Or Both at the Exact Same Time." Stories of her own adventures, mistakes, discoveries, and growth will encourage those who are pondering things relating to finances, jobs, clothes, body image, wellness, dating, emotions, and self-respect. Readers may feel a bit more ready for independence, while realizing that's not an all-or-nothing concept, after treating themselves to this text. They may choose to join other followers of Arden Rose's YouTube channel.

Featuring Francine Prose

For many reasons, Francine Prose is a perfect author for New Adults. She crosses genre boundaries as well as age boundaries. And she's a great role model in terms of both reading and writing.

Her body of work is large, most of it written and published for an adult audience. I'll start with her YA titles. *The Turning* (2012), is a retelling of Henry James' *The Turn of the Screw* (1995), a classic horror story that is often required in high school and college courses. The narrator of Prose's epistolary novel is a high school senior who is babysitting two children on an island. Students might compare this type of retelling of a classic to the writing of fanfiction (explained below), and give it a try themselves.

Several of Prose's novels have high school settings. *Touch* (2009) involves a high school girl who has been inappropriately touched on a school bus; the aftermath is complex and confusing, as issues of truth and perception are explored. *Bullyville* (2007) deals with a topic that is in the forefront in many districts, and readers can compare this story to real happenings in the schools they attend every day. *After* (2003) takes place in a school where administrators are enforcing rules to keep everyone safe. But what is the cost in terms of freedom?

Some of Prose's adult-level books may also have NA appeal. *My New American Life* (2011) has a 26-year-old protagonist from Albania, who works toward a better life than she has had, while observing new customs and trying to fit in. *Goldengrove* (2008) features a 13-year-old main character who is grieving the loss of an older sister; she develops a relationship with the sister's boyfriend (also grieving). *Blue Angel* (2000) involves a complicated relationship between a college professor of creative writing and one of his talented students. *Mister Monkey* (2016) features interconnected characters of all ages, including Lakshmi, the costume designer who is a grad student at NYU with writing aspirations.

Prose's works can be used in content area classrooms, also. *Caravaggio: Painter of Miracles* (2005) might enhance an art history class, while *Lovers at the Chameleon Club, Paris 1932* (2014) involves a teenager moving to Paris; readers will learn of the flourishing of artists and writers during the time period, as well as the political climate. The protagonist of *The Vixen* (2021) just graduated from Harvard in the 1950s, and is editing a novel based on the execution of the Rosenbergs.

Finally, I'd like to recommend a couple of examples of Prose's nonfiction. *Anne Frank: The Book, the Life, and the Afterlife* (2009) is a fascinating account of the three subjects mentioned in the subtitle. Prose takes us on her multi-faceted journey that involves both research and contemplation. *Reading Like a Writer: A Guide for People Who Love Books and for Those Who Want to Write Them* (2006) is a dream come true for both writers and writing teachers. The first chapter is titled "Close Reading," followed by chapters on words, sentences, paragraphs as well as chapters on characters, dialogue, and narration. Prose uses her own reading habits and many beautiful examples from literature as she shows readers how to carefully read and be aware of the aesthetics of literature. I reread this masterpiece regularly. It involves great teaching, without ever being didactic or sounding textbook-y.

Book Talks: Ready to Go!

Librarians call the important role of matching the right books with the right readers Readers' Advisory. The book talks throughout the chapters are designed to help you do just that. They can be shared with readers as is, either orally or in print. They can be adapted to suit your needs and purposes. Students can learn to give book talks to each other. I tried to place the book talks in the most appropriate chapters, given the chapters' primary focuses (college, careers, relationships, etc.), but many could have gone in different places, since the topics intersect. Characters in college are also forming relationships, developing a sense of their place in society, and searching or preparing for future satisfying work life. Virtually all NA books deal with the concepts of identity and values, as shown in the following samples.

Cronin, M. (2021). *The One Hundred Years of Lenni and Margot.* New York: HarperPerennial.

Lenni, at 17, comfortably fits into our NA age range. Quite uncomfortably, she is also nearing the end of her life. In the hospital, she meets 83-year-old Margot, who is dying, too. In the hospital's art room, they chronicle their combined years through pictures and stories, thereby helping us, as well as Lenni, know Margot as she began many new phases of her life.

The hospital chaplain, Father Arthur, helps both title characters (and readers) grapple with questions, emotions, philosophy, and theology. Why did Lenni's mother abandon her? What kind of God allows children to have cancer? Whose fault is it that Margot's baby had a fatal heart condition? Was it wrong that after Margot's husband left her, she fell in love with a woman? And what should she do about that now? I try to avoid spoilers in my book talks, but Father Arthur has no words for that last question. He instead writes a Bible verse on a slip of paper before walking away. When Margot borrows a Bible and looks up Ecclesiastes 9:9, dreading the chastisement she figures must be there, she finds, "Enjoy life with the woman you love, all the days of your fleeting life" (p. 319).

Father Arthur answers Lenni's questions with his friendship and love. Margot gives Lenni the love she was not able to give a child of her own, and accepts the love that Lenni expresses for her. This book is about beginnings and endings, and the one hundred years in between.

Schwab, V.E. (2020). *The Invisible Life of Addie Larue.* Waterville, ME: Thorndike Press.

The age of the title character and protagonist, 17, makes Addie's story perfect for a "New Adult" audience. Or is she over 300 years old, putting her way out of range of our NA category? Actually, Addie is both. In 1714, in an effort to escape a forced marriage at seventeen, Addie makes what turns out to be a bad deal with a god who answers after dark. She is given immortality, but cursed with the added factor that everyone she encounters will forget her as soon as the interaction is over. She travels the world, living through historical movements such as the French Revolution and the world wars of the twentieth century, never aging, and never able to establish a lasting relationship with anyone.

Until one day in 2014, when Addie meets a young man who not only can remember her from day to day, but falls in love with her. Unfortunately, he has also made a deal with the devil, and the date when the price must be paid is approaching.

Readers face life and death dilemmas along with Addie and Henry as they immerse themselves in this speculative work. Questions about the meaning and purpose of life don't get any bigger than this. That makes for a good, and meaningful, read.

Hession, R. (2020). *Leonard and Hungry Paul*. Brooklyn, NY: Melville House.

Ordinarily a novel featuring characters over 30 years of age would not be categorized as NA, but the title characters are introverts who have never left their family homes. They are just now facing circumstances that cause issues relating to independence, which many people resolve a decade sooner, to surface. Leonard's mother has recently died, leaving him grieving and lonely. He steps out of his comfort zone in hopes of building a relationship with a young woman he meets when a fire drill throws them together. Leonard writes children's encyclopedias, and Shelley happens to have a 7-year-old who is inspired by his books. That provides both hope and anxiety. (Shelley, scarred by an earlier failed relationship, has been too hurt to risk new relationships, so she is also at a point of potential growth.)

Meanwhile, Hungry Paul, a part-time postal worker who for years has enjoyed evenings playing board games with his sole friend Leonard, is getting ready for his sister Grace's wedding. She's encouraging him to move out, so his parents will have more freedom. (She has also envisioned a future where Hungry Paul might become *her* responsibility.) In addition to volunteering as a visitor at a hospital, he enters a contest that leads to a prize ceremony, which leads to a job interview, which leads to his founding of a Quiet Club, etc. Hungry Paul is on the move, on his own terms.

Both men accept themselves rather than try to fit others' definitions of normal. Hungry Paul shares some wise words with his sister that might speak to many readers:

> Grace, I know that I disappoint you. I know it but I am okay with it. Whatever happens I will do my best… I know that, more than anything, you would like me to see the world your way, to wake up to your way of looking at things and to become the version of myself that you're most comfortable with… I am not anyone's responsibility….

> We don't need a family superhero.... Maybe I'll have moved on. Maybe I'll be a hotshot. Or maybe I won't. But let's not test each other. Let's just be happy. While there is still time.

> (pp. 210–212)

Oliver, S.S. (Ed.). (2018). *Black Ink: Literary Legends on the Peril, Power, and Pleasure of Reading and Writing*. New York: Simon & Schuster.

This collection of essays, speeches, and excerpts from other texts by renowned writers is arranged chronologically, beginning with nineteenth-century authors Frederick Douglass, Solomon Northrup, and Booker T. Washington, who remind us how very precious reading was to those who risked their lives for the chance to be literate.

The section labeled "The Power" offers texts written between 1900 and 1968, by luminaries and activists including Zora Neale Hurston, Langston Hughes, James Baldwin, Malcolm X, and Alice Walker. The writers often reflect on their reading experiences while growing up and entering adulthood (sometimes including college years), making the text valuable for the New Adults reading about them now. Walter Dean Myers, reflecting on his teenage years, recounts reading books that helped him on his quest for his own identity:

> To an extent I found who I was in the books I read. I was a person who felt the drama of great pain and greater joys, whose emotions could soar within the five-act structure of a Shakespearean play.... Every book was a landscape upon which I was free to wander"

> (p. 112)

But, like many teens today, he stopped reading, unable to find characters who were like him. Luckily, he later discovered James Baldwin. Myers puts out a call for more people of color in children's books.

In the final section, "The Pleasure," we encounter memories and advice from contemporary writers including Juno Diaz, Colson Whitehead, Ta-Nehisi Coates, and Chimamanda Ngozi Adichie. In an interview with Michiko Kakutani in 2017, President Barack Obama speaks of "... the power of words as a way to figure out who you are and what you think, and what you believe, and what's important, and to sort through and interpret this swirl of events that is happening around you every minute" (p. 227). Readers can't help but come away from *Black Ink* feeling inspired, encouraged, and appreciative of the books that helped shape the contributors to this volume. The potential is there for us as well.

Strategies and Activities

One of the principles put forth in the CCCC Position Statement cited earlier in this chapter exhorts instructors to "Foster Mindful Reading to Encourage Students to Think Metacognitively about Their Reading in Preparation for a Variety of Reading in Different Contexts." Among the strategies mentioned that can work toward this goal are "Encourage reflection through reader response journals, discussion board postings, or similar approaches," and "In addition to asking students to reflect encourage them to anticipate the uses of various reading approaches in future courses and contexts."

Student choice and independent reading of NA literature are central to this book, but high school and college students also benefit from strategy instruction and participation in follow-up activities that promote further engagement with the ideas of the texts. So, each chapter will include ways for teachers and students to extend thinking, response, and application to their lives, current situations, and other courses they are taking. Walk-throughs are provided as examples, but the strategies can be adapted and/or used with different books and topics. So, for instance, an activity I introduce in Chapter 5 and apply to the books focusing on relationships could be used with the books about college life presented in Chapter 3. Possibilities are limitless, and students can practice agency as they make decisions regarding the ways they respond to and extend the texts, flexibly making them their own. I've started us off with two examples of strategies below.

Who Am I? Who Are You?

Gholdy Muhammad describes a "Who Are You?" exercise she facilitates when working with teachers. She pairs them up and has them take one-minute turns asking, "Who are you?" They alternate answers, and each time the question gets repeated, it must be answered differently. Depending on how safe and comfortable the responders feel, they sometimes share deeper, unobservable qualities and values. Muhammad points out that this exercise can be done throughout the year with students, and they can create a web or write about the aspects of their identities if they prefer.

I've adapted this activity to use on the first day of my NA literature course. Since students don't yet know each other, and they've just arrived on campus (and are probably sick of orientation games), I do it as a writing activity, letting them know it will help them when they read and respond to characters in the books we will be reading. They will not hand it in, but they will save what they write and return to it later in the semester. I put questions on the screen, and they write for one minute. (I will later give them the questions altogether, so they don't have to write them now, but could revisit them later if they want.) I'll explain that this will be an exercise in stamina, involving about ten to twelve minutes of steady thinking and writing. If they choose not to respond to a particular prompt, they can change it, or continue writing about one of the earlier ones. I'll note that these same questions will be asked and played out by the characters in the stories they will be reading throughout the course. Here are the questions:

- Who are you?
- Who are you? (Answer in a different way, with an aspect of yourself that you didn't think of the first time. Recalling pictures you have posted on social media might help.)
- Who are you in relation to others—family, friends, etc.?
- Who are you in relation to your interests and passions, your plans for the future, your hopes, and dreams?
- Who are you in relation to place—this college, your birthplace, your home?
- Who are you in relation to culture, ethnicity, religion, etc.?
- Who are you in relation to the world, the planet, the environment, and nature?
- Who are you in relation to science, medicine, art, history, and music?
- Who are you in relation to physical activity, sports, movement, and your body?
- Who are you in relation to books, reading, and learning?

Fanfiction

For readers who are not familiar with the concept of fanfiction, it's what you might guess from its name. If you are a fan of a book, or of several, you can play with them by writing your own fiction. You can extend a story into the future; you can change an ending you were upset about;

you can have characters from different novels meet each other. To get an idea of the limitless possibilities, search on the Internet for fanfiction related to J.K. Rowling's *Harry Potter* series, Stephenie Meyer's *Twilight* series, or Suzanne Collins' *The Hunger Games* series. There are fanfiction sites specifically devoted to classics, such as the works of Shakespeare or Jane Austen. Twenty-one published writers contributed to a collection edited by Tracy Chevalier called *Reader, I Married Him* (2016). If you recognize the title as the last sentence of Charlotte Brontë's *Jane Eyre* (2011), you'll know what inspired the fanfiction in the book.

Or go directly to www.fanfic.net. You can start as a follower, and then perhaps contribute something based on an original text you'd like to revise, add to, or play with. *Fangirl*, by Rainbow Rowell (2013), features a protagonist, Cath, who writes fanfiction about a fictional series (making it meta-fanfiction, I guess) about a hero called Simon Snow; Cath has a huge online following. Chapters of the fanfiction itself are interspersed throughout the novel. Simon's story proved so popular with readers that Rowell later published a trilogy called the Simon Snow Series to give her fans more of Simon and Baz.

For our first try at fanfiction, I invite you to bring together some of the characters from the books you read in the first text set above. John Green used the trope of a support group for teens with cancer; as a result, Hazel Grace met Augustus, and a unique romance ensued. So you could try that, too. Sam, Ben, D.Q., and Alice (characters from different novels in the "Facing Mortality" text set) could interact during a support group within your story. But fanfiction shouldn't come with too many directions or constraints. Feel free to bring one or more of the minor characters a few years into the future. Or tell the story's events from another character's point of view. Or find one of those miracles Cam was looking for in *The Probability of Miracles*, and save your favorite protagonist from the cruel fate their author led them to. Anything is possible in the world you create as you write.

References

Black, B. (2019). The credo second-year student transition guide: White paper. Retrieved from https://www.infobase.com/resources/the-credo-second-year-student-transition-guide-white-paper/.

Cappiello, M.A., & Dawes, E.T. (2021). *Text sets in action: Pathways through content area literacy*. Portsmouth, NH: Stenhouse.

Cart, M. (2016). *Young adult literature: From romance to realism*, 3rd edition. New York: Neal-Schuman Publishers.

Cart, M. (2013). *Cart's top 200 adult books for young adults: Two decades in review.* Chicago, IL: American Library Association.

Conference on College Composition and Communication. (2021). *CCCC position statement on the role of reading in college writing classrooms.* Retrieved from https://cccc.ncte.org/cccc/the-role-of-reading#:~:text=This%20position%20statement%20affirms%20the,their%20careers%2C%20and%20for%20their.

Fink, R. (1995/1996). Successful dyslexics: A constructivist study of passionate interest reading. *Journal of Adolescent and Adult Literacy, 43*(7), 596–606.

Gallagher, K., & Kittle, P. (2018). *180 days: Two teachers and the quest to engage and empower adolescents.* Portsmouth, NH: Heinemann.

Ivey, G. (2014). The social side of engaged reading for young adolescents. *The Reading Teacher, 68*(3), 165–171.

Krashen, S. (2013). Access to books and time to read versus the Common Core State Standards and tests. *English Journal, 103*(2), 21–29.

Lipsky, D. (2010). *Although of course you end up becoming yourself: A road trip with David Foster Wallace.* New York: Broadway Books.

Muhammad, G. (2020). *Cultivating genius: An equity framework for culturally and historically responsive literacy.* New York: Scholastic.

National Council of Teachers of English. (2019). *Position statement on independent reading.* Retrieved from https://ncte.org/statement/independent-reading/.

O'Brien, C. (2007). Stuyvesant high school commencement speech. In Eggers, D., (Ed.). *The best American nonrequired reading.* New York: Houghton Mifflin, pp. 299–304.

Prose, F. (2018). *What to read and why.* New York: HarperCollins.

Torppa, M., Niemi, P., Vasalampi, K., Lerkkanen, M., Tolvanen, A., & Poikkeus, A. (2019). Leisure reading (but not any kind) and reading comprehension support each other—A longitudinal study across grades 1 and 9. *Child Development, 91*(3), 876–900.

Wilner, A.F. (2020). *Rethinking reading in college: An across-the-curriculum approach.* Urbana, IL: NCTE.

Yoon, D. (2019). Coming of age at age 45. Retrieved from https://www.amazon.com/Frankly-Love-David-Yoon/dp/1984812203.

Literature Cited

Alcott, L.M. (2014). *Little women.* New York: Puffin.

Alcott, L.M. (1994). *Jo's boys.* London: Puffin.

Brontë, C. (2011). *Jane Eyre*. New York: HarperPerennial Classics.

Chevalier, T., (Ed.). (2016). *Reader, I married him*. New York: William Morrow.

Crutcher, C. (2009). *Deadline*. New York: Greenwillow Books.

Dickens, C. (2009). *Great expectations*. New York: Signet Classics.

Earl, E.G. (2014). *This star won't go out: The life and words of Esther Grace Earl*. New York: Dutton.

Golding, W. (1954). *Lord of the flies*. New York: Perigree.

Grealy, L. (2016). *Autobiography of a face*. Boston, MA: Mariner Books.

Green, J. (2012). *The fault in our stars*. New York: Dutton Books.

Hardy, T. (2003). *Tess of the D'Urbervilles*. New York: Penguin.

Hession, R. (2020). *Leonard and Hungry Paul*. Brooklyn: Melville House.

Honeyman, G. (2017). *Eleanor Oliphant is completely fine*. New York: Penguin.

James, H. (1995). *The turn of the screw*. Boston, MA: Bedford Books.

Joyce, J. (1996). *Portrait of the artist as a young man*. New York: Modern Library.

Montgomery, L.M. (2008). *Anne of Green Gables*. New York: G.P. Putnam's Sons.

Murphy, J. (2014). *Side effects may vary*. New York: Balzer +Bray/HarperCollins.

Myers, W.D. (2009). *Sunrise over Fallujah*. New York: Scholastic.

Nicholls, S. (2008.) *Ways to live forever*. New York: Artur A. Levine.

Obama, B. (2021). *Dreams of my father: A story of race and inheritance, adapted for young adults*. New York: Delacorte Press.

O'Brien, T. (1990). *The things they carried*. Boston, MA: Houghton Mifflin.

Ostrovski, E. (2014). *The paradox of vertical flight*. New York: Greenwillow Books.

Paulsen, G. (1987). *Hatchet*. New York: Scholastic.

Prose, F. (2021). *The vixen*. New York: Harper.

Prose, F. (2016). *Mister Monkey*. New York: Harper.

Prose, F. (2014). *Lovers at the Chameleon Club, Paris 1932*. New York: Harper.

Prose, F. (2012). *The turning*. New York: HarperTeen.

Prose, F. (2011). *My new American life*. New York: HarperCollins.

Prose, F. (2009). *Anne Frank: The book, the life, the afterlife*. New York: Harper.

Prose, F. (2009). *Touch*. New York: HarperTeen.

Prose, F. (2008). *Goldengrove*. New York: Harper.

Prose, F. (2007). *Bullyville*. New York: HarperTeen.

Prose, F. (2006). *Reading like a writer: A guide for people who love books and for those who want to write them*. New York: HarperCollins.

Prose, F. (2005). *Caravaggio: Painter of miracles*. New York: Atlas Books/HarperCollins.

Prose, F. (2003). *After*. New York: HarperCollins.

Prose, F. (2000). *Blue angel*. New York: HarperCollins.

Rowell, R. (2013). *Fangirl*. New York: St. Martin's Griffin.

Simsione, G. (2013). *The Rosie project*. New York: Simon & Schuster.

Smith, A. (2013). *Winger*. New York: Simon & Schuster.

Smith, B. (1998). *A tree grows in Brooklyn*. New York: Perennial Classics.

Stork, F.X. (2010.) *The last summer of the Death Warriors*. New York: Arthur A. Levine.

Wunder, W. (2011). *The probability of miracles*. New York: Razorbill.

Zevin, G. (2014). *The storied life of A.J. Fikry*. Chapel Hill, NC: Algonquin Books.

Zusak, M. (2005). *The book thief*. New York: A.A. Knopf.

Preparing to Launch   **2**

The High School Years

Forming Identities during the High School Years

Ponder these two quotes to prepare for reading this section:

"School starts in five days… I don't know who I am" (*Aristotle and Dante Discover the Secrets of the Universe*, p. 149). And:

> I am going to go to university in another town…. And then I will get a First Class Honors degree and I will become a scientist…. And I know I can do this because …. I was brave and I wrote a book and that means I can do anything.
>
> (Christopher Boone, in *The Curious Incident of the Dog in the Night-time*, pp. 220–221)

Think of the tremendous growth and changes that occur between the beginning of ninth grade and the end of twelfth—physical, emotional, intellectual, and spiritual. As teens are exploring new territories finding ways to adjust to new aspects of their identities, they are also seeing new challenges and opportunities ahead of them, fearfully and/or joyfully realizing increasing independence, responsibilities, and choices. They are in constant motion, even if at some points they might feel like time is moving too slowly or they are standing still. Librarians and teachers can provide literature for students who are questioning the meaning of life and their place in the world. They can encourage teens to read

DOI: 10.4324/9781003221685-2

for pleasure, while also reading to better understand other perspectives and broaden their horizons. They can demonstrate that books can be their companions as they prepare for the transition from high school to college, work, travel, or whatever else follows and will eventually lead to that place waiting for them known as *adulthood*.

This chapter offers books set during and immediately following high school. Characters and authors present different ways of behaving in relation to family and friends; various approaches to making decisions about post-graduation life; and explorations of possible ways to interact with the environment and consider, form, and act on values as knowledge of social justice issues and diversity grows. There is a text set of curated books about that iconic tradition of the high school prom, followed by a text set around the theme of the summer after high school graduation. There are multiple book talks on relevant books that readers can use as is or adapt for particular purposes and audiences. In the "Instructional Strategies and Activities" section, you'll find ideas for encouraging reading and promoting New Adult titles that will entice students to both read and talk about literature. This is followed by a strategy called "Only Connect" and another that deals with helping readers to notice, use, and appreciate texts that are outside of but relate to a focus book. All the strategies include "walk-throughs" that model the approaches in action.

TEXT SETS

As you can see from Chapter 1, there is more than one way to present a text set. The first one in this chapter uses a narrative format. Picture a librarian picking up books from a Prom display as they introduce the themed selections. Or visualize students reading the narrative as they explore the display independently. The second text set consists of a list of titles of novels that are set during the weeks after high school graduation, with an asterisk denoting those for which there are book talks in the next section. The transition time between high school and the next steps adolescents will be taking, whether those steps lead to college, an apprenticeship, a job, family responsibilities, or travel, can be crucial; and reading about how fictional characters spend those weeks can be enjoyable, comfortable, challenging, and/or thought-provoking.

The Prom

How did proms get to become, or represent, a rite of passage? While some people really do experience the magic that the special night promises, many others find themselves disappointed, anxious, rejected, confused, resistant, ambivalent, or underwhelmed. In recent years, proms have been criticized for being ridiculously expensive; for excluding teens who identify as LGBTQ+; for fostering elitism and cliques; and for exacerbating social pressures involving drinking and sex. And yet, in many high schools, the tradition continues, offering opportunities for thinking, arguing, writing, and action. There is an abundance of YA and NA literature dealing with themes and issues relating to proms, and the choices include several genres.

Let's start with short stories, where you can get a lot of different takes on the prom scene quickly. *21 Proms* is a collection edited by David Levithan and Daniel Ehrenhaft (2014). You can read about the authors and their own prom experiences in "The Prom Gallery" at the end of the book. Perhaps the most outlandish story, and my personal favorite, is Libba Bray's "Primate the Prom." I had never really thought about how I would have reacted at my own prom if one of my peers had arrived with a gorilla for a date. But after reading the story, my values are firm. With the rest of the teachers and students, I watched Ryan and Carter on the dance floor, and could hear the music as "Carter, that big ape, had this totally misty look in his big brown eyes. He had my hand cradled in his paw; his other paw rested just at my waist. We were slow dancing at the prom. Our prom. Laughing...." (p. 205).

Prom-related fiction offers great variety. There's realistic fiction, including Laurie Halse Anderson's *Prom* (2005), where a senior goes from having no interest in prom whatsoever to suddenly being responsible for it, resulting in much personal insight and growth, as well as fun. Sandy Hall's *A Prom to Remember* (2018) gives the story of one prom from the viewpoints of several different attendees. You can find a book talk in the following section for Leah Johnson's *You Should See Me in a Crown* (2020). Aimee Ferris's *Will Work for Prom Dress* (2011) features a high school artist. Several books discuss alternative proms, among them Dorian Cirrone's *Prom Kings and Drama Queens* (2008); *The Anti-Prom* by Abby McDonald (2011); and Laura Preble's *Prom Queen Geeks* (2008). (John Green's "The Great American Morp" in *21 Proms*, discussed above, also describes a fun alternative.) Julie Anne Peters, in *It's Our Prom (So Deal With It)* (2012), has socially-conscious characters working to create a prom that will be inclusive, in contrast to their school's previous proms that did not welcome prom pairs of the same sex.

For science and psychology fans, I recommend Ann Labar's *Prom Theory* (2021). You can test your own hypothesis about whether Iris's attempt to prove that love is simply chemistry—just a matter of hormones reacting to stimuli—will succeed or backfire. She's using the scientific method to get a popular track star to ask her to the prom. If you like a plot with many characters, lots to think about, and some comedy, pick up *The Night When No One Had Sex* by Kalena Miller (2021). You like a mystery? Try Michelle Kehm's *Suzi Clue: The Prom Queen Curse* (2009). Do you prefer science fiction? Chris McCoy's *Prom Goer's Interstellar Excursion* (2015) might be to your liking. Those who want a paranormal or horror prom version can check out *Prom Nights from Hell* (Meyer et al., 2009). Want a take-off on a classic? It's there in *Prom and Prejudice* by Elizabeth Eulberg (2011). Reality TV fans might choose *The Real Prom Queens of Westfield High* by Laurie Boyle Crompton (2014). Didn't I promise a prom for everyone?

There are nonfiction books that offer advice, such as *The Prom Book: The Only Guide You'll Ever Need* by Lauren Metz (2013), and those that offer critique and commentary on this billion-dollar industry, like Ann Anderson's *High School Prom: Marketing, Morals, and the American Teen* (2012).

Readers can choose from these and other readily available choices, read what and how they want, talk with readers of other selections, and make decisions about their own proms, or anti-proms. I suggest having romantic theme music playing while you read!

Summer after High School Graduation

Many New Adults would tell us that the next step after high school graduation is college, and some excited, newly admitted students would probably love to head to their chosen campus immediately. But for most, there's a summer in between, and those couple of months, whether spent traveling, working for money for the next semester, or hanging out for a long goodbye with life-long friends, can be crucial. Things happen. Surprises occur. People change. Authors of NA literature know this and have given us an abundance of stories set during the summer after senior year. Here is a sampling. The titles marked with an asterisk are book talked in the following section.

Bazay, C. (2021). *Not Our Summer*. New York: Running Press Teens.
*Culli, L.R. (2021). *Say Yes Summer*. New York: Delacorte Press.
Dhillon, N.S. (2022). *Sunny G's Series of Rash Decisions*. New York: Penguin Young Readers Group.
*King, A.S. (2014). *Glory O'Brien's History of the Future*. Boston, MA: Little, Brown and Company.
Meriano, A. (2020). *This is How we Fly*. New York: Philomel Books.
Myracle, L. (2013). *The Infinite Moment of Us*. New York: Abrams.
Niven, J. (2020). *Breathless*. New York: Knopf.
*Reul, R. (2021). *Where the Road Leads Us*. Naperville, IL: Sourcebooks Fire.
Rishi, F.N. (2021). *It All Comes Back to You*. New York: HarperCollins/Quill Tree.
Schumacher, A. (2021). *Amelia Unabridged*. New York: Wednesday Books.

Book Talks: Ready to Go!

An asterisk before a title denotes a book that is contained in one of the text sets in the previous section.

Anderson, L.H. (2014). *The Impossible Knife of Memory*. New York: Viking.
Haley, after being on the road for years with her father, who is dealing with PTSD, goes back to a public school for her senior year. Her guidance counselor, who tries to get her to sign up for the SAT exams, get recommendation letters, and look into financial aid options, does

not have an enviable job. Here's a snippet of dialogue, beginning with Ms. Benedetti telling Haley that colleges will scrutinize her senior year grades, since she hasn't been a traditional student:

> You have to step up to the plate, get in the game.
> Baseball metaphors don't work with me.
> Damn it, Haley, quit screwing around. This is your future…
> Do you get a bonus for every college application we file?.… What if I don't want to go to college? What if I don't know what I want to do? I don't even know how to think about it.

(p. 283)

A lot has to happen in this story, including the beginning of healing in Haley's home, before Ms. Benedetti has a chance of breaking through. It's a journey readers will want to be a part of.

Anderson, L. (2017). *Not Now, Not Ever*. New York: Wednesday Books. Elliot's mother expects her to attend the Air Force Academy in Colorado, where she is stationed. Her father and stepmother want her to stay near home in California and study something productive, such as law. Whichever route she chose, someone would be crushed, scared, and/or ashamed. But, "I wanted to try on my third option, the nuclear option—getting a degree that I wanted. Not close to home. Not with the military. The route that hurt everyone" (p. 113).

As a rising high school senior, she secretly heads to a camp for geniuses in Oregon, where she will have a chance to win a scholarship to the college and join their science fiction literature program.

While there, Ever (she has given herself a new identity) makes wonderful friends, begins a romantic relationship, and spends time in the incredible library that houses rare science fiction treasures. She learns that she is not the only one lying and keeping secrets. There are mysteries to be solved, competitions to win, and lessons of all kinds to be learned. And an identity to be claimed.

Bjorkman, L. (2012). *Miss Fortune Cookie*. New York: Henry Holt and Company.
How does one decide which college to go to when she can choose from among the best? It's spring of senior year at Lowell High School (a school in San Francisco that takes academic achievement seriously, for students who do the same), and Erin and Mei are struggling toward this

huge step toward independence. Mei's mother insists that she must go to Harvard, but Mei loves Darren and does not want to be a continent apart from him. Our narrator, Erin, *does* want to go to Harvard, but has promised her best friend Linny that they will be together at Stanford. Readers can weigh in on these issues and others that Erin encounters in her secret role as the advice dispenser on her Miss Cookie blog.

Erin is also navigating the beginning of her first relationship with a young man, her worries about the financial burdens related to college, her ongoing sadness over the death of her father when she was young, and her changing relationship with her mother. Her friends are Chinese American, but, though she feels Chinese due to her upbringing and love of the language and culture, she is not; she worries that she is not completely accepted because of this. In short, the story is filled with issues of identity and change; readers can weigh in with their own advice as Erin and her friends prepare to enter the world beyond high school.

Callender, K. (2020). *Felix Ever After.* New York: Balzer & Bray.
Rising senior Felix Love is participating in an art program in hopes of winning a scholarship to his dream college, Brown University. Besides that pressure, the summer's events cause him to deal with continuing identity and relationship issues. He knows he is Black, queer, and trans. But someone exhibited pictures of him pretransition, along with his deadname, causing hurt and anger. His best friend Ezra starts dating a classmate, and Felix gets caught up in an online relationship with the person he suspects posted the photos. Could he be falling for the guy he thought he hated? And could he be questioning his identity once again? He knows he isn't a girl, but "boy" doesn't exactly fit how he feels, nor does "nonbinary."

Writing and Thinking Prompt

Felix creates a series of self-portraits for his portfolio for the competition, helping him express various aspects of himself. As a reader, you get to be in on his artistic journey, as well as his search for love and acceptance. You might be inspired to paint or draw pictures of Felix and his friends as a response to the novel, and may want to create one

or more self-portraits to capture your own moods, dreams, and identities. Don't worry if you are not the talented artist Felix is. Using an
artistic medium will still help you explore what you feel and what you
want to convey. If you'd rather use words, you can create a poem, or a
description of yourself in a number of contexts.

*Culli, L.R. (2021). *Say Yes Summer*. New York: Delacorte Press.
High school valedictorian Rachel has never failed at anything. Of
course, she has only attempted things that she knows she won't fail
at. But after reading a self-help book containing her grandmother's
marginal notes, she realizes;45

> If Dr. Paula's theory is right, if we are the product of all we say
> yes to, then… I was basically the product of fear. Fear of new
> things, fear of new people, fear of new experiences, but mostly
> fear of getting hurt.

> (p. 245)

She decides to say yes, to take some risks.

Rachel's new experiences teach her, among other things, that
she is capable of inadvertently hurting others. Does she like soccer
dude Clayton, whom she had a crush on for years? Or does she
like Miles, her fellow worker on the summer ice cream truck who
turns out to be a lot more complex than she had given him credit
for? They both like her, so can't she like them both? Can she keep
kissing them both? Why not, since this is her summer to say yes to
everything? Her friend Carrie tells her, "I mean, we're all going off
in a million directions and it doesn't matter who was like what in
high school. We can all just kind of like… be who we actually are"
(p. 155). But Rachel has changed her behavior so quickly that a true
identity crisis ensues. After some mistakes and thwarted paths, she
realizes that becoming oneself is an ongoing process, with no guar-
antee that she won't get hurt.

Will readers finish this book knowing Rachel will say yes to the
next chapter of her life? Will those readers making the transition to
college or career be a bit more careful to consider the ramifications
their actions have on other people? Will they look for more literary

friends like Rachel as companions on their own journeys? I hope the answer to all these questions will be "Unabashedly, unequivocally, *yes*" (p. 245).

Gilbert, K.R. (2020), *When We Were Infinite*. New York: Simon & Schuster.

Five Asian American high school students, bound together by music and friendship, make a pact to go to the same college. What could go wrong? Beth narrates the story of senior year, with lots of college applications and auditions, and then lots of acceptances and rejections. Beth's friends watch her making mistakes, and readers do, too. She takes out her anger at her father's abandonment by blaming her mother for the divorce. She racks up a credit card bill by charging a limousine for the five friends to go to Homecoming together, which does not even happen; and later by charging a secret trip from California to New York with Jason, so they can audition at Juilliard. After witnessing Jason being abused by his father, and especially after his suicide attempt, Beth walks on eggshells, agreeing—wanting—to do absolutely anything for him. Unfortunately, her actions are not good for Jason or herself. When she is accepted at Juilliard and Jason is not, she lies and says she was rejected, too. When Jason does not treat her well, she blames herself, vowing to try harder. We worry. And her friends try to intervene, as when Sunny gently reflects, "Because when you say stuff like you think you have to sleep with him if he wants to—that really doesn't feel like the healthiest relationship in the world" (p. 250)

As the five friends all grow, change, heal, and stretch, there is a lot of pondering of identity, in terms of both individuals and groups. Beth realizes:

> … maybe in a long friendship everyone is an infinite number of different versions of themselves, and all those selves of you that you shed or grow out of, the ones you're glad you've evolved from and the ones you miss—in a long friendship there's someone who was witness to all of them, and so all those different people you were along the way, no matter what else you may have been, you were never alone.

(p. 317)

The last few chapters take us through the first couple of years of college, so you might want to predict the fate of the individuals and the group, then dive into this novel to be with the friends as they mature from adolescents into New Adults.

*Johnson, L. (2020). *You Should See Me in a Crown*. New York: Scholastic.

Senior Liz Lighty, who has avoided being noticed all through high school, has never considered running for prom queen. She's just waiting to get out of this community that values the prom so highly, to get to college where she can be in the orchestra and study to become a doctor. She's had lots of experience with doctors, since her mother died of sickle cell anemia and her brother inherited the disease.

When the scholarship she was counting on does not materialize, Liz has to re-think and adjust her plans. The winner of the prom competition will be awarded a $10,000 scholarship. Despite her fear of publicity, she's in. Can she move from twenty-fourth in the rankings to #1 by prom night? Not if top contender Rachel has anything to say about it.

This romantic comedy deals with racism; uses and abuses of social media; grief; family responsibilities and sibling relationships; competition and collaboration; evolving friendships; and more. And oh, yes, complications mount when Liz falls in love with one of the other contenders for the crown. Dare she ask Amanda to be her date, when school rules explicitly forbid same-sex couples attending?

*King, A.S. (2014). *Glory O'Brien's History of the Future*. Boston, MA: Little, Brown and Company.

There are so many aspects of identity that Glory is grappling with. She has just graduated from high school, with no college plans, no career path, and no friends other than her neighbor Ellie, who is only interested in her new relationship with a young man who lives in her commune. Will Glory follow in her mother's footsteps, taking her own life at some point? Or become like her father, who stopped painting after his wife died when Glory was four and who has done virtually nothing since? Will her newfound power after drinking a petrified bat (you'll have to read the book if you want details on that) change her life for better, or for worse?

Whenever Glory now looks at someone, she gets transmissions from their family's past as well as their future. If these revelations can be believed, there will be a second Civil War, and the aftermath will entail women and girls being sold, enslaved, and abused. Could her future possibly involve an identity as a sniper? And will her future be intertwined with that of a 22-year-old who is doing research for a psychology project at the mall?

Using her mother's dark room and her own artistic talents, Glory creates and titles photographs that help her deal with the scary, difficult aspects of her personal past, present, and near future. She may end up reclaiming more than the neighboring land that belonged to her mother and has been used by the commune for so many years. Readers will recognize that Glory deserves much more than others have provided for her, and more than she has felt herself worthy of. With or without special bat powers, Glory is a force; Glory is not her past, or what others have perceived her to be; and Glory deserves to walk into her future with hope.

Kress, E. (2021). *Dangerous Play*. New York: Roaring Brook Press.
Zoe has goals, including leading her field hockey team to a state championship, and earning a scholarship so she can play on the UNC Chapel Hill team. She's a good student, a good daughter, and a good friend. But something is not good at her high school. Girls are being sexually harassed, and the administrators are not taking their accusations seriously. After Zoe is assaulted at a party, she and her teammates decide to take matters into their own hands. There should be consequences. What would scare the boys into realizing their behavior is absolutely not acceptable? A gun might.

There is a lot of action on and off the field as both girls and boys learn some hard lessons and mature. Zoe gets support from her parents, teachers, and a new boyfriend who respects her. Readers will see the power of young women sharing their stories, becoming part of the growing #MeToo movement, and helping each other heal.

Lieber, R. (2021). *The Price You Pay for College*. New York: Harper.
The title implies that this book will provide financial advice regarding the college experience, and it does that. The author explains the systems behind the cost of college and gives practical information

regarding making a financial plan, saving and borrowing, merit aid, and appealing a financial aid award. But he puts all this in the context of the value of the college experience, devoting chapters to exploring what things are worth paying for, such as small classes led by experienced instructors who really want to teach and become mentors; well-staffed mental health centers; peers worth befriending (and possibly marrying); excellent career counseling offices; and diversity. He includes chapters about things that might appear to be money-saving but could have hidden or nonfinancial costs, such as athletic scholarships, gap years, community colleges, military programs, and study abroad.

Lieber points out ways that the pandemic of 2020 suddenly and radically changed instruction and other aspects of the college experience, calling into question exactly what was being paid for, and whether certain things were worth the costs. Some students who had wanted and expected a residential experience decided that this new kind of college was not for them. They did not return.

Lieber primarily addresses parents, but welcomes other interested parties, such as stepparents, grandparents, and high school students themselves, to whom he says, "... by all means, keep reading. None of this stuff is meant to fall into the category of proprietary parental secrets, because that would be blatant institutional adultism" (p. 11).

Lo, M. (2021). *Last Night at the Telegraph Club*. New York: Dutton Books for Young Readers.

Lily's story is set in San Francisco's Chinatown in the 1950s, when McCarthyism is at its height. Lilly attends a picnic with people suspected of being in the Communist party; subsequently, her father's naturalization papers, obtained when he served in WWII, are taken away. The threat that he might be deported to China is real. There can be no more trouble. But during Lily's senior year in high school, she is coming to realize that she is attracted to women, despite the word *homosexual* being equated with *deviant* and *perverse* in her family, community, and the larger society. She falls for Kath, the only other girl in her advanced math class, and they begin to sneak out on Friday nights to go to a lesbian bar. When the Telegraph Club gets raided and Kath is arrested, Lily must decide whether to give in to her parents' expectations in order to stay in the family and have a home, or to be true to herself and Kath.

Will her dreams of going to college and her passion for rockets and space be crushed? Will she ever belong anywhere?

Lo works a lot of history into the novel and provides further information about Chinese immigration, women working in the race to get to space, LGBTQ issues, and the "Red Scare" in the back matter.

Writing and Thinking Prompt

You followed Lily through her senior year of high school, and found out through the Epilogue that she did indeed get to college, and got back to see Kath a year later; they did not give up their passions related to flying and space travel. But they could not have ever dreamed what you see as reality now: legal gay marriage, and the beginning of space tourism. Your job is to bring one or both women into a future decade of your choice, and write a scene, perhaps at a place of entertainment, since the Telegraph Club was such a vital setting in terms of their relationship. Will they be a part of the continuing struggle for equal rights? As they get older, how do they establish families, get along in work situations, mentor young people, or find personal fulfillment and a meaningful place in the world?

Marcus, K. (2011). *Exposed*. New York: Random House.

Liz, aka Photogirl, is having a wonderful senior year. She has a forever-best friend, a boyfriend, and a portfolio she is preparing for her college applications—all schools known for their art and photography programs. Everything crashes when Kate accuses Liz's brother of raping her while on a sleepover at Liz's. One of them must be lying. How can she not believe her brother when he tells her that the sex was consensual? How can she not believe her best friend, when she explains that it was not? How can Liz support her parents as their son's trial approaches? And what will she say when she is put on the stand in court?

Liz's photography fades to the background for a while, suffering as she suffers; but ultimately, her skills and thinking and feeling as a photographer help her sort through, if not solve, difficult changes in relationships. By the time she gets her acceptance letter from Parsons School of Design, the trial is over and Liz has begun to heal; and she slowly comes to trust her point of view enough to take pictures again.

McManus, K.M. (2017). *One of Us Is Lying*. New York: Delacorte Press.
Every high school senior is on a unique path. Bronwyn is positioned to be class valedictorian, with her hopes set on Yale. Cooper's baseball skills have college recruiters as well as professional baseball teams interested in him. Addy may not be college-bound, but she's been in a relationship with Jake for three years, and she has great hair, so no problem; she will be taken care of. Nate is not so fortunate. His unstable mother abandoned him years ago, and his father is an alcoholic who is passed out most of the time. Despite being on probation, Nate is dealing drugs.

The four lives converge when they suddenly have one big thing in common. They are all murder suspects after being in an afternoon detention where their classmate Simon dies from drinking water that had peanut oil, which he is allergic to, added to it. As the investigation unfolds, many relationships change, and surprising new ones develop as they learn more about their classmates and themselves.

New Adult readers who are feeling pressure and stress about their own paths to future challenges and identities might relish the chance to delve into a complex mystery like this one. Who could have killed Simon? Who had a motive? Who had the means? Does it matter that Simon was almost universally hated by the student body, due to his posting their secrets and mistakes on a gossip app? What is the significance of some characters being able to afford lawyers, while others cannot? What is the role of the police, and of journalists? How do the clues add up?

Readers who find they thrive on being part of the solution to the mystery will be happy to discover that there's a sequel, as well as a number of other mysteries by the author. Bring on the cases!

Mendez, M. (2019). *Barely Missing Everything*. New York: Atheneum.
Not surprisingly, friends Juan and J.D. have dreams for their post-high school futures. Juan hopes for a basketball scholarship that will

get him out of El Paso, as well as out of poverty. J.D. is passionate about filmmaking. Can his camera be his ticket out? He knows that kind of dream comes true only for those with money, not for Brown boys without it. He will watch others get out, disappear to college.

> They certainly wouldn't get stuck as waitresses or cashiers… And they definitely wouldn't waste their bodies in construction or landscaping or as mechanics, not cleaning houses or hotels or chasing around kids that weren't their own…. J.D. had no shot. Zip, zero, shit.
>
> (pp. 261–262)

Readers will root for Juan and J.D., but their hopes will be tested by circumstances and by some of the boys' decisions, such as when they panic during a police raid of a party and try to run away. Juan hurts his ankle, thereby hurting his basketball participation and scholarship chances. He is arrested, and awaits his court date. Meanwhile, J.D. discovers his father is having an affair, resulting in the breakup of his family. When Juan figures out from reading letters sent to his mother that the father he never knew is in prison awaiting execution, the boys decide to drive to the prison to meet him and make a documentary. What could go wrong?

And then there's Fabi, Juan's mother. She's made her share of mistakes, too. She's been in the same dead-end waitressing job since giving birth to Juan at age 16. She has not answered Juan's questions about his father. And now, she is pregnant again. Is there any hope left?

The characters might be barely missing everything, but thoughtful readers will want to miss nothing of this journey.

*Ostrovski, E. (2013). *The Paradox of Vertical Flight*. New York: HarperCollins.

I had to employ Coleridge's "willing suspension of disbelief" as I traveled by car and boat with the characters in this novel. Jack steals his newborn baby from the hospital, naming him Socrates. He convinces his best friend Tommy as well as Jess— the mother of the infant—to accompany him as he brings the baby to meet his grandmother (who lives several states away and has Alzheimer's) before they give him up for adoption. Because our narrator Jack is of a philosophical bent, his message about the journey being a quest to find the meaning of life is less than subtle. He's terrified at the prospect of losing everything and everyone. Jess calls him her ex-boyfriend, Tommy has joined the military, his grandmother is dying, and he might never see his child again. He is afraid to grow up, afraid of change. Tommy offers some words of wisdom:

> Well, yeah, the quest keeps you together, keeps you young, but, you know, the quest can't go on forever. It can't be never-ending...Where'd the point be in that? Because, man, if it went on forever, if the evil and the monsters kept coming and coming, then you'd only get a different kind of old and a different kind of separated and that would be as bad, you know?

(p. 232)

By the way, the author wrote this book when he was 23, and majored in philosophy at Vassar College, earning a degree a year before this book was published!

Philippe, B. (2020). *Charming as a Verb*. New York: Balzer + Bray.
Henry narrates the story of his final semester of high school. Not surprisingly, much of what is on the seniors' minds and in their conversations has to do with college admissions. Who got into their dream school? Who has to be satisfied with a safety school? Who is still waiting?

Henry desperately wants to attend Columbia, which is so close to home; so prestigious; and so able to make his father, a Haitian immigrant, proud of him. Henry is keenly aware of the sacrifices his dad has made, working tirelessly as a maintenance supervisor in a Manhattan apartment building, in order to send Henry to the private Fate Academy, where students are groomed and prepared for Ivy League institutions. And Henry himself has worked hard, both academically and in extracurricular activities such as the debate team. He created a dog-walking service, which keeps him very busy. He has also honed his interpersonal skills, even consciously knowing what kind of smiles to give to certain persons and in certain contexts.

Henry is close to being the kind of student Columbia seeks, but he is worried about not being exceptional enough to be a shoe-in. And when his college interview doesn't go well, worry takes over. What else can he do? Enter Corinne, an intense classmate to whom he has not paid much attention before, but who becomes a huge part of Henry's social, ethical, and emotional learning curves at this crucial point in his life.

*Reul, R. (2021). *Where the Road Leads Us*. Naperville, IL: Sourcebooks Fire.

When we meet Jack on his eighteenth birthday and graduation day, he feels like someone who is very easy for others to leave. His brother left two years ago, after drug-related problems and a suicide attempt. His father died of a heart attack a year ago. His mother is on a book tour. And his girlfriend breaks up with him that morning.

When we meet Hallie that same day, she is dealing with news from her doctor that her cancer has probably recurred, along with news that her close friend whom she met in an online support group is close to death. When Jack and Hallie meet in the same rideshare after each has made an impulsive decision (Hallie to go to Oregon to be there for Owen's death, Jack to go to San Francisco to try to find his brother), a road trip ensues.

Turns out a lot can happen in one night: a car being stolen, a dog-napping, a trip to a tattooist, a memorable moment at the Pacific Ocean, stories shared, and fun! Jack, who wants to pursue creative writing, but feels pressure to go to Columbia and become a doctor to fulfill his parents' dream, is rethinking that plan when Hallie tells him, "Basically, you're in a real-life-choose-your-own-ending novel featuring you as the protagonist" (p. 87).

The adventure results in Hallie gaining insight into her own life, too:

> I have cancer, but it's up to me if I let it control my life or define me.... Attitude is key.... While I'm here, I want to focus on enjoying as many days between as I can get instead of dwelling on what bookends them.

(p. 242)

The road that night is not smooth, and the road ahead is not without huge obstacles. (No one who understands the concept of *quest* can be surprised by that). For readers who are on their own journeys, I can think of no better mentors to give them than Jack and Hallie. Hand them this book.

*Schumacher, A. (2021). *Amelia Unabridged*. New York: Wednesday Books.

Amelia and Jenna, with plans to attend the same college, head to a book convention to celebrate their graduation and, with luck, meet the author of their favorite fantasy book series, N. E. Endsley, who created the famed world of Orman when he was 15. Things go wrong; then Jenna dies, leaving Amelia needing to piece together what has happened, "… making a new kind of road map that will show me where I ought to go…" (p. 176). During her journey to a Michigan bookstore to try to figure out who sent a signed copy of the Orman Chronicles, she ponders the concept of being an adult, since she technically *is* one. "I'm supposed to be able to make my own life choices, be self-sufficient, and generally be more something. Mature, maybe, but I know plenty of immature adults" (p. 87).

Making choices is complicated when you have pinky promised your best friend that you would do certain things, and later realize that's not the career or academic path you want to pursue, but now that friend is dead. Amelia is grieving, but also falling in love and reclaiming a passion for photography. Is she bound to her earlier promises? What would Jenna want for her?

Amelia has always loved books, and now her life is an unfinished story. She's in the middle of it. Who controls where the story will go?

Tran, P. (2020). *Sigh, Gone: A Misfit's Memoir of Great Books, Punk Rock, and the Fight to Fit in*. New York: Flatiron Books.

In this memoir, we get to know Phuc as a child, a middle school student, and an adolescent in the 1980s and early nineties in a school district where his is the only Vietnamese family in Carlisle, Pennsylvania. What he wants more than anything is to fit in, and he tries various methods, including giving up his status as an excellent academic student in order to embrace the punk culture, where misfits at least belonged in a group with each other. Other things Phuc thought he had to eschew were his heritage, and his parents' language and values. He tells us the backstory of the harrowing escape they made from Vietnam when he was an infant, as well as the difficult and brave things they did to become independent of the resources provided by those who supported the refugees. Yet he was embarrassed by his parents; they represented all the things he thought he needed to escape in order to fit in at school.

Other than his younger brother, whom he adores and is protective of, no one, not even himself, is spared in Phuc's telling of incidents in his home life; his relationships with both parents were complicated and strained. In school, there were outstanding teachers, such as the one who drove him to see a production of his favorite Oscar Wilde play, *The Importance of Being Earnest* (1990). And then there were other teachers and administrators who did not understand him, did not protect him from racist attacks and bullying, and did not guide him well on his journey.

Phuc, not surprisingly, was searching for, as well as constructing, an identity. He figured out that he could enjoy skateboarding and punk music with his friends *and* still be the editor of the school paper, read the classics, and aspire to college. His love of literature shows in his chapter titles and themes, connecting to Kafka's *Metamorphosis* (2013), Hawthorne's *The Scarlet Letter* (2003), Shaw's *Pygmalion* (2003), and Homer's *The Iliad* (2014).

Readers will root for Phuc every step of the way and may feel like they have found a mentor as they navigate family, academic, and social situations of increasing complexity. They may want to hear his TEDx talk, "Grammar, Identity, and the Dark Side of the Subjunctive" (Tran, 2012); and to find out more about his life after graduating from high school, which is the point at which his memoir ends.

Vaughn, L.R. (2013). *OCD, The Dude, and Me.* New York: Dial Books.

When [my mother] came in my room to bring me my new Adderall prescription, she tripped on the Romantic Era section of my library, books which are alphabetized, systematized, and laid out on my floor.... Austen's works are now mixed with the Brontë sisters. I can't find Browning. Wordsworth is under my bed, and Blake and Shelley have been kicked to a pile of dirty clothes near my dresser.

(p. 3)

From this very first journal entry, written on the morning of the first day of senior year, I was rooting for Danielle. She goes to an alternative school, and we get to know her through class assignments (along with grades and teacher comments), emails, letters to and from her school counselor, and other texts. She has many issues to work through, and things are not totally resolved or magically erased by the end of the year, but Danielle is healthier and ready to begin college at UC Irvine as a creative writing major. I hope there's a sequel, so that I can follow her there. She's one friend I want to keep.

Wibberley, E., & Siegemund-Broka, A. (2020). *Time of Our Lives.* New York: Viking.
Juniper Ramírez's eyes are fixed on the future. She can't wait to get away from her siblings. She loves her parents and Tía Sofi, but she's ready for privacy and independence. So she's totally into the well-planned college tour she takes in December of her senior year with her boyfriend Matt so she can check out architecture programs. Fitz, on the other hand, is reluctantly touring colleges with his older brother because his mother insisted. He dreads the future, because genetic testing has shown that his mom will get early-onset Alzheimer's. She will need him, and he intends to go to SNHU so that he can live at home.

Fritz and Juniper meet on the tour. And—surprise—they like being together. (Juniper and Matt, on the other hand, realize they do not share the same dreams, so Matt goes home.) As they experience walks on college campuses, calls home, parties, detours, and conversations about books and language, both learn valuable lessons. Juniper is surprised when she feels homesick, realizing:

When I'm in college, I'll be finding my place and finding my people anew... I'll be deciding what parts of home to hold onto.

How I'll put myself together from the pieces of my past and my present, of old friends and new, of my family, of the two cultures I grew up in. The pressure won't just be about fitting in with everyone else—it'll be about figuring out where I *want* to fit in.

(p. 266)

Fitz learns that his love of words can be more than a hobby when Juniper arranges for them to attend a language class at Carnegie Mellon and the teacher talks about their Linguistics Program. He learns that he has been wrong about his brother in so many ways; Lewis has been making sacrifices and planning his future in a way that will pay for the long-term care their mother will need. A new mutual respect between the brothers is established on this trip. And Juniper teaches Fitz that it is okay to relish the present and not let fear about his mom's future deny him his own. She assures him that he will carry his mother's memories for her.

The book cover blurb promises "A boy desperate to hold on. A girl ready to let go." Readers who go along on this college tour will indeed find that, but also discover multiple layers in these characters, and they will finish the tour with the same thing as Fitz and Juniper: hope.

Writing and Thinking Prompt

This book can't help but make you think about the passing of time. Think about your relationship to your past and the people in it; your future hopes and plans; and your ability to live in the present. Would you say there's a good balance? What things in your past will you hold onto? What worries about others might be holding you back from being your best present self? And what changes (if any) might you think about that will allow you to care for the needs of others without sacrificing the things that will allow you to live your own dreams to the fullest? Answer one or more of these questions, or reflect on another part of the story (such as sibling relationships) that had an impact on you. Talk directly to Fitz, Juniper, or Lewis if you want to.

Instructional Strategies and Activities

Opportunity and Advertising

Reading is social, and the benefits of students reading together and being allowed to talk with others about their reading are great (e.g., Ivey, 2014; Roessing, 2019; Rose and Walsh, 2021). So it makes sense that providing time and encouragement for reading is a necessary and rewarding instructional method. You can start by structuring class or library time to include silent reading, and perhaps replacing other homework with a directive to read for pleasure for a certain amount of time (allowing for flexibility) each evening or weekend. There are many ways to challenge students to read more. I will limit suggestions here to those without external rewards. You don't need to raise money or offer prizes or grading incentives to make the idea of reading palatable. That said, keeping track of time spent reading or the number of books read, or being accountable to self or others, can encourage persistence and result in a sense of accomplishment.

Some librarians and teachers arrange some kind of readathon on a Saturday, or even overnight, so that students can come together. (What could be more fun than a sleepover in the school library, surrounded by friends and hundreds of beckoning books?) There is a variety of types of readathons and challenges available online, including Dewey's 24-Hour Readathon, Book Riot's Read Harder Challenge, and the Goodread's Reading Challenge. You can create your own version of a challenge as well, whether it be for a weekend, a summer, a semester, or an entire year. For several years I have participated in challenges created by high school teacher Krisi Bacher Amey (a former student of mine). She supplies the invitation, rules, and categories, and the rest is up to us. The categories change each year; we never know when we'll need to find a book with a map in the front, or a book over ten years old, or a book with a body count. Participants record what they read, and give their opinions or reviews, often initiating discussion among the readers. She creates a community of readers, and I am happy to belong.

There are many students who have never had a habit of reading for pleasure, or who got away from it in middle or high school as they devoted more time to homework, sports, employment, and other activities. Sadly, they might also have come to associate reading with unenjoyable worksheets and assignments, and/or with assessments that have discouraged them. They may need help rediscovering the joy of reading, as well as discovering what's out there in terms of New Adult literature that is relevant to their identities and interests. So advertising is essential. Fortunately, this can be easy and fun and can involve the whole class. The book talks throughout these chapters are meant to entice as well as inform readers. There is a near-infinite number of other forms book promotion can take. Examples include individuals, or collaborative groups, creating book trailers; posters; blogs for conversation and reviews; and book tube channels.

Walk-Through

Dr. Bütz's senior literature class is using a book club approach, adapted from Lesley Roessing's *Talking Texts* (2019). They meet twice a week for an hour and a half. In addition to the teacher's introductory and closing remarks, here's what a typical class meeting might consist of:

- *Reviews and Advertising* (twenty minutes). One student shows a book trailer she created for R.L. Culli's *Say Yes Summer*. Another shows the fan art she created after reading Malinda Lo's *Last Night at the Telegraph Club*. Two students use a Readers Theatre approach as they present a dialog-rich excerpt from Kacen Callender's *Felix Ever After*. Two more give an update on their progress in creating a book tubing channel that is close to going live.
- *Silent Reading* (twenty minutes) of books students have chosen from the text set on "The Summer after Graduation."
- *Book Clubs* (twenty minutes). Students meet with others who have chosen the same title from the text set. The unit assignments assure that all group members have read at least half the book. They follow the rule of talking only about the parts that, according to the calendar, all members should have read; if some have read ahead, they are not allowed to give any spoilers. If any students have fallen behind, they can choose to listen anyway or remove themselves to keep reading silently.
- *Whole Class Instruction/Inquiry*. Dr. Bütz gives a mini-lesson on charting characters' maturity and growth (or lack thereof) and talks about the writing assignment that will culminate the unit, where students will be writing about their plans for the two months following their graduation, as they prepare to transition to college, work, or travel. She encourages them to be thinking about how they will structure the writing piece as they finish the novels they're reading and discussing. Students ask questions related to the mini-lesson, the upcoming writing project, or other issues on their minds.

Only Connect

When author Deborah Heiligman encountered the epigraph "Only connect." in E.M. Forster's *Howards End* (2012), she thought, "That's me" (Kane, 2021a, p. 58). She explains how the phrase captures the theme of her work:

> …what I care about most in my life is connections to the people I love … not only do I like to write about connections, but I need to be connected to the people I write about …. I research so deeply that I feel like I can get inside my subjects, inside their hearts, their minds, their DNA … When a professor (you!) helps teachers of children and teens to connect with my work … it brings so much meaning to my life and my work … To think of children and teens being guided through a reading of *Vincent and Theo* [2017] and a reaction to the book that includes not only the van Gogh brothers but also me … that somewhere a student might be drawing the lines, both literally and figuratively, between Vincent's work and mine, between his heart and mine, and then connecting it to their own—well … Could you imagine if Vincent could come back and see how much people love him? How many people connect with him? With his art?
>
> (Kane, 2021a, pp. 58–59)

Inviting students to "Only connect" can stimulate readers to make connections they might not have consciously thought about without the prompt; the same words applied to texts used throughout a semester can deepen their thinking and result in the formation of connections both within and among texts. Watch their answers become richer. Be ready for the time when "Only connect" has become such a habit that students initiate the discussion of connections on their own.

Walk-Through

Mr. Vo, like Deborah Heiligman, loves connections, and not a day goes by when students in his classes are not connecting characters with themselves, characters with each other, authors with each other, fiction with real life, etc. They see connections within and across the disciplines they study. They encourage others to see and make connections. In September, Mr. Vo's classes celebrate International Dot Day by completing appropriate projects and wandering about the dedicated website to see what others in almost 200 countries have contributed; it's clear that everything is about connecting the dots. There is a large poster in his classroom that says, "Only connect." Other posters contain quotes from authors about connection, such as this one from Benjamin Alire Sáenz:

> It is ludicrous to speak of an *I* that has an existence of its own. I only matter in the context of my relationships to others and to the communities I belong to—communities that intersect and are, often, in conflict with one another—which makes the task of living more than a little complicated.
>
> (2019, p. 15)

Mr. Vo's students have read many of the books discussed in this chapter. Here is a sample of what his student responses contain:

- Ritu and Drew: We're planning a mega-prom and inviting all the characters from the prom-related books on our shelves. Guess what the prom theme is going to be: "Only connect!" If you want some hot romances and some major drama, plan to attend! Bring a date, or a friend, or Mr. Vo, or your favorite character from another book altogether.
- Bonita: After reading *Sigh, Gone*, I'm making a chart of all the ways my life and Phuc Tran's life are alike and different. I really connected to him, not just because we are both children of immigrants, but because so many times when he was trying to fit in at school, or pursue his passions, or please his parents while remaining true to himself, I felt like I knew exactly how he was feeling. His decisions are helping me think about decisions I have to make soon, as I near the end of high school and face the future—my future.
- Robyn: After reading *Felix Ever After*, Kacen Callender is my new favorite author; and I plan to make a diagram connecting all the things I learn about them—other books, reviews, speeches, their website, interviews, you name it. I don't know how the dots will connect yet, but I can't wait to make that happen. Oh, I'm going to write to the author, too—that will be a *personal* connection.
- Harrison: All semester, with Mr. Vo's help, I've been trying to make interdisciplinary connections. I'm in the process of analyzing *Last Night at the Telegraph Club*. There's history, music, math, fashion, science, engineering, language, politics, and culture. I'm working on plotting the story using the hero's journey archetype.

Using Epitext to Enrich Understanding and Response to Texts

We usually expect a work of literature to stand on its own; and we can comprehend, enjoy, and appreciate it without needing information about its author, or about what critics or reviewers have to say about it. In fact, students have been turned off when they have opinions about a book and then find out that their interpretation doesn't match some teacher's manual or answer key to a test, or that there was some hidden meaning that they had missed. Yet it's also true that bringing in resources or having readers search for things related to, but outside the text (that is, the *epitext*), can be tremendously enriching and can help readers think and feel more deeply about the original work. An author's biography or website, speeches, and interviews fit within the category of epitext, as do reviews of a book, fan letters, awards, book trailers, and advertisements. Transmedia responses to the book, using a format or genre different from the text, also count.

Witte, Gross, and Latham edited *From Text to Epitext: Expanding Students' Comprehension, Engagement, and Media Literacy* (2021), containing chapters showing the application of epitext in various instructional contexts using particular books. In a chapter I contributed, "Epitextual Analysis of Biographies: Enhancing Disciplinary Literacy," written with Deborah Heiligman, I explain how students' artistic responses and further research enabled them to make new connections to each other, the author, and the subjects of Heiligman's biographies, including Charles Darwin, Vincent van Gogh, and mathematician Paul Erdös. One class had the pleasure of meeting Deborah through Zoom. We were actually creating epitext that not only changed our appreciation of the texts we read but also affected the author herself. In her response to the chapter, she writes:

> You can't imagine how gratifying it is for an author to see her work spiraling out beyond the text into people's lives and interests and further reading. I absolutely adore the idea of readers taking the people I've written about and extending their relationships with them…. Now, after reading this, I wonder if I will also think about how readers can take what I write further into their lives and intellectual exploration. And I wonder if that will affect how I write a book….
>
> (Kane, 2021b, p. 28)

So by all means, encourage readers to go beyond the text, either before they read it or after. Show them where they can find reviews of the NA books discussed here (both by scholars in the field and by members of the general public), interviews, scholarly analyses, pertinent information on social media, and websites. They'll start initiating new projects and bringing in things you would not have thought of. That happens to me a lot, and then I learn from the students, and our thinking and pleasure go even further. Learning more about things that relate to a book can sometimes lead to re-reading, and will influence the experience and response.

Walk-Through

Let's consider using epitextual exploration related to the works of A.S. King, several of which are talked about in this book. Her style has been described as surrealistic; and readers who are comfortable with traditional stories, told in mostly chronological order, are often confused, and sometimes put off, when reading her novels. I have used *Dig.* (2019) in my classes, and I tell students up front that A.S. King will expect a lot from them. They will need to sweat, work hard, and dig deep, but the rewards will be great. They'll have to be okay with ambiguity, since they will have more questions than answers most of the way through. They will need to trust the author, even when her text and her characters frustrate them. I ask them to be conscious of their cognitive, metacognitive, and emotional reactions as they read; I invite them to keep a running commentary with the author in mind as their audience if that will help. Most rise to the challenge, but many are still skeptical when they finish the book. Did it really have to be that weird?

Together we read professional reviews, including a starred review from *Booklist*, and students begin to connect or compare their own responses to those of the reviewers. For example, lines from Kirkus Reviews resonate:

> An unwieldy list of the cast featured in each part melds well with the frenetic style of this experimental work but does little to actually clarify how they fit together; the first half, at least, is markedly confusing. However, readers able to relax into the chaos will be richly rewarded as the strands eventually weave together.
>
> (2019)

Then we watch Amy Sarig King's Printz Award Acceptance Speech on YouTube (2020) together. I cannot adequately describe the impact this experience has on the class. For some, *Dig.* takes on a whole new dimension as a result of hearing and seeing the author. If they still don't entirely get the story, they at least now *want* to, and they determine to revisit the text with the knowledge and feelings they got from the author's impassioned, angry, challenging talk about white supremacy and institutional racism.

Several years ago, I chose A.S. King's *I Crawl Through It* (2015) as our first whole class read in a Young Adult literature course. I knew it was risky, but I wanted students to grapple with strong ideas and an experimental style. Sure enough, many of the responses they came in with during our second week expressed confusion, discomfort, resistance, and worry. That was okay, even appropriate, since there is nothing comfortable or reassuring going on in the characters' lives or in their school. The picture isn't pretty. Yet the responses showed depth and creativity that went way beyond the discussion of why they liked or didn't like the book. Eventually, we read reviews and other examples of epitext that furthered understanding and intellectual inquiry. But first, I had a surprise for my class. The author visited us via a videoconference and addressed readers' questions. The results were astounding. You can read a detailed description of our epitextual experience, along with student-created poems and Amy Sarig King's response to the videoconference (another example of an author listening to, learning from, and being influenced by readers) on the blog "Dr. Bickmore's YA Wednesday" (Kane, 2018).

Once students meet A.S. King, they can't get enough of her. They read other novels by her, but they also explore her website as well as YouTube and social media sites to see what she's up to. And they look for books she recommends in her compilation of resources related to mental health in "Gracie's List" (Book Love Foundation, 2022).

For another bit of epitext based on the works of A.S. King, I encourage you to read a blog post written by Bird Cramer, a former student who crawled through *I Crawl Through It* during my class and emerged forever changed: "Mental Health and Healing through the Novels of A.S. King" (Cramer, 2020).

References

Book Love Foundation. (2022). Gracie's list. https://2167c2c5-4c77-449c-8a4a-93b13446767a.filesusr.com/ugd/f8eddb_306553e662ca4093aa7489a30830 84a2.pdf.

Cramer, B. (2020, July 8). Mental health and healing through the novels of A.S. King. Retrieved from http://www.yawednesday.com/blog/mental-health-and-healing-through-the-novels-of-as-king-by-bird-cramer.

Ivey, G. (2014). The social side of engaged reading for young adolescents. *The Reading Teacher, 68*(3), 165–171.

Kane, S., with Heiligman, D. (2021a). Impressions/expressions: Using arts integration strategies while reading a biography of an artist. In Maldonado, R., (Ed.). *Arts integration and young adult literature: Strategies to enhance academic skills and student voice.* Lanham, MD: Rowman & Littlefield pp. 49–60.

Kane, S., with Heiligman, D. (2021b). Epitextual analysis of biographies: Enhancing disciplinary literacy. In Witte, S., Gross, M., & Latham, D. (2021). *From text to epitext: Expanding students' comprehension, engagement, and media literacy.* Santa Barbara, CA: Libraries Unlimited, pp. 19–30.

Kane, S. (2018, October 1). Reading and discussing "I Crawl through It" in a YA literature class. Retrieved from http://www.yawednesday.com/blog/reading-and-discussing-i-crawl-through-it-in-a-ya-literature-class.

King, A.S. (2020). A.S. King's 2020 Printz acceptance speech. Retrieved from https://vimeo.com/434380713.

Kirkus Reviews. (2019). Review of the book Dig., by A.S. King. 1/1/2019. Retrieved from https://www.kirkusreviews.com/book-reviews/as-king/dig-king/.

Roessing, L. (2019). *Talking texts: A teacher's guide to book clubs across the curriculum.* Latham, MD: Rowman & Littlefield.

Rose, D., & Walsh, C. (2021). *Talking through reading and writing: Online reading conversation journals in the middle school.* Latham, MD: Rowman & Littlefield.

Sáenz, B.A. (2019). In the breaking, maybe something beautiful. *The Horn Book Magazine, XCV*(2), 13–16.

Tran, P. (2012, November 26). Grammar, identity, and the dark side of the subjunctive. Retrieved from https://www.google.com/search?q=phuc+tran+ted+talk&rlz=1C1GCEU_enUS888US888&oq=phuc+tran+ted+talk&aqs=chrome.0.69i59j0i22i30.6287j1j7&sourceid=chrome&ie=UTF-8.

Witte, S., Gross, M., & Latham, D. (2021). *From text to epitext: Expanding students' comprehension, engagement, and media literacy.* Santa Barbara, CA: Libraries Unlimited.

Literature Cited

Anderson. A. (2012). *High school prom: Marketing, morals, and the American teen.* Jefferson, NC: McFarland.

Anderson, L.H. (2005). *Prom.* New York: Viking.

Cirrone, D. (2008). *Prom kings and drama queens.* New York: HarperTeen.

Crompton, L.B. (2014). *The real prom queens of Westfield High.* Naperville, IL: Sourcebooks Fire.

Eulberg, E. (2011). *Prom and prejudice*. New York: Point.

Ferris, A. (2011). *Will work for prom dress*. New York: Egmont USA.

Forster, E.M. (2012). *Howards end*. Oneida, NY: Empire Books.

Hall, S. (2018). *A prom to remember*. New York: Swoon Reads.

Hawthorne, N. (2003). *The scarlet letter*. New York: Penguin.

Heiligman, D. (2017). *Vincent and Theo: The Van Gogh brothers*. New York: Godwin Books.

Homer. (2014). *The Iliad*. New York: Oxford University Press.

Kafka, F. (2013). *The metamorphosis*. New York: Modern Library.

Kehm. M. (2009). *Suzi Clue: The prom queen curse*. New York: Dutton.

King, A.S. (2019). *Dig*. New York: Dutton Books.

King, A.S. (2015). *I crawl through it*. New York: Little, Brown and Company.

Labar, A. (2021). *Prom theory*. New York: Simon & Schuster.

Levithan, D., & Ehrenhaft, D. (2014). *21 proms*. New York: Scholastic.

McDonald, A. (2011). *The anti-prom*. Somerville, MA: Candlewick Press.

Metz, L. (2013). *The prom book*. San Francisco, CA: Zest Books.

Meyer, S., Harrison, K., Cabot, M., Myracle, L., & Jaffe, M. (2009). *Prom nights from hell*. New York: HarperTeen.

McCoy, C. (2015). *The prom goer's interstellar excursion*. New York: Knopf.

Miller, K. (2021). *The night no one had sex*. Park Ridge, IL: AW Teen.

Peters, J.A. (2012). *It's our prom (so deal with it)*. Boston, MA: Little, Brown.

Preble, L. (2008). *Prom queen geeks*. New York: Berkley.

Shaw, G.B. (2003). *Pygmalion*. New York: Penguin.

Vaughn, L.R. (2013). *OCD, the Dude, and me*. New York: Dial Books.

Wilde, O. (1990). *The importance of being earnest*. New York: Dover Publications.

Navigating the College Years   **3**

The Definitive Guide to College Success Does Not Exist

The majority of the courses I teach are Education courses populated by juniors and seniors who are fairly secure in their ability to handle the academic expectations, showing varying levels of comfort and excitement as they participate in practicum settings in secondary schools and compile their resumes for teaching applications. I also teach a course I designed on the topic of New Adult literature that is limited to first-semester freshmen. This chapter may target this latter group, students who are anxious to get beyond the orientation programs, more than the students who are already thinking about their post-university life. The new arrivals may be open to learning about expectations; advice from various sources about how to succeed (and what success looks like); and the value of books in helping readers get a variety of pictures of what college life entails. The chapter could help them ponder questions about their own goals, values, identity, and hopes. The books discussed here can give them frameworks, or points of comparison, as they meet new people, explore new areas in their courses, and set about reinventing themselves (while staying true to their authentic selves).

Wilner, in *Re-Thinking Reading in College: An Across-the-Curriculum Approach* (2020), describes several scenes from her college classes showing students who give opinions without evidence from the text, or who rely

DOI: 10.4324/9781003221685-3

on strategies learned in high school rather than stretching to a higher level of analysis and interpretation. She concludes:

> Despite decades of teaching, I am regularly flummoxed by the habits and assumptions of students trying to make sense of texts. And I am far from alone. Evidence abounds that students at all levels and in all disciplines need better instruction and more practice in reading.

Readers who enter the fictional college worlds of characters in some of the books presented in this chapter, and who participate in the activities and/or answer the prompts provided, can get that needed practice in reading. Along with the characters they meet, they can mature; understand or take on different perspectives; solve problems; and become better selves.

TEXT SETS

The Gap Year

There are alternatives to going immediately from high school to college. A gap year can involve stepping away from formal education while embracing different, equally valuable, kinds of education. Professor and author Charles Wheelan (2021) is one of many proponents of the gap year for students who have completed high school. He explains:

> I teach highly motivated college students who have been running fast and jumping through hoops since middle school.... Some of those students are burned out by the time I see them. Many would have benefited from some time off after high school to mature, work, and/or reflect on why they are going to college, especially given the cost of higher education.

(p. 30)

Wheelan has credibility, having returned from nine months of travel with his family. (You'll read a book talk relating to his trip later in this chapter.) The fiction and nonfiction books I have selected for this text set show a variety of ways a gap year can play out. The selections that are marked with an asterisk are introduced in the next section on Book Talks.

*Becker, H. (2021). *Himawari House*. New York: First Second.
*Choi, M.H.K. (2018). *Emergency Contact*. New York: Simon & Schuster.
Coy, J. (2016). *Gap Life*. New York: Fewel and Friends.
Folb, P. (2020). *Find your Right Direction: The Israel Gap Year Guide*. Redwood Publishing.
Gomez, M.M. (2020). *A Year Off: How to Take a Gap Year and Travel the World Even if You Are on a Budget*. Nomadelle.
Gregory, L.S. (2019). *The Gap Year Guide: Faith-based Programs that Change Lives*. Independently published. Athens, OH: Wetknee Books.
* Ma, D. (2020). *Heiress Apparently*. New York: Abrams.
Pryor, M. (2017). *Gap Year in Ghost Town*. Sydney: Allen & Unwin.
Peetros, E. (2021). *The Unintentional Gap Year: A Memoir Chronicling my Mental Health Journey*. Independently published. ISBN: 9798592944956.
*Sheba, K. (2021). *The Marvelous Mirza Girls*. New York: Quill Tree Books.
*Wheelan, C. (2020). *We Came, We Saw, We Left: A Family Gap Year*. New York: W.W. Norton & Company.
White, K. (2019). *The Complete Guide to the Gap Year: The Best Things to Do Between High School and College*. Online: Nota Bene Press.

The College Years: Nonfiction

In this collection of titles, you'll find informational books that are filled with advice about all aspects of college, from financial to social to academic. Read them and you will succeed! Really? They might be quite helpful, but you can also learn about college from specific accounts written by people who have been through the experience. The biography and memoirs here are at least partly about the important, formative years of the memoirists' lives. Together, the two types of books will give you a lot to think about as you prepare for and make decisions related to college life. The asterisk before a title lets you know there is a book talk in the next section.

*Brenner, A.M., & Schwartz, S.H. (2019). *How to College: What to Know before you Go (and when you're there)*. New York: St. Martin's Griffin.

Brooks, K. (2021). *What Color Is Your Parachute? for College: Pave your Path from Major to Meaningful Work*. Berkeley, CA: Ten Speed Press.

*Fagan, K. (2017). *What Made Maddy Run: The Secret Struggles and Tragic Death of an All-American Teen*. Boston, MA: Little, Brown and Company.

Grimes, J. (2020). *The Ultimate College Student Health Handbook: Your Guide for Everything from Hangovers to Homesickness*. New York: Skyhorse Publishing.

Johnson, G.M. (2020). *All Boys Aren't Blue: A Memoir-Manifesto*. New York: Farrar Straus Giroux.

Lieber, R. (2021). *The Price You Pay for College: An Entirely New Road Map for the Biggest Financial Decisions your Family will Ever Make*. New York: Harper.

Tanabe, G.S. (2021). *1001 Ways to Pay for College: Strategies to Maximize College Savings, Financial Aid, Scholarships, and Grants*. Belmont, CA: SuperCollege.

Tough, P. (2019). *The Years that Matter Most: How College Makes or Breaks Us*. New York: Houghton Mifflin Harcourt.

Westover, T. (2018). *Educated: A Memoir*. New York: Random House.

White, D.A. (2021). *Healthy, Quick & Easy College Cookbook: 100 Simple, Budget-friendly Recipes to Satisfy your Campus Cravings*. Indianapolis, IN: DK Publishing.

Book Talks: Ready to Go!

An asterisk indicates that a title is included in a text set above.

Albertalli, B. (2020). *Love: Creekwood: A Simonverse Novella*. New York: Balzer + Bray.

First-year college students who are working to meet new people and become part of their college community while simultaneously missing close high school friends and lovers will read the emails in *Love, Creekwood* eagerly, especially if they have read either or both of Albertalli's previous Simonverse novels: *Simon vs. the Homo Sapiens Agenda* (2015) and *Leah on the Offbeat* (2018). They might identify with the pain and vulnerability inherent in long-distance relationships. Some readers might wonder if Simon's unhappiness when he is away from Blue is keeping him from being able to fully engage in his new surroundings. Could his dependence be unhealthy? At the other extreme, Abby and Leah are now roommates, sitting on the dorm bed together writing affectionate emails to each other. Is there such a thing as being too close? Are the high school relationships now keeping the characters from growing in college? The novella doesn't raise these questions directly, nor does it provide answers. But readers will form conclusions, and perhaps ponder the pluses and minuses of various ways of balancing former relationships and new experiences.

*Becker, H. (2021). *Himawari House*. New York: First Second.
Nao, born in Japan but raised in the Midwest of the United States, defers college in order to spend a gap year in Tokyo, relearning the language and reconnecting with her roots. She shares a house with Hyejung, from Korea, and Tina, from Singapore, as well as two Japanese brothers. As the young adults get to know each other and share food, memories, cultural routines, family stories, experiences in Japanese language school, and dreams, they become strongly bonded. For a long time, Nao feels more conflicted by her biracial identity than ever, feeling like there is nowhere she will completely belong. But her comfort and confidence levels grow along with her fluency in Japanese, and by the time she is scheduled to return to the United States, she can't imagine leaving what has become her home.

The graphic novel panels are filled with illustrations showing the characters' emotions, and the speech bubbles contain whatever language the characters are speaking. The English is written phonetically to match the pronunciation of the speakers. The friends have conversations about language, noting that they change the way they speak depending on context and whom they are interacting with. Readers who visit Himawari House will leave enriched in so many ways, and will not forget the close friends who live there for a year, flourishing.

*Brenner, A.M., & Schwartz, S.H. (2019). *How to College: What to Know before you Go (and When You're There)*. New York: St. Martin's Griffin.

If there are high school graduates who like to check off boxes on a list as they accomplish tasks, this book will help them make good use of the summer before they head off to college. The authors cover a lot of territory when giving helpful advice and tips, as well as provide quotes from college students, who offer a different kind of credibility. While assuring readers that they do not have to have their whole lives figured out and planned before beginning their first semester, nor should they succumb to stress or pressure, Brenner and Schwartz explain numerous ways people can prepare for the academic, social, and financial issues that are part of college life. They encourage an explorer mentality.

The authors talk to readers directly, recognizing that no two individuals will have the same needs or will experience college in the same way; thus, they allow for flexibility, discernment, making mistakes, and changing one's mind. While encouraging growth and active working toward an identity that will be different from a high school version of oneself, they stress the importance of knowing and keeping one's core values, as "They will ground the decisions you will have to make and prepare you to thrive in your college environment" (p. 18).

There's a section consisting of three chapters on taking care of oneself. The concept of wellness is explored; eating well, sleeping well, and playing well are discussed, as are spiritualty, time management, and stress reduction. Readers are even encouraged and taught how to practice napping the proper way!

Some readers will try out every exercise, seriously consider all the self-assessments, and begin to make changes before they leave home. Others might peruse the book, reading sections randomly or depending upon what appeals to them at certain times. Returning to the book during the course of the first semester would be beneficial for both kinds of readers. Contexts will help determine the best ways to make meaning of and apply the many suggestions in *How to College*.

*Choi, M.H.K. (2018). *Emergency Contact*. New York: Simon & Schuster.
Things we learn about Penny: She's organized and responsible. She feels deeply but does not show that. She feels like she has had to take care of her flighty, immature mother. She loves creative writing. She is happy to be at college, 79 miles from her mother. (However,

when her mother overdoses on marijuana-laced brownies and lands in the hospital, Penny feels she needs to go home to check on her once again.)

Things we learn about Sam: At 21, he has dropped out of college, despite having a passion for filmmaking. He loves to bake, and lives over a bakery. He struggles financially. He loves his mother, though she is flawed and unstable. His ex-girlfriend is pregnant, and Sam is determined to offer support in every way.

Things we think we know about Penny and Sam: They are perfect for each other! They are falling in love through their texts, though they are supposed to be emergency contacts only. Maybe by the end of the book, if we hurry, they will realize what we realize, and there will be a happy resolution (oh, we hope).

Both protagonists have things to figure out about their identities and relationships with others. Penny's Creative Writing professor helps her find her first-person voice. But ironically, it's Penny's mother who is able to break through to her:

> It's good to have high standards. I worry because you hold yourself against these standards too. You're way too hard on yourself. This analysis and thinking and plotting and figuring out, it's stopping you from living your life. Just be, Penny. Don't push people away.
>
> (p. 379)

Wisdom for her daughter and for readers alike.

Ellen, T., & Ivison, L. (2018). *Freshmen*. New York: Delacorte Press.
On his first day of college, Luke breaks up with his girlfriend of three years. He hadn't realized his gradual falling out of love, partially due to the gradual increase of Abbey's clinging neediness. Well, college is the time for new beginnings.

Phoebe just happened to have picked the same college as soccer star Luke, whom she had a crush on throughout high school. Amazingly, they sign up for Quidditch Club together, swap phone numbers, and shake an agreement to go to the first meeting. Not so amazingly, Luke doesn't show. Hmmm.

Freshmen takes us through a semester of characters trying new experiences, forming friendships, making mistakes, and growing. We don't hear much about classes or studying; the focus is on the social-izing. There are opportunities to grapple with social justice issues and take a stand, as when the girls respond to the misogynistic behavior of the soccer team with a unique form of protest.

Here are a couple of examples of self-reflection that happen toward the end of the semester. Luke tells Abbey, "It's like I haven't been thinking all semester. I've just been... blindly moving forward, smashing into stuff as I go" (pp. 306–307). Phoebe, whose friend confronts her with evidence that she has been confusing her high school fantasy version of Luke with the much more flawed real thing, refuses Luke's invitation to be a couple, suggesting authentic friendship instead, recognizing that her eighth-grade self would have died from shock at this turn of events.

Maybe there are readers of this book who have made no mistakes during transitions to new stages of their academic lives; but those who have goofed up, or know they are bound to do things they will regret, can gain hope from Luke's words to a girl who left the campus in shame. He admits that he made a mess of the first semester more than anyone. "But *I* was still coming back. I told her we should both look at it like first semester didn't happen. Like, next semester we were starting again from scratch" (pp. 328–329).

Ah, freshmen.

*Fagan, K. (2017). *What Made Maddy Run: The Secret Struggles and Tragic Death of an All-American Teen*. Boston: Little, Brown and Company.

> Exactly when do our young people have time to develop their own sense of self? When are they able to be alone, to understand how they think, what they really want—without the pretense of how it might look on a college application?
>
> (p. 173)

This is one of many questions the author asks as she tries to make sense of the suicide of college athlete Madison Holleran. Despite access to Maddy's social media accounts, email, and other writing, along with access to the family members and friends who loved Maddie, she knows that neither she nor anyone else will ever know the answers. What part did the pressure of being on the track team at an Ivy League school play? How much of a factor was Maddy's activity on social media? ("We put time into our social media because we believe that it affords us the unique opportunity to fashion our own identity" [p. 237].) Could her depression have been recognized earlier as being debilitating, and could intervention have helped?

Fagan intersperses sections that tell of her own experiences, as well as information and analysis of current situations encountered by today's college students. Some athletes, like Maddy, face not only the stigma that still exists relating to mental illness but also the stigma around quitting. Maddy could have quit track; she could have quit college. But she "… had never before quit anything, let alone her dream since she had started playing sports at age seven" (p. 208). Fagan recognizes that it is often hard to determine whether quitting or persevering is the right way through a crisis. She notes that, at times, stopping competition when it is no longer fun is the best answer. "But more often, if student athletes push through the discomfort of the first year, they grow stronger, and later, those thoughts of quitting come to seem like the notions of someone else entirely" (p. 221).

This book could open up valuable, necessary conversations among high school and college students, teachers, counselors, coaches, and parents. There are measures being taken at the University of Pennsylvania and other campuses to better meet the needs of students who are dealing with depression and anxiety. Readers may recognize themselves or friends as they learn of Maddy's struggles. They might listen differently, and act differently. That's what Kate Fagan hopes. That's what Maddy's parents hope.

Iloh, C. (2020). *Every Body Looking*. New York: Dutton Books.

This novel in verse is narrated by Ada; we travel with her through her first months as a freshman at a historically Black college. We watch her struggle to become acclimated to the campus, and to her classes, including accounting, which she can neither understand nor care about. We see her get a job, and enter a relationship with a boy—more things she does not understand or care about. Who *is* Ada? We get a sense of her identity when we see her watch a young woman dancing, and when she finally meets Kendra and attends dance classes with her.

Interspersed with the chapters set at college are others where we get flashbacks of Ada in sixth grade, second grade, and twelfth grade; we see how her identity has been influenced by her religious father from Nigeria; her troubled mother, who, despite not living with her, manages to harm her self-esteem and induce guilt; and her auntie from Nigeria who visits, offering a role model and some sense of culture. We learn of her being sexually abused as a child by a male relative. We get glimpses of the hundreds of drawings Ada has secretly produced of Magic, a dancer whose body and face look surprisingly like her.

This is a book about a young woman negotiating her sexuality, her academic decisions, and her life in a way that calls for having the courage to free herself from the expectations of others. Can Ada succeed? As the end of the book approaches, we see evidence of the answer.

Kade, S. (2018). *Finding Felicity*. New York: Simon & Schuster.
Caroline made *so* many mistakes in high school, including inventing fictional friends based on her favorite TV show so that her single mother wouldn't worry about her; and choosing a college because Liam, her high school crush, will be there. Her counselor warns her:

> Caroline, college is certainly a common time for reinvention. However, most adolescents are using that space and newfound freedom to become more of who they perceive their true selves to be. My concern is that you seem to want a version of yourself that has little grounding in who you really are.

> (p. 42)

Caroline's bold plan seems to work, until she spends a night in Liam's room only to find out he does not love her or feel any sense of commitment. She's devastated, but soon finds out that everyone else has been making mistakes, also. Her roommate Lexi has been betrayed by a boy; Tory drinks to the point where she is hospitalized for alcohol poisoning; Liam apologizes and admits that he is lonely and sad after hearing his high school girlfriend has already found someone else. Maybe Caroline can survive her first semester after all; maybe she is actually beginning to make real friends, and maybe there are clubs that match her interests.

In the Acknowledgments, the author identifies with Caroline, explaining that she too was introverted, that she took comfort in fictional characters, and that she was determined to reinvent herself in college. Readers can think about and discuss what an appropriate balance would be. How can they improve themselves in the new context college provides, while remaining true to their core values so they don't become fake? By answering these questions before college is upon them, they might be ready to face challenges and spare themselves some of the hard lessons Caroline has to learn through her messy experiences. (Yes, we can learn from fictional characters, without blurring the lines between fiction and reality.)

*Karim, S. (2021). *The Marvelous Mirza Girls*. New York: Quill Tree Books.

On the night of her high school graduation, Noreen finds out that her mother's work could take her to India for a few months. She realizes she wants to defer her admittance to college (for screenwriting) so that she can go, too. She has been grieving the death of her favorite aunt, and she has been unable to write, so she welcomes the opportunity for a change of place, culture, people, and experiences.

And what a change! Artist Kabir becomes her guide, friend, and lover. He takes her to many historic and sacred places. She writes letters to the jinn and leaves them in the cracks of the ruins; once she stands in a luminous doorway where she feels the presence of her aunt and knows she is at peace.

> To think, she'd visited beautiful churches and masjids and temples all over the world and never felt the presence of God. But there… inside a vast and ruined masjid inside a crowded village inside a polluted city, God had found her.

(p. 322)

The #MeToo movement is strong in New Delhi, and Kabir's father is accused of inappropriate behavior with a woman who works for him, so Noreen has to figure out how to best support Kabir as he decides whether to stay silent (as his father expects him to do) or go public with a response showing his support for women. There are many events that lead to Noreen growing and maturing. She certainly would not have predicted that she would become a stand-up comedian, but… a gap year can bring anything!

Writing and Thinking Prompt

When Noreen's grandparents hear of her decision to go to India rather than head straight to college, they tell her it is a bad decision, and Noreen understands their point of view. "To her grandparents, education and work were a matter of duty, necessity, stability, and respect, not emotional fulfillment. Choice meant choosing your medical specialty. If school or work didn't make you happy, what did it matter…" (p. 33). Think about and make a list of the pros and cons of a person taking a gap year. It can be Noreen, or another character you've met through our literature selections, or someone you know—perhaps a sibling, friend, or even yourself. Then, write a piece that represents your opinion. It could be a letter to a fictional person who has asked for your advice, a journal entry reflecting on your own options and wishes, an article for your school newspaper, or another genre of your choice.

Lee, K.R. (2022). *Required Reading for the Disenfranchised Freshman.* New York: Crown.

Savannah's mother has sacrificed for many years so that her daughter would have opportunities for a life beyond poverty. Now it's Savannah's turn to make sacrifices. She's only 17, and she wants to go to the historically Black college ten miles from her home. But, having worked really hard in high school and earned a full scholarship to an Ivy League school, off she goes to a place far away, with few Black students. She will try.

As she and her mother are getting her side of the dorm room settled, the mother of Savannah's new roommate comments, "It's nice that they're adding more diversity to the campus. When I went here, there weren't very many African Americans. N-not that I see color or anything" (p. 21).

The microaggressions continue, along with overt racist behavior. Did this girl from the hood make a mistake coming here, pursuing her mother's dream instead of her own? Join Savannah as she figures out where she belongs and how to respond to the challenges of her freshman year.

*Ma, D. (2020). *Heiress Apparently.* New York: Abrams.

One reason for taking a gap year between high school graduation and the beginning of college is to gain experience and take the time that will allow people to know themselves better, so that they will be more focused and prepared for the next major step toward a satisfying career path. Despite her parents' misgivings, Gemma defers admission to UCLA to pursue her love of acting. When she lands a role in a movie that will be filmed in Beijing, she faces more identity issues than she had planned on. She needs to separate the roles she plays from her true self, and figure out ways to challenge scenes that reinforce stereotypes and bias. She has to interact with family members she didn't know existed and who do not welcome her presence in their country. (But isn't it her country, too?)

Gemma finds herself embroiled in a mystery involving politics, scandal, art, activism, and fashion. Her parents had forbidden her to go to China, never revealing that her mother had been a twin who had been kicked out of the family. History becomes alive for Gemma as she visits Tiananmen Square, and learns that her grandfather is a high-ranking Communist official. Ethics questions abound. Who is Gemma in relation to her new family, and to her parents? Is her look-alike cousin trying to bribe her, threaten her, or embrace her? Is it right to be falling for Eric, whose family has been feuding with her family since the days of the Cultural Revolution?

Identity issues are at the heart of the plot and subplots of *Heiress Apparently*. Readers may ponder the roles they play in their own lives after following Gemma on her literal and archetypal journey.

Montgomery, C. (2019). *By Any Means Necessary*. Salem, MA: Page Street.

Like many 18-year-olds, Torrey views college as his way out of his hometown and his stifling home life. But he returns home almost immediately after arriving for orientation week, deeply conflicted about his responsibilities. He had recently inherited an aviary from his uncle Miles, and has just found out that his grandfather (a bitter man who cannot accept the fact that Torrey is gay) has not kept up with payments on the land, which is now going into foreclosure. Readers will want Torrey to go to classes, make new friends, and reconnect with his middle school boyfriend Gabriel who has come to the same college. But they'll come to understand his love and appreciation for his bees, as well as his commitment to the promise he made to his dying uncle to protect them. Plus, his mother is lying comatose in an institution as a result of becoming addicted to pain killers through no fault of her own. Torrey is not going to leave her to die alone. So how important can college be, anyway? Sigh.

Though Torrey feels alone, he gets support both at home and at school. Aunt Lisa does not want him to stay in the toxic environment his grandfather has created, and takes steps to make her own life and Torrey's better. And then there's Dr. Lily Anderson, the professor who locked him out of class on the first day. (Okay, he was a little late.) When he meets with her after class he thinks, "Like, I've only met one college professor in my life so far, and if they're all this intimidating, I'm going to have to rethink my interest in higher education" (pp. 70–71). He agrees to her condition to visit her in her office an hour before each class, and that turns out to be the best decision he ever made.

The story leads us through a lot of close calls, mistakes made, and tough conversations and decisions before there is a resolution to Torrey's seemingly unresolvable dilemma. But we learn a lot along the way about the behavior and importance of bees; about sleazy characters who offer to help but really have no one's best interests in mind except their own; and about trust, hope, love, and new beginnings.

Roache, K. (2018). *Frat Girl*. Toronto: Harlequin Teen.

It's hard enough figuring out identity issues when you're a first-semester freshman, but when you've gone under cover to write an exposé of a fraternity, that adds complications. Cassie starts out as a confident feminist, convinced that her participation in this research project in return for a scholarship from a foundation is for the good of women. But she hadn't realized how hard it would be to live a lie, or that the project would prevent her from forming real friendships. She definitely hadn't planned on having fun with her fraternity brothers, or falling in love with one of them (prohibited by house rules plus *really* bad for the study!)

Cassie makes numerous mistakes throughout her freshman year. She finds herself drinking too much, sometimes dangerously so, trying to keep up with the boys. She forgets her responsibility to support her best friend, the only one who knows the real reason for her pledging the fraternity. She is biased against and judgmental about sororities, generalizing about the girls who belong to them, considering them all to be frivolous Barbie dolls. Her former roommate calls her out about her hypocrisy, pointing out that sinking to the level of the frat boys was *not* feminism. Another girl adds:

> I am sooo sick of you and your white feminist bullshit.... do you know what happens to black girls that try to join Greek life?.... There are plenty of barriers all sorts of women face just trying to live... you are not *my* feminist hero.

(pp. 328–329)

But Cassie learns and matures, too. She tries to stop her field notes from being published, arguing that she now knows she needs to talk about nuance, and to wrestle with the question of whether the misogyny so prevalent on college campuses has more to do with the fraternity system or with the larger society. "But when we're talking about social equality… we're talking about changing hearts and minds" (p. 403).

By the way, Kiley Roache wrote this book while she was in college, and the dedication goes like this:

> To the friends I've made in college.
> You're feminists.
> You're frat boys.
> But most important, you're family.

(unpaged)

Writing and Thinking Prompt

Cassie's story offers opportunities to discuss ethical issues connected to social science research and journalism. Was it okay for Cassie to deceive the fraternity members, secretly writing and sending field notes to outside sources? Was her research tainted from the start because she went in looking for trouble and expecting to find it? What would you say to Cassie if she came to you seeking friendship, support, or advice?

Rowell, R. (2013). *Fangirl*. New York: St. Martin's Griffin.

When I was reading Rainbow Rowell's *Fangirl*, I wanted to be Cath's roommate. Her twin sister had refused, saying it was time they met new people and did some things separately. The roommate Cath got was so not like Cath, not at all. Every aspect of this arrangement made Cath uncomfortable.

I eventually had to admit that even though I felt like her soulmate, I probably would have made Cath anxious, too. The reason is simple: she has an anxiety disorder. Online, however, things are different. Cath is a writer of fanfiction, and she has thousands of followers. The world that another author has created, and that Cath has entered, is where she feels safe, empowered, and happy. Why would she ever leave it to interact with people on campus?

Her professor in a fiction-writing course pushes the issue, not allowing any fanfiction yet lavish with her praise about Cath's potential. Cath starts co-writing with a young man in the class and is eventually betrayed by him; he turns the story in as his final assignment.

> It really was his story. It was nothing Cath would have ever written on her own. Stupid, quirky girl character. Stupid, pretentious boy character. No dragons. It was Nick's story. He'd just tricked her into writing it. He was an unreliable narrator, if ever she'd met one.
>
> (p. 212)

Professor Piper is astute in her recognition of Cath's talent, and willing to trust this freshman writer. She gives her every opportunity to succeed, even at the risk of allowing her to fail.

Ukazu, N. (2018). *Check, Please! Book 1: Hockey*. New York: First Second. In this graphic novel, Eric Bittle (aka Bitty) begins narrating the story from his freshman dorm at Samwell University. He hasn't even had orientation, but the hockey team has begun its preseason training. In colorful panels, he introduces us to his teammates, including team captain Jack, who gives him private tutoring on how to handle the physical "checking" that is allowed in college hockey, and that Bitty is terrified of. Bitty chose this college because of its reputation of being an LGBTQ-friendly campus, and he does indeed find acceptance. However, since he seems to be breaking his own rule against falling in love with straight guys, he keeps his feelings for Jack to himself. When not playing hockey or doing schoolwork, Bitty spends time in the kitchen baking pies, which further endears him to his teammates.

The book takes us through Bitty's freshman and sophomore years, at the end of which Jack is graduating and preparing to move on to professional hockey. The romantic cliffhanger ending (sorry, any more than that would constitute a spoiler) will assure that many readers will immediately go looking for *Check, Please! Book 2: Sticks and Scones* (2020, First Second).

The Foreword illuminates the author's writing process. Ukazu had intended during a seminar to write a screenplay about a hockey player who falls in love with his best friend, "But being a Texan, a woman, and a first-generation Nigerian, I knew that writing about a white, Boston-born hockey bro would require weeks of anthropological study" (unpaged). After attending Yale hockey games and interviewing players, she realized she had become obsessed with hockey; and *Check, Please* became "...a love letter to college hockey, the bonds you form in undergrad, and self-acceptance" (unpaged).

*Wheelan, C. (2021). *We Came, We Saw, We Left: A Family Gap Year*. New York: W.W. Norton & Company.

The shortest version of this travel account is told right on the cover: "Nine Months. Six Continents. Three Teenagers." Halfway through the book, Wheelan provides specifics from the tally he kept in the back of his journal, adding information like "Search parties looking for us: 2" and "Family meltdowns: 5" (p. 136). But lists can't do what stories can, and the chapters are filled with accounts that bring readers into canyons and homes; up mountains; across cities and bodies of waters, and into the minds and hearts of the five members of Team Wheelan.

As with any quest, the Wheelans encounter obstacles. The flesh-eating parasite that was picked up by 18-year-old Katrina while they were in South America, finally correctly diagnosed when they were in Southeast Asia, and treated in Europe, was perhaps scarier than any dragon could be. But Katrina returned from her gap year a hero: healthy, strong, and independent. (When she left a few weeks later for Williams College, 120 miles from her home, she chose to go by herself, by bicycle.)

One of the hardest parts of the trip turns out to be the "homeschooling" of eleventh-grader Sophie and eighth-grader C.J. For some reason, they were not as interested in their schoolwork as they were in the adventures they were living. It was hard to meet deadlines for online courses, but the academic obstacles were eventually overcome. There are so many valuable lessons and opportunities for growth and connection throughout the book. Charles credits his wife and teammate Leah with managing and holding them to their budget, and sharing all responsibilities as they experienced months of "parenting on steroids: the good, the bad, and everything in between.... This trip was the ultimate family dinner" (pp. 261–262).

Writing and Thinking Prompt

Choose one option, or adapt one of them to suit your needs related to the topic of travel and/or a gap year:

A. If you are not yet in college or in a steady job, think about the possibility of deferring future plans for a year. Assume that you will have to be careful with money, but you have the means to accomplish what you desire. What will you choose to do with that gift of time? Will you travel alone or bring others with you? How will you assure that you take advantages of opportunities for growth, and that you will not only take from others, but do something productive that will (now or later) give back to others and make the world a better place?

B. If you are in college or in a job now, look ahead and decide when you would like to take a gap year. (For example, my son Christopher lost his job during the 2020 pandemic, and decided to use those months of isolation to walk the Appalachian Trail.) Assume that you have enough money to take you through a year if you handle your finances carefully. Where will you go? Whom will you invite along on your adventure? What will you learn, an what can you offer others along the paths you take on your quest?

Winn, R. (2018). *The Salt Path*. New York: Penguin Books.
Why am I including a nonfiction book featuring a husband and wife in their fifties in a book about New Adult literature? The first reason is that it demonstrates beautifully that our lives will have *many* new beginnings; we can look at the lives of famous people and of older people we know from the lens of new beginnings. Often, those new beginnings are not chosen willingly, but rather precipitated by loss. Raynor and her husband Moth find themselves homeless and poor after they lost their farm and livelihood in a court decision following a bad financial investment. Oh, and Moth also receives a diagnosis of corticobasal degeneration, CBD, a painful, progressive, and terminal illness. What kind of new beginning could there be for this couple?

They decide to walk away from everything—literally. They take off on England's South West Coastal Path, with virtually no preparation. They didn't even bring hats or sunblock! What they did have was love, determination, the support of each other, an appreciation for nature, and an ability to learn along the way:

Excited, afraid, homeless, fat, dying, but at least if we made that first step we had somewhere to go, we had a purpose. And we really didn't have anything better to do at half past three on a Thursday afternoon than to start a 630-mile walk.

(p. 39)

Eating places served hot water for free, so they bought tea bags. They ate a lot of noodles. They endured stares and comments from others on the path who did not have faith in their ability to backpack and wild camp. You can follow their adventure with its high points and low points by reading the book, but I will fast forward to near the end, to explain why I included *The Salt Path* in the chapter about the college years. Since their money problems continued to worsen and no new home was magically appearing, I kept wondering what the solution would be as they finished their walk. I never would have guessed the answer, which involved Moth deciding to go to university. They could live on his college loans. Talk about new beginnings!

You'll need to check out the sequel, *The Wild Silence* (Winn, 2021, Penguin Books) to see what that new beginning leads to.

Instructional Strategies and Activities

Online Reading Conversation Journals

Teachers and students corresponding in writing about books and reading is not new. Both formal and informal correspondence between readers and mentors has been going on for centuries. My colleagues and I have been collecting and responding to reading response journals for decades, sometimes with grading involved, sometimes not. When the pandemic caused schools to shut down in 2020, electronic journal submissions and electronic responses from teachers increased. A year later, *Talking through Reading and Writing: Online Reading Conversation Journals in the Middle School*, by Daniel Rose and Christine Walsh (2021) was published, providing a rationale, resources, and encouragement for teachers at all levels who wish to begin or continue enhancing students' skills and fostering relationships through digital discussion.

Rose, based on his own experiences using online reading conversation journals, offers a number of benefits to the method, including the low-risk environment that some readers prefer to a face-to-face conversation; the ability to give precise and deliberate feedback that is not possible in the more rushed classroom setting; the ease of record-keeping; and the ability to differentiate instruction naturally as information from students' journals comes in that allows teachers to make recommendations based on students' interests and identities, as well as give instruction based on data relating to skills. The online conversation journals can enhance student–teacher relationships, encourage metacognitive processes, and provide incentive and purpose for reading widely and deeply. This approach will only work if teachers are active readers and writers themselves. Choice is another essential element of Rose's classroom.

Walk-Through

I'll give an example of online journal correspondence between Mr. Rose and a student reader, followed by examples from my college classes.

Kaylee offers this in her journal:

> I am currently reading *The Graduation of Jake Moon*…. the character Jake Moon is fighting with the fact that his grandfather's Alzheimer's is controlling his life. Whatever or whenever he tries to do something new, his after school "job" always gets to him…. Me as a reader I like to read to myself, I'm kind of a slow reader but I love to read…. *The Graduation of Jake Moon* is a fantastic book and I am completely into it and cannot wait to find out what happens at his graduation.
>
> (p. 26)

Here is an excerpt from Mr. Rose's response:

> I am so happy to hear that you are enjoying this book. Barbara Park is one of my favorite authors. If you have not read *Mick Harte was Here* yet, please read that book next! I bet you don't read slowly all of the time. I would bet that you take extra care when you come to an exciting moment, or a moment full of tension, or a sad moment. That is what great readers do—they read quickly or slowly or mediumly (not a word!) when they need to, or when the writing tells them to….
>
> (p. 26)

Here is a response from an undergraduate to Joy McCullough's *Blood Water Paint* (2019), which you will learn more about in Chapter 6:

I think Joy McCullough did an amazing job with this novel. I found myself putting sticking notes throughout the whole novel on aspects I found interesting or even some quotes that I found beautiful and relatable. Artemisia's story is one that needs to be heard, and I for one am so happy I got the chance to read this novel and learn about the story and life of Artemisia.

I am an artist myself, so I found myself comparing the studio and the words written to my own feelings with art. One's studio can be a sanctuary, and Artemisia's was taken from her, in multiple ways. I have an art area and it's my safe place, as Artemisia's father's studio was her sanctuary until that horrible man took it from her. She was able to gain some of her sanctuary back when her innocence was proven, but it will never fully return. Although I don't believe in how everything was worked out in the end, I still loved every part of this novel.

I had so many emotions throughout this novel, some good, and of course, some not so good. I even found myself tearing up at the end. I felt that I went through everything with Artemisia, I felt as if I was standing next to her the whole time but unable to speak and help her. After finishing this novel, I also found myself wanting to learn more about Artemisia. She is a strong woman and through this novel that is proven multiple times. Artemisia deserved so much better than what she was given, but even with everything that came her way, she told her story. She may have felt broken, but she never was. Her story is an inspiration to me for so many reasons, not just because she is an artist but because of the way she handles everything. She stood up for herself in a time that was not common at all. She fought for herself, and she won.

I have a friend who is an artist and a book lover like me and when I told her about this amazing novel, she put it right onto her list to read! I will suggest this book to as many people as I can, artist or not this is a story that needs to be heard.

(Sydney Lawton, used with permission)

Here is part of my response: You made valuable contributions to our class discussion. I'm so glad you have met Artemisia. There are many other YA books that connect to art and artists. You'll be able to make great connections.

Color the College Experience!

The college freshmen in my New Adult literature courses are initially skeptical, then delighted, when I pass out paints, crayons, colored pencils, and markers and encourage them to use color to respond to the texts we are reading. Sometimes I give little direction, just saying that I'd like them to keep the utensils and paper handy as they read their next book at home, and to have at least part of their response to be in color. They could doodle as they proceed through the chapters, and see what results when they put their drawings together at the end.

Sometimes we brainstorm first, with prompts such as the following:

- Use color to create an image or words that convey what your college experience has been so far.
- Think of books you've read that have the name of a color in the title, such as *Purple Hibiscus* (Adichie, 2003), *Brown Girl Dreaming*, (Woodson, 2014), *The Black Flamingo* (Atta, 2020), *All Boys Aren't Blue* (Johnson, 2020), or *A Clockwork Orange* (Burgess, 1995); and/or color imagery in the story. Students might mention the green light in *The Great Gatsby* (Fitzgerald, 2004), or the emblem Hester Prynne must wear in Nathaniel Hawthorne's classic *The Scarlet Letter* (2005). What might they signify? How are colors used to create a mood or to evoke a setting in books you've read?
- Think of the main characters and secondary characters of the last book we read, and assign a color to each, with a short rationale accompanying it. Then get into small groups to see if your decisions matched others, or to understand why responses differ.

Students can initiate other ways to bring color into their responses throughout the semester. They might use colored tissue paper to make a collage, or create something digitally using a painting app. They could match famous paintings that are known for their colors to books or characters within a story. Once the strategy catches on, you can ask them to reflect on the ways their thinking in color enhances or changes their thinking about the literature.

Walk-Through

Anna Roseboro shares an activity in a blog post, "Colors, Arrangement and Stories" (2019) that shows how teachers can implement assignments involving color to help students think critically about texts. She asks students to look carefully at the painting "Nine Colors" by Ellsworth

Kelly (which can be found online), then apply what they have thought and heard others say about it to literature. Here are the first three steps:

1. Keep notes as you answer the questions about ways colors in this painting could portray people, place, and events in your chosen story.
2. Create an artistic imitation of the Ellsworth Kelly painting that shows your choice of rearrangement to portray characters, places, or events in a book you've recently read. Label your artwork so someone viewing will know what your choices represent.
3. Write a one-two page paper explaining your choices. In your opening paragraph, include the title and author of story, and the title and artist of the painting. Use quotations from your story to support your choices. Include adjectives on the color symbolism chart(s).

Roseboro gives examples of students' explanations of and textual support for the colors they assign to characters, such as the following:

> **DARK BLUE** (depression). Felicia was morose. (p.17) She hadn't been invited to the first party of the year and feared no one would ask her to the Halloween dance to be held in the school gym. (p. 25)
>
> **ORANGE:** (enthusiasm, demanding of attention) She saw a note taped to her locker. Hope filled her with anticipation, until she read and saw it was simply a reminder to pick up her little brother from pre-school. (p. 28)

For a complete description of Roseboro's color activity, check out her blog, "Teaching English Language Arts."

References

Rose, D., & Walsh, C. (2021). *Talking through reading and writing: Online reading conversation journals in the middle school.* Latham, MD: Rowman & Littlefield.

Roseboro, A. (2019, January 22). Color, arrangement, and stories. Retrieved from https://teachingenglishlanguagearts.com/colors-arrangement-and-stories/.

Roseboro, A. "Teaching English language arts" blog. Retrieved from https://teachingenglishlanguagearts.com/anna-roseboro-bethany-kim/.

Wheelan, C. (2021). *We came, we saw, we left: A family gap year.* New York: W.W. Norton & Company.

Literature Cited

Adichie, C.N. (2003). *Purple hibiscus.* Chapel Hill, NC: Algonquin Books.

Albertalli, B. (2018). *Leah on the offbeat.* New York: Balzer + Bray.

Albertalli, B. (2015). *Simon vs. the Homo Sapiens agenda.* New York: Balzer + Bray.

Atta, D. (2020). *The black flamingo.* New York: Balzer + Bray.

Burgess, A. (1995). *A clockwork orange.* New York: Norton.

Fitzgerald, F.S. (2004). *The great Gatsby.* New York: Scribner.

Hawthorne, N. (2005). *The scarlet letter.* New York: Barnes & Noble Classics.

Johnson, G.M. (2020). *All boys aren't blue: A memoir-manifesto.* New York: Farrar Straus Giroux.

McCullough, C. (2019). *Blood water paint.* New York: Penguin Books.

Woodson, J. (2014). *Brown girl dreaming.* New York: Nancy Paulsen Books.

Job Exploration and Entry   4

Careers and Passions

Mike Rose, a researcher who followed various types of workers and interviewed them about their thoughts and feelings related to their occupations, reminds us:

> ... young people are at the stage where they're realizing how important work will be in their lives, how it will frame who they are and what they can do in the world. They are desperate to be somebody, to possess agency and competence, to have a grasp on the forces that affect them... the desire quivers within adolescent life.
>
> (2004, p. 186)

Many students nearing the end of high school or beginning college do not know what they want to do for a living, and they should not be pressured into committing themselves too soon. However, it's a good idea to explore, imagine, research options, and perhaps do some preliminary planning. Reflecting on how they like to spend their time and what topics interest them is a great place for New Adults to start. Reading books and other resources about various jobs and opportunities is another excellent step. Librarians and teachers need to be careful not to limit resources and discussions to professions requiring academic degrees. Military service is a route some high school graduates will consider pursuing. And opportunities for satisfying and challenging careers in the vocational realm

DOI: 10.4324/9781003221685-4

abound. Lisa, a welder whom Rose studied, compares what she does to a flower; it has an aesthetic dimension. "There's a certain beauty... an art to it. It's not just metal joining metal" (p. 116). Speaking of technical education, she says, "There's this idea that academics and the trades don't go together, but they do. A vocation combines theory and practical application" (p. 124).

This chapter will introduce books that demonstrate people investigating or working toward a career or other work-related goals; figuring out or constructing identities in terms of work and social structures; making and recovering from mistakes; and growing in maturity, skill, and wisdom. We will examine the ethical dimensions of work through story. We will make connections to twenty-first-century skills: How are the characters in NA literature measuring up in terms of collaborating; navigating social media; thinking critically and creatively; using technology; and so forth?

TEXT SETS

Becoming

Scientists are not born scientists; military leaders, entertainers, inventors, teachers, astronauts, accountants, environmental activists, and sports superstars are not born into those identities. What influences and character traits come together to cause people to become adults performing certain jobs or being known for particular ways of interacting in the world? Authors have given us many biographies, memoirs, and works of fiction that look back on famous figures' growing up years to note patterns of behavior, early passions, family and peer group relationships, mentors, social conditions, and sometimes surprises on the paths to adult accomplishments or notoriety. For example, Ilyasah Shabazz wrote novels exploring the lives of each of her famous parents before they were her parents, and before they were famous as Civil Rights activists. X: A Novel (2015), written with Kekla Magoon, is based on Malcolm Little's life up until his early 20s, showing the numerous influences, including those from his family as well as societal ones, that led to his beliefs as well as to actions that caused him to be imprisoned. Betty Before X (2018), written with Renée Watson, addresses her mother's adolescent years, dealing with her mother's rejection by others, her faith, and her growing social consciousness. *The Awakening of Malcolm X*, written with Tiffany D. Jackson (2021), shows her father in prison, learning much and converting to Islam, emerging as Malcolm X.

Many authors call attention to the formative years of their subjects by placing the word *Becoming* in the title of their biographies or memoirs, or by using other words that allude to that concept. This text set provides examples. Students can read about the early influences of political leaders, sports figures, entertainers, authors, and business leaders, as well as individuals who might not be famous but wish to tell about the impact that events or interests during their youth had on the people they became.

Students can read the books that interest them, perhaps predicting what a subject's early life was like before beginning to read; perhaps seeing themes within and among the biographies; and maybe wondering about things they hadn't thought of before. They might be led to explore other biographies in order to learn more about famous people when they were closer in age to those doing the reading now. Readers might also be inspired to write about their childhood and adolescence, pondering the choices they are making in relation to family modeling and expectations; early and evolving values and interests; talents and skills; and people and experiences who have been important to their becoming the persons they are and want to be.

Before listing individual titles, I'll mention the Masters at Work Series, published by Simon & Schuster, introduced on its website this way:

> Choosing a profession begins with imagining yourself in a career. The Masters at Work series, written by acclaimed long-form journalists, reveals how experts in their field got to where they are. It's rarely a straight path. These essential guides impart practical knowledge about the risks and rewards of our dream jobs. This is the best virtual internship you'll ever have. Discover what leading practitioners actually do every day. Here is the job as it is performed, not as it is taught.

You'll read a book talk for *Becoming a Baker* later in this chapter, and another book talk in Chapter 8 will introduce you to *Becoming a Climate Scientist* (Dickman, 2021). There are more than two dozen other titles, profiling professionals and offering guidance to readers who are curious about or who have aspirations to become a veterinarian, real-estate agent, private investigator, yoga instructor, sports agent, midwife, venture capitalist, architect, interior designer, firefighter, or a number of other possibilities.

Asterisks indicate that there are book talks in the next section that give more information about the titles.

Abdul-Jabbar, K. (2018). *Becoming Kareem: Growing Up on and off the Court*. Boston, MA: Little, Brown.

Anonymous. (2020). *Becoming Duchess Goldblatt*. Boston, MA: Houghton Mifflin Harcourt.

Burton, S., & Lynn, C. (2017). *Becoming Ms. Burton: From Prison to Recovery to Leading the Fight for Incarcerated Women*. New York: The New Press.

*Coulombe, J., with Civalleri, P. (2021). *Becoming Trader Joe: How I Did Business My Way & Still Beat the Big Guys*. New York: HarperCollins Leadership.

Callahan, P. (2018). *Becoming Mrs. Lewis: The Improbable Love Story of Joy Davidman and C.S. Lewis*. Nashville, TN: Thomas Nelson.

Downing, A.M. (2021). *Saga Boy: My Life of Blackness and Becoming*. Minneapolis, MN: Milkweed Editions.

Freedman, R. (2013). *Becoming Ben Franklin: How a Candle-Maker's Son Helped Light the Flame of Liberty*. New York: Holiday House.

Freehling, W.W. (2018). *Becoming Lincoln*. Charlottesville, VA: University of Virginia Press.

Goddu, K.P. (2019). *Becoming Emily: The Life of Emily Dickinson*. Chicago, IL: Chicago Review Press.

Grey, J. (2011). *Becoming Marie Antoinette*. New York: Ballantine Books.

Jones, B.J. (2019). *Becoming Dr. Seuss: Theodore Geisel and the Making of an American Imagination*. New York: Dutton.

Kigel, R. (2017). *Becoming Lincoln: The Coming of Age of our Greatest President*. New York: Skyhorse.

*Leonard, T. (2017). *Becoming Bach*. New York: Roaring Brook Press.

*Levy, D. (2019). *Becoming RBG: Ruth Bader Ginsburg's Journey to Justice*. Illus. W. Gardner. New York: Simon & Schuster.

Lipsky, D. (2010). *Although of Course You End Up Becoming Yourself: A Road Trip with David Foster Wallace*. New York: Broadway Books.

Mann, W.J. (2012). *Hello, Gorgeous: Becoming Barbra Streisand*. Boston, MA: Houghton Mifflin Harcourt.

*Manzano, S. (2015). *Becoming Maria: Love and Chaos in the South Bronx*. New York: Scholastic.

Nutt, A.E. (2015). *Becoming Nicole*. New York: Random House.

*Obama, M. (2021). *Becoming, Adapted for Young Readers*. New York: Delacorte Press.

Pak, J.H. (2020). *Becoming Kim Jong Un: A Former CIA Officer's Insights into North Korea's Enigmatic Young Dictator*. New York: Ballantine Books.

*Patterson, J., & Alexander, K. (2020). *Becoming Mohammad Ali*. New York: JIMMY Patterson Books.

Poe, H.L. (2016). *Becoming C.S. Lewis: A Biography of Young Jack Lewis*. Wheaton, IL: Crossway.

Schlender, B., & Tetzelli, R. (2016). *Becoming Steve Jobs: The Evolution of a Reckless Upstart into a Visionary Leader*. New York: Currency.

Schulman, M. (2017). *Her Again: Becoming Meryl Streep*. New York: Harper Paperbacks.

Spence, J. (2007). *Becoming Jane Austen: A Life*. New York: Continuum.

*Straczynski, J.M. (2021). *Becoming a Writer, Staying a Writer: The Artistry, Joy, and Career of Storytelling*. Dallas, TX: BenBella Books.

Voiklis, C.J. (2018). *Becoming Madeleine: A Biography of the Author of A Wrinkle in Time by her Granddaughters*. New York: Farrar Straus Giroux.

Williams, K. (2010). *Becoming Queen Victoria: The Tragic Death of Princess Charlotte and the Unexpected Rise of Britain's Greatest Monarch*. New York: Ballantine Books.

Food: A Passion? A Career?

Wars have been fought over food. People have fallen in love over food. Food helps form us and define us. Foods can teach us about various cultures and can broaden both our tastes and horizons. There is plenty of evidence to show that food is a popular topic that appears in conversation; in essays, poems, and books; and in movies and TV. This text set consists of titles that can be relevant for

New Adults, who may be at college or traveling or in new jobs and other situations where they have opportunities to go beyond what has been typical food fare during their growing up years. They are having all kinds of new experiences, and if they step out into new culinary territory, their lives can only be enriched. There are novels with characters representing diverse ethnicities, and those with characters who are experimenting with cooking and restaurant work. There are memoirs and nonfiction books that will interest readers with aspirations to bake or to pursue a career in food management. Some of the books will stimulate critical thinking about nutrition, and about how our food choices and behavior influence, and will be increasingly influenced by, the environment. And, of course, there are cookbooks. Bon appétit!

Aronson, V. (2021. *The Asian Market Cookbook*. San Francisco, CA: Page Street.

*Acevedo, E. (2019). *With the Fire on High*. New York: HarperTeen.

Capetta, A.R. (2021). *The Heartbreak Bakery*. Somerville, MA: Candlewick Press.

*Delliquanti, B., & Ho, S. (2018). *Meal*. Chicago, IL: Iron Circus Press.

Donovan, L. (2021). *Our Lady of Perpetual Hunger: A Memoir*. New York: Penguin.

Ellgen, P. (2017). *The 5-Ingredient College Cookbook: Easy, Healthy Recipes for the Next Four Years and Beyond*. New York: Rockridge Press.

Farrow, J. (2021). *The Official Harry Potter Baking Book: 40+ Recipes Inspired by the Films*. New York: Scholastic.

*Gregorio, I.W. (2020). *This Is My Brain in Love*. New York: Little, Brown.

*Hall, A. (2021). *Rosaline Palmer Takes the Cake*. New York: Forever.

*James, V. (2020). *Wine Girl: The Obstacles, Humiliations, and Triumphs of America's Youngest Sommelier*. New York: HarperCollins.

Jarrow, G. (2019). *The Poison Eaters: Fighting Danger and Fraud in our Food and Drugs*. Honesdale, PA: Calkins Creek.

Kemp, L.Z. (2021). *Somewhere between Bitter and Sweet*. New York: Little, Brown Books for Young Readers.

*MacNicol, G. (2019). *Becoming a Baker*. New York: Simon & Schuster.

*Manansala, M.P. (2021). *Arsenic and Adobo*. New York: Berkley Prime Crime.

* Mihaly, C., and Heavenrich, S. (2019). *Diet for a Changing Climate: Food for Thought*. Minneapolis, MN: Twenty-First Century Books.

Michalak, J., & Florence, D.M. (2021). *Niki Nakayama: A Chef's Tale in 13 Bites*. Illus. Jones, Yuko. New York: Farrar.

Namey, L.T. (2020). *A Cuban Girl's Guide to Tea and Tomorrow*. New York: Atheneum.

*Onwuachi, K., with Stein, J.D. (2021). *Notes from a Young Black Chef: A Memoir. Adapted for Young Adults*. New York: Delacorte Press.

Scott, S. (2022). *Fix Me a Plate: Traditional and New School Soul Food Recipes from Scotty Scott of Cook Drank Eat*. San Francisco, CA: Page Street.

Straczynski, J.M. (2021). *Becoming a Writer, Staying a Writer: The Artistry, Joy, and Career of Storytelling*. Dallas, TX: BenBella Books.

*Sharma, N. (2021). *Radha & Jai's Recipe for Romance*. New York: Crown.

Tila, J. (2022). *101 Thai Dishes You Need to Cook Before You Die*. San Francisco, CA: Page Street.

*Weissman, J. (2021). *An Unapologetic Cookbook*. New York: DK.

*Yen, J. (2021). *A Taste for Love*. New York: Razorbill.

Book Talks: Ready to Go!

Here you will find book talks for fiction featuring characters who are navigating new physical, intellectual, spiritual, and emotional spaces as they explore trades and/or enter careers; biographies and memoirs; and informational books offering guidance about how to succeed and flourish in various trades and types of work.

Arash, J., and Reedy, T. (2021). *Enduring Freedom*. New York: Algonquin.

Joe's life changed more than those of most of his Iowan classmates as a result of the events of September 11, 2001, since he had previously enlisted in the National Guard as a way to pay for college. He had to leave college in 2003 when the war in Afghanistan began. He entered the country as a Private First Class, knowing little about the Afghan people, and little about the restorative mission his unit was supposed to accomplish.

Baheer knows a lot about farm work, and he knows he wants an education to break free from a life of farm work. He knows little about Americans, or what they are suddenly doing in his village in May of 2003. Baheer and Joe meet; gradually, as their friendship grows and they begin to realize how they need each other and can help each other, misconceptions and biases are replaced with understanding and trust. By November, the Christian Americans and the Muslim Afghans are praying together and learning about the commonalities in their religions and sacred texts. Soon after, the groups are fighting together to fend off an attack by the Taliban, their common enemy.

I'll let the co-authors finish my book talk. In the back matter, Jawad credits the presence of American and coalition soldiers with opening windows for millions of his country's people:

> Before what the Americans called Operation Enduring Freedom, men, boys, and especially women and girls were deprived of education and other basic freedoms. Now ... my country still faces many problems. But we will not go backward ... . We are filled with a new creativity and hope.

(pp. 357–358)

Trent confesses to readers that, like the protagonist PFC Joe Killian, he held hurtful and ignorant perceptions of Afghanistan and Muslims:

> Like Joe, my beliefs quickly changed once I met the Afghan people ... . We [Trent and Jawad] reasoned that showing a character's heartfelt change from anger, hatred, and prejudice toward a more fair, informed, and friendly understanding of Afghanistan would be a more effective means of challenging the lingering prejudice that our readers might encounter in America than to present soldier characters who never faced that internal struggle for change.

(p. 360)

Becker, H. (2020). *Emmy Noether: The Most Important Mathematician You Never Heard of.* Illus. Kari Rust. Toronto, ON: Kids Can Press.
Imagine being told you can sit in on classes, but you can't take tests or get a degree. That's what 18-year-old Emmy Noether, who loved math, was told. Years later, the rules changed and she graduated from a university in Germany. But then she wasn't allowed to be a professor or

teach men. She taught without being paid and had to stand by while men took credit for her accomplishments.

This book explains how Emmy solved a problem with Einstein's general theory of relativity that neither he nor others could figure out. The brilliant Emmy "… went on to figure out new math concepts that would be used by scientists to help them understand atoms and by future mathematicians to develop computer software" (unpaged).

Readers will also come to understand how Emmy's life was affected by the rise of Hitler and the Nazi party. The obstacles she faced were huge. Her accomplishments were monumental. This book does a great service in bringing her life to light. We are the better for it, and aspiring mathematicians may find strength knowing how she persevered.

Beil, K.M. (2019). *What Linnaeus Saw: A Scientist's Quest to Name Every Living Thing*. New York: W.W. Norton & Company.

How to describe the personality of Carl Linnaeus, the brilliant scientist who gave us a classification system for plants and animals? It depends on who's giving the description. His students came home from day-long hikes he led proclaiming, "Vivat Linnaeus! Long live Linnaeus!" (p. 190). However, Beil tells us that his colleagues, whose classes were not as popular, perceived him as egotistical; a letter written by the secretary of the Royal Swedish Academy of Sciences notes, "…everybody valued Linnaeus, but 'hardly anyone loves him…'" (p. 191).

This biography recounts Linnaeus's life from early childhood and includes photos of portraits, documents, his drawings of plants and animals, and his residence and gardens. For our purposes, I'll tell a bit of what I learned about his adolescence and early adulthood. Carl hated high school, often skipping classes to look for interesting plants in the fields surrounding the boarding school and write in his precious notebook. Struggling with classes in ethics, theology, and Hebrew, his future as a clergyman (his parents' dream) was destined to not be achieved.

But, oh, how he loved collecting and observing plants! Mentors over the next few years helped Carl to develop his hobby into serious study. Beil explains:

> What questions he pondered, at nineteen, are lost to history.… Whatever his questions were then, one answer would become clear to Carl Linnaeus over time: in the natural world, the most important

trait was a plant's ability to sustain life by making more plants. This key understanding would eventually guide all of his life's work.

(pp. 41–42)

What questions will NA readers ponder as they read about Carl Linnaeus, and in what ways might those questions come to guide their future work and play?

Burling, A. (2021). *What You Need to Know about Job Searching*. New York: Rosen YA.

You have to find the one right job that's out there waiting for you. Employers frown upon resumés that indicate frequent job changes. You can't switch careers once you've begun one. JUST KIDDING! Burling replaces these common myths with facts showing otherwise. Some information might be surprising, such as just how important first impressions can be:

> Many human resource professionals say that interviewers make up their mind about a job candidate in the first thirty seconds .... They spend the rest of the interview trying to come up with ways to prove or disprove their decision.

(p. 41)

By starting with this short, reader-friendly volume in *The Teen Guide to Adulting* series, readers can gain confidence, think about the examples provided, and decide which of the many further resources offered to pursue.

There is advice about crafting a resumé, as well as a sample; there's advice about interviewing, along with a list of questions to ask an interviewer; and there's a checklist to complete to help someone decide whether to accept a job offer.

Burling recommends taking a proactive approach, from developing an action plan based on your passions and skills at an early searching stage, to assessing whether you are making good contributions and experiencing job satisfaction after you've been employed for a while.

Cimino, L. (2021). *The Incredible Nellie Bly: Journalist, Investigator, Feminist, and Philanthropist*. Illus. Sergio Algozzino. Trans. Saura Garofalo. New York: Abrams ComicArts.

Any young person who aspires to be the kind of journalist who can really make a difference in the world will find hope and encouragement from reading this biography in graphic novel format, framed as a series of interviews granted to a fictional student at the Columbia School of Journalism. Though ill, Nellie answers Miriam's queries about her undercover investigative reporting, which involved feigning insanity and spending ten days locked up in an asylum for mentally ill women. She recounts tales from her 72-day trip around the world, a feat that had been thought to be impossible.

Miriam learns of Nellie Bly's 1888 interview of Belva Ann Lockwood, the first female candidate for president of the United States. Nellie gave a voice to workers in the Pullman Factory strikes and interviewed anarchist Emma Goldman, as well as Socialist Eugene V. Debs and suffragist Susan B. Anthony. Where the activists were, there was Nellie. And she went to war, creating correspondence from the Serbian Front, trying to bring meaning to the destruction and loss all around her.

Miriam comes to realize, "She's the one who opened the door for women in journalism" (p. 134.) The book ends with a double-page spread with illustrations and captions about nine famous female journalists from around the world. "It is also thanks to Nellie that the concept of journalism as a democratic instrument, one that can change the conditions of the vulnerable, has grown stronger" (p. 140).

*Coulombe, J., with Civalleri, P. (2021). *Becoming Trader Joe: How I Did Business My Way & Still Beat the Big Guys*. New York: HarperCollins Leadership.

What makes a good grocery store? What would be the characteristics of an ideal grocery store, a utopian grocery store? Many New Adults have worked, and perhaps still work, in grocery stores. Virtually all have shopped in them, and sometimes have a loyalty to a particular store or chain. Asking these questions could result in interesting discussions.

Joe Coulombe thought about the questions raised above for years, as he founded (in his 20s) and managed a chain of convenience stores called Pronto Markets. In this memoir, he recounts when, how, and why he made decisions that led to the birth and growth of the specialized chain of stores branded as Trader Joe's. Chapter after chapter detail obstacles that he and his people turned into opportunities, and creative risks that paid off. As we follow Joe's route to success, we get lessons in economics, politics, business management, wine making, advertising, social skills, retail marketing, and more. Joe provides a sampler of stories relating to some of his best deals, including maple syrup, wild rice, almond butter, and kibble.

Young entrepreneurs will find this book especially valuable and stimulating. But all of us can find enjoyment as we read this anecdote-filled success story.

Delliquanti, B., with Ho, S. (2018). *Meal*. Chicago, IL: Iron Circus Comics. [Character Book Talk]

I'm Yarrow, and I'm into entomophagy. I've been harvesting insects and refining my cooking skills for a while, and I earned certification from a culinary school. Now my goal is to be hired in a new restaurant, La Casa Chicatana. The problem is that I seem to have gotten off on the wrong foot with the owner and chef. Chanda says I have the wrong attitude, and has given me the challenge to prepare a taco appropriate for the restaurant's customers. I also have not impressed my neighbor, Milani (who's a really great artist, and very attractive to me). Care to join me as I look for specialty ingredients such as ant larvae, grasshoppers, tarantulas, and mealworms? And then work magic with them? If you do, you'll be rewarded with recipes at the end. (Plus you'll see if I make any headway toward a relationship with Milani.)

Here are some words from an essay by Soleil Ho, co-creator of this graphic novel:

> Reducing insect cuisine to a spectacle, to a reaction to climate change or industrialized food production, erases the fact that it's been a meaningful part of many cultures throughout the world.... When we talk about insects being the "future" of food, we're also talking about other people's past and present. It's only the future for us because we chose to ignore and belittle what was right in front of us all along.
>
> (pp. 135–136)

Dorian, C. (2020). *Darwin's Rival: Alfred Russell Wallace and the Search for Evolution*. Illus. H. Tennant. Somerville, MA: Candlewick Press.

Most of us know much more about naturalist Charles Darwin than we do about naturalist Alfred Wallace; that is a shame, since they independently "... came up with one of the greatest scientific discoveries of all time, the theory of evolution by natural selection" (p. 52). They had made voyages and collected data at different times and in different places, but both came to the same conclusion.

Alfred's love of science and nature began in his teens, and he became an avid collector of beetles. At age 25, he began what would become a series of voyages to and explorations in South America. Readers get to share his amazing discoveries in the Amazon rainforest, as well as experiences of being shipwrecked, losing his precious specimens, and hearing the roar of tigers that he might encounter as he collected and studied hundreds of species of beetles.

The illustrations of Wallace at work collecting butterflies and birds, along with maps and pictures of tools, collectors' equipment, and animal specimens, help make this book an immersive, interactive experience for those who choose to go along on the adventure.

Eves, R. (2021). *Beyond the Mapped Stars*. New York: Alfred A. Knopf. *"Per aspera ad astra.* Through hardship to the stars." These words are on the dedication page. And they are given to aspiring astronomer Elizabeth in 1978 by Dr. Henry Morton, the president of Stevens Institute of Technology, as they anxiously wait with astronomer Maria Mitchell and others to witness an eclipse (p. 123). Elizabeth is not at all sure she should be in Colorado. It's the first time she has put her own wishes ahead of her family responsibilities and the expectations of her religious community in Utah. She worries, "Does being a person of faith—particularly a Mormon—disqualify me for scientific rigor? What if my training as a scientist makes me question, even abandon, my faith?" (p. 309).

Elizabeth definitely does not want to marry the older man who has expressed interest in her, despite his being married already. She has no desire to be a second wife; and she suppresses her growing feelings for her neighbor Samuel because she thinks that she has to be either a wife and mother *or* a scientist. Readers will want to assure her she can be both; and through the experiences she has on her journey, she does come to that realization and others:

> I've felt lifted by religious faith and prodded by scientific questions, and I don't know if I can sift through my life and pinpoint the moment where they diverge. Maybe they don't diverge at all—maybe they're part of the same vast system, but I don't see all the connections yet…. Maybe I have been looking at everything wrong, seeing "or" where I should have seen "and."

(pp. 324–325)

This work of historical fiction might well help contemporary New Adults discern their purpose and have confidence that they will find a way to grow spiritually and emotionally as they follow their passions for meaningful work.

Forman, G. (2021). *We Are Inevitable*. New York: Viking.
When we meet our narrator Aaron, he has been reading a book about the extinction of dinosaurs. But he tells us that dinosaurs still exist, and they look like this: "A father and son in a failing used bookstore, spending long, aimless days consuming words no one around here buys anymore" (p. 2). His friends have gone to college, but we learn that the money meant for Aaron's education was used in attempts to treat his brother Sandy's drug addiction, to no avail. After Sandy's death, their grieving mother left home. Aaron doesn't look forward to taking away one more thing from his father, but sees no way out of the debt his father has incurred trying to keep the store afloat through credit card loans.

It doesn't take long for readers to love the store, too, and to think selling the store simply cannot be the right answer, though we may not have alternative solutions at the ready. The name of each chapter is the title of a relevant book. Aaron simply cannot sell the store out from under us, especially to that greedy woman who already owns the rest of the neighborhood and does not understand the spirit of literature.

As often happens in the books Aaron has grown up with, new people are introduced, and the situation gets more complex. Chad, a former friend of Sandy who is now paralyzed as the result of an accident, finds people to build a ramp to make the store accessible. Hannah, a musician who is also knowledgeable about books, shows an interest in Aaron, which would be great if he weren't so burdened with economic woes. Isn't the demise of the store inevitable? After all, this is realistic fiction, not fantasy.

Seemingly insoluble problems call for creative thought and action. Readers' minds will get a workout once they join the team determined to give new life to a store and to people who didn't know they had any dreams left.

*Gregorio, I.W. (2020). *This Is My Brain in Love*. Boston, MA: Little, Brown and Company.
Jocelyn's father agrees to let her take measures to improve the situation at the family's failing Chinese restaurant, so she hires aspiring journalist

Will, who has computer skills and an enterprising spirit. Together they create a business plan and find new advertising and marketing avenues. What they hadn't planned on was falling in love—partly, it seems, with the help of food. Jocelyn's grandmother makes the best pot stickers, and Will brings over some Nigerian food; Jocelyn enjoys eating egusi stew with chopsticks.

The efforts to bring in more customers and get the food out to more venues are producing results, but it looks like the lease for the restaurant property will not be renewed. Jocelyn faces further challenges when her participation in a competition results in her being accepted into a university Junior Business Program, but without a scholarship. Plus, her father catches her and Will kissing; he fires Will and takes measures to assure that Jocelyn cannot see or contact him.

Mental health issues play a large part in this story. Will, who for years has been in treatment for anxiety and panic attacks, recognizes signs of depression in Jocelyn, but she doesn't take kindly to his observations or gentle suggestions to seek help. Jocelyn knows there is a stigma related to mental illness, and Will has had to keep his visits to the therapist a secret from his mother's side of the family. The benefits and drawbacks of taking drugs for anxiety and depression are discussed within the story, as well as in the Author's Note. I. W. Gregorio, a surgeon, shares her own history with mental illness, and shares resources for readers, including those from diverse backgrounds who might have difficulty finding therapists who understand unique cultural backgrounds. She tells readers that this book is her way of breaking her decades-long silence, to let readers experiencing mental health difficulties know they are not alone:

> You are not broken.
> There is no shame in being who you are.
> When you are ready to speak your truth, there will be people to listen
> (p. 374)

*James, V. (2020). *Wine Girl: The Obstacles, Humiliations, and Triumphs of America's Youngest Sommelier*. New York: HarperCollins.
Victoria James was told during her training, "The sommelier should always be the smartest person in the room" (p. 157). She certainly shows throughout this memoir that she was intelligent, as well as persistent, passionate, generous, resilient, courageous, ambitious, and

self-reflective. Her childhood was filled with poverty and neglect, but she found ways to survive and take care of her younger sister.

As a teenager working in a restaurant, Victoria listened carefully to advice about how only happy people can give good hospitality, and that giving good hospitality and genuinely loving people in turn can make the server happy. She loved learning about wines and cocktails and found ways to take classes in addition to working eighty hours per week. She won competitions that resulted in wine trips to France and other destinations; she learned how to network and then take advantage of opportunities for advancement.

Her jobs were not always safe; she faced danger, even assault. Victoria recounts her share of mistakes as well. But she turned obstacles into opportunities for growth. One of the biggest things she had to learn was how to care for herself. Once, when she lost a job, she spent the rest of the summer foraging in the woods, learning about medicinal herbs, barks, and roots.

> I hadn't realized how much I needed this time in nature, far away from the unnatural world of fine dining … . I found an ability to cultivate a sense of wonder…. The ability to appreciate the natural world eventually set me apart from my peers.

(p. 245)

Readers can learn valuable lessons from the young woman who was a certified sommelier by age 21 and soon found ways to make a difference in the lives of others, especially women, in the industry. They can apply these lessons to whatever job they have, and beyond. Victoria is as true a mentor in her writing as she is in her life.

*Jarrow, G. (2019). *The Poison Eaters: Fighting Danger and Fraud in our Food and Drugs*. Honesdale, PA: Calkins Creek.

This frank, detailed look at the history of those who worked and fought for the safety of our food and medicine, along with fascinating information about those who currently do so in various capacities, could give readers ideas for their own futures. It is partly a compilation of examples of horrendous conditions and misinformation regarding the handling and advertising of food and drugs in the past two centuries (cocaine toothache drops, lead added to wine and candy, and radioactive medicine that caused bones to crumble). It's partly a biography of Dr. Harvey Washington Wiley, founder of the Food and Drug Administration (the existence of which so many take for granted today); and partly stories of activists, lawyers, advertisers, business leaders, politicians, journalists, fraud detectors, and critical consumers of the past and present.

Perhaps a reader will become fascinated by the science of food and drugs, and decide to explore a future as a chemist, pharmacist, or food scientist. Another might get absorbed in the extensive descriptions of Dr. Wiley's experiments early in the twentieth century involving dozens of young male volunteers—the "Poison Squads" who ate free food supplied along with capsules of borax and boric acid, in order to determine how much of a preservative caused discomfort or physical harm. Still another could become interested in working in food growing or preparation. Virtually all readers might pay more attention to what they are putting in their bodies. Are there additives? Is the food adulterated? What are the pros and cons of preservatives? Are we, like the generations before us, ingesting poisons without knowing it? Is it possible that there could be medicines today that kill rather than cure? What are ways to combat misleading advertising and food fraud? What responsibilities do we have as eaters?

The Poison Eaters could be the first of many texts and resources readers consume for their own health and that of their families, community, nation, and world. It could truly be a life-changing book.

Kantor, J., and Twohey, M. (2021). *Chasing the Truth: A Young Journalist's Guide to Investigative Reporting.* Adapted by Ruby Shamir. New York: Philomel.

The authors begin by differentiating investigative reporting from other forms of journalism and give examples from their careers showing how this line of work can lead to societal change and legal reform as well as justice for individuals who have been wronged. Megan had reported on abusive doctors and on the mistreatment of female inmates. She uncovered the not rare underground practice of adoptive parents giving away the children they had adopted, without any government regulations or knowledge. Jodi's work led to better conditions for workers, including those at Amazon and Starbucks.

The chapters in this book provide information about the steps and procedures of investigative reporting through the story of how Megan and Jodi handled the case that eventually led to the downfall and criminal conviction of Hollywood producer Harvey Weinstein. Their story illustrates how phone calls and interviews were handled; how they persisted in their attempts to uncover secrets and find witnesses; how they documented and confirmed sources and claims; the ways they followed up on tips and pursued new leads; how they handled pushback by powerful, angry people; and how they wrote and broke their story. In the epilogue, after describing the courtroom procedures and the verdict (guilty on two counts of rape) and the sentence (twenty-three years in prison), the authors sum up:

> The courtroom was the last stop in a through line: from the women who mustered the courage to break their silence, to the work of investigative journalists who chased the truth, to a report that was airtight and unassailable and nurtured by an institution devoted to questioning the mighty, the New York Times. That line extended even further back, to the system designed by America's founders, to the First Amendment, which protects the public's right to confront abuses of power.

> (pp. 213–214)

The backmatter includes tips on chasing the truth, organized into categories relating to uncovering abuses, following the facts, finding and researching sources, preparing for interviews, establishing ground rules, recording conversations, and never giving up. I wonder how many readers will be inspired to investigate this career as a result of discovering this guide by two highly credible and successful investigative reporters.

Kantorovitz, S. (2021). *Sylvie*. Somerville, MA: Walker Books.
Many students in high school and college agonize over their choice of career, especially if what they are passionate about does not match the values or goals of their parents or guardians. Sylvie is one of them. Growing up in France, Sylvie knew how important it was to pass the baccalaureate exam that would allow her to further her education at a university. When she started high school, she had to choose among courses of study focusing on philosophy, literature, and art; or on math and sciences. Though she loved art, she was pressured by her parents (both teachers) to choose the math and science track. She complied.

As the book draws to a close, we are with Sylvie as she meets an artist who mentors her and helps her see that she could study art and truly become an artist. The last section of this memoir in graphic novel form is titled "My Future in my Hands." She resists her mother's urge to pursue math studies, as well as to find a good husband—perhaps a "nice Jewish pharmacy student" (p. 325). She decides that a practical course of action would be to work toward earning a teaching degree in three years and then applying for art study at the Beaux-Arts.

Readers are given the gift of seeing Sylvie's long, difficult decision-making process throughout this book. So we can feel hope when we see an illustration of Sylvie carrying her bags toward her future. "And now, after a summer full of preparations, I was on my way to my little student room in Paris. On my way to independence! Tomorrow would be my first day at teaching school" (p. 337).

Keys, A., with Burford, M. (2020). *More Myself: A Journey*. New York: Flatiron Books.

Alicia Keys has a long list of accomplishments as a singer, songwriter, actor, musician, nonprofit founder, and other identities. Fans familiar with her smash debut album *Songs in A Minor* from when she was nine-teen years old, and/or her more recent work, may think they know her well. Yet she calls herself a "… person in process, from the me I once was to the me I am now" (p. 5). She adds:

> I'm also a breathing set of contradictions: a child who has known the greatest love there is, and one who longed for an affirmation that eluded me. I've been a builder of inner walls and a burier of feelings. I've been both someone in denial and a free spirit, an artist in hiding and a 'hood hippie…. I'm discovering who I am at my core—and becoming, day by day, more myself.
>
> (p. 5)

The first few chapters recount moments and memories from Alicia's childhood. Her love of the piano began when she was tiny and never left her. Her mother's love was another constant. But she did not trust her mostly absent father, and gradually her recognition of others' assessments caused her to begin losing herself as she tried to please others. She uses the metaphor of a mask to describe how she kept others from knowing her fully. Only in her diary did she reveal her true thoughts.

Alicia describes events and aspects of her late teens and early 20s that influenced her evolving identity. She had skipped two grades and graduated as valedictorian of her high school class, but floundered at Columbia University because she had signed a record deal with

Columbia Records, and she could not succeed at both endeavors simultaneously. First, she left the university; and eventually, when people at the record company insisted on changes to her image and music that she knew contradicted the girl she truly was, she knew she had to break free in order to live her own dream.

The chapters go on to tell other key points of her journey to the place where she is now, but each begins with an observation or reflection by a friend, family member, mentor, co-worker, or someone else who has interacted with Alicia. Michelle Obama remarks, "There was none of the pretense, none of the thirst that often accompanies celebrities. There was simply Alicia—light and sweetness, creativity and power, peace and hope. I saw then that it was real, all of it" (p. 237).

Writing and Thinking Prompt

Use the framework of Alicia Keys' *More Myself: A Journey* to chronicle some key moments or relationships of your childhood and adolescence that helped shape who you are today and your dreams for the future. Then think about how others might have described you at those points. Write a paragraph in the persona, or voice, of at least one of those people. Will what they have to say match your own truths, or might they reveal discrepancies that could help you understand yourself better, and someday be able to tell about your own journey along the paths that will lead you to be "more yourself"?

Kobabe, M. (2020). *Gender Queer*. Portland, OR: Oni Press.
Through the panels and pages of this graphic memoir, we follow the author's often painful, often frightening, often confusing, and often joyful road to self-knowledge and self-acceptance. Maia did not feel comfortable identifying as a girl, nor as a boy. It took years of learning about nonbinary expressions of gender; experimenting with clothes and ways of interacting with others; and many stages of coming out to family and friends as genderqueer before e was ready to use eir talent and training as a comics creator to write and illustrate eir story.

Maia still struggles with decisions about how much to share. Since 2017, e has taught comics workshops at libraries, wondering if e should introduce eirself using eir chosen pronouns, worrying that eir identity is too political for a classroom, fearing that the parents of the kids might not accept em as a nonbinary person. Speech bubbles convey eir thoughts: "I wonder if any of these kids are trans or nonbinary, but don't have words for it yet?" "How many of them have never seen a nonbinary adult?" "Is my silence actually a disservice to <u>all of them?</u>" (p. 237).

Maybe this memoir is an answer to those questions. Though Maia might not make public eir gender identity during comics classes, this comic book can get into the hands of readers who may see themselves, or others, more clearly as a result.

*Leonard, T. (2017). *Becoming Bach*. New York: Roaring Brook Press. This biography ends when Johann Sebastian Bach—who would go on to become, according to some, the greatest composer of all time—turns 19. The story of the years preceding his first job as a church organist is narrated by the musician himself. He was born into a family where members had been musicians for 200 years, so he was always surrounded by music. Music helped him cope with the deaths of both parents before he turned 10. Bach learned to play multiple instruments, and loved to copy music. The growing boy tells us of his fascination with patterns, and of being amazed that with just seven notes, each of which makes a different sound, he could invent and combine patterns in an infinite number of ways to create beauty and evoke emotion.

Leonard's illustrations bring the text to life in a variety of ways. He uses patterns, too, combining music notes to create images of people and a castle. Bach's sounds come out of the organ pipes as colors, and as curved patterns, evoking images of creatures and plants. The final spread shows people from different historical periods listening to Bach's music notes; one contemporary boy wears glasses and a t-shirt with Bach's name and image. Leonard tells us in "A Note from the Author" that this child is a self-portrait.

There's a lot to look at, and appreciate, in this picture book. It could be a springboard leading to students exploring more biographical information to find out what happened next.

*Levy, D. (2019). *Becoming RBG: Ruth Bader Ginsburg's Journey to Justice*. Illus. Whitney Gardner. New York: Simon & Schuster.

Of the many biographies of the great Ruth Bader Ginsburg (RBG), this graphic novel version might become a favorite. Ruth is shown throughout her childhood participating in all aspects of literacy. She listens well as her parents discuss anti-Semitism and the horrors of World War II; and she listens to her mother's encouragement to be independent. She reads voraciously about strong women, both real, such as Amelia Earhart, and fictional, such as the March sisters in *Little Women*. She performs poetry; she becomes editor of her school newspaper in eighth grade and writes for her synagogue's newsletter.

The pictures and text in the panels show Ruth learning more and accomplishing more throughout high school and college. There is much sadness, including her mother dying from cancer, as well as many obstacles put in her way because of her gender. There is love, as she becomes engaged to fellow Cornell student Martin Ginsburg, a man who appreciates her intelligence and encourages her personal and professional growth.

Further chapters help us to know Ruth as a law student, wife, mother, teacher, law clerk, and advocate for people being discriminated against by unjust laws. Readers will see how her values, response to opportunities, perseverance, and decisions to work for justice all led to her becoming the Supreme Court Justice and the icon who is still so revered. This book was published the year before Ruth's death, but the timeline and an extensive bibliography are helpful in understanding her very full, rich, and inspiring life. Those who wish can search online for obituaries and speeches that will add to the awe and respect they will already be feeling from experiencing the book. And that could lead to more young people following in RBG's footsteps.

*MacNicol, G. (2019). *Becoming a Baker*. New York: Simon & Schuster.

Quick quiz question: If you ran a bakery, which choice represents how you would prepare for a holiday?

a. Make more cakes, pies, and bread than were ordered, and risk having to throw some out at the end of the day.
b. Make the number of products ordered, and risk having dissatisfied walk-in customers.

According to Mary Louise Clemens, owner of Ladybird Bakery in New York City, the correct answer is b. She learned to run the risk of running out of a product rather than overstock. The cost of wasted ingredients and labor can result in a small business going under. In addition to this economics lesson, I learned things related to the science of baking, as well as the history of baking. Other disciplines come into play, too. "If baking is a great math equation, then each cake is a construction project," notes MacNicol (p. 102). Add advertising, marketing, physical therapy, and art to the list. The role of TV, movies, and social media with regard to baking is addressed.

What type and level of education are required to become a master baker? This book tells the stories of graduates of the Culinary Institute of America along with those who chose the apprentice route. What level of physical and mental fitness is required? The answer might be surprising to readers whose experience with baking is mostly at the consumer end. Baking is demanding, requiring long hours of standing, sometimes in uncomfortably warm temperatures with few breaks. Clemens loves decorating cakes, but after years of doing it, her knees are shot. The emotional toll of long hours of redundant steps (beginning long before dawn) and going home exhausted can be high. But baking is a vocation, and if one loves it, all that goes into it is worth it. The author ponders, "Is there another profession so devoted to bringing happiness to other people's lives? It's difficult to imagine a simpler, more direct way to bring some goodness into the world on a daily basis" (p. 6).

After reading this book and pausing over the drawings of baked goods, I ate a cupcake.

*Manansala, M.P. (2021). *Arsenic and Adobo*. New York: Berkley Prime Crime.

Lila has returned to her small hometown after a break-up with her fiancée in Chicago. Just temporarily, of course. She's helping her Tita Rosie try to save her floundering restaurant so that her landlord doesn't oust her. She briefly reconnects with her old boyfriend, but that doesn't work out; and Derrick, now a food critic, is trashing the restaurant with his bad reviews. Oops, make that past tense. Derrick collapses, then dies, after eating in Tita Rosie's place with his step-father (who happens to be the landlord mentioned above). Lila finds herself the prime suspect. Since the police seem to be too busy trying to pin the murder on her to look for the real killer, Lila decides to investigate the crime herself. Why was arsenic found in the food, and in Derrick's body? Who could have planted drugs in Lila's locker?

Readers who join the hunt will encounter a couple more dead, or near-dead, bodies. They'll also be trying to figure out a mystery within the main mystery: Who will turn out to be Lila's love interest? Amir, her best friend's older brother who is a lawyer? Or the young dentist who has recently started a practice in town? Another subplot involves best friend Adeena, who wants nothing more than for Lila to open a café with her. Maybe Lila can reflect on goals and relationships if she can just keep herself from going to prison!

You might not think there would be room in such a packed plot for descriptions and discussions of food and drink, but oh, they are there. You'll smell the aromas and visualize the main courses and desserts; you'll want to taste what the characters are tasting. Because it's all good. Very good.

Mihaly, C., and Heavenrich, S. (2019). *Diet for a Changing Climate: Food for Thought*. Minneapolis, MN: Twenty-First Century Books.
We are told in the Introduction, "Following a diet for a changing planet requires rethinking what we consider food" (p. 4). This book serves as both stimulus and resource enabling us to do just that, by showing readers the benefits to them, the global population, and the planet of eating radical edibles. The chapter titles can be a bit intimidating: "Eat the Pushy Invasive Plants," "Bugs for Lunch," "Crickets are the Gateway Bug," and "Rustle up Some Grubs." But the authors provide rationales for broadening our view of what is good to eat and assure us that it is possible to change attitudes. Lobsters, now considered a delicacy, were once considered "cockroaches of the ocean" (p. 7) and were ground up as fertilizer and fed to pigs.

You can try out the book's recipes on friends and family: dandelion flower pancakes, roasted crickets, secret bug sauce, chirpy-chip cookies, mealworm tacos, and beetle croutons. Be a trend-setter!

There's new vocabulary in this book. For example, in the dedication, the authors write, "We hope that our words will help inspire new weed-eaters, invasivores, and entomophagists." If context and your knowledge of morphology are not enough to help you figure out the meanings of unfamiliar words, there's a glossary you can go to.

Photographs can help students realize that the movement is already underway, with positive reception. Under a photo of a normal-looking cafeteria line, the caption reads: "Professor Joe Roman organizes a popular meal ... at the University of Vermont, where he teaches marine ecology. The entire meal focuses on invasive fish species, and students love it!" (p. 55).

This book shows that people do not have to give up meat to help the environment. So go ahead and enjoy that lionfish, and those wild boar ribs. Do your part. Bon Appétit!

*Manzano, S. (2015). *Becoming Maria: Love and Chaos in the South Bronx*. New York: Scholastic.

Shortly after she enters New York City's High School of the Performing Arts, Sonia gets an assignment to write about her hopes and dreams. She answers the prompt honestly:

> My mother's childhood during the Depression in Puerto Rico makes Oliver Twist's childhood sound nice.... So she came to this country, but she's poor here, too. Still we are really, really poor.... Some people think home is a good place no matter what. Not me. My father drinks and beats up my mother every chance he gets. I wish my parents would get a divorce so I can come from a broken home—these are my hopes and dreams.
>
> (p. 200)

Sonia brings her readers into her many childhood homes, all filled with both love and violence. (There's a recurring image of her mother hiding the knives in the oven each night.) Sometimes her mother leaves her father, but always takes him back, much to Sonia's bewilderment and dismay. And why does her mom keep having more babies?

She also brings us to school with her. One teacher explains to the class that there are three kinds of people: white, black, and yellow. The children look around, and ask what about brown? No, that's not one of the categories. But another teacher takes Sonia and a few others to see *West Side Story*, where Sonia is overcome with emotions she didn't know existed. Another teacher arranges for her to audition for the High School of Performing Arts, and her talents finally lead (on the last three pages of the book for us) to her audition for a role on Sesame Street. Her final line, "Then I go home, because there is nothing else to do but wait for the next thing to happen" (p. 262), made me want to head to Sesame Street episodes featuring Maria so that the story could continue.

Menon, S. (2017). *When Dimple Met Rishi*. New York: Simon/Pulse.
If the young women in your courses have few models for pursuing careers in the STEM subjects, introduce them to Dimple Shah, who is passionate about coding, and confident that she can develop an app at Insomnia Con, the camp she attends the summer before college, which will jumpstart her career and advance healthcare. If there are boys in your class who love comics but don't think it's practical to consider a career in art, introduce them to Rishi Patel, who initially believes he must respect his father's expectations that he will follow in his mathematical footsteps, but learns to embrace the field for which he has the talent and passion. If your students are interested in reading about romantic relationships with memorable beginnings, invite them to begin Sandhya Menon's debut novel to find out what happened *When Dimple Met Rishi*. There's a not-so-subtle clue on the back of the cover jacket, which depicts a girl tossing coffee in a boy's face.

Readers will become invested as they follow Dimple and Rishi through the academic and social aspects of the six-week program, complete with a talent contest and a competition that will result in the winning team getting support to market the app they created. They will learn about first-generation Indian American young adults negotiating cultural traditions and values involving arranged marriages, diet, and other lifestyle choices. They'll ponder issues relating to career opportunities, obligations to elders, peer pressure, competition, collaboration, dedication, and destiny. But perhaps the questions uppermost in their minds as they read will be more along the lines of, "Will Dimple and Rishi ever be compatible? Can their love survive their different life goals? Will this be a summer romance with an inevitably sad parting, or is there hope for a lasting romance for this coder/comic artist pair?"

Morkes, A. (2020). *Cool Careers in Science: Computer Game and App Developers*. Philadelphia, PA: Mason Crest.
If your idea of a good job involves spending days playing video games, but the adults in your life scoff at you, this book can be

a great support. You can point out that you learned that the median annual salary for software application designers and lead app developers is over $100,000. Full-time computer game developers often get benefits, including health insurance and vacation days. Plus, the book provides descriptions of what a day in the life of an app developer and a game developer looks like, and both are the kind of challenging but fun days you could picture for yourself.

The book is user-friendly and interactive. There's an assessment checklist near the beginning that will let you know if a career in computer science seems right for you. It describes steps to take to enter the field, such as becoming an app or game tester, attending a coding camp or related program, serving an apprenticeship, and researching colleges that are known to have good video design programs.

The book further discusses building a portfolio, checking out job boards, joining professional organizations, participating in competitions, and building skills and motivation.

The author addresses the problem of the lack of women in the field of game development; only about one-fifth of developers are women. He describes steps that the industry is taking to encourage and support females, along with providing the names and addresses of organizations and resources that support women in computer fields.

Readers who learn the basics from this book can take advantage of the "Further Reading" list and the Internet resources provided that can take them to the next level. Gamers like to level up, so it makes sense that those who desire to work in the field will, too.

*Obama, M. (2021). *Becoming. Adapted for Young Readers*. New York: Delacorte Press.

"I'm not sure… that you're Princeton material" (p. 65). How does that sentence make you feel? How might you respond to being told something similar regarding your first choice of a college? Well, that's the sentence that Michelle Obama heard from her high school guidance counselor during her senior year. It's one of those defining moments she selected to include in her memoir. She notes that the counselor was just trying to do her job, as she suggested that

Michelle lower her sights, which is the opposite of the message her parents instilled in her throughout her childhood and adolescence. Guess who won.

Memoirists reflect on people and events that made them who they are. So we see Michelle as a child within her family, her school, and her neighborhood. We see her playing with dolls, jumping rope, being embarrassed when she makes mistakes in school, and becoming aware of matters of class and of race.

Michelle also worried. "My biggest worry about high school was, *Am I good enough?*" (p. 55). Since her brother went to a different school, she had to figure out who she was on her own, and where she fit among all the smart (and sometimes, unlike her, rich) kids she observed. She slowly grew in confidence, maturity, and determination.

Since the memoir is told linearly, we next get chapters about Michelle's college years. The student population at Princeton was mostly male and mostly white. So the pattern continues: Michelle has to figure out where and how to fit in. She talks about how she needed the camaraderie of other Black students on campus; she recounts the satisfaction of her work-study job as an assistant to the director of the Third World Center, which supported students of color. Predictably, "Home began to feel more distant, almost like a place in my imagination" (p. 82). But she came to understand her cultural history and heritage better. She visited the South, realizing that she was probably a descendant of slaves. She remained serious about her studies, always focused on the future.

> Beneath my laid-back college-kid demeanor, I lived quietly but unswervingly focused on achievement, bent on checking every box.... If there was a challenge to meet, I'd meet it. Such is the life of a girl who can't stop wondering, *Am I good enough?* and is still trying to show herself the answer.

> (p. 87)

That guiding question remained with her in law school and in her first job in a law firm. What does the question, and Michelle's journey, mean for readers? She addresses us directly in a note placed at the very beginning:

So I hope that as you're reading my story, you'll also think about your own—because it's the most beautiful gift you'll ever have. The bumps and bruises, the joys and triumphs and bursts of laughter—they all combine to make you who you are. And who you are is not some static, unchanging thing. It will change every day and every year, and none of us know what shape our lives will ultimately take. That's what becoming is all about. And just like you, I still have a lot of becoming left to do, too.

(pp. x–xi)

Writing and Thinking Prompt

Using the motif of "becoming" that Michelle Obama employs in her memoir, create an outline or a Table of Contents for your present or future memoir, recognizing that the point you are at now is only a stop on the way to additional changes, not the final destination. Who and what influenced your values and behavior at various stages of your development? Was, or is, there a guiding question that leads you on your search for meaning and fulfillment? What forces did you resist, and what obstacles blocked your path? How did your path converge with those of others? In what ways have you supported others on their journeys?

*Onwuachi, K., with Stein, J.D. (2021). *Notes from a Young Black Chef: A Memoir. Adapted for Young Adults*. New York: Delacorte Press.
When a 26-year-old publishes a memoir that begins with a description of the day his new Washington, D.C. restaurant is opening, with a $185 menu price, one might expect that the story will be focused on victories and successes. But this author points the lens at many serious obstacles and mistakes along his journey as well. He doesn't hesitate to tell us about emotional and physical abuse by his father; or the blatant racism he has encountered while driving and while working; or his own involvement in dealing drugs. There are constant questions and ponderings about recognizing and constructing

identity, as well as reinventing oneself. For example, "I knew how to be black in Nigeria, black in SoHo, black in Harlem and the Bronx. But I didn't know how to be black in the South" (p. 103). And "When I closed my eyes, when the cameras were off, when there was no one but myself, who was I then? What Kwame did I want to be?" (p. 202).

Not surprisingly, the author's relationship with food is threaded throughout the memoir. His childhood experiences with his mother in the kitchen were memorable. As an assistant chef on a ship, he gained a passion for cooking. After seeing Obama on TV after winning the 2008 election, Kwame recognized the contrast with his own life. "I was hungover, strung out, and depressed. When I looked at what my life had become, at who I had become, I felt a total estrangement" (p. 98). So what did he do? He went to the grocery store for ingredients, then made a delicious chicken curry! He explains, "I wasn't just cooking a recipe, I was regaining my sanity" (p. 99).

Writing and Thinking Prompt

Kwame is not afraid to bring love into his story. "It didn't matter what continent I was on, in my mind food and love were being mixed together" (p. 61). Reader, how have food and love been intertwined in your life? And what other things are mixed together with love, things that might lead you to a satisfying and successful career like this young Black chef has built? Feel free to munch on some energizing snacks as you write about your own connections between love and food.

*Patterson, J., & Alexander, K. (2020). *Becoming Mohammad Ali.* Illus. D. Anyabwile. New York: JIMMY Patterson Books.
Was Mohammad Ali destined for greatness? When did he realize, or first proclaim, that he was the greatest? This co-written historical novel, alternating between prose chapters narrated by Cassius Clay's boyhood friend Lucky and poetry in the voice of Cassius himself, shows us the future champion's journey from childhood to the age of seventeen. We learn of his difficulties in school, ranging from

trouble with reading to getting into trouble for daydreaming about boxing and neglecting homework to train for boxing. We learn of the love and support he got from his family; and of events, such as the murder of Emmett Till (who was close in age to Cassius) that helped him realize the extent of racism and injustice in our country. We learn of his growing determination and confidence, and his entry into the adult level of boxing championships.

In a "Final Round," the adult Lucky, now a journalist, fills us in on some highlights of the rest of his best friend's life. He mentions the Gold Medal at the 1960 Olympics and the name change after joining the Nation of Islam. Lucky gives us his take on Ali's refusal to be drafted into the army in 1967:

> It was one thing to fight another man in the boxing ring—but the idea of killing people in a far-off country was not in Ali's nature .... knowing Ali, I realized that [refusing to enlist] was the only thing to do—even though we both understood that it might be the end of his boxing career.

(p. 302)

This fictionalized biography could be enjoyed by middle-grade readers, but I believe it reaches into our NA category because it shows Ali's coming of age, detailing the fights (in and out of the boxing ring) that represented the leaving of adolescence and entering adulthood. It shows how Cassius becomes Ali.

*Sharma, N. (2021). *Radha & Jai's Recipe for Romance*. New York: Crown.

This book delivers on the title promise, but the changing relationships in Radha's life go far beyond romance. Her mother takes the concept of *dance mom* to an extreme. When Radha learns that her mother has been sleeping with one of the judges, she walks away from a kathak dance competition and gives up performing. She does, however, move from Chicago to New Jersey with her mother after her parents get divorced. She needs a fresh start, away from her old dance community.

Surprisingly, Radha develops a closer relationship with her father when they are apart. His long work hours and commitment to his Indian restaurant meant that he had not always been there for

Radha while she was growing up, but now they have video chats as she learns to cook using the family recipe book he handed down to her. Perhaps she is discovering a new passion.

Jai, meanwhile, is trying to lead his Bollywood Beats dance team to victory during their senior year. Though he has a passion for medicine and would love to go to Columbia University, he has committed to working full-time at his family store after graduation. Since an accident left his father paralyzed, all the family members have struggled financially and emotionally. If the spectacularly talented Radha would be the lead dancer in their showcase, there's a chance for prize money that could make his dream a reality. But Radha gets panic attacks. Can he request this of her? He has seen her "dance joy," but has promised to support her decision to not perform.

This story is filled with opportunities for characters to forge new friendships, forgive, find inner strength, and be kind to themselves as well as to others. It's a recipe for constructing an identity one can feel proud of. And speaking of recipes, the chapters begin with recipes for the Indian foods Radha cooks while talking with her father.

Roach, M. (2016). *Grunt: The Curious Science of Humans at War*. New York: W. W. Norton & Company.

A military career often combines with another area of expertise. In the introductory chapter, Mary Roach recognizes that there are a number of excellent books on topics related to war, such as PTSD, artillery, and strategies for fighting. She is content to leave those subjects to the historians and memoirists. Her interests lie not where the war movies take us, but in the "…quiet esoteric battles with less considered adversaries: exhaustion, shock, bacteria, panic, ducks" (p. 15). She explains, "This book is a salute to the scientists and the surgeons, running along in the wake of combat, lab coats flapping. Building safer tanks, waging war on filth flies. Understanding turkey vultures" (pp. 15–16).

Hence we get chapters with titles such as "Leaky Seals: Diarrhea as a Threat to National Security"; "The Maggot Paradox: Flies on the Battlefield, for Better and Worse"; "Old Chum: How to Make and Test Shark Repellent";

Second Skin: What to Wear to War." Roach tells stories of courage, such as that of Angus Rupert, a Navy flight surgeon who flew upside down and blindfolded to test a vibrating suit that could help pilots who become disoriented or blinded to fly by feel. Captain Herschel Flowers, who worked in the Army Medical Research Laboratory, tested the possibility of building immunity by injecting cobra venom into himself. Roach demonstrates through anecdotes like these that, "Heroism doesn't always happen in a burst of glory. Sometimes small triumphs and large hearts change the course of history.

(p. 17)

It won't be just students considering entering a branch of the military who will appreciate this book. It's a fascinating, thought-provoking read.

Siegel, S.C. (2021). *Tiny Dancer*. Illus. Siegel, Mark. New York: Atheneum.

We often identify people by their careers: teacher, architect, engineer, hotel manager, chef, office assistant, painter, politician, police officer, nurse practitioner, accountant, contractor, social worker, truck driver, journalist, musician. When someone identifies with a particular life path since childhood, and that dream falls through, what is left?

Siena has loved ballet forever and feels most alive when she is dancing. She excels at the art form and gives up many parts of a more typical childhood and adolescence to improve her talent and achieve success in prestigious venues. When she lands wrong and badly injures her ankle, her world comes crashing down. A ghost dancer is what is left.

This memoir in graphic novel format takes us inside Siena's mind and heart as she struggles to come back from her injury, working hard to regain strength and confidence while watching her peers land great parts and achieve what she no longer can. Slowly, she realizes she has alternatives. There may not be words to describe her anguish and fears, or her growth and self-acceptance. Fortunately, the illustrations convey the emotions exquisitely. The epilogue is almost entirely wordless, and when words do come back in, they are perfect.

*Straczynski, J.M. (2021). *Becoming a Writer, Staying a Writer: The Artistry, Joy, and Career of Storytelling*. Dallas, TX: BenBella Books. Many readers of YA and NA literature have aspirations of following in the footsteps of their favorite writers, and they have learned to read like a writer. They observe an author's techniques, tropes, and styles. They evaluate how well the crafting works in particular texts. That's all wonderful. This book will provide some mentoring, including encouragement and practical advice. Readers will begin immediately to learn something about Straczynski's stylistic choices as they peruse the table of contents, offering chapters such as, "In Which We Discuss Murdered Typewriters, Lost Loves, and the Writing Impulse," "Shark Alert!", "How to Build a Monster in Three Easy Lessons," and "The Thick Plotens." The author establishes credibility by naming some of the various kinds of writing he has done for more than four decades, but also recalls his days as a fledgling writer, as he assumes his audience may be. He does not sugarcoat the obstacles and challenges, both from the outside and from within, that writers will inevitably experience; but, in addition to assuring readers that their writing can have a significant effect on the world, he promises the possibility of profound joy:

> Every day, I step into my home office where I get to do what I love for a living. Every day I am surrounded by fascinating people saying the most amazing things, characters who only I can see and hear until I put their words down on paper and make them real to others. Every day, I travel to distant worlds whose coordinates have never been triangulated by equations or imaged by telescope.
>   Every day, I live in joy.
> This is your invitation to join me there.
>
> (pp. 3–4)

*Weissman, J. (2021). *An Unapologetic Cookbook*. New York: DK. Where do you get butter, ketchup, English muffins, graham crackers, peanut butter, cheese, and hot dog buns? After reading this book, your answer might no longer be the grocery store. The author is a professional chef who can be seen performing on TikTok, Instagram, and Facebook as well as on his own YouTube channel. Joshua explains in his introduction that cooking is an expressive art form, and he encourages readers to develop their culinary intuition.

"If you understand how and why various cooking techniques and ingredients behave the way they do, then there is no boundary or barrier of entry for any idea you could ever have in food" (p. 9).

The first part of the book provides instructions for creating staples from scratch. From there we can progress from breakfast foods to desserts, with appetizers, sandwiches, salads, soups, snacks, and main dishes in between. The accompanying illustrations are a visual treat that may challenge readers to see if they can match or top the models. Apprentices of Joshua Weissman just might unapologetically announce that they intend to head to culinary school or to teach themselves in a way that will lead to a career in preparing and serving original culinary creations for the good of the world.

Wiggs, S. (2020). *The Lost and Found Bookshop*. New York: William Morrow.

We're faced with many choices when we reach adulthood. Should we take risks, or opt for safety and security? Once we decide, do we have to live with the consequences, and possible regrets, for the rest of our lives? Natalie Harper, having grown up with a mother who struggled to keep the independent bookstore she founded and loved alive, picked a career that did not make her happy, but provided a steady paycheck and benefits. She was also dating a man who was steady and good to her, but she realized the relationship was not thriving. When both her mother and boyfriend die in a plane crash, Natalie has to deal with a lot of grief, but also is thrust into a life of second chances. Could she rescue the bookstore? Could she build new relationships? Could she find true love this time around?

Just as Natalie finds comfort and wisdom in books as she takes over the bookstore, New Adults who read *The Lost and Found Bookstore* might realize that they can trust themselves to embrace opportunities that will allow them to follow their passions and commit to new adventures. Life will present challenges, but it will offer surprises, wonders, and treasures as well.

Wyckoff, A., & Harris, M. (2019). *Career Programming for Today's Teens: Exploring Nontraditional and Vocational Alternatives*. Chicago, IL: ALA Editions.

"What do you want to be when you grow up?" Students who have been guided by librarians who use ideas presented in this book might give answers that include veterinary technology, machine manufacturing, culinary arts, video game design, massage therapy, radiology, restaurant management, salon owner, tattoo artist, recording artist, sports trainer, app designer, air traffic controller, nuclear technician, funeral service manager, web developer, wind turbine service technician, or medical equipment repairer.

Wyckoff and Harris provide evidence indicating that many teens today feel ready to begin a career and contribute to society, preferring to forego a college education due to the time involved, financial burdens, or lack of interest in traditional classwork. They note the high need for:

> individuals who can fill middle-skill careers—jobs that require more than a high school diploma, but less than a four-year degree .... People with specialized training and skills that can be acquired from an Associate's degree program or certificate program.

> (p. 3)

Why then do we regularly hear of college fairs being offered in schools, but less often hear of trade school fairs or vocation fairs?

This book is filled with resources and program ideas for librarians wishing to meet the needs of the noncollege bound, the students who love working with their hands as well as their minds, the adolescents with a particular passion or goal that requires something other than what most colleges have to offer. Examples of programs that have been implemented in libraries are combined with information about apprenticeships and internships, as well as resources that can be passed on to young people seeking guidance about preparation for a particular career, or ideas about possible career paths to explore.

*Yen, J. (2021). *A Taste for Love*. New York: Razorbill.
Liza has a passion for baking, and she dreams of going to a culinary school. Ironically, her parents forbid this because they want to spare her the kind of nonstop work that they have experienced running the Yin and Yang bakery and restaurant. Dating is another thing they disagree on. While her mother will only accept Asian boyfriends, Liza wants to be able to make her own choices, and does not appreciate her mother's matchmaking attempts.

Readers who love baking shows and light romance have come to the right place. The plot of this novel revolves around a baking contest Liza's mother is in charge of. Liza is one of the judges, and it doesn't take long to figure out that her mother has chosen contestants who are possible suitors. After many twists and turns, the resolution satisfies both mother and daughter. Along the way, they have a frank discussion. Mrs. Yang has felt that Liza was trying to be like everyone else, to be more American, to the extent that she was not proud of her own culture and background. Liza, recognizing that her mother wants the best for her, is able to assure her, "I know who I am, Mom, and I'm proud of it. All of it" (p. 260).

Some readers will most appreciate the great descriptions of delectable foods that are described during each of the subcategories of the baking contest. But in her Acknowledgments, Jennifer Yen talks directly to her readers, hoping that Liza's story will inspire them. "Life may give you a path to walk, but you can choose the destination. Dream big, and believe in yourself. Be afraid, but do it anyway" (unpaged).

Instructional Strategies and Activities

Write Your Way into Your "Becoming"

When asked in an interview what drew him to the kinds of projects he is best known for (adaptations of classic literature into a graphic novel format), artist Gareth Hinds explained:

> I went to art school for illustration and I found myself increasingly drawn to comics as my medium of choice. I would do my own comics and I would always feel like the writing was the weak link. So initially, for my senior thesis, I decided to do an adaptation of a Brother's Grimm fairy tale. I really enjoyed that adaptation process, so I thought I would try it again with something more ambitious, which was *Beowulf*. *Beowulf* not only was enjoyable, but then I discovered there was an educational market for it.
>
> (DeHart, 2022)

The books featured in the section above offer varied examples of how real and fictional individuals followed unique paths and actively worked at constructing an identity or becoming themselves in terms of work and beyond. Some of the authors are looking back on their journeys. We see some characters reacting to circumstances and other people, as well as making decisions that result in their becoming somehow different from their former selves. Librarians and teachers can invite students to think about the outside and internal forces that have shaped who they are so far, and then to envision the next steps on their quests for an identity. What might they encounter on the road to becoming whatever they aspire to? How can they play an active role in their own construction of their future selves at work and beyond?

Walk-Through

Here is a sample assignment from high school science teacher Mr. Nayeri:

Biologist Sy Montgomery wrote *How to Be a Good Creature: A Memoir in Thirteen Animals* (2018) and adapted it for younger readers in *Becoming a Good Creature* (2020). Now that you have explored some of the books in our "Becoming Text Set," choose one of the following options. Feel free to use a graphic format, with panels and speech bubbles, if that works for you.

A. What would your memoir about the people and events that make you who you are today look like? How might you structure the chapters? Looking ahead, what do you anticipate might be some key points in future chapters? Write ideas down to discover and share your story. (If you have already started this project by answering the prompt in the book talk for Michelle Obama's *Becoming* above, you can use this opportunity to go further. Perhaps draft a prologue or the first chapter.)

B. Choose a well-known person (historical or contemporary) in the field you are pursuing, and research their early lives and influences. What caused them, or enabled them, to become the person they are today, or that they became noted for in history? How would you approach writing a "Becoming" essay or book about them?

C. Interview a parent, guardian, relative, or other adults to find out about what personal characteristics or interests, events, and people influenced them throughout their childhood, adolescence, and early adulthood. Explain that you are interested in the concept of *becoming*, and would like their opinions about how people can grow into the best versions of themselves, how to match careers and passions, and what qualities young people should be developing and nurturing. As you listen, take notes, and ask probing questions if appropriate. How did they decide on or land the job they are in? What are their hopes for the future? What advice would they like to offer to you and your friends who are at an earlier stage of *becoming*? Be sure to thank them for the valuable gifts of their time and thoughts. Later, write a reflection based on what you heard.

Using a Youth Lens as a Critical Approach

We've employed the construct of *becoming* a lot in this chapter, and now we're going to explore a critical approach that asks us to disrupt the notion that adolescents are merely *on their way* to something presumably better and fuller, i.e., adulthood. This might seem contradictory, but the lens of becoming and the youth lens can also be seen as intersecting, or complementary.

In 2015, *English Journal* published an issue devoted to the theme, "Rethinking 'Adolescence' to Re-imagine English." The guest editors ask readers to recognize the stereotypical ways texts and people tend to view adolescence monolithically, as a universal experience, when actually, adolescence is a construct rather than something that objectively exists that can describe behaviors of all teens. We and our students can become aware of language (often negative) used to depict adolescents as immature, risk-taking, irresponsible, governed by raging hormones, and incapable (Sarigianides, Lewis, and Petrone, 2015). We can analyze such depictions in literature, movies, and classroom discourse, troubling the stereotypes. "Re-imagining adolescents as capable, knowledgeable, complex, and contradictory—affordances we allow for adults—affects one's position in relation to youth in the classroom and in the world" (p. 18).

We can look critically at the books discussed in this chapter, even those in the "Becoming" text set, to see how the adolescents and New Adults are portrayed by authors, as well as viewed by other characters. The approach can also be applied to the books noted in earlier chapters. It's not hard to find examples of parents who don't give their nearly or newly grown children credit for the deep thinking they are doing and the actions that show responsibility and maturity. Teachers, employers, and other adults can also fail to recognize the complexity and uniqueness of teens and college-age students. Both Ruth Bader Ginsburg and "Wine Girl" Victoria James were demeaned and discriminated against because of their youth as well as their gender in professions where many would rather have excluded them. Students can analyze Emoni in Elizabeth Acevedo's *With the Fire on High* (2019) through the Youth Lens. Where others might see only a teen who got pregnant early in high school, her grandmother, some teachers, and readers see a hard-working, responsible senior caring for her 2-year-old, appreciating her grandmother, and aspiring to become a chef against daunting odds. The Youth Lens can be threaded through a whole semester, helping readers to see the incredible diversity of the young people they meet, as well as unfair assumptions and perceptions others often have of adolescents, and barriers they erect that prevent the young people from valuing themselves and succeeding in their goals.

Walk-Through

Ms. Vega is a librarian who has taught lessons in several high school classrooms about reading texts critically and using a Youth Lens to analyze novels. More than a dozen students meet weekly in the library to discuss NA literature, and Ms. Vega has modeled using the Youth Lens with specific texts, offering articles about this critical approach. Book club members copied and displayed quotes they particularly liked, such as the following:

> Contrary to mainstream views that read youth as in a state of "becoming" and "developing," we see youth as already engaged in conversations around issues from which our communities are not protecting them (e.g., immigration policies, racial and ethnic biases, homophobia, misogyny).... We see youth as intellectually invested global citizens ready for curriculum that encourages them to cultivate cosmopolitan habits of mind such as cooperation and hospitality, dialogue and curiosity.
>
> (DeJaynes and Curmi, 2015, p. 75)

Book club members encourage each other to find examples in stories of assumptions about adolescents and ways that certain characters in NA books refute the stereotypes about teens. Here are samples of what responses from readers might sound like:

ROGER: Well, we all know that teenagers are all the same—NOT! I think Rainbow Rowell does a great job in *Fangirl* of showing twins who are so different they shatter that notion. Also, which one is the more mature? Depends on the circumstances. Wren is way more independent, self-confident, and able to interact with people as they start college. But Cath studies and makes other wise choices throughout freshman year, while Wren parties to the extent that she is hospitalized for alcoholism.

Now I'm thinking about how differently they react when their mom, who abandoned them when they were 9, comes back into the picture. Wren forgives all and is eager to be part of her mother's life again. Cath doesn't let her mother off so easily, refusing to act like her leaving was no big deal. Who's more mature? The jury is still out on that one. But I think both twins are more mature than their mother!

PRIYA: Radha's mother Sujata in *Radha & Jai's Recipe for Romance* should definitely read up on the Youth Lens. She tries to control and manipulate every aspect of Radha's life to fulfill her own needs. Granted, she has regrets about her own aborted dancing career, but she needs to realize her daughter has a life of her own. She has pushed and pressured Radha for years. And her behavior is what causes Radha to walk away from dance. I don't care what her complicated reasons were for sleeping with a competition judge. It caused her daughter shame, and now Radha isn't even confident that she won all the earlier competitions on her own merit.

But I digress. That's now in the past, and Radha is finding her own way at the Princeton Academy of the Arts. Since she has decided not to perform anymore, she negotiates an agreement with her teacher to fulfill that requirement by taking on the role of choreographer. We can see how mature she is becoming, but her mother still doesn't respect her choices. Finally, Radha confronts her mother directly about why she has been keeping secrets from her.

> "I didn't want your help, Mom. I don't want your help unless I ask for it. I'm almost eighteen, and you still make everything about what *you* want me to do, and I lose my dance joy. Being a part of Bollywood Beats brought it back for me, and I really think that it was because you weren't involved".
>
> (pp. 308–309)

References

DeHart, J. (2022). An interview with Gareth Hinds. Retrieved from http://www.yawednesday.com/weekly-posts/an-interview-with-gareth-hinds-graphic-novels-and-the-classics.

DeJaynes, T., & Curmi, C. (2015). Youth as cosmopolitan intellectuals. *English Journal, 104*(3), 75–80.

Rose, M. (2004). *The mind at work: Valuing the intelligence of the American worker.* New York: Viking.

Sarigianides, S.T., Lewis, M.A., & Petrone, R. (2015). How rethinking adolescence helps re-imagine the teaching of English. *English Journal, 104*(3), 13–18.

Literature Cited

Acevedo, E. (2019). *With the fire on high.* New York: HarperCollins.

Dickman, K. (2021). *Becoming a climate scientist.* New York: Simon & Schuster.

Montgomery, S. (2020). *Becoming a good creature.* Illus. Green, R. Boston, MA: Houghton Mifflin Harcourt.

Montgomery, S. (2018). *How to be a good creature: A memoir in thirteen animals.* Illus. Green, R. Boston, MA: Houghton Mifflin Harcourt.

Shabazz, I., with Jackson, T.D. (2021). *The awakening of Malcolm X.* New York: Farrer Straus Giroux.

Shabazz, I., with Magoon, K. (2015). *X: A novel.* Somerville, MA: Candlewick Press.

Shabazz, I., with Watson, R. (2018). *Betty before X.* New York: Square Fish.

Changing Relationships

5

Nothing Stays the Same

What do we mean by the word relationship? Ponder how one literary character thinks of it. "Relationship. That was a vague term if ever there was one. It could describe just about anything." (Sáenz, 2021, p. 48)

Relationships are always evolving, and changes might be especially dramatic or significant in the age range that New Adult (NA) literature encompasses. How do relationships deepen, shift, or end as both New Adults and NA characters develop and take on new roles and identities? Parent–child relationships must inevitably transform as grown children leave home, whether that happens gradually or suddenly, amicably or with tension or hostility. If they don't move out, or if they move back at some point after living away, things are still different. Relationships between and among life-long friends alter as they go to separate colleges, devote themselves to different jobs or causes, question the values of their youth, etc. And new or deeper types of relationships, often including romance and long-term commitments, beckon. There are numerous NA books that help us ponder the issues relevant to changing relationships, and we will investigate some in this chapter. Of course, many of the books explored in previous chapters would also fit this chapter; we have certainly seen a variety of relationships among characters. Our topics intersect in literature, as they do in our lives.

DOI: 10.4324/9781003221685-5

TEXT SETS

Family

New Adults at some point come to the startling realization, "My parents grew up!" Children and teens, as they work toward gaining independence, often do not, or cannot, understand the perspectives of the adults in authority whom they perceive as curtailing their freedom, not wanting them to have any fun, treating them like babies, smothering them. New experiences do indeed provide freedom, but also have consequences and teach valuable lessons. New Adults often come to appreciate their guardians and mentors in different ways. On the other hand, young people entering adulthood can realize that their parents truly are flawed, some very much so, and the New Adults must make decisions about being patient, forgiving, and/or supportive. Some conclude that they need to assert their right to be respected, or even break ties in order to protect themselves.

Moving out of the home inevitably changes the relationships New Adults have with guardians and siblings, whether those siblings are younger or older. The books in this text set explore all kinds of changing family relationships and can stimulate readers to step back and think about how relationships within their family have affected their own identities and values. What would they like to strengthen, change, or abandon? The titles preceded by an asterisk will be discussed in book talks in the next section.

*Acevedo, E. (2020). *Clap When You Land*. New York: HarperCollins.
*Ali, S.K. (2021). *Misfit in Love*. New York: Salaam Reads.
*Anderson, L. (2017). *Not Now, Not Ever*. New York: Wednesday Books.
*Benway, R. (2017). *Far from the Tree*. New York: HarperTeen.
*Kann, C. *Let's Talk about Love*. New York: Swoon Reads.
*Kaur, J. (2021). *If I Tell You the Truth*. New York: HarperCollins.
*King, A.S. (2021). *Switch*. New York: Dutton Books.
*McCullough, J. (2021). *We Are the Ashes, We Are the Fire*. New York: Dutton..
*McCauley, K. (2020). *If These Wings Could Fly*. New York: Katherine Tegen Books.

Sánchez, E.L. (2017). *I Am Not Your Perfect Mexican Daughter*. New York: Alfred A. Knopf.
*Straub, E. (2020). *All Adults Here*. New York: Random House.

Fake Dating

Have you ever been involved in a fake-dating situation? How did that work out for you? Many authors of NA literature have employed this trope. But really, how many possible variations on the theme can there be? How many outcomes? Don't the stories become predictable, and therefore no longer challenging? Readers can compare the books in this text set to evaluate how well the authors manage to create a new story with rich characters who surprise the readers, as well as other characters, and perhaps themselves. They can pay attention to the writer's craft and be conscious of their own thinking as they follow the characters' decisions and dialog. They can be interactive, talking to the characters, offering criticism or advice. Or they can just go along for the ride, enjoying the plot and, as they encounter the uncomfortable situations fake daters inevitably get themselves into, feeling happy that it's not them!

Asher, A. (2022). *Not the Witch You Wed*. New York: Griffin.
*Bellefleur, A. (2020). *Written in the Stars*. New York: Avon.
*Bhuiyan, T. (2021). *Counting Down with You*. Toronto, Ontario: Inkyard Press.
*Boulley, A. (2021.) *Firekeeper's Daughter*. New York: Henry Holt and Company.
Chao, G. (2020). *Rent a Boyfriend*. New York: Simon & Schuster.
Hazelwood, A. (2021). *The Love Hypothesis*. New York: Jove.
Jaigirdar, A. (2021). *Hani and Isu's Guide to Fake Dating*. Salem, MA: Page Street.
Light, A. *The Upside of Falling*. New York: HarperTeen.
*McQuiston, C. (2019). *Red, White and Royal Blue*. New York: St. Martin's Griffin.
Menon, S. (2020). *10 Things I Hate about Pinky*. New York: Simon Pulse.
Yoon, D. (2021). *Frankly in Love*. New York: G.P. Putnam's Sons.

Book Talks: Ready to Go!

Here you will find book talks for fiction featuring characters who are navigating new physical, intellectual, spiritual, and emotional spaces as they fall into and/or out of love, as well as form new friendships and relate to their families in different ways. Biographies, memoirs, and informational books will offer guidance on how to establish and promote healthy, loving relationships. An asterisk indicates that the book is part of a text set above.

*Acevedo, E. (2020). *Clap When You Land*. New York: HarperCollins.
Forgiveness. It's easy to recognize its value in the abstract. And so many counselors, religious leaders, and self-help books tell us it is necessary for healing and moving on in our lives. BUT, when it's called for in specific circumstances, it's often not easy at all. Camino's Papi lived a lie, involving a second marriage and family in New York. Yahaira's Papi betrayed her and her mother, by marrying another woman in the Dominican Republic and spending summers there. It isn't until the man both girls called Papi dies in a plane crash that they learn about each other's existence. It's hard to forgive such a transgression, such a secret. And how can the girls express their anger toward him when their beloved father is dead?

This novel in verse alternates between Camino's and Yahaira's narration. We feel empathy toward both these 17-year-old sisters. But perhaps the person who has to work the hardest for forgiveness and acceptance is Yahaira's mother, the betrayed wife. Can she ever accept the now-orphaned Camino?

The book asks hard questions, and readers must contemplate answers as they watch the characters grieve and make decisions. Class, gender, and cultural issues are raised, even as Papi is being buried in his homeland. Important concepts are grappled with. Maybe especially forgiveness.

*Ali, S.K. (2021). *Misfit in Love*. New York: Salaam Reads.
This is a book for those who love wedding stories. It's the summer between Janna's high school graduation and the beginning of college, and she is excited about her brother Muhammad marrying Sarah. But as guests begin to arrive for the weekend, she realizes that things—and people—are changing all around her. Just as she is ready to tell

her friend Nuah that she now can reciprocate the feelings he expressed earlier and can commit to a relationship, she discovers that he met someone at college and now sees Janna as just a good friend. She sees that her father is exhibiting racist behavior, and she wants no part of being near him. Her mother seems to be more interested in spending time with a male friend and his children than with Janna, leading to feelings of jealousy and insecurity. While in high school, Janna had been sexually assaulted by a young man in her mosque, and now the people who supported her and helped her feel safe seem to be moving on.

As Janna meets new people and the weekend events unfold, Janna's world and list of possibilities grow much larger. She has an epiphany.

> Maybe that's what I need to secure before I go to college—not a boy, not a relationship, not romantic love, but learning how to act and take risks and first steps and be decisive and become bolder and move out of the safety of my head and into the disruptive and messy realm of making life better. For me and for others, too.

(p. 287)

Readers who have read Ali's *Saints and Misfits* (2017, Salaam Reads) will be encouraged by Janna's continuing healing and courage. Those who start with this stand-alone sequel may choose to go back to meet her at a younger age and explore her background more extensively. Either direction will offer rewards.

*Anderson, L. (2017). *Not Now, Not Ever*. New York: Wednesday Books. Elliot's mother expects her to attend the Air Force Academy in Colorado, where she is stationed. Her father and stepmother want her to stay near home in California and study something productive: i.e., law. Whichever route she chooses, someone will be crushed, scared, and/or ashamed. But, "I wanted to try on my third option, the nuclear option—getting a degree that I wanted. Not close to home. Not with the military. The route that hurt everyone" (p. 113).

As a rising high school senior, Elliot secretly heads to a camp for geniuses in Oregon, where she will have a chance to win a scholarship to the college there and join their science fiction literature program.

While on campus, Ever (she has given herself a new identity) makes wonderful friends, begins a romantic relationship, and spends time in the incredible library that houses rare science fiction treasures. She learns that she is not the only one lying and keeping secrets. There are mysteries to be solved, competitions to win, and lessons of all kinds to be learned. And an identity to be claimed.

*Bellefleur, A. (2020). *Written in the Stars*. New York: Avon.
Her mother refers to Belle's new girlfriend Darcy as *the actuary*. "Mom had a terrible habit of reducing everyone to their professions. Jane, the pharmacologist. Daniel, the software engineer. Lydia, the dental student. She could only imagine what mom referred to her as. Elle, the disappointment" (p. 172).

Actually, Darcy also scoffs at Elle's job as horoscope reader/writer and astrology-related app creator. Later, while stargazing with Elle during their fake relationship meant to keep Darcy's brother from setting her up with any more dates, Darcy finds out that Elle had been in a Ph.D. program in astronomy, but had dropped out when she realized the program had taken the magic out of learning. By this time, Darcy is discovering aspects of Elle that go beyond her job, her awkwardness, her messiness, and her habit of buying boxed wine—aspects that just might be causing Darcy to fall in love for real. Elle is a person who refuses to let others make her into anything other than her true self. And Elle "… woke up every morning and hoped for the best instead of anticipating the worst" (p. 206).

This novel, with allusions to *Pride and Prejudice* (2003) as well as charts based on Zodiac signs, explores family dynamics, parental expectations and pressures, the risks and rewards of romance and job choices, and other aspects of identity. Each of the protagonists makes mistakes as she learns about loving another who is not perfect, but who may be perfect for her.

*Benway, R. (2017). *Far from the Tree*. New York: HarperTeen.
The jacket cover asks, "What does it mean to be a family?" and the characters seek answers to this question as they uncover secrets and forge new relationships. Grace pours all her love into the baby inside her before making the unselfish choice to allow adoptive parents to raise Peach. She herself has been raised by loving parents who adopted her, but when she discovers that she has siblings, she sets out to find both them and her biological mother. She meets Maya, who was adopted as a baby by a couple who shortly after that had a daughter who grew up to look like them, so Maya feels insecure about her status. Together they

meet Joachin, the eldest sibling, who, after experiencing a dozen foster care settings, has learned, "I know when I'm not wanted, you know?" (p. 164). He has learned to not trust others and to not risk loving.

As they follow the siblings on their journey to find their mother, readers will come to understand why Grace, having faced shame, cannot open up about her pregnancy and her baby; why Maya breaks up with her girlfriend Claire, though everyone (including the reader) realizes how good Claire is for her; and why Joachin is doing all he can to sabotage his relationship with the foster parents who truly love him and want to adopt him. The complexities of family dynamics that are explored in this story offer opportunities for readers to listen and observe carefully to figure out how each person is influenced by their background and prior experiences.

*Bhuiyan, T. (2021). *Counting Down with You*. Toronto, Ontario: Inkyard Press.

Our narrator, Karina Ahmed, is very sure of what she wants. She wants to study English and writing at Columbia University. She wants to date— for real—Ace Clyde, the white boy whom she has been tutoring and fake dating. And she wants to please her loving parents. The problem is that she cannot have her third wish if she embraces the first two goals. Her Muslim parents expect her to refrain from dating (until they find a suitable mate), and become a doctor. She is terrified of disappointing them and riling their anger.

Karina uses coping strategies to handle her anxiety; they include counting downward, writing down her thoughts, breathing consciously, and yoga. But she seems unable to deal with the causes of the anxiety, most of which have to do with her parents. They treat her younger brother as though he is perfect, and give him much more freedom, while Karina feels she can never be good enough for them. While her parents are away for a month visiting Bangladesh, Karina becomes closer to Ace and helps him communicate with his parents and brother in order to make their family dynamics better. And it works! Could the same work for her?

That turns out to be not so easy, but Karina does find support from her grandmother. As readers count down the twenty-eight days of the parents' absence with Karina, they'll have plenty to think about, plenty of opinions, and plenty to say. They might be amazed to find out that the author is 21, and may decide to follow her on social media.

Writing and Thinking Prompt

Karina's friends provide strong support for her as she makes choices. In order to do what she wants, what she comes to know is right for her, she has to lie to her parents. Choose one of the following options to write about:

A. Play the role of a friend of Karina or another character in this book. Write a dialogue between your character and at least one other. You can use the scene where Karina's grandmother intervenes by talking with her parents as a model:

> You treat her as less than she is, and she never says a word.... you kill her dreams... What would Allah say about this? You are supposed to love your children unconditionally.... Where in the Quran does it say she has to be a doctor?
>
> (p. 440)

You'll have to determine what you think is the correct course of action. Does Karina have the right to choose her own major and career? Do her parents have the right to restrict her dating, at least while she is still in high school and being supported by them?

B. Think about relationships and/or college and career choices, in terms of yourself or someone you know. Should a young person's goals take precedence over the expectations of parents, guardians, or other adults? Is deception ever an acceptable way to deal with conflicts? How can you find support for yourself, and/or provide support for others who are in a bind because of conflicting values within a family? Place yourself in the position of parents, at least for a while, so that you really try to understand their perspective and reasons for their behavior. Write an opinion piece, or craft a dialog that grapples with these questions.

*Boulley, A. (2021.) *Firekeeper's Daughter*. New York: Henry Holt and Company.

Can a relationship survive and thrive if one or both partners have assumed a false identity? While Daunis is guiding the newcomer to the hockey team around the community, she realizes she is attracted to him; but, knowing Jamie has a girlfriend already, she will not let herself act on her feelings. When she finds out that he is actually an undercover agent for the FBI (and that the girlfriend was just part of his fictitious background story), she agrees to be a confidential informant. She is grieving the meth-related death of her uncle and the murder of her best friend, and so wants to help track down the network of drug dealers on the reservation. This requires that she act as if she is Jamie's girlfriend. Is he falling for her, too? How can she tell what is real and what is part of his act? Can a relationship that began with deception turn into something truthful?

While Daunis is trying to figure these things out, she's also spying on suspects; dealing with injuries she has been keeping a secret; learning the science behind meth production and healing plants; visiting her dying grandmother in a facility; supporting her grieving mother; taking college classes; and analyzing clues as more of her friends become victims. As the lies add up, the danger and violence increase.

This thriller brings to light many of the social problems that some Native populations have had to face in the past and that continue today, including rampant violence against Native women. But it does far more. In the Author's Note, Boulley tells us:

> I sought to write about identity, loss, and injustice… and also of love, joy, connection, friendship, hope, laughter, and the beauty and strength of my Ojibwe community. It was paramount to share and celebrate what justice and healings look like in a tribal community: cultural events, language revitalization, ceremonies, traditional teachings, whisper networks, blanket parties, and numerous other ways tribes have shown resilience in the face of adversity.

(pp. 490–491)

Caletti, D. (2021). *One Great Lie*. New York: Atheneum.
"All of you is different before and after heartbreak. All of you is different before and after betrayal," (p. 344) Charlotte is told by a researcher who is helping her uncover the mysteries of her Renaissance ancestor Isabella di Angelo, whom Charlotte suspects was the writer of a famous poem that her famed male lover took credit for. The truth of those words hits Charlotte hard while she is in Italy participating in a summer writing workshop led by her favorite author, Luca Bruni.

Charlotte learns about women writers in the Middle Ages and the Renaissance who had virtually no power, but nonetheless found ways to write, even if they had been locked in a convent by a father or brothers for economic or other reasons. Learning about the lives of women and the injustices done to them helps her to understand how in school they study the works of Tasso, while history has forgotten Isabella. If Charlotte can find evidence that Tasso stole the words of Isabella, that would be a huge step toward justice.

Charlotte does not immediately see that history is being repeated during the workshop, though astute readers will see the signs clearly and want to warn her. A powerful man is taking things from the young women who trusted and revered him, and he is getting away with it. What will happen if the girls go public with reports of his seductions, indiscretions, lies, and sexual harassment? Does Charlotte owe that to Isabella, to herself, to other women?

I can give no answers here. In fact, we are told that Charlotte doesn't have answers about her future, "…and any story that ends with answers is a lie anyway" (p. 372). Maybe it's enough that readers will leave with some of the wisdom and maturity Charlotte paid a heavy price to attain. Maybe that will lead to fewer women having to say, "Me, too."

*Coles, J. (2021). *Things We Couldn't Say*. New York: Scholastic.
Gio hasn't seen his birth mother since he was 9, when she abandoned the family. At 17, he's not feeling supported by his remaining parent, either. His father is a pastor who is often drunk, and who does not accept that Gio is bisexual. Now nearing the end of high school, Gio is handling things as well as he can, taking care of his younger brother, playing on the basketball team, and making playlists.

And then, his birth mother walks back in, wanting love and acceptance from her G-Bug. He finds he can't just run back into her arms. He also can't concentrate on basketball or schoolwork. Life becomes even more confusing when the new guy on the team, David, asks him out on a date.

Readers may weigh in along the way about what choices Gio should make. Is forgiveness in order? Or does that need to be earned first? Is it time to come out to more people than his family and close friends? How will David react if he keeps trying to keep their relationship a secret?

Gio learns that, although both parents are flawed, others are there whom he can depend on, including his wise stepmother, who might be the reason his father is attempting to change for the better. Though his mother leaves again, Gio is not devastated this time. He realizes, "The future is uncertain, but looking at each person around me, I know that I've found my light. Light that'll carry me forward through whatever life brings" (p. 308).

Johnson, L. (2021). *Rise to the Sun*. New York: Scholastic.
Music lovers and those who thrive in the atmosphere of festivals will immerse themselves in the weekend at the Farmland Music and Arts Festival with the two narrators and their friends. Olivia has begged her best friend Imani to come with her and has promised to refrain from her usual behavior that involves constantly falling in love and starting new relationships. There have been far too many, and the last one ended particularly badly when her boyfriend posted near-naked pictures of her on social media. She must decide whether she is going to testify against him the following week, effectively dashing his hopes for an athletic scholarship.

Toni is three days away from the start of college. Her heart is not in it, nor in much of anything else. She's grieving the death of her father; she was with him eight months ago when he was the victim of a random shooting. He was a musician who often went on tours, leaving his family to fend without him. Toni loved him so much, but also missed him and needed him to be home for her. She feels conflicted about this and hopes that a weekend at the festival she and her dad attended every year will help her figure out what to do with her life.

When Olivia meets Toni, her promise to Imani about a best friends' weekend is quickly forgotten. This time it's different; this time it's real love. Toni and Olivia make beautiful music together, literally. Toni, who was guarded even before her father was killed and since then has let no one close enough to have the potential to hurt her, begins to melt. Does she dare trust Olivia? Love is frightening, but now so is the thought of not having Olivia in her life. She falls fast, and she falls hard.

Both girls make mistakes over the two days of this whirlwind romance, leading to new questions about whether forgiveness is possible, and whether love is worth the hurt that inevitably accompanies it. Readers will feel helpless as Olivia lies, as Toni runs away, as Olivia cheats, and as Toni builds that wall around her again. Maybe by reading to the end they'll be able to salvage the promising relationship from the wreck that it becomes at one point. And maybe the magic of music will help.

*Kann, C. *Let's Talk about Love*. New York: Swoon Reads.
College sophomore Alice has spent a lot of time figuring herself out and is now comfortable with who she is. But that doesn't seem to be good enough for other people. When her counselor asks her to talk about her family, she tells him, "You might want to strap in for this ride I like to call *Not Black Enough to Be the Black Sheep of Black Excellence*" (p. 158). Her parents insist that she must go to law school in order to continue getting financial support from them. But Alice's skills and passions are leading her to a major in interior design, which her mother refuses to see as anything other than a hobby.

Alice is also comfortable with being asexual, but will she ever be in a romantic relationship with someone who is also okay with it? As she falls for her co-worker Takumi, she tells her counselor, "When I compare myself to him, I'm not good enough anyway. And I don't really get why he's bothering with me in the first place" (p. 157).

Readers might want to have sticky notes at hand so they can write to Alice as they follow her journey. They can tell her when they're laughing (because she *is* very funny); or they can give her advice or sympathy. If they actively listen to what Alice tells herself and others as she discovers paths to happiness, they just might discover some things that will help them with their own issues and relationships.

Kenwood, N. (2020). *It Sounded Better in my Head*. New York: Flatiron Books.
Perhaps readers who are feeling insecure about multiple aspects of their identities will find comfort knowing that young people in Australia are going through similar struggles. Eighteen-year-old Natalie is waiting to hear about her acceptance into the University of Melbourne. Throughout high school she dealt with severe acne; though medication and time have improved the situation, she is scarred both physically and emotionally. As the novel begins, she

finds out her parents are separating. Her two best friends are now a couple. She is a natural worrier, and all these things combine to make everyday life and thoughts about her future troublesome.

Here are a few sentences from our first-person narrator that will help you get a feel for the way Natalie's mind works:

> I don't know what I want to be. I mostly trained myself to do well at school as an antidote to all the dark thoughts.... No one likes you very much, and You have nothing to show for your life except schoolwork, and You have the face of a monster.

(p. 22)

As if things couldn't get more complicated, Alex, 19 and much more experienced, begins to pay attention to her. Natalie really likes him, but now has to figure out the whole dating thing. She finds herself making mistakes, second-guessing herself, and pushing him away when that's the last thing she wants to do.

Many readers will understand Natalie's anxiety and will cheer as she takes steps that can lead to a coherent identity and hope for new dreams and relationships.

*King, A.S. (2021). *Switch*. New York: Dutton Books.
Fans of A.S. King will not be surprised that some pretty bizarre things occur in *Switch*. Time has stopped due to some weird fold in the universe; the Becker's house is turning/flipping; some individuals (Anomalies, as they come to be called) develop abilities such as flying; and high schools have added "Solution Time" to their daily schedules so that teams of teenagers can figure out an answer that will start time up again. The Becker family is clearly dysfunctional. Our narrator Tru's father is building boxes around rooms in their home; her mother, a psychic, has walked out on the family; her brother Richard, once having been accused of being a pedophile, is uncommunicative and is sneaking out at night. Little by little we learn that all of the family members, as well as others, have been hurt by Tru's older sister Karen's destructive lying. (You might want to look for informational resources on compulsive lying to give to NA readers.)

Tru, when she is not busy breaking world records in javelin throwing and removing the nails her father has been putting into his barricades, is pondering problems of both time and identity. She recognizes anomalies in every person she observes in the hallways, concluding:

> Abnormal is what high schoolers do, no matter how normal we may seem/it's our job.... The minute they put us in this building we're expected to be something we aren't. Interested/ engaged/athletic/baby grown-ups with the will to be social and succeed in life.

> (p. 182)

Tru believes the answer to the time problem has to do with "People giving a shit about other people" (p. 221). She understands that everything has to do with energy; she demonstrates much positive energy in her interactions with others, and eventually, in her self-acceptance and love. This book can be taken as a challenge. Are we ready to flip the switch?

Linmark, R.Z. (2019). *The Importance of Being Wilde at Heart*. New York: Delacorte Press.

Ken Z is in the last semester of high school in the impoverished Pacific Island nation of South Kristol. He's in a book club with several close friends and a teacher, all of whom appreciate the life and works of Oscar Wilde. He is supported by a loving, but often silent mother, who won't share anything about his father or why she moved to South Kristol and never saw her relatives again. When he meets Ran, a fellow Wilde enthusiast from North Kristol, he falls in love and discovers things about himself and the world that deepen both his knowledge and his sadness.

When Ran disappears, never returning his messages, Ken Z writes haiku and list poetry to cope; sort out his feelings; and ponder issues including freedom, military regimes, homophobia, obsession, censorship, friendship, and more. Did Ran use him? Why did he keep so many secrets about himself? How will he handle the forced military conscription awaiting him? Were Ran's messages to him blocked? Did the messages Ken Z sent get Ran in serious trouble?

Oscar Wilde (somehow) appears periodically to answer Ken Z's questions and offer advice. Ken Z, after researching Wilde's life, expresses fury at him for continuing in what Ken Z considers an abusive relationship, among other things. Wilde gives thoughts on love and moving on to new beginnings. Ken Z continues to read, and concludes that Oscar Wilde's stories and plays have taught him that, "We are never who we are. Just a bunch of bunburyists inventing identities to get the most fun out of life…. But how many 'I's' do I need to start feeling good about myself again?" (p. 217).

There are perhaps more questions than answers in this book, which is maybe a good thing. Readers will have to delve into many resources, including some within themselves, to seek answers and continue the important work of understanding soul and heart. Resources relating to Oscar Wilde are provided in the back matter.

McBride, A. (2021). *Me (Moth)*. New York: Feiwel and Friends.
Moth narrates her story through verse. She doesn't understand why she survived the terrible car accident that took the lives of her parents and brother. She figures she had lived too hard, and in her grief and guilt, she stops the dancing that has always been a part of her.

Moth suffers another loss when her aunt, with whom she lived after the accident, abandons her, leaving only a note on the refrigerator explaining that she can't stay, and asking for forgiveness. Moth understands, since she hates herself, too, but she can't forgive.

A new boy appears at school. Sani *gets* her, accepts her. And after Moth witnesses him being abused by his stepfather, they run away in his jeep, heading toward the Navajo Nation where his father lives. Moth realizes, "Steps in new directions are the hardest to take…" (p. 80).

I'll stop there, so you can join Moth and Sani on their journey, one filled with surprises and healing.

*McCauley, K. (2020). *If these Wings Could Fly*. New York: Katherine Tegen Books.
Leighton, entering her senior year of high school, is an aspiring journalist. She is researching information about crows, following the rising crow population in her Pennsylvania town, and writing about the topic for the school newspaper. She has applied to New York University, and is starting to date Liam, a star football player; artist; and genuinely kind and loving person. At the same time, her home life is filled with violence. Her father is abusive, and Leighton is trying to protect her mother as well as her younger sisters from him. Somehow, the town's crow problem and the family's dysfunction are connected. And when Leighton's essay using the crows as a metaphor for the town members'

refusal to see or become involved in domestic disputes wins first place in a contest and gets published, situations escalate.

Leighton uses what she has learned about writing to make sense of her world. In trying to understand why her mother keeps forgiving her father, even at the expense of endangering her children, she concludes, "Mom's thesis statement became, 'My life has meaning because he is in it,' And now every move she makes supports that claim" (p. 64). Leighton chooses a different stance. "I refuse to write in feelings. Journalists seek the truth" (p. 64). She overcomes fear to bravely write her truth. The book ends with hope.

In the Author's Note, Kyrie McCauley explains, "I wrote the book I would have liked to read when I was fifteen—when I didn't know it was domestic violence" (unpaged). There are resources offered for readers experiencing violence at home or in dating situations. *If These Wings Could Fly* may help readers to recognize difficulties their friends could be having and offer ways to assist them in getting the help they need.

Murphy, J. (2021). *If the Shoe Fits*. New York: Disney Enterprises.
At age 22, recent college graduate Cindy is at a crucial stage of her identity development when she has a revelation:

> When I was in elementary school and Mom died, and then again in high school when Dad died, my everyday life was almost the same. I still went to school and took the bus home. But this adult version of my life? It's my second act—my sophomore collection—and neither of my parents will ever be in the audience. I have to find a way to move through all these new experiences without forgetting them. And I have to find a way to create again. All the pieces are there inside me.
>
> (pp. 227–228)

Readers, along with the fictional viewers in the novel, follow Cindy as she competes in a reality TV show that will culminate with a suitor, the current Prince Charming, proposing to one of the contestants. Cindy, the first plus-size woman in the show's history, becomes a big hit with fans, as well as with Henry himself. But is he really falling in love (as she, to her surprise, is) or is it all part of the script, the act? Will she be able to get beyond the disappointment if she is not the chosen Cinderella? Will she regain her confidence, her giftedness in fashion design, and her ability to choose joy for herself as an independent adult?

Rajurkar, A.D. (2021). *American Betiya*. New York: Alfred A. Knopf. Many young readers will discern before Rani does that there are early warning signs in her relationship with fellow artist Oliver. They'll want to tell her to slow down, pay attention, and be careful! There's no question of their mutual physical attraction, and he says he loves her. But when he calls her Princess Jasmine, and when he seems obsessed with wanting her to wear a sari, Rani makes excuses and tries to please him instead of calling him out and explaining that his actions are microaggressions. She deceives her parents and behaves in ways that she knows they would not approve of. Is she gaining independence, or is she losing herself?

Predictably, Rani finds herself in uncomfortable, and then dangerous, situations as she becomes more deeply involved with Oliver. When she finds overwhelming evidence that he has betrayed her trust, she finally gets it. Though the pain is great, the lessons learned are valuable. A summer in India mourning the death of her grandfather, along with her first year of college, help Rani mature and attain real independence and self-confidence. Her story may prompt readers to ask themselves questions about the relationships they are in. Is either party too controlling, demanding, or needy? Is there mutual trust and respect? Is the relationship fostering the personal growth of each partner, or inhibiting it?

Rani's first love was intense, but not quite right. When she has a chance to start over with Oliver, she reluctantly, but wisely, chooses to move on instead. She is a person of integrity, and we readers can trust that she will be more than okay, as she works toward her goals and embraces the future.

Reed, C.H. (2020). *The Black Kids*. New York: Simon & Schuster. Ashley's parents have tried to protect her and her older sister Jo from the hardships they and so many of their Black family members and friends have experienced. They are well off financially and go to a good school. Ashley has been close friends with several White girls most of her life. Only now, as she is waitlisted for Stanford during her senior year, does a series of events cause her to question her friends, her values, and her goals for the future.

The setting is important to this novel: Los Angeles, 1992. The trial of the police officers who brutally killed Rodney King ends in acquittal. Riots ensue. Ashley's uncle's store is vandalized, while her sister is off in another neighborhood doing some vandalizing herself. Can her sister be protected from conviction and imprisonment?

Meanwhile, Ashley faces drama in friend territory. She begins a rumor about LaShawn, a popular Black athlete who has been accepted at Stanford. (Why did she do that?) She becomes involved with her friend Kimberly's boyfriend. (Why did she do that?) And how should she react to Kimberly's reaction, which involves calling her a racial epithet? Who is she, and who does she want to become?

I'll offer one passage that shows Ashley's growing insight: "And with the rejection letter goes some version of myself that I had imagined, but there are new versions to imagine. Other schools .... Each of them hold other future versions of me. Maybe better versions, even" (p. 346).

Read *The Black Kids* to join Ashley on her journey to new friends, new ways of loving, and new ways of constructing a self in a challenging, inequitable time and place. Join her in hope.

Rivera, G. (2021). *Juliet Takes a Breath*. Illustrated and adapted for Comics by Celia Moscote. Los Angeles, CA: Boom! Box.

Readers who appreciated this coming-of-age novel in the original print version (2019, Dial Books) will be eager to dive into the graphic novel adaptation. Those who experience this one first will likely want to meet the Juliet of the first version. We meet the title character on the evening before she leaves her Bronx home for an internship with a feminist author she adores. She comes out to her family as a lesbian, but her mother is in denial, believing that Juliet has been led astray by a book written by Harlowe Brisbane; that she is confused because she has never had a boyfriend; that this is just a phase. Juliet leaves for Portland, Oregon not knowing if her mother will disown her forever.

Juliet finds Harlowe to be overwhelming and radical, but decides, "I can handle her hippie white lady stuff" (unpaged) and throws herself into her duties as an intern, embracing new adventures in the community. She sets up a reading date for Harlowe in Powell's Bookstore, and does research in the Multnomah Library. She meets interesting, caring people who can support her when she gets a break-up letter from her girlfriend. Unfortunately, Harlowe says something at her public reading that makes Juliet realize that Harlowe does not understand her and has been using her; this epiphany effectively crushes Juliet's crush on Harlowe, sending her into even newer territory in her search for identity and belonging. Readers will travel with her willingly, rooting for her all the way. She returns home after what has truly been a hero's journey.

Rooney, S. (2018). *Normal People*. New York: Hogarth.
We meet Marianne and Connell when they are seniors in high school. Though set in Ireland, the story will feel familiar to many American New Adults. Connell plays sports and has a group of friends he hangs out with. Readers are let in on his insecurities, which his classmates don't seem to be aware of. Marianne is not part of any group and doesn't appear to care that others perceive her as strange, at times abusing her verbally. Connell's single mother is the housecleaner for Marianne's wealthy, widowed mother. Inside that house, Connell and Marianne develop a friendship, then a romance. But Connell does not try to bring her into the school group, and indeed asks someone else to the summer dance.

   Readers will watch both characters make mistake after mistake in their on-again, off-again relationship over the next several years at Trinity College. It's clear they love each other, but both have problems that keep their relationship from being stable. There are numerous opportunities for readers to gain an understanding of depression and grief. They'll ponder questions such as whether the parental and sibling abuse Marianne was subjected to in childhood will leave her forever damaged, unable to love herself or consider herself worthy of love. They will wonder if Connell can ever overcome the feeling of not belonging due to the economic hardships of his youth. It will be frustrating for readers who follow two academically gifted individuals who have to learn social skills the hard way. But they will be invested, and they will be rooting for a happy ending.

Sáenz, B.A. (2021). *Aristotle and Dante Dive into the Waters of the World*. New York: Simon & Schuster.
"You're not such a boy anymore. You're on the edge of manhood. 'It feels like I'm at the edge of a cliff'" (p. 37). Aristotle is in love, and both he and Dante have supportive parents. So why is he approaching adulthood with so much trepidation? The year is 1987, and gay men

are facing discrimination. Too many are also facing death, in the midst of the AIDS epidemic, about which so little was known. Ari can't imagine a future where he and Dante could be open about their love, enabling it to flourish; he's afraid there is no future for them, and he can't face a future without Dante's love. He writes his worries in the form of letters to Dante that serve as a journal.

Dante's world is expanding; he has a new baby brother, Sophocles, a true wonder. He has applied for a summer art fellowship in Paris. But readers can pick up clues that he is scared, too. As we follow both boys along with new friends they are hanging out with, we see that everyone is searching for meaning, and purpose, and they support each other in those quests. For example, Gina and Susie give Ari a silver cross on a chain as a Christmas present, writing on the accompanying card, "We know that you think God hates you... you shouldn't blame God for all the stupid and mean things people say. And we're both pretty sure God isn't homophobic" (pp. 320–321). Ari wears the cross, figuring that God contains all the mysteries of the universe. One thing he and Dante have in common is that they ask questions no one has the answer to. New Adults joining the boys on their deep dive will have questions of their own. This book may give them the courage to keep asking them, to keep struggling to find out who they are, and to find comfort in Ari's realization that "... yes, we were all connected. And we all wanted to have a life that was worth living" (p. 441).

Stohl, M., & de la Cruz, M. (2020). *Jo & Laurie: A Romantic Retelling*. New York: G.P. Putnam's Sons.
This is fanfiction at its best. Margaret Stohl and Melissa de la Cruz must have had so much fun deciding what could or would happen between the originally published version of Louisa May Alcott's *Little Women* and its sequel (which later was combined with the first to become what we now have as one novel of that name).

Jo March and Theodore Laurence (Laurie), having grown up together and shared many adventures, are best friends. When Jo struggles with the sequel her readers and editor are demanding after the wild success of *Little Women*, Laurie invites her to New York for a week of adventures, including attending a public reading by Charles Dickens! But when Laurie makes his intentions clear, hoping Jo will agree to marry him, she refuses:

How could she make him understand that she would never marry, would never become someone's property, never give up her name and her writing, to play house with any man. Not even for him. No matter how she felt about him.

(p. 192)

That happens halfway through the novel. Where's there to go after that? Well, that's the beauty of fanfiction. You can be true to the text you're riffing off of when it works for you, and you can alter the story when it serves your purposes. In "A Brief Historical Note" after the text, the authors explain that they tried to follow the spirit of the novel that inspired *Jo & Laurie*, and:

> When we chose to depart from the world of the established fiction, or from explorations based on questions raised by the established fiction (see: Jo and Laurie's romance), those decisions were usually inspired by Alcott's personal history or the letters of Louisa, Bronson, and May Alcott.

(pp. 363–364)

This book can be read as a stand-alone, but may also serve as a treat for readers after they finish *Little Women*, or may lead readers to the classic. They'll be ready to critique film versions of *Little Women* and might just end up writing a sequel to *Jo & Laurie*, adding their own adaptations to the rich world built by Louisa May Alcott and continued by others during the next century and a half.

*Straub, E. (2020). *All Adults Here*. New York: Random House.
The ages of the characters range from 13 to approaching 70; flashbacks and memories give us glimpses of them at various points of their physical and emotional development. It's a story of changing family dynamics; it's a story filled with mistakes, regrets, lessons learned, and some things done right. Eighth-grader Cecelia, bullied at school after she tried to protect her friend Katherine from a predator whom Katherine met online, is living with her widowed grandmother Astrid in order to get a fresh start at a new school. Astrid comes out as bisexual to her three adult children; she and Birdie are ready to have their relationship publicly recognized. We follow Elliot and Nicky as they negotiate marriage and parenthood,

as well as Porter, who has chosen to become pregnant and take on the challenge of raising a child without a partner.

Secondary characters do not remain static. Birdie, who has never had children, becomes a player in the lives of Astrid's family members. Cecelia's new friend, supported by her both in and out of school, changes clothing (from pants to a dress), names (from August to Robin), and pronouns (from he to she). Throughout the book, relationships deepen, and people mature as events occur and contexts change. It's evident that there is really no magic point at which childhood is left behind, and we know what to do in every situation since we are "adults." This story can help us reflect on our pasts; dream about our futures; and, perhaps most importantly, decide the kind of people we want to be in the here and now.

Werlin, N. (2021). *Zoe Rosenthal Is not Lawful Good*. Somerville, MA: Candlewick Press.

How does one make sure to choose the right college? Zoe goes about it methodically, creating a color-coded spreadsheet for the thirty-two colleges she and her boyfriend Simon are considering. (*Of course* they will go to the same college.) Though Zoe, self-proclaimed perfect girlfriend, is so sure of her life plan, readers will pick up on red flags from the first page, as Zoe is boarding a plane to attend DragonCon, where she can watch the Season 2 premiere of her favorite TV series, *Bleeders*. She had to tell Simon she was home with a headache, since he thinks fantasy TV is ridiculous. Hmmm.

One comic convention leads to another. One lie leads to another. Zoe is having a fantastic time with new friends, participating in cosplay competitions, parades, and sessions with celebrities, "Everybody wearing their inside on their outside! Which is how life should always be" (p. 12). She loves being a fangirl and doesn't recognize the gap that is growing between her interests and Simon's more serious projects, which include working on a political campaign.

Lots of fun, and much drama, including Zoe kidnapping (only in the strictest sense of the word) Simon's younger sister, occurs before her second life catches up to her and her secrets go public. She loses what she thought was her life plan, but she has gained wonderful friends, and new dreams are forming.

Where does Zoe end up for college? You'll know by the end of the story.

Instructional Strategies and Activities

Seeing New Adult Literature as Windows, Mirrors, Doors, Curtains, and Telescopes

Several decades ago, Rudine Sims Bishop offered a metaphor that gave us a new lens with which to think about literature and how it relates to readers. She writes:

> Books are sometimes windows, offering views of worlds that may be real or imagined, familiar or strange. These windows are also sliding glass doors, and readers have only to walk through in imagination to become part of whatever world has been created and recreated by the author. When lighting conditions are just right, however, a window can also be a mirror. Literature transforms human experience and reflects it back to us, and in that reflection we can see our own lives and experiences as part of the larger human experience. Reading, then, becomes a means of self-affirmation, and readers often seek their mirrors in books.
>
> (1990, p. ix)

Since that time, teachers, researchers, librarians, and authors have used the extended metaphor, adapted it, reflected on it, and interacted with it (e.g., Rezvi, Han, & Larnell, 2020; Suzuki, Diuguid, & Ward, 2021; Aronson, 2021). We've heard from many authors who say one of the main reasons they write is that they never saw themselves in books when they were growing up. And teachers in schools where the population consists mostly of white students have become increasingly aware of how important it is to introduce literature with characters of various ethnicities to broaden their students' worlds. Teachers and librarians are encouraged to give their collections a diversity audit, and then use funds to fill in gaps, so that all their students will experience books as mirrors, and will be able to enter through "sliding glass doors" to experience things beyond their own classrooms and communities. The metaphor has become even more popular since the We Need Diverse Books campaign was started in 2015.

Debbie Reese, founder of American Indians in Children's Literature (Reese a) finds the metaphor useful, but has added the image of curtains as a way to discuss the issue of some tribes not wanting certain religious or other practices written about publicly, partly because of a history of having practices not treated as sacred, or misrepresented. For a fuller explanation, check the website above, or see and hear Dr. Reese on YouTube (Reese b).

Toliver (2021) extends the metaphor by speaking of mirrors, windows, and telescopes with regard to fantasy. She explains:

> Mirrors transform the human experience and reflect it back to the reader, and telescopes use multiple mirrors to gather light from hazy futures and clouded otherworlds to make faraway, liberatory ideas clearer and brighter. Windows offer views of real, imagined, strange, or familiar worlds, and provide views of liberating futures and otherwise worlds. Through telescopes children—especially those whose access to futures and fantasies has been distorted by violence and oppression—will be able to see that those futuristic and fantastical landscapes are actually closer than they first appeared to be.
>
> (p. 30)

How might Rudine Sims Bishop's metaphor, or an adaptation of it, be applied to NA literature? The short answer is the same way it's applied to literature for age ranges below or above the one we are concerned with. The NA category is based on the premise that the years between late teen and early 20s are crucial in terms of identity and new beginnings, so giving our NA readers this helpful and fascinating lens could provide a valuable thinking tool, or even a lifeline. You can give students Sims Bishop's original article, as well as other resources explicating and employing the lens. The beauty of the method is that the answers change constantly. Different readers will see and feel various aspects as they read, partially depending on what they bring to the text. A particular book can be a mirror for students who see characters they can identify with, while providing a window for others who bring limited knowledge about a demographic represented by characters in the story to the text. All readers will be enriched as they read the varied and nuanced identities of the people they meet in literature.

Walk-Through

Mr. Radhakrishnan's classroom library is well-stocked with diverse books, and he introduced the metaphor of books serving as windows, mirrors, and sliding glass doors early in the semester. He hears his students applying the lens as they talk in book clubs, and he sees references in their writing. Here are examples of comments that demonstrate their thinking and feeling.

STACY: I'm struck by the title of *The Black Kids*, because it reminds me of how some people think all Black kids are alike, but then the story presents so many different individuals! Ashley is figuring out what it means to be Black, as she has mostly hung out with white kids because of the school she went to. I have had to ask myself questions similar to those Ashley faces, not only about others but about herself. So I guess that makes this book a mirror for me. I'm going to go back for another look, I'm sure.

RODNEY: When I read *American Betiya*, I did kind of feel like I was looking through a window. At first, I didn't see anything wrong with Oliver calling Jasmine "Princess Jasmine," and I thought his wanting her to wear a sari was a compliment, showing appreciation of her culture. But as I looked more carefully, and paid attention to Jasmine's reactions, I realized he wasn't treating her with respect. I think I'll be better able to recognize microaggressions when I see them in our school now.

CARMEN: I was interested in Debbie Reese's introduction of the "curtains" image that our librarian told us about last week, so I searched to learn more about it. After reading her post about first giving Rebecca Roanhorse's *Trail of Lightning* a positive review, and then reconsidering and reversing her recommendation (Reese, 2018), I was intrigued. I found a similar critique of the novel in a review in the Anishinabek News (Hele, 2019). This connects so much to our ongoing discussion of the #ownvoices movement. I've ordered *Trail of Lightning*, because it sounds really exciting, but I am going to keep the controversy in mind. My thinking about whether authors have the right to tell stories involving characters outside their own identities is still evolving. I mean, where do you draw the line? If we can never write outside our own identities, won't that limit the stories that get told?

Creative Summarizing

The ability to summarize and share information succinctly is important in academic settings and beyond. Sometimes telling a story, real or fictional, with lots of detail is desirable, but at other times brevity is necessary.

Asking students to capture the gist of a text in a playful way can produce surprising and memorable results. Can readers write a seventeen-syllable summary in haiku form? Can they compose a short dialog between characters at the end of their story using texting bubbles? Can they write a Twitter review adhering to the maximum limit of 280 characters? Absolutely. You can find dozens of examples of sixty-second book talks on YouTube.

Is it possible to shrink an enormous classic down to a list of a dozen words? The Cozy Classics series of board books has done just that with *Moby Dick, Pride and Prejudice, War and Peace, Great Expectations*, and other literary works. After watching a YouTube clip about the series (Cozy Classics, 2016), students will welcome the challenge to choose twelve key words as a way of summarizing and responding to a book they've read. They may choose to draw accompanying scenes.

One format that teachers have made great use of for over a decade is the six-word memoir. To find out about its origin and some of the collections that have been put together, check out the work of Larry Smith in "The Evocative World of the Six-Word Memoir" (Smith, 2012a). You might want to follow up with Smith's *Things Don't Have To Be Complicated: Illustrated Six-Word Memoirs By Students Making Sense of the World* (2012b); *The Best Advice in Six Words* (2015); or some of his earlier titles. There are topical applications and adaptations of the format, such as Smith's *Six Words Fresh off the Boat: Stories of Immigration, Identity, and Coming to America* (2017); and *Six Word Memoirs on Jewish Life* (2012c), as well as *6 Word Wonder: Stories, Poems, Memoirs, and Jokes to Entertain and Amuse in only Six Words*, by Weller (2020).

Walk-Through

Sidney has finished Robin Benway's *Far from the Tree*, and has created six-word memoirs in the voices of the five teen-aged characters at the end of the story.

GRACE: From baby to siblings to hope!
MAYA: I'm adopted, different, but truly belong!
JOACHIN: Finally able to love and trust.
CLAIRE: My girlfriend is more complete now.
LAUREN: I claim Maya's new siblings, too!

Sidney can't resist adding his six-word response to the novel, directed to the characters he has come to know: Let's all go to college together!

References

Aronson, M. (2021). Nonfiction windows so white. *Horn Book Magazine, 97*(2), 12–16.

Bishop, R.S. (1990). Mirrors, windows, and sliding glass doors. *Perspectives, 6*(3), ix–xi.

Cozy Classics. (2016). Cozy classics by Jack and Holman Wang. Retrieved from https://www.youtube.com/watch?v=j1jFDURdQLM.

Hele, K. (2019). Book review: Trail of Lightning. Retrieved from https://anishinabeknews.ca/2019/08/01/book-review-trail-of-lightning/.

Reese, D. a. American Indians in Children's Literature. Retrieved from https://americanindiansinchildrensliterature.blogspot.com/.

Reese, D. b. (2016). Retrieved from https://www.youtube.com/watch?v=ctOJtK-ONgo.

Reese, D. (2018). Concerns about Roanhorse's TRAIL OF LIGHTNING. Retrieved from (https://americanindiansinchildrensliterature.blogspot.com/2018/08/concerns-about-roanhorses-trail-of.html).

Rezvi, S., Han, A., & Larnell, G.V. (2020). Mathematical mirrors, windows, and sliding glass doors: Young Adult texts as sites for identifying with mathematics. *Journal of Adolescent and Adult Literacy, 63*(5), 589–592.

Smith, L. (2017). *Six words fresh off the boat; Stories of immigration, identity, and coming to America.* Glendale, CA: Kingswell.

Smith, L. (2015). *The best advice in six words.* New York: St. Martin's Griffin.

Smith, L. (2012a). The evocative world of the six-word memoir. Retrieved from https://blog.ted.com/the-evocative-world-of-the-six-word-memoir-a-qa-with-new-ted-ebook-author-larry-smith/.

Smith, L. (2012b). *Six word memoirs on Jewish life.* Larry Smith.

Smith, L. (2012c). *Things don't have to be complicated: Illustrated six-word memoirs by students making sense of the world.* New York: TED Conferences.

Suzuki, T., Diuguid, D., & Ward, B. (2021). Mirrors, windows, and sliding glass doors: Exploring the 2020 Rainbow Book List. *Children & Libraries, 19*(3), 3–6.

Toliver, S. (2021). On mirrors, windows, and telescopes. *NCTE Council Chronicle, 31*(1), pp. 29–30.

We Need Diverse Books. Retrieved from (https://diversebooks.org/).

Weller, D. (2020). *Six word wonder: Stories, poems, memoirs, and jokes to entertain and amuse in only six words.* Independently published.

Literature Cited

Alcott, L.M. (2014). *Little women*. New York: Puffin Books.

Ali, S.K. (2017). *Saints and misfits*. New York: Salaam Reads.

Austen, J. (2003). *Pride and prejudice*. New York: Barnes & Noble Classics.

Benway, R. (2017). *Far from the tree*. New York: HarperTeen.

Roanhorse, R. (2018). *Trail of lightning*. New York: Saga Press.

Sáenz, B.A. (2021) *Aristotle and Dante dive into the waters of the deep*. New York: Simon & Schuster.

Civic Responsibilities and Taking Action for a Better World

6

Can NA Literature Help Save the World?

As they leave adolescence behind, many New Adults become keenly aware of the responsibilities they have to their communities, countries, and the world. Librarians and teachers can help them learn how important it is to speak out for justice, truth, and equity; to stand against hate and anything else that can harm others; to take positive action to protect and restore the environment; to love life and the planet we live on. Maureen Johnson exhorts us to *"Read widely and often: It's one of the best defenses against totalitarianism"* (2018, p. 198). Fortunately, there is an abundance of NA literature dealing with these topics and offering ways people might participate in and contribute to the good of society. Those are the kinds of books this chapter will investigate.

TEXT SETS

Saving the Planet/Protecting the Environment

The responsibility for caring for the Earth and resisting anything that threatens it should not fall to any one age group, or to any other specific population. We all need to be aware and be active in our efforts to stop and reverse the damage that has already caused tremendous devastation and has led to many people giving up hope for the survival of life. Teachers, librarians, counselors, and

---

DOI: 10.4324/9781003221685-6

others guiding youth must be careful not to inundate them with bad news and scary predictions to the point where they feel helpless and immobilized. Yet they have a right to know what is happening. Promoting literature that is truthful and that offers solutions and suggestions for changing their own behavior and influencing others is one way we can mentor New Adults as they enter a world in need of healing. At the same time, of course, we should model behavior that shows a positive approach to fighting for the only home we have, and to creating, appreciating, and nurturing beauty and goodness. The following books are representative of texts that can lead to understanding and determination. An asterisk indicates that the following section contains a book talk for that title.

*Cavalier, D., Hoffman, C., & Cooper, C. (2020). *The Field Guide to Citizen Science: How You can Contribute to Scientific Research and Make a Difference*. Portland, OR: Timber Press.

*Dickman, K. (2021). *Becoming a Climate Scientist*. New York: Simon & Schuster.

Doerr, A. (2021). *Cloud Cuckoo Land*. New York: Scribner.

Gilio-Whitaker, D. (2019). *As Long as Grass Grows: The Indigenous Fight for Environmental Justice, from Colonization to Standing Rock*. Boston, MA: Beacon Press.

*Goodall, J., & Abrams, D. (2021). *The Book of Hope: A Survival Guide for Trying Times*. New York: Celedon Books.

*Jahren, H. (2020). *The Story of More: How We Got to Climate Change and Where to Go from Here*. New York: Vintage Books.

Kimmerer, R. W. (2013). *Braiding Sweetgrass*. Minneapolis, MN: Milkweed Editions.

*Klein, N. (2021). *How to Change Everything: The Young Human's Guide to Protecting the Planet and Each Other*. New York: Atheneum.

*Love, A. (2021). *DIY Sustainable Projects: 15 Craft Projects for Eco-Friendly Living*. London: Welbeck.

Lowman, M. (2021). *The Arbornaut: A Life Discovering the Eighth Continent in the Trees Above Us*. New York: Farrar, Straus and Giroux.

*McPherson, S. S. (2021). *Hothouse Earth: The Climate Crisis and the Importance of Carbon Neutrality*. Minneapolis, MN: Twenty-First Century Books.

Nakate, V. (2021). *A Bigger Picture: My Fight to Bring a New African Voice to the Climate Crisis*. Boston, MA: Mariner Books.

Thunberg, G. (2019). *No One Is Too Small to Make a Difference*. New York: Penguin.

*Zissu, A. (2021). *Earth Squad: 50 People who are Saving the Planet*. Illus. Lê, Nhung. Philadelphia, PA: Running Press Kids.

Youth vs. Nazis

Sometimes we wonder how much one individual can do against institutional injustice, against evil. The problem is so much bigger than we are, and the risks are great. Teens and New Adults have every right to feel this way, since they often are given little agency and can feel virtually powerless. Yet we can provide literature that shows them the bravery of young people in the midst of grave situations throughout history as well as in contemporary society. This text set focuses on one place and one time, when evil appeared to be almost certain to overcome good. The books feature people, many of whom had not yet reached adulthood, who refused to accept that seeming inevitability. An asterisk indicates that there is a book talk for the title in the next section.

Bascomb, N. (2020). *How an Outcast Driver, an American Heiress, and a Legendary Car Challenged Hitler's Best*. New York: Scholastic Focus.

Batalion, J. (2021). *The Light of Days: The Untold Stories of Women Resistance Fighters in Hitler's Ghettos*. New York: William Morrow.

Brady, T. (2021). *Three Ordinary Girls: The Remarkable Story of Three Dutch Teenagers Who Became Spies, Saboteurs, Nazi Assassins and WWII Heroes*. New York: Citadel.

Brown, D.J. (2015). *The Boys in the Boat: The True Story of an American Team's Epic Journey to Win Gold at the 1936 Olympics*. Adapted for Young Readers by Gregory Mone. New York: Viking.

Cameron, S. (2021). *The Light in Hidden Places*. New York: Scholastic.

Demetrios, H. (2021). *Code Name Badass: The True Story of Virginia Hall*. New York: Atheneum.

Donner, R. (2021). *All the Frequent Trouble of our Days: The True Story of the American Woman at the Heart of the German Resistance to Hitler*. New York: Little, Brown and Company.

Eder, M. (2021). *The Girls who Stepped out of Line: Untold Stories of the Women who Changed the Course of WWII*. Naperville, IL: Sourcebooks.

*Freedman, R. (2020). *We Will Not Be Silent: The White Rose Movement that Defied Adolf Hitler*. New York: Clarion.

Hendrix, J. (2018). *The Faithful Spy: Dietrich Bonhoeffer and the Plot to Kill Hitler*. New York: Harry N. Abrams.

Hoose, P. (2015). *The Boys who Challenged Hitler*. New York: Farrar Straus Giroux.

Loftis, L. (2021). *The Princess Spy: The True Story of World War II Spy Aline Griffith, Countess of Romanones*. New York: Atria Books.

McCormick, P. (2018). *The Plot to Kill Hitler: Dietrich Bonhoeffer: Pastor, Spy, Unlikely Hero*. New York: Balzer + Bray.

Sharenow, R. (2012). *The Berlin Boxing Club*. New York: Balzer + Bray.

Strass, G. (2021). *The Nine: The True Story of a Band of Women who Survived the Worst of Nazi Germany*. New York: St. Martin's Press.

Taylor, J. (2020). *The Paper Girl of Paris*. New York: HarperTeen.

Wein, E. (2012). *Code Name Verity*. New York: Hyperion Books.

*Wilson, K. (2020). *White Rose*. Boston, MA: Houghton Mifflin Harcourt.

Book Talks: Ready to Go!

This section contains book talks for fiction featuring characters who are navigating new physical, intellectual, spiritual, and emotional spaces as they take a stand for justice, or work toward better communities, governments, and societies. It includes biographies and memoirs; poetry; novels; and informational books offering guidance about how to become an activist, and how to care for the environment. An asterisk preceding a title means that it is part of a text set in the previous section.

Ahmed, S. (2018). *Love, Hate & Other Filters*. New York: Soho Teen.
Can a camera offer security and protection? Can a camera *affect* events as well as document them? Can a camera inspire a dream for a far-away college and a career? For narrator Maya Aziz, the answer is a strong yes to all these questions. She loves filmmaking and has been

accepted at NYU, though her parents think she is staying near her home in Illinois for college.

The events of senior year are movie-worthy, ranging from two very different young men showing interest in beginning a romantic relationship with Maya to a terrorist attack that leads to hate crimes against Maya's Indian-born, Muslim parents as well as an assault on her. Maya must figure out how to deal with the clash between her loving, protective parents' values and her own desires and beliefs.

Readers will empathize with Maya as she makes difficult personal decisions: Can she defy her parents, knowing that she will be disowned? Can she leave her first love for a chance to be in a film program that could open new worlds for her? Readers will also recognize that this is more than one person's story; it is a larger story of racism and Islamophobia, as well as of community and police support.

*Dickman, K. (2021). *Becoming a Climate Scientist*. New York: Simon & Schuster.

Perhaps you've considered a career in geomorphology. Cathy Wilson trained in this and added expertise in modeling, a highly technical field involving computer programming. She's working on a project that requires her to travel to the Alaskan arctic to collect samples and data that will allow her team to "make global climate models that better predict the world's future" (p. 5).

This book transports us into the field (commuting via a herd of musk oxen to an Alaskan research site) and the laboratory with senior scientist Wilson and many other climate scientists. We learn about permafrost, and so much more. We end up in a Los Alamos mall, where Cathy gives a slide show presentation to high schoolers on the topic of how the melting Arctic will affect our future.

Dickman provides further resources for those interested in pursuing any of the varied paths to a career as a climate scientist:

> But if you have an aptitude and interest in math and science, are eager to travel and to contribute to our understanding of the crises created by climate change, and want to work in a rapidly expanding field, consider yourself encouraged.
>
> (p. 137)

Indeed.

Dionne, E. (2020). *Lifting as We Climb: Black Women's Battle for the Ballot Box*. New York: Viking.

The stories in this nonfiction book make clear that the suffragists our textbooks teach us about, those dedicated women who fought for decades for the right of women to vote, did not always have *all* women in mind during their meetings, speeches, and protests. Sadly, many of the white leaders did not welcome Black suffragists into their ranks. This led to the rise of Black women's suffrage clubs, and to Black female leaders who worked tirelessly against racial discrimination and segregation at the same time they fought for voting rights. This book includes shaded sections providing biographies highlighting the contributions of Ida B. Wells-Barnett, Mary Church Terrell, Mary McLeod Bethune, and Amelia Boynton Robinson, among others. Many of the women started their careers of activism while young.

The photographs throughout the book are striking. There's a political cartoon from 1913, with two women holding identical signs pleading for votes for women; yet the white woman is separating herself and motioning for the Black protester to get away from her. The caption beneath the photograph of Fannie Lou Hamer trying to register to vote for the first time tells of how she was forced to copy Mississippi's state constitution and explain the meaning of each section, along with answering a trick question about the meaning of "de facto law," a meaningless phrase.

NA readers may come away from this book with a desire to learn more, and a commitment to continuing the fight for equal rights in the area of voting as well as other aspects of civil life.

*Freedman, R. (2016). *We Will Not Be Silent: The White Rose Movement that Defied Adolf Hitler*. New York: Clarion.

Readers meet Hans and Sophie Scholl as teens who initially participated in the Hitler Youth Movement enthusiastically, but became disillusioned when they witnessed repression and learned of Nazi atrocities. After compulsory work for the regime, they became university students; Hans went into medicine, while Sophie studied philosophy and biology. College encourages the exploration of big questions, and they discussed with close friends how responsible citizens living in a dictatorship should act. (Earlier family experiences had already helped form their commitment to social justice.) The result was the founding of the White Rose movement, devoted to writing and disseminating leaflets exposing Nazi evils and calling for fellow students and other citizens to resist. Readers can imagine the turmoil Sophie experienced during her summers, forced to work at a munitions factory to further the war effort.

We feel grief and agony for the whole family as the photos show us places central to Hans and Sophie's valiant work, while the text recounts their trials and convictions. Before their executions, their father told them how proud he was of them, promising, "You will go down in history... There is such a thing as justice despite this..." (p. 76). Freedman's book helps keep this history alive, while offering young people of today a model of speaking truth to power.

Girma, H. (2019). *Haben: The Deafblind Woman who Conquered Harvard Law*. Boston, MA: Twelve.

If I had to capture the theme of this book in one word, I'd choose *positivity*. The author assures us from the start that she does not feel deprived because of her disability (a word she promotes over others that try to mask what it is). "I like my Deafblind world. It's comfortable, familiar. It doesn't feel small or limited. It's all I've known; it's my normal" (p. 12). She structures the book using chronologically ordered scenes from her childhood, adolescence, and 20s that help us know her, interspersed with her commentary that helps us understand that what seem to be limitations in what disabled people can do really have more to do with limitations of a system that excludes them rather than supporting them. "Blindness is just the lack of sight, but people... assume incompetence, intellectual challenges, and an inability to contribute.... Wherever I go, regardless of how hard I work, I keep encountering ableism" (p. 170).

In a conscious effort to not be trapped by her loss of hearing and sight, Haben takes lessons in dance; uses public transportation; uses power tools, including a radial arm saw, in woodworking class; travels to Mali with a school group to build a schoolhouse; spends a summer in an intensive blindness program at the Louisiana Center for the Blind; learns how to work with a guide dog; and climbs icebergs in Alaska. She doesn't let her own fears or the worries of others deter her.

Haben gradually learns how to advocate for herself and others. In college, the people in charge of the dining hall were resistant when she asked to have the daily menus sent to her so she could convert them to Braille. She patiently and repeatedly gave suggestions and tried to help them; but finally, after studying the Americans with Disabilities Act (ADA), she informs the manager in writing of their legal obligation, and asks him to comply with the law against discrimination, or face legal action.

The memoir continues with stories and insights from Haben's years at Harvard Law School and beyond, one highlight being her introduction of President Obama at the White House celebration of the twenty-fifth anniversary of the ADA. We see Haben in relationships; we appreciate her humor. The book ends with a guide on how to increase access for people with disabilities.

Writing and Thinking Prompt

Choose one or more of the following questions to help you make connections and applications after reading Haben's memoir.

A. What struck you about the way Haben went about her learning at various levels of education? What interactions with or responses from other people surprised you, or caused you to reflect on ways *you* perceive or interact with people with disabilities, or ways people have perceived you in terms of a disability?
B. What experiences described by Haben remind you of things that have happened to you or someone close to you; or of decisions you have made in the face of challenges or obstacles? What resolutions have you made as a result of getting to know this remarkable woman?
C. What are your thoughts about how groups, institutions, or other aspects of society are structured in terms of accessibility and equity? Imagine an ideal world or at least a near future where we have made some changes in our attitudes, actions, structures, and laws that affect people with disabilities of any kind. Where will you start?

*Jahren, H. (2020). *The Story of More: How We Got to Climate Change and Where to Go from Here*. New York: Vintage Books.
The author explains that she uses the structure that is evident in the title to frame the whole book because we have to see where we are in order to ask ourselves if this is where we desire to be. Most readers, after reading anecdotes about our natural world and about garbage production; historical information about population growth and meat production; scientific explanations of the collapsing food chain; and stories of human cost and loss due to

greed, will answer the question emphatically in the negative, and will be ready to hear practical suggestions as to how we can begin the only possible way to save the planet and humanity, which boils down to Jahren's mantra, *"Use Less and Share More"* (p. 88).

Readers entering adulthood might take pause at Hope's conclusion that presently, we are choosing ourselves over our own grandchildren. If they were to think like the children they were just a short time ago, they could react angrily at how their parents' generation and those before them have left them and their future children in such a precarious plight. But now, this will be combined with the knowledge that they have responsibilities, and agency. How can they become part of the solution? In the Appendix, titled "The Story of Less," they'll read about many small changes they can make to reduce their energy consumption; eat, travel, and spend money in ways that will help better the atmosphere and waters; and, after starting in their home, expand out from there in ways that can make a global difference. The author speaks directly to readers as she provides encouragement. "…we are ultimately endowed with only four resources: the earth, the ocean, the sky, and each other. If we can refrain from overestimating our likelihood of failure, then neither must we underestimate our capacity for success" (p. 189).

Johnson, M. (Ed.). (2018). *How I Resist: Activism and Hope for a New Generation.* New York: Wednesday Books.
This book is ideal for those who feel overwhelmed by the huge problems in the world, or else helpless, confused, too young, or scared. The contributing authors to this collection offer—through interviews, essays, music, letters, poetry, or cartoons—such a variety of advice that readers are bound to find some recommendations that feel doable. Here are a few samples from authors whose works include books that fit the NA category:

- Jason Reynolds, while believing that "…there's a generational groundswell of young people who together are impenetrable" (p. 38), cautions youth to resist hopelessness and to resist the unhealthy addiction to being on their phones all the time.
- Malinda Lo, noting that her parents had grown up in Communist China, cites phone calls, protests, and voting as examples of ways to resist, but she also pays attention to her parents' advice to

her to keep doing what she has been doing. So she continues to create art, writing fiction about people of color and queer teens, in order to resist despair as well as threats of hatred and evil.

• Jacqueline Woodson tells readers not to let fear eat them from the inside out, but rather to live life fully and "… know you have the right no matter who you are to walk through the world" (p. 131).

Editor Maureen Johnson advocates reading widely and often as a defense against totalitarianism, so reading this book is an excellent way for readers to begin, or continue, their commitment to activism.

Kaur, J. (2021). *If I Tell You the Truth*. New York: Harper.
We first meet Kiran in 2001. She has recently arrived in Canada from Punjab to begin college. She had been raped by a police officer in Punjab, and was not believed by her fiancée. She has been disowned by her parents after deciding to keep the baby that resulted from the rape. She has almost nothing, but she does have the support of a new friend and the friend's mother. And the love she has for her child, Sahaara, gives her the courage to keep going despite the poverty, restrictions, and fear caused by her illegal status after her student visa expires.

We get to know Sahaara through the poems she writes throughout her school years, as well as from prose chapters. She's frustrated by her mother's unwillingness to talk about her past, as well as by what seems to be her overprotective behavior. When Sahaara turns 18, in theory it is possible that she could do something about her mother's undocumented status. But that will take money, and saving that money will take time.

When Kiran is apprehended and taken to a detention center the day before Sahaara is about to begin college on an art scholarship, circumstances cause more of the truth to emerge, as well as opportunities for both mother and daughter to go public with their experiences. Accusations against a powerful man who is now running for the highest office in Punjab will be extremely dangerous. Will Kiran, who has depended on silence and invisibility for two decades, be able to become an activist in order to help other women who have no voice? Will Sahaara, who can see her monster father's features every time she looks in a mirror, be able to confront him and call him a liar and a rapist?

This powerful book explores many aspects of identity; Sahaara says, "My identity was a question mark" (p. 130). The story shows how difficult it is for marginalized populations to have the agency to construct positive identities and change the circumstances that prevent them from succeeding. It also presents a mother, a daughter, friends, and advocates who offer hope for a time when women will not have to worry about their safety from men who feel they are entitled to whatever they want to take, and when the slogan "ALL HUMANS ARE LEGAL" (p. 248) is a reality recognized by all.

Kendall, M., & D'Amico, A. (2019). *Amazons, Abolitionists, and Activists: A Graphic History of Women's Fight for their Rights*. New York: Ten Speed Press.

When did the history of the battle for women's rights begin? Six girls in an A.I. history class are transported to 4500 BCE to find out. Their teacher shows them artwork and artifacts by women in ancient times and teaches historical information comparing and contrasting various rights and restrictions in Sumer, Egypt, Greece, Rome, the Mayan Empire, Vietnam, and Celtic lands. In subsequent chapters, they learn about female warriors and rulers around the world and throughout the centuries. Attention is given to the fight for civil rights, voting rights, and corporate rights in the United States. The teacher does not shy away from complex issues, such as the transphobia and transmisogyny that exists within some feminist communities.

Some panels show the students responding to what they are learning; these can invite readers to be aware of and express their own reactions and further questions. By the end of their tour, the students in the story commit to work for justice by running for office, joining an environmental activist group, coaching a girls' team, volunteering for transgender rights, etc. Readers will feel that they have completed a comprehensive course, and will, hopefully, feel energized to continue the work that is calling to them.

*Klein, N. (2021). *How to Change Everything: The Young Human's Guide to Protecting the Planet and Each Other*. New York: Atheneum.

This book shows respect for its target audience by refusing to downplay the crisis our planet faces or shield readers from vital information. The author also emphasizes climate justice, explaining how poorer people and marginalized groups suffer disproportionately, and showing who is to blame for past and present injustices.

Yet it is a hopeful book, at least for those readers willing to follow the example of the many climate activists highlighted and to follow the specific, practical suggestions Klein offers. Early chapters provide some history that helps us understand how we got to the dangerous point we are at, as well as scientific explanations of key concepts related to the use of fossil fuels and the resulting harm. Shaded pages provide stories of young activists who faced political backlash and even ridicule, but who made a difference by standing up for what they knew was right.

For those who doubt that rapid, radical, and large-scale social change can happen, Klein points to the 2020 pandemic:

> The biggest lesson I see from the coronavirus pandemic is that everyone, from individuals and families to government leaders, made difficult but necessary changes—changes none of us could have imagined before this. And many people rose to the challenge in creative and generous ways...

(p. 297)

Klein calls on us to use creativity, energy, and resources to fight injustice and climate change, and to work for a future that is fair.

After reading this book, I have made a commitment to plant a tree.

Kuklin, S. (2019). *We Are Here to Stay: Voices of Undocumented Young Adults*. Somerville, MA: Candlewick Press.

Taking a picture walk through this book is a jarring experience. There are photographs, with captions, showing the cities of Nogales, Mexico, and Nogales, USA divided by a fence; signs cautioning that smuggling and illegal immigration could be going on; surveillance equipment; trails through desert areas that refugees use; detention centers; and a campsite of "No More Deaths/No Más Muertes," where volunteers offer medical care, water and food to crossers. But there are other pages where there is a frame but no photo, something readers don't often encounter. The author explains that the book was scheduled for a 2017 publication with colored portraits of the young interviewees; but in September of that year the president repealed DACA, and the publisher stopped the presses. The stories needed to be told, but in order to protect the now even more vulnerable undocumented participants, names, identifiers, and photos were removed.

Readers can't help but note how different the stories of the nine immigrants featured in this book are. But they all are aware of ongoing issues relating to identity and values. For example, G- came to this country from Seoul, South Korea when she was eight. After fifteen years here:

> Mathematically I'm more in tune with American culture than Korean culture. But I'm very proud of who I am, my roots, my inner-core values. I feel most comfortable identifying myself as a Korean-American. I don't think it will ever be a perfect balance. All I know is, we have the freedom to identify ourselves as who we are, as who we want to be.

> (pp. 155–157)

What gives undocumented persons the courage to be open about their status? College student Y- explains that many people grow up with anxiety and shame about being undocumented, but that activism is important to her for that reason. She was a part of a campus group known as the DREAM team and agreed to be on a panel for parents:

> … because it's an opportunity to pull in allies. Maybe next time they hear someone railing about how terrible immigrants are, they'll think about me. I'm a real person. I go to school with their kids. I have a wonderful family.

> (p. 22)

This collection of inspiring and thought-provoking interviews should spark discussion, further exploration (resources are provided), and understanding. It can be used as a mentor text for readers who are honing their own interviewing, listening, and writing skills. Be sure to look for an updated edition, since Susan Kuklin's hope is that "… we can one day republish this book with the participants' names, places, and photographs fully intact" (unpaged).

LeZotte, A. C. (2021). *Set Me Free*. New York: Scholastic.

Mary Lambert is younger than most of the protagonists introduced in this book. But in this historical novel set in the early nineteenth century, she faces responsibilities and burdens that test and hasten her maturity. An aspiring schoolteacher, she chooses to leave the relative comfort of her home on the island of Martha's Vineyard, where her deafness is not seen as a disability, to answer the call to help a young deaf and mute child on the mainland whom no one has been able to communicate with or to control. She finds the young girl chained in an upstairs room of a mansion, cared for (or neglected by) a set of servants who have been put in charge of her welfare.

Here are a few questions Mary must answer: How is she to teach the child when she is prevented from going to the upstairs room? Is it right to use another's key to let herself in? How should she react when she is attacked by the girl? How and when did this 7-year-old learn to read and write? Where is she from? Is there any family left? And, in order to prevent further abuse, does she dare to kidnap young Beatrice and flee?

Readers find out Mary's answers as the plot unfolds. I'll leave you with a question concerning her own identity and her affirmation of her purpose in the world:

> I've thought I was meant to be many things. Dutiful daughter, devoted sister, writer of tales. I will finish the history of the deaf on our island community. But is writing enough without courageous action?.... The difference between victims and survivors is whether you're found in time. We cannot swim while the other sinks.... The shackles that cowed me are broken.
>
> (pp. 264–265)

*Love, A. (2021). *DIY Sustainable Projects: 15 Craft Projects for Eco-Friendly Living*. London: Welbeck.

We are often encouraged and reminded to reuse and recycle, as well as to reduce the number of materials and things we buy. This book gives examples of how that might look in practice, using everyday objects to create usable and aesthetically pleasing objects. It's a terrific resource for teachers and librarians who guide students in maker spaces. The author expresses confidence in her readers' commitment to the repair and protection of the planet, and she promises, "This book is a way to make rituals around sustainable practices, contextualizing how individual behaviour and making greener choices within your environment scales to bigger and bigger communities" (p. 8).

Readers can choose from a variety of projects, including building crate furniture, upholstering a chair, creating a solar lamp, making shampoo and conditioner bars, and designing and decorating an insulated lunch bag. They can add life to their living spaces with a hanging planter made from gutters, a wine crate greenhouse, and a ladybird house for outside. Each project includes a list of materials and tools that will be needed, along with clear directions and photos showing the stages of development and the finished product. After trying a few of the craft projects and showing friends and family members the results, young people might decide to continue in their identity as a "sustainable maker" (p. 155) for the rest of their lives.

McCullough, J. (2018). *Blood Water Paint*. New York: Dutton Books. We travel back to the seventeenth century in this verse novel where we meet 17-year-old Artemisia Gentileschi, grinding pigments and serving as a model in her widowed father's studio. A better artist than he, she often improves his paintings, though her female status keeps her from getting appreciation or respect. Artemisia's mother prepared her for the power inequities she would face by telling her daughter stories of biblical women, including Susanna and Judith, who found ways to combat the abuses of men. Thus, after Artemisia is raped by a tutor, she demands justice, though it will be achieved— if at all—at a great price.

Readers will want to know what happens next. They can discover the famous paintings of the adult Artemisia, which explore the themes of courage and revenge, sometimes depicting Susannah and Judith. They might wonder, as Joy McCullough does in some of her interviews relating to her novel, in what ways Artemisia's life as an apprentice and a courageous young woman influenced her life's work. *Blood Water Paint* is an emotionally difficult read, but ultimately an inspiring and thought-provoking one. There are resources relating to sexual assault listed at the back of the book.

McCullough, J. (2021). *We Are the Ashes, We Are the Fire*. New York: Dutton Books.

Narrator Em is hurting from the beginning of this story; life has been really hard for her whole family since her sister Nor was raped while at college. At least there was some justice, with Craig being found guilty in court. But since the day of the sentencing, when the judge, praising Craig's honesty and remorse, and noting the negative impact the media attention has had on Craig as well as on Nor, decided on **no jail time**, Em has not known what to do with her fury. Added to that is her guilt; she was the one who used her journalism skills to publicize what happened; she was the one who convinced Nor to speak publicly about her horrible ordeal in order to have Craig brought to trial. And now Nor is facing more harassment, as athletes band together and effectively make it impossible for her to live on campus.

We readers only get as much of Nor's story as Em can give us; *We Are the Ashes, We Are the Fire* lets us into only Em's mind and heart during the following months. She quits the school newspaper, so that outlet is gone. But when she learns through a new friend about a medieval woman, Marguerite de Bressieux, who avenged herself, her sister, and other women who had been raped in their castle after a siege during the Hundred Years War, she decides to write Marguerite's story, giving *her* the revenge that was not available to Nor, her family, and other women throughout history who were used and abused by privileged men.

The contemporary story is told in prose; the parallel medieval story is told in verse. Often the last line of a section is cut short, when Em's writing is interrupted by events in real time. We get to see the writing process and can hope that the writing will provide some resolution and healing. Except—while there are signs indicating that Nor is doing better, we get worrisome red flags about what's happening to Em. She becomes obsessed with Marguerite's story. Her research leads her to take sword fighting lessons, and she begins sleeping with a dagger under her pillow. Is her quest for revenge going to destroy her? Readers will wonder: if revenge isn't the answer, what is?

This novel can lead to intense discussions and insights, as well as the possible commitment to activism. It shows the power of writing, as well as the power of people loving each other and courageously working together to right wrongs and change society.

McLemore, A. M. (2021). *The Mirror Season*. New York: Feiwel and Friends.
Would you like to walk into a pastry shop and meet a server who can sense which sweet treat is right for you, and can maybe even provide some love magic for you? Ciela works in her family's pastelera, and she has this gift. Unfortunately, that ability is one of many losses she suffers after being sexually assaulted at a party. Her life is shattered, her body is shattered, her heart and mind are shattered. And things are shattering around her: flowers turn to glass, and shards enter her. Will she ever be able to heal?

Ciela has to deal with her assaulters every day at school, as well as whenever they come into the pastelera. She knows nothing will happen if she reports the crime, since they are the rich kids whose parents give money to the school. They taunt her, constantly reminding her of her degradation. There's a new development when a new boy, Lock, enrolls in her school. She had met him at the fateful party; she had driven him to the hospital after he had been sexually assaulted at the same time she was and had left him there. Lock had been drugged, and now has no memory of what happened. What should Ciela do now? Is there any possibility of a relationship? Could they help each other heal? Is it kinder to tell him the truth, or keep it from him?

Readers will be struggling with those questions and rooting for Lock and Ciela as they recover. Ciela recognizes, "That night left each of us holding pieces of broken glass. And ever since, we have been gripping them. We have been clenching our fingers around them, the edges cutting into our palms...." (p. 303). But she recognizes something else, something that can lead toward healing, which I will let readers learn for themselves as they read this re-imagining of the tale of the Snow Queen.

In the Author's Note, Anna-Marie McLemore, a nonbinary, queer, Latinx writer, explains that this fictional story is also their story. They and a boy were assaulted by the same person, and at the time of publication they and John Doe (the name used by the legal system) did not know if they would ever get justice. They talk directly to their readers about how reporting the crime proved to be a big step away from being broken and toward finding their voice.

*McPherson, S.S. (2021). *Hothouse Earth: The Climate Crisis and the Importance of Carbon Neutrality*. Minneapolis, MN: Twenty-First Century Books.

The first few chapters of this book are nothing less than frightening. Readers learn of terrible disasters that have already happened and the certainty of future death and destruction due to the climate crisis caused by carbon emissions and other human-caused factors. We are living in what scientists are calling the Anthropocene, and the picture isn't pretty.

Fortunately, the author does not leave us without hope. Rather, the book as a whole can be considered a call to action, and there are many climate heroes featured throughout the pages who are already leading the way. For example, renowned botanist Joanne Chory and her colleagues are using genetic manipulation to evolve plants that will hold carbon in their roots, thereby decreasing erosion and improving soil. If these plants were grown across the globe, atmospheric carbon dioxide levels could fall dramatically every year. Chory believes, "It's a philosophical issue, too.... If I take pain now [make sacrifices], maybe my great-grandchildren might see a benefit. People choose no pain now, and that's why we've done nothing about climate change" (p. 54)

Readers will want to take action; and the book, in addition to giving a lot of information about things that are happening now to prepare for an uncertain future, such as developing renewable energy, and using robots and artificial intelligence to solve ecological problems, offers suggestions for things we all can do right now. Some involve personal choices and decisions, including eating less meat, using less electricity, and recycling. The book gives stories of young activists and groups that have protested, gone to court, and otherwise made their voices heard. *Hothouse Earth* can be part of the solution to the crisis it explains.

Ribay, R. (2019). *Patron Saints of Nothing*. New York: Penguin Books. Nearing the end of his senior year of high school, Jay has a lot of issues related to identity. His best friend even forgot that Jay was half Filipino, since he acted like all the other kids at school—that is, white, the default. After learning of his cousin Jun's death in the Philippines, Jay feels shame and guilt, both for stopping their correspondence that had been going on for years and for not having paid attention to the politics and struggles going on in his father's home country. He decides to go to the Philippines to visit relatives and find out what really happened to 17-year-old Jun. Why was there no funeral? Was he really a drug dealer? Was he killed by the police? Jay concludes that adults have told a lot of lies, and that growing up will involve peeling back layers of lies. He wants the truth, and "Truth is a hungry thing" (p. 29). He believes Jun's father, a police officer, knows the truth. He has been instructed not to mention Jun when in his uncle's house. Hmmm.

Once there, Jay realizes that many things, including not knowing how to speak Tagalog, and not having read books that are required reading for his cousins, add up to his being "not Filipino enough" (p. 74). The mysteries surrounding Jun's death multiply, and Jay's knowledge of current events and corruption, as well as his convictions relating to social justice, increase. Readers will want to stay with him as he grieves, and matures, and maybe finds a way to begin healing through taking action, telling his truth.

The book ends with a list of Recommended Reading for those wanting to know more about the situation in the Philippines, along with website addresses for those wishing to get involved.

Robb, L., & Roberts, R.B. (2020). *The Suffragist Playbook: Your Guide to Changing the World*. Somerville, MA: Candlewick Press.
What is the cause to which you feel most committed? Whether it be racial justice, protecting the environment, addressing the systemic causes of poverty, or something else, the authors of this book have advice and encouragement for you. Rather than give a chronological narrative of the decades-long Suffragist Movement that finally achieved victory with the passing of the Nineteenth Amendment in 1920, they give highlighted (literally) tips for achieving goals related to making society better.

With every bit of wisdom comes a story of a suffragist who exemplifies it. We are told we must be willing to speak up, and then we learn about the first woman to make women's suffrage a full-time job: Lucy Stone. Her classmates at Oberlin (the first American college to accept women) chose her to write an essay for graduation; but Lucy was forbidden to read it to the audience, since both men and women would be present. She went on to become a public speaker, lecturing against slavery and arguing for women's rights. We hear another story about Lucy Stone in the chapter about recruiting and using allies to your cause. Henry Blackwell (brother of Elizabeth Blackwell, the first woman to graduate from medical school in the United States), was impressed by both the speeches and the woman. Stone was singularly committed to her causes and did not intend to marry; but after two years of patience and showing his good qualities, they married, with Stone becoming the first woman to legally keep her own name after she married.

The personalities of the featured suffragists shine through in the vignettes offered. Readers are told that "Sometimes a little stage-craft is necessary" (p. 94); this is modeled by Susan B. Anthony, who voted in a presidential election, and then stretched out her hands for handcuffs when a deputy marshal came to her home to arrest her. The judge at her trial told the jury to find her guilty, then asked Anthony if she could give any reason why that sentencing shouldn't happen. She could indeed, and later printed and disseminated the proceedings. Anthony began speeches from then on with the words, "I stand before you a convicted criminal!" (p. 95).

As guides to changing the world go, this is an entertaining and persuasive one.

Shabazz, I., with Jackson, T.D. (2021). *The Awakening of Malcolm X.* New York: Farrar, Straus Giroux.

Our narrator, Malcolm, brings us to his trial, his sentencing, and his first days in prison in the opening chapters of this novel based on the life of Malcolm X. Through his dreams, we learn back matter, such as his growing up in a large family where his mother provided much love and wisdom. She taught her children that the principles that define them were Self-love, Self-reliance, and Unity. "You are Black, like your papa.... Proud, smart, and Black. Beautifully Black, Scholarly Black, Lovingly Black. You hear me? You are a child of God, strong and protected by the universe" (p. 28). Will his mother's words be enough to sustain this 21-year-old through years of prison?

Malcolm tells some details about the abuse from the guards, the filth, the isolation, the cold, and the nightmares. It's not hard to imagine the things he's leaving out. He also tells of visits and letters from family members, who are all praying for him. But he can't fathom a God who would allow such injustice and evil. He argues with God, who seemed not to care as Malcolm's friend was sent to Death Row. Through family letters, he learns that his brothers have found a God who cares for Black people, whose Arabic name is Allah. Malcolm keeps hearing a voice telling him he doesn't belong in prison; but where *does* he belong?

After a transfer to a prison that actually believes in rehabilitation, Malcolm becomes an avid reader and a lover of language and learning. After receiving letters from Elijah Muhammad, Messenger of Allah, Malcolm has a mission. "Nothing can stop me" (p. 244). Subsequent chapters tell of numerous ways in which his faith is tested. But the ending is filled with promise and hope, as Malcolm X is freed from prison; receives his ministry as chief spokesperson for the Nation; and, on the last page, is introduced to Sister Betty X.

Readers can round out their knowledge of the "New Adult" years of Malcolm and the woman who would become his wife in Shabazz's other books, *X: A Novel*, co-written with Kekla Magoon; *and Betty Before X*, co-written with Renée Watson. Shabazz is the daughter of Malcolm X.

Watson, R. (2021). *Love Is a Revolution*. New York: Bloomsbury.
Rising senior Nala agonizes over questions of identity throughout the summer. Her cousin and others in her circle seem to think less of her because she doesn't join the social justice group Inspire Harlem. In fact, their smugness ("But when you know better, you do better," p. 34) as they try to convince her that she has bought into the patriarchy because she straightens her hair and wears make-up causes her to be even more resistant. Her cousin Imani is busy going to meetings and working on environmental issues, but it is Nala who spends time visiting her grandmother in her home for seniors and interacting with Grandma's friends. Shouldn't that count for something?

Nala wants to be accepted by Tye, a boy who seems to like her, and finds herself mirroring his values; she says things implying that she is vegetarian, and that she actually *works* at her grandmother's residence, doing service projects. Of course, her lies catch up with her, threatening her new relationship. But Tye asks a crucial question, "Why don't you just want to be yourself?" (p. 175). Nala imagines there might be a college course on How to Be Yourself, but meanwhile, her grandmother offers wisdom to the cousins that guides her thinking. "You two are family. Family. That alone ought to be enough for you to respect each other. You're also two women, Black women. The most radical thing you can do is love yourself and each other" (pp. 215–216).

Writing and Thinking Prompt

Nala reflects in writing about her growth process, which involves loving herself, doing things that make her happy, and keeping a gratitude journal. Using Nala's method, write down things you love about yourself as a way toward revolution. Her examples can prompt introspection and provide inspiration. Here's one:

> My mind. It is strong and holds all of who I am. It is still forming and growing and in so many ways, still the same. My mind. It is expansive, and there is so much room to fill, so much more to know. (p. 269)

Watson, R., & Hagan, E. (2019). *Watch Us Rise*. New York: Bloomsbury. Jasmine chronicles her junior year of high school as she supports her father during his last months of life; deals with the hurt inflicted by others over her weight, even though she feels positive about her body; begins to have romantic feelings toward her forever friend Isaac; and co-founds a school club, "Write Like a Girl," with her friend Chelsea. Chelsea chronicles the same year as she supports Jasmine during this time of loss and grieving; wrestles with her belief in feminist principles while falling for a boy who already has a girlfriend; and creates ways to actively call out the injustices perpetuated in her high school and stand up for equity and respect.

Both girls are talented and committed to changing the world for the better. They offer blog posts, poetry, and art throughout the story. They are wonderful models for readers who want to be activists but might need a little urging and coaching. Students could just begin by inviting their teachers and administrators to read and talk about this novel with them and then collaborate to identify and promote change in their schools.

Wiles, D. (2020). *Kent State*. New York: Scholastic.

I got to know four college students as I read this book. I met Sandy, who scrapbooked years of vacations, dances, movies, songs, and family. Her father was a Holocaust survivor. She was studying to be a speech pathologist. I met Jeff, who loved music, motorcycles, math, and the Mets. Jeff was a drummer in a band, and a DJ for a college radio station. He went to Woodstock! Oh, and Bill, who loved geology since he was a boy, discovering arrowheads and fossils. He loved so many things—basketball, poetry, football, the Rolling Stones. He drove a green Fiat, and majored in Psychology. He was in ROTC. Finally, I met Allison, with her love beads, her fur coat. She went sledding on campus; she was reading *One Flew over the Cuckoo's Nest*.

Readers meet them, but they've already lost them. These four young people died on May 4, 1970, killed on the Kent State campus by National Guard soldiers. How could this have happened? What really did happen? Deborah Wiles researched thoroughly in the archives of Kent State, and gives voice not just to *two* sides, but to *many* perspectives. Positioning on the page, along with varying fonts and letter sizes, helps readers keep track of groups that totally defend the students' behavior while totally faulting the guards and soldiers; other groups of town residents, firefighters, and witnesses who claimed to have no opinions; and people who carried weapons and were trained to obey orders. There were Black students who were protesting, and there were Black residents. They saw and perceived things the white students and soldiers and town residents missed. There was so much misinformation, and so many contradictions. Did the young feel one way, and older people another? It's not that simple. Some students and soldiers conversed, and now the students are reminded by those who had weapons, "Some of us were your age. Don't you understand? We were forced to be there" (p. 79).

The text is structured as a recounting told to someone new at the scene, who is invited to listen, and make up their own mind as to whether it was a tragic mistake or a calculated government assault. Near the end, the book becomes interactive, when we are suddenly confronted as the listener, and told to "INSERT YOUR NAME HERE" (p. 87).

In an afterword, Deborah Wiles reminds us that with any story, "There will be as many versions of the truth as there are people who lived it" (p. 121). She extols the May 4 Collection on the campus and encourages readers to delve into the digitized material that is available online. Some readers might be moved to visit Kent State someday to take part in the annual vigil.

A class or theatre group could perform this text, using Readers Theatre or a choral reading adaptation. It would be powerful to take on different voices, perhaps especially those representing roles that readers least identify with. Writers could use this multiple-voiced text to examine and tell the nuanced story of other historical events.

*Wilson, K. (2019). *White Rose*. Boston, MA: Houghton Mifflin Harcourt.

In the Author's Note, Kip Wilson tells of first learning about the White Rose resistance movement when she was in high school German class. Years later, she saw Sophie Scholl's artwork and letters in Munich, retraced Sophie's steps from her flat to the university where her act of distributing leaflets took place, and visited her grave. Now, more than a decade later, she has given us this novel in verse.

Most of the poems are narrated by Sophie. The first scene takes place in 1943 at Gestapo Headquarters, where she is being interrogated. The poems go back and forth in time, so that we get to know Sophie as a teen growing up under the reign of Hitler but before the outbreak of the war. We learn how she falls in love with a young man who is conscripted into Hitler's army; and how she watches as her Jewish neighbors lose privileges and undergo persecution, then decides she must join her brother in secret acts of resistance. And the poems set during and after Sophie's trial never let us forget that she paid the highest price for her bravery and commitment to justice. We hear from Sophie as she is awaiting her execution.

Was her sacrifice worth it, readers may ponder? Wilson provides further resources for investigation. I'll share just one fact Wilson leaves us with. "Smuggled leaflets also made it to the Allies, and more than five million copies were reprinted and dropped by aircraft over German cities" (345).

*Zissu, A. (2021). *Earth Squad: 50 People who are Saving the Planet.* Illus. Lê, Nhung. Philadelphia, PA: Running Press Kids.

Readers will feel impressed, inspired, and empowered by this collection of chapters featuring people of all ages, ethnicities, and talents. The commonality that unites them is their devotion to and willingness to work for preserving and bettering the environment. Many have multiple roles; they have used their main careers and educational backgrounds to fight for our world in unique ways. We learn of Pete Seeger speaking out through his music; hip-hop artist Xiuhtezcatl pressuring politicians and spreading awareness as a climate activist; waste expert Annie Leonard making the film *The Story of Stuff* (Fox, 2007); architect William McDonough serving as a sustainability consultant; pediatrician Philip Landrigan advocating for environmental health. Angela Merkel is both a scientist and the chancellor of Germany. Inka Saara Arttijeff is both a reindeer herder and a presidential advisor. Vanessa Hauc combines journalism and environmentalism. And Lamya Essemlali is a pirate as well as an ocean activist.

After every profile, there are suggestions for following the lead of the people featured in this book. Readers are encouraged to strike to call attention to climate change, as young Greta Thunberg modeled; and to plant trees as Wangari Maathai has done in Kenya. Several stories show us that we can make a difference by buying less; eating locally grown foods; reducing our consumption of meat; writing letters; planting gardens at home and school; and collecting litter to make art.

Environmental problems are complex, but some of the solutions are simple. Perhaps after reading this book, classes can take action to join the Earth Squad, and create their own record of ways they have spoken up and acted for the good of the planet. As this book shows, we can change the world.

Instructional Strategies and Activities

Make Good Trouble

In 2020, in Selma, Alabama, on the fifty-fifth anniversary of Bloody Sunday, Congressman John Lewis urged us to, "Speak up, speak out, get in the way. Get in good trouble. Necessary trouble, and help redeem the soul of America" (Cole, 2020). What exactly is good trouble? Isn't that an oxymoron? Readers can reflect on the phrase and verbalize what it means to them. They can read others' interpretations, analyses, and applications. And they can read the entire speech he gave that day, as well as earlier speeches and quotes from interviews or essays. They can come to know John Lewis as a child, adolescent, and young man by reading the graphic trilogy consisting of *March, Book One* (2013); *March, Book Two* (2015); and *March, Book Three* (2016), all co-written with Andrew Aydin, and illustrated by Nate Powell. They'll be eager to follow him into later years in *Run* (2021), which was published posthumously. They will love watching his acceptance of the National Book Award for *March, Book Three* (Lewis, 2016).

The lens of good trouble, necessary trouble, can be applied to virtually any NA novel, memoir, or biography, and can be a recurring theme throughout a course. Students can apply it to their own creative writing or report writing, and it can be a catalyst to help them reflect on their own lives and make decisions in various situations. You can have a poster of the quote displayed in the classroom. (There are t-shirts available with the saying as well.) Encourage students to channel John Lewis's call as they face challenges, think critically, and strive to do what is right and just, to make the world better.

Walk-Through

Ms. Polinsky teaches social studies and ELA in a rural high school. John Lewis is her hero, so her students are very familiar with his accomplishments and his life story through the literature and other resources in her classroom. The mantra "Make good trouble" is a thread throughout the academic year, and her students are helping to spread the message throughout the school through their words and actions. Here are what readers' comments sound like as they grapple with particular books in light of John Lewis's charge.

ANGELIA: I read *Love from A to Z*, by S.K. Ali. In the beginning, Zayneb hates her social studies teacher—for good reason, since he is blatantly anti-Muslim. But she acts out of anger and hurt; she draws an image that is perceived as threatening, and ends up suspended. No good came out of that, so I don't think that's *good trouble*. But throughout spring break she corresponds with classmates, making plans to bring Mr. Fencer down. And he *should* be fired; no one who is Islamophobic belongs in a school. This time, the students calculate their actions and are acting with the right motive, so I think by the last part of the book they are making good trouble, working for justice rather than revenge.

JORGE: Wow, I just finished *Kent State*, by Deborah Wiles. Talk about good trouble! The student protesters were so brave; they could have dispersed at the first sight of the troops with guns, similar to how John Lewis and the people he led over the bridge into Selma could have scattered before they were beaten up and arrested. The Vietnam War was the thing that caused the protest at Kent State to be necessary trouble. Doing nothing would not have stopped the war. A terrible result, a terrible sacrifice, but very good trouble.

TRINITY: I was really feeling the dilemma Kiran and Sahaara faced in Jasmin Kaur's *If I Tell You the Truth*. Kiran kept the baby after being impregnated by rape. She fled, endured shame and poverty and estrangement from her family, and did everything she could to give her daughter a good life. Now, eighteen years later, Kiran, who is undocumented and extremely vulnerable, is being asked to go public about the rape because the rapist is vying for the highest office in Punjab. And Sahaara is being called on to confront her rapist father. Isn't that too much to ask, of both of them? Getting in *good* trouble often means risking everything. But the *good* that could result from their sacrifice and courage helps me understand multiple meanings of the adjective *good*. I think Kiran and Sahaara are *good*. I hope I can be as *good* when I have the opportunity to stand up for the rights of myself and others. *Good* book!

Combining Nonfiction Accounts with Historical Fiction Treatment of Topics

Which is better, nonfiction or historical fiction? Which can better help students learn about curricular material? Which genre do readers prefer? Of course, the answer to all these questions is "It depends." The quality of writing in books of any genre varies greatly. Plus, some students would rather read fiction, while their classmates would usually choose nonfiction. Perhaps the best answer for teachers is to offer narrative nonfiction (which can tell every bit as good a story as fiction) along with well-researched fiction (which can teach just as much information as nonfiction) together. As students respond to the texts cognitively, emotionally, and metacognitively, they will absorb and interact with the information in meaningful ways. They'll notice differences in structures, and in authorial choices. They might notice contradictions or inconsistencies and want to pursue further resources to resolve their new questions.

There is no right order in terms of which genre should be read first. If students read a totally factual account first, they'll bring background knowledge to their reading of the fictional account, perhaps appreciating characters' dialog added that was not available from sources, but that remains true to what the author was able to find. (Susan Campbell Bartoletti chose to tell 16-year-old Helmut Hubner's story this way in *The Boy Who Dared* [2016], since the archives did not supply his words, but she wanted to give him a voice.) Conversely, if readers get to understand and appreciate a character through a fictional story first, they'll bring more to a nonfiction treatment that may help them comprehend new information at a deeper level, or read the material more critically.

Depending on their purpose, teachers can simply display the nonfiction and fictional texts together and give book talks so that students can decide whether to read one or the other, or both. Or they can require that both be read, and provide specific tools for comparing, contrasting, and synthesizing.

Walk-Through

The following is an example of part of a discussion a group of students might have after reading Kip Wilson's novel-in-verse *White Rose* and Russell Freedman's *We Will Not Be Silent: The White Rose Student Resistance Movement that Defied Adolf Hitler.* You can find book talks for both earlier in this chapter.

MARGARITA: Wow, Sophie Scholl is my new hero. Can you believe how brave she was? I was terrified as I read the first poem of *White Rose* on page 3, when she was handcuffed and hauled into Gestapo Headquarters.

RAPH: Yeah, that was pretty cool how the author started the story (through the poems) in February of 1943, the month she and her brother were executed, and then went back and forth to fill us in on how they got to that point.

ROMEYN: That was really different from the chronological approach of *We Will Not Be Silent*, where we get to know Hans and Sophie as kids. Hans joined the Hitler Youth, even though his father disapproved. We followed the steps of his journey from being a leader in the movement to founding a resistance movement.

MARGARITA: I think the saddest part for me was learning in Kip Wilson's Author's Note that Sophie's hope that the executions of the White Rose members would stir other students to rebel didn't happen. Her university classmates were just too scared. Did they feel guilty about that? I'm afraid that I would have been one of the ones who kept silent, even though I know that's not what I *should* do when confronted with an evil regime.

TERRY: Well, these two books are making sure that Sophie and Hans and the others aren't forgotten. Wouldn't you love to visit the places pictured in *We Will Not Be Silent*? I want to walk under the sign at Munich's University Square: Geschwister-Scholl-Platz (Scholl Sibling Square), and see the White Rose leaflets in the cobblestone pavement at the university memorial.

References

Cole, D. (2020). John Lewis urges attendees of Selma's 'Bloody Sunday' commemorative march to 'redeem the soul of America' by voting. Retrieved from https://www.cnn.com/2020/03/01/politics/john-lewis-bloody-sunday-march-selma/index.html.

Fox, L. (Director). (2007). *The story of stuff* [Film]. San Francisco, CA: Free Range Studios.

Johnson, M. (Ed.). (2018). *How I resist: Activism and hope for a new generation*. New York: Wednesday Books.

Lewis, J. (2016). National Book Award Acceptance Speech. Retrieved from https://www.youtube.com/watch?v=uqmYNOPVyO4.

Literature Cited

Bartoletti, S. (2016). *The boy who dared*. New York: Scholastic.

Lewis, J., Aydin, A., Fury, L., & Powell, N. (2021). *Run, book one*. New York: Abrams ComicArts.

Lewis, J., Aydin, A., & Powell, N. (2016). *March, book three*. Marietta, GA: Top Shelf Productions.

Lewis, J., Aydin, A., & Powell, N. (2015). *March, book two*. Marietta, GA: Top Shelf Productions.

Lewis, J., Aydin, A., & Powell, N. (2013). *March, book one*. Marietta, GA: Top Shelf Productions.

Shabazz, I., with Magoon, K (2015). *X: A novel*. Somerville, MA: Candlewick Press.

Shabazz, I., with Watson, R. (2018). *Betty before X*. New York: Square Fish.

So You'd Rather Be Reading

7

A Literary Guide through the Disciplines

The Value of Literature in Content Area Classrooms

Does the following quote from artist Winfred Rembert (2021) resonate with you, or with any young readers you know? *"I got to find a way to make myself successful by getting out of what has been planned for me into something I want to do myself"* (p. 52). There are books related to science, the arts, economics, politics, math, technology, the humanities, computer science, psychology, and other fields that fit the New Adult (NA) literature category. This chapter will help you think about learning new content, disciplinary ways of thinking, and vocabulary through story. Many biographies and works of historical fiction are available, and you can focus on the benefits of examining the early adult years of famous people, which can provide both surprises and life lessons. Readers will see how all school subjects can be taught through or with literature. You may have noticed that the books introduced in previous chapters often featured characters who had an interest in or even a passion for a particular discipline. There have been aspiring musicians, journalists, scientists, artists, poets, environmentalists, actors, and activists. The books recommended in this chapter will deal with topics addressed earlier, including relationships, academic pursuits, and career exploration. NA literature reflects the world, and can teach about the world. In short, reading for pleasure can make us smarter.

I am passionate about using literature in all subject areas at the secondary level. A previous book, *Integrating Literature in the Disciples* (Kane, 2020), focuses on this topic and contains hundreds of book talks divided into genre

DOI: 10.4324/9781003221685-7

categories as well as subject categories. You can get an idea of what a typical day in a school espousing this practice might look like by checking out a blog post I wrote for Dr. Bickmore's YA Wednesday (Kane, 2019).

Reading NA books for pleasure can help with virtually all curricular studies. Reasons for using trade books in disciplinary courses include enhancing the learning of content and disciplinary ways of structuring thinking and writing; creating opportunities for challenging discussions; enabling the teaching of content from multiple perspectives and sources; stimulating interest and motivation to read and learn; and increasing the volume of reading, including independent reading. Think of how important those things will be when students enter or proceed through college. Now, imagine a teacher–librarian collaboration that invites high school seniors to participate in a NA literature book club, with books representing common disciplines in General Education requirements at many colleges. Or picture a senior elective on NA literature that uses the same kinds of books. Many seniors have virtually finished their high school requirements and are just biding time until they can enter the next stage of their education. The NA books we can give them in high school might help them realize what areas they would like to pursue in college, or could even provide the incentive and encouragement some students need to apply for college admission, while helping others to realize there are valuable paths they can take after high school that don't involve higher education.

The previous chapters have been about the love of learning and pursuing knowledge; passions and careers; relationships; activism and working for justice; and figuring out the meaning of life and our place in the world. All of these can be connected to the disciplinary fields studied in high school and college. And, we can look at the classics and other texts in new ways, asking how they connect to NA literature, maybe even claiming some, or parts of some, as NA. One example would be to read biographies through a Youth Lens. (Remember that strategy in Chapter 4?) Readers can note the childhood and adolescent influences on people, and also contemplate the reverse direction—how have youth influenced adults, and history, and science, and art?

TEXT SETS

Doing (and Loving) Science and Math

Beckman, M. (2022). *Math without Numbers.* Illus. M. Erazo. New York: Penguin.

Cantor, J. (2020). *The Code for Love and Heartbreak*. New York: Inkyard Press.

*Greenfield, A.B. (2021). *The Woman All Spies Fear: Code Breaker Elizabeth Smith Friedman and her Hidden Life*. New York: Random House.

Jahren, H. (2017). *Lab Girl*. New York: Vintage Books.

Kaplan, A. (2020). *We Regret to Inform You: An Overachiever's Guide to College Rejection*. New York: Ember.

McCully, E.A. (2019). *Dreaming in Code: Ada Byron Lovelace, Computer Pioneer*. Somerville, MA: Candlewick Press.

*Mlodinow, L. (2020). *Stephen Hawking: A Memoir of Friendship and Physics*. New York: Pantheon Books.

Morris, B. (2019). *Slay*. New York: Simon & Schuster.

Singh, S. (2017). *Pi of Life: The Hidden Happiness of Mathematics*. Latham, MD: Rowman & Littlefield.

*Sorrell, T. (2021). *Classified: The Secret Career of Mary Golda Ross, Cherokee Aerospace Engineer*. Illus. Donovan, Natasha. Minneapolis, MN: Millbrook Press.

Su, F., & Jackson, C. (Contributor). (2020). *Mathematics for Human Flourishing*. New Haven, CT: Yale University Press.

Yuki, H. (2016). *Math Girls³ Gödel's Incompleteness Theorems*. Trans. Tony Gonzalez. Austin, TX: Bento Books.

Cool Collective Biographies

Anderson, B. (2020). *The Book of Awesome Woman Writers: Medieval Mystics, Pioneering Poets, Fierce Feminists and First Ladies of Literature*. Miami, FL: Mango.

Bagieu, P. (2018). *Brazen: Rebel Ladies who Rocked the World*. New York: First Second.

Bolden, T. (2020). *Changing the Equation: 50+ Black Women in STEM*. New York: Abrams Books for Young Readers.

Croll, J., & Buchhole, A. (2016). *Bad Girls of Fashion: Style Rebels from Cleopatra to Lady Gaga*. Toronto: Annick Press.

Freeman, M. (2020). *Born Curious: 20 Girls who Grew Up to Be Awesome Scientists*. Illus. Wu, Katy. New York: Simon & Schuster.

*Grimes, N. (2021). *Legacy: Women Poets of the Harlem Renaissance*. New York: Bloomsbury.

Hood, S. (2018). *Shaking Things Up: 14 Young Women who Changed the World*. Illus. Alko, S., Blackall, S., Brown, L., Hooper, H., Martin, E.W., Mora, O., Morstad, J., Palacios, S., Pham, L, Robinson, E.K., Roxas, I., Strickland, S., & Sweet, M. New York: HarperCollins.

Ignotofsky, R. (2017). *Women in Sports: 50 Fearless Athletes who Played to Win*. Berkeley, CA: Ten Speed Press.

LaBarge, M. (2020). *Women Artists A to Z*. Illus. Corrigan, Caroline. New York: Dial Books.

Montillo, Roseanne. (2021). *Atomic Women: The Untold Stories of the Scientists who Helped Create the Nuclear Bomb*. Boston, MA: Little, Brown.

*Murray, J. (2018). *A History of the World in 21 Women*. London: Oneworld Publications.

*Porath, J. (2016). *Rejected Princesses: Tales of History's Boldest Heroines, Hellions & Heretics*. New York: William Morrow.

Wilson, J. (2018). *Young, Gifted and Black: Meet 52 Black Heroes from Past and Present*. Illus. Pippins, Andrea. Minneapolis, MN: Wide Eyed Editions.

Skeers, L. (2017). *Women who Dared: 52 Fearless Daredevils, Adventurers, and Rebels*. Naperville, IL: Sourcebooks Explore.

Ottaviani, J. (2020). *Astronauts: Women on the Final Frontier*. Illus. Wicks, Maris. New York: First Second.

Art Is Pervasive

Cagan, K. (2018). *Art Boss*. San Francisco, CA: Chronicle Books.

*Cagan, K. (2017). *Piper Perish*. San Francisco, CA: Chronicle Books.

Corthron, K.L. (2017). *The Truth of Right Now*. New York: Simon Pulse.

Gaiman, N. (2018). *Art Matters*. Illus. Chris Riddell. New York: William Morrow.

Gibson, E.V. (2020). *Together we Caught Fire*. New York: Simon & Schuster.

*Greenberg, J., & Jordan, S. (2020). *World of Glass: The Art of Dale Chihuly*. New York: Abrams.

Linn, L. (2016). *Draw the Line*. New York: Margaret K. McElderry Books.

Lippincott, R. (2020). *Five Feet Apart*. New York: Simon & Schuster.

Menon, S. (2018). *From Twinkle, with Love*. New York: Simon Pulse.

Mukherjee, S. (2016). *Gemini*. New York: Simon & Schuster.

Nelson, M. (2022). *Augusta Savage: The Shape of a Sculptor's Life*. New York: Christy Ottaviano Books.

*Rembert, W., as told to Erin. I. Kelly. (2021). *Chasing me to my Grave: An Artist's Memoir of the Jim Crow South*. New York: Bloomsbury.

*Sidman, J. (2018). *The Girl who Drew Butterflies: How Maria Merian's Art Changed Science*. Boston, MA: Houghton Mifflin Harcourt.

Sports

Bush, C.A. (2022). *Every Variable of Us*. Mendota Heights, MN: Flux.

Deming, S. (2019). *Gravity*. New York: Make Me a World.

Gibson, T. (2020). *Off Track*. Kingston 6, Jamaica: Blouse & Skirt Books.

Ibtihaj, M. (2018). *Proud: Living my American Dream*. New York: Little, Brown and Company.

Jarzab, A. (2021). *Breath like Water*. New York: Inkyard.

Jones, K., & Segal, G. (2021). *Why We Fly*. Naperville, IL: Sourcebooks Fire.

McGinnis, M. (2020). *Heroine*. New York: HarperCollins.

Méndez, Y.S. (2021). *Furia*. Waterville, ME: Thorndike.

Patel, S. (2021). *The Knockout*. Mendota Heights, MN: Flux.

Yang, G.L. (2020). *Dragon Hoops*. New York: First Second.

Book Talks: Ready to Go!

This section contains book talks for texts connected to disciplines that New Adults are already passionate about or that might entice readers who are not yet sure what areas might interest them when they search for work in their post-high school years, or what subjects they would like to pursue in college. They can supplement textbooks and other resources typically used in courses, or be used to motivate students to investigate curricular topics with enthusiasm. Of course, the books can be read for pure pleasure, with any learning that happens being natural and coincidental. Books marked with an asterisk appear in the Text Sets above.

Ackmann, M. (2020). *These Fevered Days: Ten Pivotal Moments in the Making of Emily Dickinson*. New York: W.W. Norton & Company.
The author knows the life and writings of Emily Dickinson well; for years she taught a course about her in the Dickinson Homestead in Amherst, MA:

> My Mount Holyoke students discussed Dickinson in the very rooms where the poet created her work. Sitting around that seminar table, the students demonstrated that they understood Dickinson's life and work more deeply when our conversation centered on an important moment in the poet's life.
>
> (p. xvii)

So, she structured this biography in the same way.

The first chapter focuses on the teenaged Emily announcing to her friend in a letter that all was ready; she was prepared to seriously start her work. In the following chapter, we see the 21-year-old Emily at Mount Holyoke Female Seminary, which she would soon be leaving; after much consideration, after puzzling over the seemingly contradictory goals of the founder, Mary Lyon, Emily knew that she would not be making the commitment to Christianity that was expected of the residents. How could Lyon preach independence, ambition, and using one's mind, while simultaneously expecting the girls to join the flock? Emily's response involved the shunning of categories and classifications. "She made her decision. She had discovered a way to take religion seriously while also remaining independent. She neither accepted faith nor rejected it. Emily decided to continue questioning" (p. 48).

The third chapter focuses on the publication of Emily's first poem, when she was in her late 20s, along with the increase in the volume and intensity of her writing. Subsequent chapters use the same framework involving pivotal moments.

Writing and Thinking Prompt

Choose choice A or B:

A. Research someone who has made valuable contributions to a particular discipline, or who is significant in another way. As Martha Ackmann did in her biography of Emily Dickinson, choose several incidents you would consider "pivotal" moments in the person's youth and early adulthood to introduce others to them.

B. Begin an autobiographical account, using the "pivotal moment" framework to reflect on events or decisions in your life that have led you to where you are today and helped form you into the person you have become, or are on your way to becoming. Think about your beliefs and the projects you embrace.

Beckman, M. (2021). *Math Without Numbers*. Illus. Erazo, M. New York: Dutton.

Let's start with a couple of questions. First, how many shapes are there? Dozens? Hundreds? Millions? An infinite number? Second, if you accused your math teacher of overthinking things, do you think they'd be offended? Mathematician Milo Beckman would agree with you. "It's sort of what we do. We take some concept that everyone understands on a basic level, like symmetry or equality, and pick it apart, trying to find a deeper meaning to it" (p. 3). He exemplifies this by talking at some length about the concept of shape, listing lots of simple questions, including "How many shapes are there?" Turns out that one is not easy to answer. A version of the question, the generalized Poincaré conjecture, has been tackled for more than 100 years, without a solution. A mathematician won a million dollars for solving one part of it! (p. 4)

This is Beckman's introduction to the field of topology, one branch of mathematics that he plays with in this book. Others include analysis and algebra. True to the title, he does not use numbers, though there are plenty of drawings. Treat yourself to this nonnumerical discussion of a fascinating discipline. I can't help but think that the young protagonist Milo who explores math and words in Norton Juster's *The Phantom Tollbooth* (1996) would love to be further guided by the Milo who wrote this book.

Cagan, K. (2017). *Piper Perish*. San Francisco, CA: Chronicle Books.
Our high school readers can commiserate with and learn from the
narrator of this novel as she shares the story of her last few months
of senior year. Piper is accepted by a prestigious art school in New
York City, but there are obstacles to achieving her long-standing
dream of escaping Texas with her best friend and her boyfriend.
Kit is rejected by the institute, and Enzo decides to stay in Texas
after falling in love with a young man. Piper's parents, while supportive, cannot afford the college tuition, partly due to her older
sister Marla's pregnancy and subsequent return home from college.

Piper negotiates family problems (including her sister's emotional
illness and abusiveness), changing peer relationships, and a budding
epistolary friendship through her art. Her art teacher is a wonderful
example of a mentor. Readers who come together to discuss *Piper
Perish* will have a choice of issues to pursue, even as they prepare to
embark on their own journeys toward college, career, and passion.
They'll want to head to New York with her in the sequel, *Art Boss*
(2018, Chronicle Books).

Clapsaddle, A.S. (2020). *Even as We Breathe*. Lexington, KY: Fireside
Industries.
This work of historical fiction is narrated by an old man. Cownie
Sequoya relates his experiences between high school and college,
during the summer of 1942. The 19-year-old, wanting to escape his
Cherokee land, as well as his uncle Buddy's control, takes a summer
job at a resort in Asheville where high-level prisoners of war are
housed and guarded. While there, he falls in love with Essie, who is
also seeking freedom from the restrictions of the reservation. Based
on circumstantial evidence, betrayal, and information given by Essie,
he is suspected of murdering the child of one of the "guests." On visits
home, he grieves the death of his grandmother Lishie, who raised
him; and eventually of Buddy, whose family secrets come to light.

The events and relationships cause Cownie to think deeply about
his identity. A high school teacher had told him that we are bits and
pieces of the people we meet. And on his first day on the new job,
he realizes, "We had a chance to do everything new and fresh and
start our lives away from the suffocating safety of the familiar...."
and hopes that he has within him "... the courage to step into one's
true self, whoever that might be" (p. 40).

On Cownie's last day, he receives help from his Asheville boss, who gives him a letter of recommendation for his college applications; money; and perhaps most important of all, words that imply trust in Cownie's next steps. "Consider it a graduation present. Just not sure if it is a late high school graduation present or an early college graduation present... either way" (p. 218).

Readers will learn about the discrimination and injustices inflicted upon the Cherokees during World War II, and may realize that, like Cownie, they can learn to forgive and forge ahead with an indomitable spirit.

Donoghue, E. (2020). *The Pull of the Stars*. New York: Little, Brown and Company.

Julia, a nurse working on a maternity ward in Ireland for women who have influenza, is about to turn 30. Bridie, a volunteer helper who was raised in an orphanage, is (probably) around 22. And the characters who become new mothers during the three days of the story range from 17 to mid-20s. Readers today will find much that seems familiar, though the setting is 1918. There are signs everywhere urging people to cover their coughs, wear masks, stay out of public places, and stay distant while keeping socializing at a minimum. "IF IN DOUBT, DON'T STIR OUT" (p. 170). The pandemic is resulting in tragic deaths, shortages of workers, exhausted medical staffs, and much grief. One day Julia manages to save a mother but not her baby; the next day she saves a baby only to watch his mother succumb to the disease.

Meanwhile, the Great War continues. Julia's brother Tim was discharged from the army and now lives with her, but he is mute as a result of the trauma of the battlefield. Are the two devastating forces connected? There is much to learn from this story in terms of politics, ethics, history, and medicine. You might not think there would be time for romance, but love finds a way.

Engle, M. (2020). *With a Star in my Hand: Rubén Darío, Poetry Hero*. New York: Atheneum.

Rubén Darío might prove to be an inspiration and hero to young readers who are figuring out their own identities as they transition from childhood to adulthood. The precocious Darío earned a reputation as the "Child Poet," causing him to wonder what that means once he is approaching twenty. Poetry helps him navigate this and other challenges.

Margarita Engle (whose given name, matching the title name of Darío's famous fairy tale "A Margarita Debayle," was chosen because the poet was so important to generations of her family) has created a fictionalized biography in verse based on the poet's autobiography. She assures us that the events are factual, as are the emotional aspects, since "Darío wrote so clearly about his childhood and youth" (Author's Note, unpaged). We see how greatly influenced Darío was by his feelings of abandonment during years of believing his parents were dead, and later finding out they were alive. We see how he dealt with problems and uncertainty in some unproductive and destructive ways, often including alcohol.

Perhaps most importantly, we see his early and continuing use of writing to understand himself as well as express his emotions and convictions. Several of Engle's poems, including "Traveling with Invisible Mentors," "When I Write Poetry," and "When I'm Asked to Describe the Process of Writing," could help readers analyze their own writing styles and goals.

With a Star in my Hand brings Darío to the point where he is "No Longer a Teenager" (p. 139), and when he publishes his first book, *Azul*. The penultimate poem relates some other key accomplishments in his life, while the closing poem looks to the future. Now, Margarita Engle has used her lens and creativity to make Darío accessible to today's youth. His legacy continues.

Engle, M. (2021). *Your Heart My Sky: Love in a Time of Hunger.* New York: Atheneum.

Is it possible to live courageously in a dangerous time? This is one of many questions Liana must try to answer. There's also the dilemma she shares with everyone on the island of Cuba in 1991, the "special period in times of peace" (p. 1), which is what to do when treasured scraps of food are found—devour them, or save some for others. Should she defy the government and risk punishment by growing food in her home? Should she consider joining those who are building makeshift rafts to attempt to escape to the shores of Florida?

Amado faces all these decisions, plus another. Should he give himself over to the mandatory military service waiting for him and all young males, or should he refuse? His brother did the latter, and is now languishing in a prison with horrendous conditions.

This historical novel in verse is both a record of the near starvation that Cubans faced as the government prepared to host the Pan Am Games in a manner that would hide the conditions from the rest of the world, and a love story. Liana and Amado face their privations and fears together, and make their decisions based on their love for one another.

Margarita Engle, who has given us two memoirs of her growing up as a Cuban American, tells us in the Author's Note that she visited relatives in Cuba in 1991, and continued throughout the decade to deliver food and vitamins. She explained what caused the crisis. "Shortages of food resulted from a combination of the sudden loss of Soviet aid; inefficient collective farming; bizarre laws that prohibited individuals from growing, buying, and selling agricultural products; and a brutal US trade embargo" (p. 207). She has empathy for those cousins who became refugees as well as for those who "… stayed in their homeland, inventing solutions to daily problems" (p. 207). Her story, set during a devastating time, offers hope and shows the beauty of the people she loves.

*Greenberg, J., & Jordan, S. (2020). *World of Glass: The Art of Dale Chihuly*. New York: Abrams.

Aspiring artists who love to experiment with color, medium, and size will be enthralled with this book's photographs of Dale Chihuly's glass installations as well as with his life story. Dale's childhood involved drawing with crayons, visiting the exotic plants in a glass-house botanical conservatory, watching sunsets, and searching for sea glass. But these did not magically evolve into a career in glassblowing. During his teenage years, he lost both his older brother and his father. With the encouragement of his mother, he worked a number of jobs to be able to attend college, where he took a course in weaving.

Many 20-something readers will nod at Dale's realization at the age of 21 that, without a passion or goals, he was wasting money and time. He wandered Europe, then Turkey, and had a life-altering experience working on a kibbutz in Israel. Returning to college, he won an award for his art; graduated and got a job; and developed an obsession for learning the skill of glassblowing. He had a new path, one he has stayed on and forged throughout his adulthood.

Readers can follow Dale's journey and his artistic contributions along the way through this combination biography-art appreciation text. They'll be amazed not only by Dale's talent and brilliance, but also by his persistence and resilience. Due to a car accident, he lost an eye; in a body surfing accident, he dislocated a shoulder. In 2017, hoping to help others with chronic illnesses realize that shouldn't stop them from being successful, he disclosed that he has had bipolar disorder since his early twenties.

The authors conclude, "Dale's gift to himself in both good times and bad has been following his passions and fulfilling his creativity…. Dale's gift to the world is the joy of his creations" (p. 51).

*Greenfield, A.B. (2021). *The Woman All Spies Fear: Code Breaker Elizebeth Smith Friedman and her hidden life.* New York: Random House.

Elizebeth wanted to go to college. Her father thought that was a waste of time for a girl, though he finally relented enough to give her a loan, which she was to pay back with 6% interest. After college, she took a job with a millionaire cracking codes and ciphers at his private estate. There she met her future husband, William. Both would go on to lives as cryptanalysts, working for various government agencies in crucial roles, including during wartime. Elizebeth cracked codes used by the Nazi spies in South America; she became a spy herself. She and her husband were both involved in top secret work, so they could never share what they were doing with each other. But they had a strong, loving, supportive relationship.

Readers learn a lot of history through the lens of cryptography. And at the end of the chapters, they get lessons on various types of codes. It's a challenging, exciting, and inspiring text.

Though much of the book is about Elizebeth and William in their adult years, it can be used in classrooms and in school coding clubs. The pair had to struggle with many ethical issues. "When was it okay to eavesdrop? What did you owe your allies? If you were protecting your country, did the ends justify the means?" (p. 243)

Both during her life and beyond, Elizebeth opened up opportunities for other female code breakers, including about 11,000 who were critical to the Allied victory in WW II. Who knows how many more young people will become fascinated with codes and codebreaking after reading this biography?

*Grimes, N. (2021). *Legacy: Women Poets of the Harlem Renaissance.*
New York: Bloomsbury.

The author begins with a brief history of the Harlem Renaissance, noting especially the contributions of women who are often left out of historical accounts and school curricula. She sets out to highlight some of the gifted female writers of the time, who laid a foundation for Black women artists who worked closer to today, such as Gwendolyn Brooks, Toni Morrison, and Maya Angelou, among many others.

Grimes structures the book using three main themes: Heritage, Earth Mother, and Taking Notice. Within each section, she provides a poem created during the Harlem Renaissance, and follows it with a poem of her own using the Golden Shovel form, in which one takes a *striking line* from the original poem and works it into a new poem. Grimes chooses to put one word of the striking line (which can be multiple lines, or a short poem in its entirety) at the end of each of her own lines. For example, Anne Spencer's "Earth, I Thank You" begins with the repetition of the title, followed by "for the pleasure of your language" (p. 41). This poem is followed by Nikki Grimes' "Sweet Sister," in which the last words of each line are *earth, I, thank, you, for, the, pleasure, of, your*, and *language*, all of which are bolded.

The book also contains photographs of paintings by various artists. Biographical sketches of both poets and artists can be found at the end of the book.

Writing and Thinking Prompt

Of the Golden Shovel technique, Nikki Grimes says:

> This is a very challenging way to create a poem, especially to come up with something that makes sense, and I love it for that very reason! In this form, the poet is bound by the words of the original poem, but the possibilities for creating something entirely new are exciting.
>
> I continue to find this form a joy to create. I hope you'll give it a try, too!

(p. 8)

Nikki Grimes has invited you to write a Golden Shovel poem. Choose a poem from this collection, or one of your favorites from another source. Find a short section you will consider as your *striking line*. Then, create a poem of your own, fitting the original words in it (perhaps at the end of every one of your lines, as Grimes chose to do) and then bolding those words. Find a work of art that you feel accompanies your poem thematically or emotionally, or paint or draw an illustration of your own. We will display the poems made in this classroom for a few weeks, and then bind them into a book for our classroom library, and/ or create a digital collection.

Hoffman, A. (2019). *The World that We Knew*. New York: Simon & Schuster.

Some of the characters in this story, set in Europe between 1941 and 1944, fit firmly in the age group of NA literature's range of late teen-early 20s. Some are a bit younger at the story's start, but after the harrowing events related to trying to escape persecution and death, and/or resisting Nazi occupiers, those that make it have certainly emerged as adults. As for one of the main characters, Ava, her age is unclear, or irrelevant, or unknowable; she was created in secret from clay by the daughter of a rabbi, for the purpose of protecting the young Jewish girl Lea and leading her to safety. Lea received instructions from her mother, who sent her away right before she herself was taken away to a place from which she would not return, to kill the Golem. That's what always had to happen.

Readers know that some of the characters whom we come to care for, and who care for each other, will die. The history that the novel is immersed in will demand it. Ava is just one of the many we have to wonder about, root for, hoping for the best while bracing for the worst. The book teaches about history and humanity, inviting readers to look further for more stories of the Golem. In addition, the heron on the front cover, presumably the same heron we meet in the text, will stay with many readers, who will appreciate heron encounters on a new level after learning of the heron's role in this haunting, enchanting journey involving many intersecting lives of various kinds of young heroes.

Jackson, H. (2020). *A Good Girl's Guide to Murder*. New York: Delacorte. Aspiring journalist Pippa decides to analyze the court records and news stories involving a murder that took place several years ago in her town. As her research proceeds, she grows increasingly suspicious about whether the police got it wrong, and she begins interviewing people close to both the victim, Andie, and the supposed murderer, Sal, who took his own life several days after the murder. It seemed like the puzzle pieces fit: Sal was Andie's boyfriend, and witnesses say they were having disagreements. There was even a written confession and apology. Pippa and Sal's brother Ravi team up to check out leads and form new hypotheses. What if Andie, whose body was never found, is still alive? What if Sal didn't actually write the note, and was a murder victim himself? Could the evidence they are uncovering about drugs being slipped into girls' drinks at parties be connected to their main case? Where did these and other drugs come from? Is the killer still on the loose?

The answer to the last question would seem to be yes, since Pippa keeps getting threatening notes telling her to drop her snooping. Pippa and Ravi place themselves in considerable danger as they continue their investigation. So much is at stake. Readers will be guessing and plotting the next steps right along with these amateur sleuths, and some of the hunches will be about the present rather than the past. Might Pippa and Ravi be falling for each other? Would that be wise during a quest where everyone must be suspect, and maybe some lies need to be told? Hmmm....

Jackson, H. (2021). *Good Girl, Bad Blood*. New York: Penguin Random House.
In this sequel to *A Good Girl's Guide to Murder* (2020), Pip is trying to keep the promises she made to give up the detective work that caused so much pain and destruction, and concentrate on finishing high school. But she and her boyfriend/co-investigator Ravi can't refuse to help when 24-year-old Jamie goes missing, and the police refuse to take it seriously because of his age and past history of disappearing. They post information and ask for help from listeners of Pip's podcast. The tension increases as they gather clues, interview potential suspects, put themselves in dangerous situations, research past crimes, and form hypotheses.

Pip is not perfect. She is filled with rage at the outcome of the trial of Max Hastings, who in the previous book confessed to Pip that he drugged and raped a girl. Pip's recording is not allowed in court; she cannot control her anger over justice being denied. Pip becomes obsessed with her new case; how could she not, with Jamie's life at stake? We armchair detectives can cheer her on and admire her perseverance, determination, and skill. But we can question her judgment and behavior, also. Young readers can ponder and discuss issues related to psychological concepts and ethical principles as they guess whether Jamie is alive, whether he is guilty of crimes, whether he is being held against his will, and why his behavior seemed to change so drastically over the past few weeks. (The Jamie constructed from the evidence does not match the Jamie they know. What does that have to say about identity?) They will probably not have to guess whether Pip will solve the mystery. The uncertainties involve only how she will do it, and what the cost will be.

Khor, S.Y. (2021). *The Legend of Auntie Po*. New York: Kokila.
What role did Chinese immigrants play in the history of logging camps in the United States during the nineteenth century? If your answer, like mine, began with "Umm...," this graphic novel is for you. Teen-aged Mei lives with her father, Hao, who is the chef in a logging camp, and every day she helps him feed one hundred lumberjacks as well as forty other Chinese workers who are not boarders. She bakes wonderful pies, and manages the kitchen. Though she would love to go to a university, she is realistic enough to realize her future will probably entail becoming the head cook when her father can't handle it anymore.

It's 1885, and though the boss, Mr. Anderson, values and appreciates Hao after years of service, and promises to protect him, there comes a point when the company gives orders to not hire Chinese workers; if he disobeys the mandate, there will be a boycott of the mill, or worse. They could shut down the camp, or even burn it. What would you do faced with this ethical dilemma?

Join Mei and her friend (more than a friend?) Bee, the foreman's daughter, as they face challenges, and receive assistance from the unlikely source of Auntie Po, come to life from a tall tale.

In the Author's Note, Shing Yin Kohr explains how difficult the task of researching working-class Chinese in lumber camps was. She acknowledges the scholars whose sources she read, adding:

> Ultimately, where I took liberties with history, I chose to do so because when our histories have been repressed and our people were not deemed worthy enough to document, I feel that we have the obligation to return ourselves to the narrative. If history failed us, fiction will have to restore us.

(p. 286)

Lee, S. (2019). *The Downstairs Girl*. New York: G.P. Putnam's Sons.
1890, Atlanta. What is life like? For 17-year-old Jo Kuan, life is very difficult, for she is Chinese, and there seems to be no place for her. She and Old Gin, the man who raised her, live secretly in the basement of the family that publishes one of the city's newspapers. She has been dismissed from her job in a milliner's shop, though she is skilled. As she negotiates a new job as a personal maid to a girl with whom she grew up (though never as equals), she uncovers secrets about people prominent in society, and solves mysteries about her parentage.

Jo discovers, or rather constructs, another part of her identity when she begins writing letters of advice for the newspaper in the persona of "Miss Sweetie." She tackles subjects ranging from the advantages of girls remaining single to racial tensions. Miss Sweetie makes enemies, for sure, because her ideas are upsetting to those in a class that benefits from the present social arrangement. But her column is also resulting in subscriptions soaring!

Through Jo's eyes, we learn about the Reconstruction era and the beginning of the Jim Crow laws that would make life even worse for persons of color. We meet suffragists and other courageous activists standing up to the many injustices of this time and place. We are inspired.

*Mlodinow, L. (2020). *Stephen Hawking: A Memoir of Friendship and Physics*. New York: Pantheon Books.
It might seem strange that I'm including a book about Stephen Hawking in the category of NA literature. He died in 2018 at the

age of 76, and most people outside the field of physics knew of him only after *A Brief History of Time*, published when he was in his late forties, brought him fame. After that, many followed his life and career at least partly because of his success in not only keeping death at bay despite having ALS, but continuing to work productively, travel, communicate, and nurture relationships while almost completely paralyzed. There are three reasons I consider this combination memoir/biography as NA.

First, Stephen's life as a young man is intriguing and instructive. Mlodinow introduces us to Stephen as the coxswain of his college rowing club, and as a bored student who spent little time on ridiculously easy (for him) academic assignments, who replaced study with listening to classical music and reading science fiction:

> He had no ambition, no goals, no direction. And like most of his fellow students, Stephen drank too much. That was before he went to Cambridge for graduate school, before he got his death sentence, and before he found physics.

(p. 28)

Stephen was diagnosed with the progressive degenerative disease at age 21. Death from ALS usually occurs within five years of diagnosis. Of course, he experienced grief and depression, but readers may be affected by what he was able to tell his co-writer and friend decades later:

> Stephen told me that his illness guided him to something new, too. "We all know we will die. For most, that is an abstract thought. It is not abstract for me," he said. It inspired him to value each of his remaining days.

(p. 41)

My second reason for including the book is as a reminder that NA is not necessarily limited to a certain age range. It's a category focusing on new beginnings, entering new territories. Stephen solved problems that arose as he lost more and more mobility; he rebounded after each near-death episode. He continually grew and welcomed experiences and relationships. When his second marriage ended in divorce in 2006, a sad Stephen "… typed something out on his computer, then smiled as he played it for me in his computer voice. His message was, 'I'm never getting married again'" (p. 189). However, in 2013, Stephen was in love again, and became engaged.

A third reason I'm promoting this book to NA readers is that it is beautifully written and could serve as a mentor text when students experiment with combining their own story with that of another. We get to know Leonard really well as he brings us into his professional collaboration and his deep friendship with Stephen. He is a master of metaphor:

> To those who knew Stephen from afar it could appear that, for him, just to live was to climb Mount Everest. After I got to know him it struck me that he *was* Mount Everest. An immovable giant, immune to the passage of time and able to withstand even the most violent storms nature hurls at it.

(p. 218)

Readers might follow up by reading other books Mlodinow has written, including *A Drunkard's Walk: How Randomness Rules our Lives* (2009, Vintage) and *Elastic: Flexible Thinking in a Time of Change* (2018, Pantheon Books).

Moyes, J. (2019). *The Gift of Stars*. New York: Pamela Dorman Books. Alice marries a man she hardly knows, thinking she has escaped her parents' control and her restricted life in England, only to discover that her new life in rural Kentucky offers even less freedom and stimulation. That is, until she joins other young women delivering books on horseback as part of the WPA packhorse librarian program in the late 1930s. She learns about the lives of coal miners' families, and sees the results of poverty, racism, classism, and gender discrimination. She learns the power of reading, the power of friendship, and the power of love. Readers ride up those mountains with Alice, sharing her adventures, and figuring out with her the solutions to seemingly insurmountable obstacles. How can she get out of the loveless marriage that was never really a marriage? How can she help her friend and lead librarian from being wrongfully convicted of murder? Answers must be found in the Kentucky hills.

There is no better way to learn American history than through the stories of the people who lived it. This story is a gift.

*Murray, J. (2018). *A History of the World in 21 Women*. London: Oneworld Publications.

When my students arrived one day, they found a timeline across the whiteboard running the length of the side wall, with one end labeled "Antiquity," and the other "The Present." I asked them to make a list at their seats of twenty-one women who impacted history, and then to write their names, with approximate dates, on our class timeline to represent the history of the world. Many struggled for a bit, but seeing others' contributions stimulated their own thought. Once they started thinking of categories, such as rulers, artists, authors, scientists, and political activists, their pens began to flow, and our timeline filled out. They were ready to hear about *A History of the World in 21 Women*.

Jenni Murray emphasizes that the women presented in this book are her personal choices; the book is not all-encompassing. But it can be a great start, which can be added to by readers who have chosen other role models or admire different women of the past and present. They will recognize Joan of Arc, Catherine the Great, Marie Curie, Toni Morrison, Hillary Rodham Clinton, and Madonna; their worlds might be broadened after reading chapters on Artemisia Gentileschi, Clara Schumann, Golda Meir, Margaret Atwood, Angela Merkel, and Anna Politkovskaya. The chapters can serve as mentor texts for students who research and then write about famous early or contemporary women. Soon, students will have no trouble filling out a timeline with ten times the twenty-one women they started out with. It will be beautiful.

*Porath, J. (2016). *Rejected Princesses: Tales of History's Boldest Heroines, Hellions & Heretics*. New York: William Morrow.

In the Introduction, Jason Porath assures us that, contrary to what most textbooks would lead us to believe, history does not lack for strong-minded women. He proves it in this collection of biographies of women who were underestimated, undervalued, underappreciated, and/or neglected in the telling of history, but who deserve to be remembered, and who can serve as role models for girls today.

Porath provides an illustration depicting each of the hundred featured females in action, along with art notes explaining his choices for symbols and scenes. I jumped around in the text, reading about scientists, pirates, spies, athletes, mathematicians, warriors, poets, healers, political leaders, and religious leaders.

Many of the stories were inspirational. For example, Annie Jump Cannon was an American astronomer who created a classification system for the stars that is still in use. She worked seven days a week until her death at age 76, noting that her almost total deafness gave her the relative silence that allowed her to concentrate fully. Her words on the eve of WW II might resonate with readers today. "In these days of great trouble and unrest, it is good to have something outside our own planet, something fine and distant and comforting to troubled minds. Let people look to the stars for comfort" (p. 42).

There is further information about the women in these biographies, as well as new entries about more amazing women on the companion website (Porath). There truly is no end to what we can learn and enjoy.

O'Neal, K. (2021). *Lycanthropy and other Chronic Illnesses*. Philadelphia: Quirk Books.

Sometimes, we need a bit of fun or fantasy added to our reading diets. This novel provides both, despite dealing with the heavy but important topic of illnesses and disabilities that can keep New Adults from being successful and reaching their goals. Priya was a pre-med student at Stanford, but several months after being bit by a tick and contracting Lyme disease, she is now back in New Jersey, in constant pain and depending on her family to care for her physical needs. Her dream of being a doctor now seems unobtainable, and she is not at all happy with her new identity. Fortunately, she joins on online support group, and her new friends, fighting their own battles with conditions including cerebral palsy, endometriosis, digestive issues, and depression, offer support and encouragement. They understand her; they listen without judgment, accepting her as she is. Gradually, she lessens the pressure she has always put on herself, realizing, "Maybe it's okay to just focus on being a person. Maybe that's enough" (p. 159).

Priya offers support to others, too, especially Brigid, whose undiagnosed condition causes her to turn into a werewolf once a month. (Didn't I promise fun and fantasy? As if this isn't enough, there's a cute animal control guy who joins their team, too.) As she searches for answers that could help Brigid, Priya discovers she loves the research aspect of medicine; and when her father gives her resources about doctors who have illnesses themselves, she sees potential career paths opening up, giving her hope.

This novel does not downplay the struggles associated with having a chronic illness, but it does show characters who refuse to let those illnesses define them or defeat them.

*Rembert, W., as told to Erin. I. Kelly. (2021). *Chasing me to my Grave: An Artist's Memoir of the Jim Crow South*. New York: Bloomsbury.

Winfred Rembert's memoir shows a person with many identities: abused child, prisoner on a chain gang, drug dealer, father, artist, and storyteller. A Black person in rural Georgia who told himself at about age 14, *"I'm in a prejudiced world and I really don't have no one to talk to about it. I just got to figure out my next step, on my own, in a White world"* (p. 265).

One of the heroes of this story is Patsy, the girl he met while working in the fields as a prisoner. He asked her for a glass of water. She waited for him to be released, and their relationship grew through letters. They married and had eight children. When Winfred was serving a sentence after being convicted of drug dealing, Patsy pleaded with a judge to let him out, and the judge listened. Patsy convinced Rembert that he had talent, and could tell his story through painting on tooled leather.

The book is filled with photos of those story paintings. Some, like the ones showing lynchings, made the artist physically sick as he cut the leather and applied the paint. Some are joyful, such as the ones showing Patsy and him together. The art is filled with motion: the scenes at a pool hall, and dancing in a church, and prisoners shoveling or picking cotton. The words and pictures in this book tell a story of one man's exterior and interior life, as well as a history of the rural South in the Jim Crow era.

We are lucky to have this book. Winfred died before his memoir was published. In a Collaborator's Note, Erin I. Kelly explains that she interviewed Winfred when she was working on a book focusing on the philosophy of criminal justice in 2015. They met regularly from 2018 to 2020 so that he could tell his story to her through interviews. In the Preface, Winfred explains that he had wanted to tell his story for a long time, but was afraid:

> I was worried about whether people would believe me or care and whether the real people I name might in some way or other retaliate. I wasn't sure how to talk about my search for my mother's

love or the bond I feel with Patsy. But my time in this world is up, so there is no better time. This may be the perfect time.

(p. xvi)

Now is indeed a perfect time for readers to appreciate the gift Winfred left us.

Sabic-El-Rayess, A., with Sullivan, L.L. ((2020). *The Cat I Never Named: A True Story of Love, War, and Survival*. New York: Bloomsbury.

Amra loved learning, and she loved school. Her accomplishments and high test scores did her no good, however, once war came to Bosnia in the early nineties. People became too busy trying to survive to keep schools going, and it wasn't safe to go anywhere. How could it be that people who were her friends and neighbors were now her enemies, wanting her family and all other Muslims dead? Readers become witnesses to many hardships and dangers Amra's family faces, including gunfire, severe food shortages, bombings, the threat of being captured and sent to rape camps, grieving for fallen friends, and loss of freedom. They had to flee their home; Amra's father was sent to the front to dig ditches and do other heavy labor, despite his worsening diabetes. Her mother loses her hearing, and almost her life, as the result of a bomb hitting their home.

Amra goes from the serious student with aspirations for higher education to someone who can say to us that she doesn't know if she believes in miracles anymore. When the citizens of her town of Bihać manage to drive back a Serb offensive in 1993, she proclaims:

> I know that means they are just going to regroup and come back harder, but every day above the ground is a good one. Every day brings hope that the world will finally see and put a stop to this.

(p. 185)

Hope and help come in the form of a stray cat that follows Amra home, becomes part of the family, and repeatedly causes family members to have to make decisions that end up saving them from harm. When Amra's father has to take the cat away to save his store from being closed down, she finds her way back against all odds. The cat becomes a main character in the author's memoir, and a crucial part of the plot and resolution.

Without giving away too much of the ending, I'd like to share a quote that could give present-day readers much to think about in terms of our immigration history, as well as serve as encouragement and a call to action for creating just policies for the near future, as more people are forced by war to seek asylum. Twenty-year-old Amra has just landed in Philadelphia to pursue a college education with the help of a scholarship that finally came through. The customs agent stares at her Bosnian passport, stares at the gaunt, frightened woman, and finally stamps the passport ADMITTED, saying to Amra, "I'm sorry for what's happened to your country. You're safe now, ma'am. Welcome to the United States of America" (p. 336).

*Sidman, J. (2018). *The Girl who Drew Butterflies: How Maria Merian's Art Changed Science*. Boston, MA: Houghton Mifflin Harcourt.
We learn very early in our education about the life cycle of the butterfly. We know what a caterpillar turns into. But in the seventeenth century, when Maria Merian was observing this phenomenon as a curious child firsthand, it was not generally known. Butterflies were known as "summer birds," thought to emerge from under the earth. And females who showed intense interest in creeping things could be hanged as witches.

This biography chronicles the life of an extraordinary scientist and artist. She learned engraving, drawing, and painting from her father, and she collected and studied bugs, recording her findings. But women were considered adults at age fourteen back then, and females were not allowed to pursue academic studies or have any measure of independence. For Maria, there was marriage, and more constrictions.

End of story? Absolutely not. Readers will be spellbound as they learn of Maria's accomplishments as a scientist and author; of her escape (with her daughters) from her husband; of her travels to Surinam to study different species; of her continued work until her death at age 69 (when the life expectancy of the time was around 40).

In addition to photographs of Maria's stunning paintings, Sidman begins each chapter with a poem, and includes excerpts from Maria's journals. "Patience is a beneficial little herb" (p. 110). There is much to appreciate in this exquisitely told story of the woman whom many call the world's first ecologist.

*Sorell, T. (2021). *Classified: The Secret Career of Mary Golda Ross, Cherokee Aerospace Engineer*. Illus. Donovan, Natasha. Minneapolis, MN: Millbrook Press.

How hard would it be for you to keep your job a secret from your family and friends? How difficult would it be for you to go through an educational program where the other students exclude you, treat you as invisible, or mock you? What if the mission of your work team was to take the theoretical and make it real? These were all challenges that Mary Golda Ross faced. How did she succeed? "Do the best you can and search out available knowledge and build on it. I started with a firm foundation in mathematics and qualities that came down to me from my Indian heritage," she said at the age of 99 (unpaged).

This picture book shows us Mary hard at work in school, despite the gender discrimination she faced in a program dominated by men. We see her as a teacher, and then as a mathematician for the Lockheed Aircraft Corporation. As she designed spacecraft as an engineer, the men on her team respected her ability to collaborate as well as her problem-solving abilities and intellect. It was when she joined the Skunk Works division that her work became top secret. But she managed to recruit women and American Indians into the fields of math and science.

Readers are sure to be impressed as they read, "… Mary worked on projects that people had only imagined and some no one had ever thought of before" (unpaged). As they look at the illustrations showing math problems, and tools for designing plans, they may be inspired to consider a STEM career. In a way, that would mean that Mary Golda Ross, even though she died in 2008, is still recruiting!

Instructional Strategies and Activities

Follow the Author's Research Path

High school students need to understand the research process, and many teachers model and expect students to do their own academic research and write what has come to be known as *the dreaded research paper*. This looks different in social studies, English, and science classes, of course, but students often find the endeavor overwhelming, as they search for primary and secondary sources and try to curate, evaluate, and analyze the sometimes huge amounts of data to find meaning and come to conclusions. But they don't have to start from scratch. Bober (2021) suggests having students tag along as they read historically based literature resulting from an author's research.

> Unlike independent research, following the author's path is meant to illuminate the path the writer took in the creation of their story. The process of students searching for and investigating resources can elevate that role as part of the writing process leading to a better understanding of the text and potentially impact their own future writing.
>
> (unpaged)

Doesn't it make sense to take advantage of the months and years of legwork authors have already done for us? And their enthusiasm for research will squelch any mutterings from students who up to this point have considered research boring. Watch and listen to Deborah Heiligman and Karen Blumenthal as they present highlights of their research on MacKids Streaming Schoolhouse (MacKids) and you will catch the love.

Walk-Through

Mr. Patel challenges his history class to explore documents that will immerse them in the time of the Civil Rights Movement. He provides guides to help them: the authors of award-winning books set during that era that are based on extensive research and contain primary and secondary sources within the book and in resources related to the book, such as author interviews or YouTube clips. He uses Kekla Magoon's *Revolution in our Time: The Black Panther Party's Promise to the People* (2021) as he introduces the process of tagging along with an author on their research journey. He projects some pages of the book on a screen, showing photographs of people, posters, newspaper articles, flyers, quotes, the Black Panther Party Book List, and drawings. He muses, "I wonder how she found all this?" and then reads from a post on Kekla's website just before her book was launched. "The Panthers' story is incredibly powerful, but has often been misunderstood or deliberately misrepresented. Digging for the truth has been fascinating. The research process took me all around the country!"

Mr. Patel then takes students to the web page dedicated to the book (Magoon). The class listens to relevant songs from the playlist Kekla has curated to get the feel of the passion of the movement. Students are then ready to explore the many resources listed on the website, and to read the book itself. They will be awed by the more than thirty pages of Source Notes, as well as by the narrative Kekla has written. They will want to look for interviews so they can hear even more of her thinking; they'll be interested in reviews of the book and awards it received.

And they are now prepared and eager to follow some other authors' research paths. As they use their new skills to investigate other books about the Civil Rights Movement, they'll see some of the same photos and documents, as well as new ones. They'll understand that authors make choices as they use various lenses to tell the stories of history.

But it doesn't end there. Students can follow the research processes of authors/mentors in their other subjects. Their science classroom library is filled with books from the Scientists in the Field series by Houghton Mifflin Harcourt, so they can tag along with authors as *they* tag along with contemporary scientists doing research in particular areas. There are also recently published biographies of scientists who lived in the past. The librarian, Ms. Castrovilla, is excited to show the science class her new acquisition, *Dragon Bones: The Fantastic Fossil Discoveries of Mary Anning* (Marsh, 2021). Students can follow the research processes of both the nineteenth century scientist and the author, Sara Glen Marsh. They'll study the detailed, complex illustrations of Maris Wicks, and learn "How to Be a Paleontologist" in the back matter.

Meanwhile, Mr. Hrab's ELA class is in the middle of reading Laura Amy Schlitz's *Amber and Clay* (2021), which takes place in ancient Athens. Once again, the librarian is there! Ms. Castrovilla shares information from a Q and A session about the author's research and writing. Schlitz explains:

> I didn't know much when I started this book. I had to dig in. After a year or two, I had to buy a new bookcase to accommodate all the Greek books I bought. I drew maps, made lists, filled notebooks and tried to make clay pots. I went to museums and stared at things for long periods of time. I went to Greece. I tried to learn the language....
>
> (Piehl, 2021)

She uses illustrated images of historical artifacts and museum placards as part of the narrative.

> As I was writing the story, I wanted to be able to drag children to a museum and say, 'See? That's what I'm talking about!' I wanted the

reader to feel a little bit like an archaeologist, to have to search for the story behind each artifact.

(Piehl, 2021)

Using Picture Book Biographies as Mentor Texts

Many students, and even some teachers, consider picture books to be appropriate only for children, and therefore think that they have aged out of that genre. Not so! In recent years, there has been a proliferation of sophisticated picture books that have appeal for all ages. After reading one of these, ask students if they have learned anything. If the answer is yes, that is evidence that the genre should not be perceived as beneath them.

Provide an opportunity for students to read several picture book biographies that *could* be read by children but that can provide knowledge and enjoyment for older readers as well. A school librarian might be able to visit a class with a cart filled with possibilities. Or a teacher can spread books out and have students do a gallery walk or just peruse the displays and pick up biographies about people who interest them. Ask them to pay attention to the artwork, and to jot down thoughts and feelings as they read. Perhaps an art teacher can give some book talks, pointing out artistic decisions, styles of illustration, the significance of color schemes, etc. This could easily be a collaborative, interdisciplinary project.

Students can then research a person in the discipline they are studying, or a hero or anti-hero of theirs, and create a picture book that could be read by children but also could stimulate thoughts and emotions from teenagers and New Adults. Below is a text set with examples of picture book biographies that are appropriate for readers in the NA age range. Students can talk with each other as they peruse the books, perhaps beginning to brainstorm ideas for their own books. You can have students share drafts in a writing workshop setting, and revise based on feedback from peers and teacher.

Walk-Through

Ms. Méndez's high school classroom has a bookstore look about it. Intriguing picture books are on display in multiple spaces, and she changes the arrangements regularly depending upon her curricular objectives and pedagogical purposes. Here is an example of a writing project her students are involved in.

Directions: After looking at several picture book biographies from the text set I have compiled (see below), choose someone you have been studying, or someone whose life you would like to investigate. Compile facts and anecdotes from several resources, then decide the stance you will take, and craft your text. State your facts succinctly, so that there is not too much text on any page. Use citations when necessary. You can illustrate each page, or use non-copyrighted pictures from the Internet. Add an Author's Note if you wish. Plan on 10–20 pages. Design a cover page. When this activity is finished, we will have our own classroom library of volumes we will arrange alphabetically by the last name of our subjects.

TEXT SET

Exemplary Picture Book Biographies and Informational Books for a NA Audience

Amescua, G. (2021). *Child of the Flower-Song People: Luz Jiménez, Daughter of the Nahua*. Illus. Tonatiuh, D. New York: Abrams.

Azúa Kramer, J. (2021). *Dorothy and Herbert: An Ordinary Couple and their Extraordinary Collection of Art*. Petaluma, CA: Cameron Kids.

Becker, H. (2020). *Emmy Noether: The Most Important Mathematician You've Never Heard of*. Toronto: Kids Can Press.

Dunbar, E.H. (2017). *Never Caught: The Washingtons' Relentless Pursuit of their Runaway Slave, Ona Judge*. New York: 37 Ink/Atria.

Gilberti, F. (2021). *Banksy: Graffitied Walls and Wasn't Sorry*. New York: Phaidon.

Heiligman, D. (2013). *The Boy Who Loved Math: The Improbable Life of Paul Erdös*. New York: Roaring Brook Press.

Sis, P. (2021). *Nicky and Vera: A Quiet Hero of the Holocaust and the Children He Rescued*. New York: Norton Young Readers.

Steptoe, J. (2016). *Radiant Child: The Story of Young Artist Jean-Michel Basquiat*. New York: Little, Brown and Company.

Todd, T.N. (2021). *Nina: A Story of Nina Simone*. New York: G.P. Putnam's Sons.

Westergaard, A. (2021). *A Life Electric: The Story of Nikola Tesla*. New York: Viking.

Winter, J. (2019). *Our House Is on Fire: Greta Thunberg's Call to Save the Planet*. New York: Beach Lane Books.

Enhancing the Reading Experience through Peritextual Analysis

Pick up a nonfiction book you have near you, or think of a couple you have read. What do you think of the cover? Is it appealing? Does it give any clues about the main text? What do you think of the title? Does the title or the author's name have larger font? What might this tell you?

Do you like to read the blurbs on the back covers, and/or the text on the front and back flaps? Do you pay attention to the endpapers inside the book cover? Do you read the Table of Contents whenever one is provided? What about things like the preface, foreword, and introduction? How about the back matter, perhaps consisting of an Author's Note, a glossary, a timeline, source notes, a bibliography for further reading, and an index?

All of the above questions have to do with the *peritext* of a book, consisting of anything within the book surrounding the text proper. Witte, Latham, and Gross created a Peritextual Literacy Framework that can be used as a teaching and critical thinking tool. The authors note that readers often skip most of the peritextual elements, and thereby haven't gotten the full advantage of all the additional layers of meaning that surround the text within the book. The chapters of their edited book, *Literacy Engagement through Peritextual Analysis* (2018), give examples of ways teachers and librarians have implemented strategies that help readers examine and critique aspects of the peritext of a book or of media, such as a movie, as well as to navigate complex text and gain a rich appreciation of the whole work. Engaging with the peritext of the NA literature featured throughout the chapters of this book could result in readers who notice significant details, such as symbols and colors worked into the cover image; ask critical questions about the decisions of authors and publishers; construct meaning and synthesize print and visual features; and become more knowledgeable about authors' research and collaborative processes. Such engagement may make readers eager to then go beyond the text to explore a book's *epitext*, which you may recall is discussed in Chapter 2 of this book.

Walk-Through

I'll model a think-aloud as I examine Amra Sabic-El-Rayness's *The Cat I Never Named* (booktalked above) with my NA Literature class. After they see and hear me model this, they will take a book they have chosen for our nonfiction exploration and engage with their book's peritext.

> I'm looking carefully at the cover. In the foreground is an artist's rendering of an adolescent girl with bright red curls, carrying a calico cat over her shoulder. The background is much less colorful, and shows rubble, including the fallen minaret of a mosque. The subtitle lets me know it's a true story, and the title makes me wonder why the author never named the cat (*her* cat?) and why that fact is significant enough to put in the title. The back cover continues the illustration, featuring mostly sky and smoke (I assume from bombs). There are quotes from two starred reviews of the book. Promising!
>
> The front flap gives a book talk of sorts, letting me know enough that I think I will find the story of this girl and the cat that got separated from refugees entering the city in 1992 interesting. The back flap gives information about the author (including that she has LOTS of education from prestigious U.S. universities, further assuring me that she survived the war and even thrived afterward). Two websites are provided in case I want to learn more about her. I won't go to them right now, because I am exploring *peritext*, not *epitext*, at the moment, so have to stay within the confines of the book itself.
>
> On to the pages themselves. After an illustrated title page, there are four lines that read like a poem, comparing the war's approach to that of a cat. The Table of Contents is helpful because it has dates. I know the author will age about six years during the span of this book, from 1992 to 1998. Next, there is a map of Bosnia and Herzegovina, with two cities marked, and the surrounding countries identified. Good, I needed that.
>
> After another couple of pages with the title (again) and illustrations, Chapter 1 begins; we are no longer in the peritext. I flip to find where the peritext picks up again. The Epilogue ends on page 367, so I turn to find Acknowledgements. Ah, peritext! Amra weaves her thank-yous through a narrative that gives me information about her now—she has two daughters, one of whom had to react to a friend who told her all Muslims were terrorists, and one who asked, "Mom, what will happen to children like me if Muslims are rounded up in America?" (p. 358).
>
> Her children gave her a purpose for going through the emotional turmoil of recalling her war years. We find out what has happened

to Amra's father, mother, and brother since the war. She thanks the unsung heroes who sacrificed their lives for the freedom of Bosnia, and she acknowledges the love others have given her, for, "To overcome hatred and trauma, love is a prerequisite" (p. 358).

There's more! The author provides a page of information about Bosnia and Herzegovina today, followed by a page about her writing of the book (promising more stories of the beloved cat someday). In "A Note from the Author," Amra stresses the importance of education (which certainly reinforces what the main text has shown us), and confronts Islamophobia and the prevalent stereotype of Muslims as terrorists. She connects what she experiences with the Black Lives Matter movement and the #MeToo movement. She talks directly to her readers.

Finally, there is a list of resources for further reading, and a list of movies about the Bosnian War. The peritext offers a way to continue our exploration. And the story has given me that desire.

References

Bober, T. (2021). Pairing children's literature and primary sources. Retrieved from https://www.slj.com/?detailStory=pairing-childrens-literature-and-primary-sources.

Kane, S. (2020). *Integrating literature in the disciplines: Enhancing adolescent learning and literacy*. New York: Routledge.

Kane, S. (2019). *Librarians, teachers, and school leaders can promote YA literature in all disciplines*. Retrieved from http://www.yawednesday.com/weekly-posts/librarians-teachers-and-school-leaders-can-promote-ya-literature-in-all-disciplines-by-sharon-kane.

MacKids Streaming Schoolhouse. (2020). Social studies class with Deborah Heiligman and Karen Blumenthal. Retrieved from https://www.youtube.com/watch?v=oWT7xB1i5Y8.

Magoon, K. (website) https://revolutioninourtime.com/.

Piehl, N. (2021). *Laura Amy Schlitz*. Retrieved from https://www.bookpage.com/interviews/25992-laura-amy-schlitz-childrens/.

Porath, J. Rejected Princesses. https://www.RejectedPrincesses.com.

*Rembert, W., as told to Kelly, E.I. (2021). *Chasing me to my grave: An artist's memoir of the Jim Crow South*. New York: Bloomsbury.

Witte, S., Latham, D., & Gross, M. (2018). *Literacy engagement through peritextual analysis*. Chicago, IL: ALA Editions.

Literature Cited

Hawking, S. (1998). *A brief history of time*. New York: Bantam Books.

Juster, N. (1996). *The phantom tollbooth*. Illus. J. Feiffer. New York: Random House.

Magoon, K. (2021). *Revolution in our time: The Black Panther Party's promise to the people*. Somerville, MA: Candlewick Press.

Marsh, S.G. (2021). *Dragon bones: The fantastic fossil discoveries of Mary Anning*. Illus Wicks, M. New York: Roaring Brook.

Mlodinow, L. (2018). *Elastic: Flexible thinking in a time of change*. New York: Pantheon Books.

Mlodinow, L. (2009). *A Drunkard's walk: How randomness rules our lives*. New York: Vintage.

Sabic-El-Rayess, A., with Sullivan, L.L. ((2020). *The cat I never named: A true story of love, war, and survival*. New York: Bloomsbury.

Schlitz, L.A. (2021). *Amber & Clay*. Somerville, MA: Candlewick Press.

Best Foot Forward   **8**

Stepping into New Stages with Care and Delight

What's Next?

If you have read the chapters leading up to this one and explored some of the books introduced through book talks or recommended in the text sets, you are on your way to becoming an expert on the category of New Adult (NA) literature. Perhaps you have gotten some books in the hands of other readers as well. Now it is time to bring this book to a close. That's a difficult thing for me to do, since there are so many other quality NA books available. And new titles appear in the bookstores every week. It's my hope that NA becomes as vibrant and well-known as the categories of Middle-Grade literature and Young Adult literature. People in their late teens and early 20s certainly need and deserve to be served by librarians and teachers as much as their younger counterparts.

This chapter is about books that can engage readers as they continue to construct their identities; to love and care for themselves physically and emotionally; to grow intellectually and spiritually; and to seek ways to relate to others and interact lovingly with the world. Ponder this quote from Jane Goodall in *The Book of Hope* (2021) to help set the stage for exploring the ideas that will follow. "I don't believe in fate or destiny. I believe in free choice…. I believe that opportunities arise and you can seize them, reject them—or simply fail to notice them." (p. 209).

DOI: 10.4324/9781003221685-8

TEXT SETS

Self-Care and Wellness

Schools at all levels are giving increased attention to social and emotional aspects of learning (SEL). If students are overly stressed or worried about things happening in school or at home; or if relationships are causing them harm; or if they are struggling with their identity or concerns about their changing bodies, learning will be difficult. Anxiety impedes learning, as does depression, and a number of other conditions. The whole community should be involved in making sure the school atmosphere is safe and positive for everyone. Professionals, including counselors and social workers, are needed. While librarians and teachers can't solve every problem, they can use their resources and their Readers' Advisory skills to get literature relating to SEL issues into students' hands, minds, and hearts. The books discussed in previous chapters feature characters grappling with situations involving empathy, respect for others and self, perspective-taking, relationship skills, building confidence, self-acceptance, anger management, and social awareness. This text set offers titles that could be just what certain New Adults need to help them think about problems and possibilities in their present circumstances or can help prepare them for future stages of their personal quests. Books can provide comfort, advice, encouragement, and healing words. Let's fill our shelves with literature that promotes wellness and self-care. For further resources, look for the wonderful compilation that author A.S. King curated and the Book Love Foundation provides online called "Gracie's List."

An asterisk before a title indicates that you can find a book talk later in the chapter.

*Ashton, J., with Toland, S. (2019). *The Self-Care Solution: A Year of becoming Happier, Healthier, and Fitter—One Month at a Time.* New York: William Morrow.

*Bosh, C. (2021). *Letters to a Young Athlete.* New York: Penguin Press.

Dellitt, J. (2019). *Self-Care for College Students: From Orientation to Graduation, 150+ Ways to Stay Happy, Healthy, and Stress-Free.* Avon, MA: Adams Media.

*Grant, A. (2021). *Think Again: The Power of Knowing What You Don't Know*. New York: Random House.

Gross, E.L. (2020). *What Next?: Your Five-Year Plan for Life After College*. Avon, MA: Adams Media.

*Hugstad, R. (2021). *Be You, Only Better: Real-life Self-care for Young Adults (and Everyone Else)*. Novato, CA: New World Library.

*Man, C. (2021). *Continuum*. New York: Penguin Workshop.

Pollan, M. (2015). *The Omnivore's Dilemma: The Secrets behind what you Eat, Young Readers Edition*. Adapted by Richie Chevat. New York: Dial Books.

Suzuki, W., with Fitzpatrick, B. (2021). *Good Anxiety: Harnessing the Power of the Most Misunderstood Emotion*. New York: Simon & Schuster.

*Whitney, D. (Ed.). (2021). *You Don't Have to Be Everything: Poems for Girls Becoming Themselves*. Illus. González, C., Mockford, K., & Singleton, S. New York: Workman Publishing.

Spirituality and Philosophy

New Adults ponder large questions. What is the meaning of life? What is my purpose? How can I live a good life? Again, books provide tools for questioning, words of solace and wisdom, frameworks for making decisions, and ideas from various worldviews. The answers to the big questions will differ from person to person, just as the ways individuals develop their identities depend on their values, circumstances, desires, and interests. Temple Grandin, in Sy Montgomery's (2012), *Temple Grandin: How the Girl who Loved Cows Embraced Autism and Changed the World* (2012), gives us her answer:

> When I get to do something to improve treatment of animals, when I get to help a mother with her autistic kid, when I help one of my students get a good career…Well, that's the meaning of life for me. It's that simple.
>
> (p. 129)

This text set offers a sampling of books that deal with philosophical, religious, and spiritual perspectives, so that readers can continue to search for and construct their own answers. An asterisk indicates that there will be a book talk in the next section for that title.

Brundage, V., Jr. (2018). *Shoot your Shot: A Sport-Inspired Guide to Living your Best Life.* Independently published.

Dominguez, M. (2020). *Inklings on Philosophy and Worldview.* Columbus, OH: Wander.

*Feder, T. (2020). *Dancing at the Pity Party: A Dead Mom Graphic Memoir.* New York: Dial Books.

*Garcia, H., & Miralles, F. (2021). *Ikigai for Teens: Finding your Reason for Being.* New York: Scholastic.

Gay, R. (2019). *The Book of Delights.* Chapel Hill, NC: Algonquin Books of Chapel Hill.

* Goodall, J., & Abrams, D, with Hudson, G. (2021). *The Book of Hope: A Survival Guide for Trying Times.* New York: Celadon Books.

Gorman, A. (2021). *The Hill We Climb: An Inaugural Poem for the Country.* New York: Viking.

*Green, J. (2021). *The Anthropocene Reviewed: Essays on a Human-Centered Planet.* New York: Dutton.

Oliver, M. (2020). *Devotions: The Selected Poems of Mary Oliver.* New York: Penguin Books.

*Paulsen, G. (2021). *Gone to the Woods: Surviving a Lost Childhood.* New York: Farrar Straus Giroux.

Rūmī, J. (2018). *The Book of Rumi: 105 Stories and Fables That Illumine, Delight, and Inform.* Translated and edited by Mafi, M. Charlottesville, VA: Hampton Roads Publishing Company.

Stiefvater, M. (2017). *All the Crooked Saints.* New York: Scholastic.

*Sullivan, M., & Blaschko, P. (2021). *The Good Life Method: Reasoning through the Big Questions of Happiness, Faith, and Meaning.* New York: Penguin Press.

Thich Nhat Hanh. (2012). *You Are Here: Discovering the Magic of the Present Moment.* Boulder, CO: Shambhala Library.

West, P. (2020). *Just Think: Philosophy Puzzles for Children Aged 9 to 90.* Woking, Surrey, UK: Nielsen UK.

Book Talks: Ready to Go!

*Ashton, J., with Toland, S. (2019). *The Self-Care Solution: A Year of Becoming Happier, Healthier, and Fitter—One Month at a Time.* New York: William Morrow.

In addition to having a medical practice and being a nutritionist and the ABC News Chief Medical Correspondent, the author identifies as a self-improver. She likes collecting and analyzing data, and decided to track a year of monthly challenges she gave herself. The chapters are labeled by the month and structured the same. Dr. Ashton tells her own story relating to each issue, then gives the science explaining the drawbacks of some habits and the benefits of others. Finally, she gives tips for the reader who wants to take on the challenge. One could actually speed read through all the headings, subheadings, and topic sentences, and walk away with a lot of good information, though without the enjoyment of the anecdotes and details.

In January, Ashton gave up alcohol. In February, she concentrated on two specific exercises: planks and push-ups. March's focus was on meditation, and April's on cardio fitness exercises. In May, she changed her diet to include less meat and more plants, followed by concentrating on hydration in June. In July, she focused on increasing her walking; the August chapter deals with mindful use of technology. In September, she cut down on sugar, in October she did more stretching, and November was devoted to getting more sleep. The December goal was to add laughter and fun to her usually serious life. There you have it!

The book makes the challenges seem doable, since they have an endpoint. Ashton found that she carried the good habits into the following months, even if not with the same intensity or level of commitment. One of the valuable lessons she learned came from her failure during September; she craved sweets and broke her promise to herself more times than she should have. She realized how powerful sugar addictions and cravings can be, and developed more empathy for her patients.

Overall, the author achieved a new level of health and well-being. She wishes the same for her readers, exhorting us to strive for wellness and to find joy around us and within us.

Writing and Thinking Prompt

Come up with an outline or table of contents for a book you could write after following Jennifer Ashton's program of completing monthly self-imposed challenges for one year. You could start with whatever month follows the one you are living through at present.

You can take the challenges she provides, though you don't have to go in order. If you want to start easy and think you could handle the hydration challenge, begin there. You can eliminate any of the topics you don't need, and replace them with different challenges, such as spending more time outdoors, appreciating nature. (I am currently participating in a virtual challenge called the Circumpolar Race around the World, so I do not need to add any steps to my days. I've got that covered.) Best wishes on following through! Consider writing to the author to let her know how you are applying her advice, and to share a story or two of your own.

*Bosh, C. (2021). *Letters to a Young Athlete*. New York: Penguin Press.
Don't let the title narrow the audience to whom you recommend this book. The advice Chris Bosh offers applies to anyone who wants to excel in an area they are passionate about, whether that be sports, art, academics, creative writing, or another endeavor that will require dedication, commitment, and hard work. He tells his own story, explaining how he became the great professional basketball player he was. And then how his career was gone in an instant when his doctors told him he could never play again, due to a medical condition involving potentially fatal blood clots. There is not a bit of self-pity expressed as the story unfolds, though Bosh does discuss how difficult that news was to hear and bear.

Bosh talks directly to his readers, establishing a relationship with them early on.

> You see, you're at a crossroads in your life. You have two paths ahead of you, and you can only take one. I want to make sure you take the right one, the one that helps you get the most out of yourself, out of this game—whatever that game is for you.
>
> (p. 5)

Bosh provides chapters on key aspects of achieving success, including hard work and persistence, teamwork, finding purpose, dealing with criticism, communication, and leadership. He devotes a chapter to cultivating the mind. He advocates reading, thinking, and being open to all kinds of learning. Another chapter deals with the care of one's body, and includes tips on nutrition, sleep, exercise, and listening to bodily cues.

As Bosh makes each point, he gives anecdotes from his own life or that of his former basketball teammates, or athletes in other sports. We learn of LeBron James's habits of stretching, meditation, self-care, ice baths, nutritional decisions, and reading to keep up with the science of taking care of the body. Bosh explains those things are the reasons LeBron's career has been durable and exceptional. He works tirelessly to remain in prime condition.

Bosh wants readers to think about not just the sport or other activity they love, but about the meaning and purpose of life. Recognizing all that basketball taught him and the lasting riches that are now a part of him, even though he's off the court, he shares the big picture of his own life, which includes his five children, as he encourages readers to envision their futures:

> And I look forward to thinking about what's next for myself—because the way I see it, basketball was just the first quarter of my life. Now I'm on a mission to find the new things that will bring out my best and keep teaching me in the way the game did.
>
> (p. 216)

Writing and Thinking Prompts

Choose one of the following prompts, or combine them, and write for a few moments in response to them and the text.

A. Since Chris Bosh wrote a letter to you, write back to him, noting the advice that you needed to hear the most or that feels new or valuable to you. Outline a plan that will show him some of the little or big changes you intend to make as a result of his suggestions, stories, and mentoring. (You can write again at a later point to talk about how you have followed through, or faced challenges.)

B. Bosh is upfront early on about this text not being about drills or skills development to make you a better athlete. His letters focus on the bigger issues, such as what you will do with the talent you have been given. He tells his own story, complete with heartbreak and pain, so that his words do not come across as preachy, so that his is not just another voice telling you what you should do without the credibility that comes from being there. Perhaps you have been very focused on your performance in one sport, or on one team, or your academic achievements or aspirations to pursue a certain career. Now broaden your lens, and think about balance. How will being open to new experiences beyond your narrow goal enrich your life? If you wish, bring yourself into a future where the sport or other activity is no longer the center of your life. The world is large; embrace it as you write to explore or make a commitment to contribute to it in new ways.

DiCamillo, K. (2021). *The Beatryce Prophecy*. Illus. Blackall, S. Somerville, MA: Candlewick Press.

Once in a while, a children's book comes out that has something of significance to say to all ages. I believe *The Beatryce Prophecy* is a book that could appeal to the NA population, as it provides an adventure while simultaneously dealing with themes of identity, integrity, love, courage, and justice.

Young Beatryce is found by a monk on the grounds of the monastery of the Brothers of the Order of the Chronicles of Sorrowing. She remembers only her name. When Brother Edik discovers that Beatryce can read and write, he knows she is in danger; he cuts her hair and disguises her as a monk for her protection. But the other monks are afraid to have her stay, knowing there is a prophecy that a young girl will unseat a king, and that the king is searching for her. Beatryce finds herself on a journey to be a scribe to a dying man who needs his sins written down. She's joined by Jack Dory, a young boy whose parents have been killed; Brother Edik, who follows despite his superior's orders to the contrary; and Answelica, a contentious goat whose soft ears provide comfort to Beatryce.

Readers will rightfully be afraid when Beatryce, having recovered memories of her brothers being killed and her own life threatened, decides that, rather than flee or hide, she will go to the king and confront him. Will she be able to keep her promise to teach Jack Dory how to read, or her promise to write a story about a seahorse for Brother Edik? Will she ever find her mother? What will Beatryce say to the king when they are together in the dungeon? Readers will find resolutions in "Book the Last." Beatryce finds her purpose, and perhaps readers will also as they stand on a cliff looking out at the sea with Beatryce and Jack Dory.

DK. (2021). *How to be a Global Citizen*. New York: DK Publishing.
Many New Adults may have heard numerous calls to be a global citizen, but do not have a good understanding of what that looks like in action. This book gives a definition early on:

> Global citizenship goes beyond national borders to unite people as members of humanity. Global citizens are aware of what's happening in the world, they care for each other, and they understand that today we are all more interconnected than ever before. They have an appreciation for different ways of life and respect for diversity.... The idea of global citizenship can encourage people to take action locally, nationally, and globally to build a more tolerant, diverse, sustainable, and peaceful world for everyone.
>
> (p. 18)

The middle chapters are filled with text and visuals exemplifying that definition with concrete information on society, politics, the environment, our digital lives, and other topics. Sections are sometimes labeled with a question: What is culture? Is everyone equal? What is ableism? What is marginalization? Why do we pay taxes? Specific young change-makers are championed; and case studies provide concrete examples of personal and collective agency. Dozens of ways we can protect nature, animals, and the land are offered, accompanied by photos.

Chapter 6, "Calling All Global Citizens," presents suggestions for readers without overwhelming them by implying they have to take on every problem discussed in the book. The first step is for individuals to find their cause, reflecting on what they care about: animal welfare? Helping the homeless? Climate action? Combatting discrimination? Human rights? Digital safety? Other? The next step involves planning and preparing, followed by taking action. Readers are assured that each choice counts, whether that involves visiting people with dementia; initiating or joining hashtag campaigns; boycotting companies whose policies are discriminatory or harmful to the environment; volunteering for local or global preservation projects; or another cause that ignites the reader's passion. "... even small differences can lift community spirit and change lives. Working together, we can all make the world more fair and sustainable for everyone" (p. 143). Let's begin.

*Feder, T. (2020). *Dancing at the Pity Party: A Dead Mom Graphic Memoir*. New York: Dial Books.

Tyler was a college freshman when her mother Rhonda was diagnosed with ovarian cancer, and a sophomore when her mother died. Through drawings, photographs, and words, she captures her own fluctuating emotions as she helps us feel like we know Rhonda. Tyler offers childhood memories and lists of things her mother loved; dialog that occurred in the hospital; and her grief during the months and years after the death. She teaches about Jewish mourning and burial traditions. She talks about how awkward her social interactions were after the loss of her mother and offers charts with examples of helpful things people can say to someone who has lost a loved one, as well as comments that should be avoided.

It's clear that Tyler's life was in upheaval, and that the process of grieving was not linear or simple. Some of the panels are cute and humorous, but at the same time, she doesn't try to hide the pervasive sadness. She shares things she does to keep the memory of her mother alive and to come to an acceptance that she will be motherless forever. There's a series of panels showing Tyler visiting her mother's grave, placing a pebble on her headstone ("Jews use rocks instead of flowers," p. 185), and lying on the grass. "If I close my eyes, I can picture that she's lying there next to me" (p. 186). She ponders the spiritual implications of death, explaining that she doesn't know where her mom is now. Playing Scrabble in the sky? Haunting her old favorite places? Reincarnated as a bird? Energy reabsorbed into the earth, making other living things more beautiful?

Ultimately, this is a comforting and reassuring book. What happened was a horrible thing. Yet Tyler is still dancing.

*Garcia, H., & Miralles, F. (2021). *Ikigai for Teens: Finding Your Reason for Being*. New York: Scholastic.

Finding the mission that will give one's life meaning sounds pretty serious, and it is. Yet completing the exercises in this interactive guide to choosing a path that will combine what you love, what you are good at, what the world needs, and what can be financially rewarding could be fun, and even lead to some laughter. Imagine a classroom of students sharing some of the things they put down on their "WHAT AM I NOT GOING TO DO WITH MY LIFE?" list

(p. 27), intended to help narrow the options. Similar prompts about what will not happen in a text can help writers get unblocked.

The authors offer practical suggestions for taking beginning steps once readers have determined what they want to be. Aspiring scientists can read articles; journalists might publish in a local paper or start a blog; singers can join music groups and take part in competitions; chefs can invite friends over for tastings and feedback. If someone thinks that a job has to be drudgery, this book assures them that they can work on things they love, an activity that leads to a flow state that is not tiresome.

Every chapter is filled with practical tips. Note the difference between the phrase *good luck*, which is a typical way we wish others well, and the Japanese encouragement "Ganbarimasu," which translates to "Do the best you can!" (p. 76). The latter phrase refers to something within our control. There are questions to help determine things you love to do, and seven rules to follow if you want to live happily for one hundred years. There's a template for a letter readers can write to themselves fifty years down the road, thanking that person for specific things that contributed to the wellbeing of the world.

Who could ask for anything more?

*Goodall, J., & Abrams, D, with Hudson, G. (2021). *The Book of Hope: A Survival Guide for Trying Times*. New York: Celadon Books.

You are invited to a conversation between renowned naturalist Jane Goodall and author Douglas Abrams. They started the conversation in person in Tanzania, and were scheduled to finish it in Jane's home; due to the pandemic, they ended up talking remotely. After an introductory section defining and discussing the concept of hope, the chapters in the following part are titled using Jane's reasons for hope in our times, which include the human intellect, nature's resilience, the power of young people, and the human spirit, believed by Jane to be indomitable. The third section details Jane's journey from being a shy young woman to a global public speaker and messenger of hope for the world and concludes with a message of hope from Jane to readers.

Doug probes Jane about her spiritual beliefs, and she recounts incidents in her life and those of others that convince her that there are no coincidences, that her life has been a mission that began as an invitation, and that she had been given certain gifts to follow the path that has been mapped out for her. She references other great scientists as she explains how she reconciles her spiritual orientation with her scientific mind, confiding that "… she truly welcomes this convergence of science and religion and spirituality" (p. 214).

Jane is also forthright about her feelings about death. Doug's last paragraph reflects his hope that Jane would be strong enough to be with us for many more years:

> And I also knew that there would be a day when she would begin her next great adventure, binoculars and notebook at the ready. And that the indomitable human spirit in all of us would finish what she could not.
>
> (p. 223)

Grande, R. (2018). *A Dream Called Home*. New York: Atria Books. Reyna's parents left her in the care of her grandmother in Mexico when they entered the United States. At age 9, she was able to cross the border to reunite with them. But her family was fractured, and Reyna's teenage years were filled with obstacles. She used writing as a coping strategy and as a way to obtain her goals.

But we learn that background later. Reyna begins her memoir as she is heading to Santa Cruz for college, having chosen a creative writing major. There were so many things she had to negotiate alone. She watched other students being dropped off by parents; others who knew where and how to get food, to buy books, to make friends, and to endure classes where teachers demeaned her by not even trying to pronounce her name correctly. Every time she mastered some aspect of college, a new challenge would arrive. She rescued her younger sister Betty from trouble by bringing her to Santa Cruz, trying to support them both and serve in a guardian role to a teenager who did not appreciate the value of school as Reyna did.

In subsequent chapters, we follow Reyna as she makes mistakes, finds mentors, works amazingly hard, and triumphs. She graduates; she writes; she takes on various jobs, including teaching, to provide a good life for her baby, whom she is raising as a single mother. She falls in love. She shows integrity, refusing to sell her first book manuscript to a publisher who wants her to change her protagonist from a Mexican immigrant to a U.S.-born Latina. No!

Like many immigrants, for years Reyna felt neither fully Mexican nor fully American, resting uncomfortably somewhere between those identities. Yet she found a new way of looking at the situation. When she told her Spanish professor after a visit to Mexico that people treated her as not Mexican enough, her teacher explained, "'If they treat you differently in Mexico it is because you *are* different…. You are now bilingual, bicultural, and binational. You are not less. You are more'" (p. 96). Throughout the memoir, we see a reflective, determined woman who continues to develop her multiple identities, not the least of which is that of an author.

*Grant, A. (2021). *Think Again: The Power of Knowing What You Don't Know*. New York: Random House.

People experiencing a mid-life crisis could find this book very helpful; it gives guidance for self-assessment and advice for making decisions and changing the course of career or life paths in order to grow and become more skilled at sustaining strong interpersonal relationships; more open to listening to others' opinions and influencing the thinking of others; and better able to build cultures of learning at work. If New Adults read the text and heed Grant's message, maybe they can avoid some of the typical pitfalls the author describes.

Grant explains that many young people, unwilling to accept uncertainty about who they want to become, commit to a career path too early, without having explored options and listened to mentors. "I've noticed that the students who are the most certain about their career plans at twenty are often the ones with the deepest regrets by thirty. They haven't done enough rethinking along the way" (p. 331).

Many of the tips Grant offers, such as replacing the pursuit of happiness with the pursuit of meaning and the pursuit of joy, are accompanied by stories of people he's worked with who serve as examples. Then, he offers thirty succinct practical takeaways at the end of the book. I'll list a few that I think are especially good for New Adults:

- "Think like a scientist" (p. 355)
- "Beware of getting stranded at the summit of Mount Stupid" (p. 356)
- "Learn something new from each person you meet" (p. 357)
- "Don't shy away from constructive conflict" (p. 358)
- "Throw out the ten-year plan" (p. 363)

There is great value in knowing what we don't know. It's the first step that lets us think again, and become better because of it.

Green, J. (2021). *The Anthropocene Reviewed: Essays on a Human-Centered Planet*. New York: Dutton.

Many of the essays in this collection will speak to a NA audience. Fans of John Green who have read his novels during their adolescence; seen the movie adaptations of his novels *The Fault in Our Stars* (2012) and *Paper Towns* (2008); supplemented their high school curricular courses with his Crash Courses; or followed him via podcast or vlog will love the background stories and discussion of his writing process that he provides. He is very open about past and present relationships, as well as struggles with OCD, anxiety, and depression. He shares opinions on art, nature, travel, technology, and music. There is no question he is a master storyteller, whether the genre is fiction or nonfiction.

Apprentice writers can choose almost any essay to serve as a mentor text. After reading "Super Mario Kart," they could write a review of their favorite video game. They can give their expert opinion of an app in response to John's take on "The Notes App." "Piggly Wiggly" could inspire them to look critically at and then review a small independent store, or a mammoth store that is part of a chain. After reading "Sunsets," they could add their personal creations to the ongoing body of poems, essays, photographs, paintings, and stories about the sun or another aspect of nature. They can enjoy John's personal thoughts on *Penguins of Madagascar* and *Harvey*, then write about personal connections to movies, especially ones they have watched multiple times.

The Postscript, as well as the book as a whole, deals with essential questions about the meaning of life and our purpose in the grand scheme of things. John ponders:

I have tried here to map some of the places where my little life brushes up against the big forces shaping contemporary human experience, but the only conclusion I can draw is a simple one: We are so small, and so frail, so gloriously and terrifyingly temporary.... I will, sooner or later, be the everything that is part of everything else. But until then: What an astonishment to breathe on this breathing planet. What a blessing to be Earth loving Earth.

(pp. 273–274)

Haig, M. (2020). *The Midnight Library*. New York: Viking.
Sometimes we make big decisions, or big mistakes, that impact our futures in ways we can't reverse. We may wonder what might have happened had we reacted to a situation in a different way, or chosen a different path from the one we are now on. When Nora Seed tries to end her seemingly unfulfilled and unfulfilling life, she finds herself in the Midnight Library, a place where she can/must enter alternative universes where she discovers how her life and those of others unfold after she chooses different options from the ones in the life she has just departed from. Time after time, she finds disappointment, disillusionment, and insights that send her back to the library of possibilities. Through these experiences, she discovers that she does indeed want to live—in fact, passionately so. But is it too late? Has one drastic decision made it impossible to try her former life again, this time with a more positive attitude and with grace?

Readers will perhaps find hope and resolve as they travel—by means of the strange books in the Midnight Library—with Nora to the potential lives she tries on. If they use their imaginations as they read, they may recognize that the life they are in is filled with possibilities as well as challenges, and that they have the strength and determination to deal with the situations they cannot change, while working toward righting wrongs and making life better for themselves and others in creative ways. That's the value of living other lives through literature.

Higuera, D.B. (2021). *The Last Cuentista*. Hoboken, NJ: Levine Querido.
Many of the books we've explored feature people who are looking ahead to a near future, and stepping into an exciting, but perhaps

uncertain future, filled with possibilities and challenges. Petra is facing a far more distant future. The story begins as she and her family are boarding a spaceship in 2061, about to leave Earth, which they know will be hit by a comet the next day. They are heading for the distant planet Sagan, which they will reach in 480 years, where they will be revived after their long "nap," or period of induced stasis.

Petra is indeed revived, but all is not as she had been promised. Petra and readers recognize the signs of a dystopia. The ship has been taken over by the Collective, and the new arrivals have been reprogrammed. Feelings are gone, everything is fake, and Petra must pretend that she has become the new version of herself that the leaders have tried to form. She discovers evidence that her parents and brothers have been "purged," and she knows that if humanity is to survive, she must resist the Collective, escape with other children, and help them recover their memories and identities through her storytelling. A monumental task.

The Last Cuentista is science fiction that offers ethical dilemmas at every turn. Readers will be actively trying to solve mysteries and technical problems, while cheering when Petra succeeds in tricking the leaders and grieving with her when she is betrayed. They will appreciate the value of books (virtually wiped out in this colony) and of freedom of thought (considered most dangerous to the regime). Their hearts will be pounding with suspense, and yearning for the return of love. The author, like the protagonist, works wonders through storytelling.

*Hugstad, R. (2021). *Be You, Only Better: Real-life Self-care for Young Adults (and Everyone Else)*. Novato, CA: New World Library.
Readers who pick this book up at a time they are open to suggestions for improving their physical, emotional, social, and/or financial health will find that the author comes at these things from a number of directions. She presents scenarios of young people who have struggled, and then improved, in these areas. She gives the science connected to some of her claims, including that exercise is good for mental health and self-esteem; experiencing nature changes the brain and reduces stress and depression; journaling improves physical health; good sleep can raise exam grades; and nature makes people kinder.

Hugstad, a certified grief recovery specialist and credentialed health educator, provides practical tips and exercises, such as using a daily planner and keeping a log of sugar consumed each day, which readers can begin to work on immediately. After sharing a chart showing the effects of drinking a can of cola, she adds, "Now, if you replace the cola with your favorite energy drink, you multiply the harmful effects by two or three times" (p. 57). She suggests soda water with a bit of juice and a lemon slice or flavored carbonated water instead.

Chapters deal with relationships, exercise, time management, money management, being mindful and grateful, and embracing and enhancing hope. Hugstad both encourages readers to be willing to ask for help when needed and provides mental health resources. Her final thoughts include asking readers to be appreciative of all that they encounter, and also grateful for themselves:

> As much as this book is about making changes, it is also about making room for self-acceptance. It may seem like a paradox: In order to change, you must accept the person you are. But like most paradoxes, it is true. As the title of the book suggests, *Be You*.
>
> (p. 136)

Lewis, S. (2014). *The Rise: Creativity, the Gift of Failure, and the Search for Mastery*. New York: Simon & Schuster.

Youths making the transition from the teen years to adulthood often tend to feel confused about the choices facing them and afraid about making mistakes. What if they fail? *The Rise* is here to assure them that, not only will the sky not fall, but the failures could actually lead to success later on. Failure can be good for us. How reassuring!

Lewis makes the claim, "Many of our most iconic endeavors—from Nobel-prize winning discoveries to entrepreneurial invention, classic works of literature, dance, and visual arts—were in fact not achievements, but conversions, corrections..." (p. 8). Stories throughout the chapters demonstrate her point. The near-win in Olympic competitions, vulnerability in the presence of pain, being patient with incompleteness, surrendering to forces we can't conquer, all get a positive spin in *The Rise*.

In a chapter titled "Deliberate Amateur," Lewis tells of two physicists who initiated "Friday Night Experiments" in their lab, where scientists and students can work on outlandish ideas that the academic world might deem foolish with freedom from criticism or rules. At times these wild explorations have led to scientific breakthroughs.

Readers may choose to embrace the concept of "radical play" (p. 157) promoted in this book, and be happier, maybe even successful, because of it.

*Man, C. (2021). *Continuum*. New York: Penguin Workshop.
Remember the "Who Are You?" activity way back in Chapter 1? That reminded us that none of us is a single, unchanging identity. We describe ourselves differently depending on the context, our purpose, and our audience. Chella Man, 21 years old at the time of writing this memoir, reflects on his multiple identities as Chinese, Jewish, pansexual, Deaf, and genderqueer. He shares experiences throughout his school years, often uncomfortable or hurtful, that helped him understand various aspects of his authentic self in relationship to others. Social media sites helped him find communities and cultures that made him realize he was not alone, that he could fit in, and that offered hope.

When the author was accepted at Parsons School of Design through an early admittance program, he was able to skip his senior year of high school and move to New York City, where "Trans individuals were not mythical but real people I could befriend" (p. 43). He attended art events for the Deaf community, and he began to heal. "I belonged here, a place where people rejected the limitations of binaries" (p. 44). We readers may benefit from Chella's lens of a continuum to look at his past, present, and future. We can join him in a process of what he calls endless discovery, for our stories, like his, are "far from over" (p. 62).

*Paulsen, G. (2021). *Gone to the Woods: Surviving a Lost Childhood*. New York: Farrar, Straus Giroux.
The very young boy sang in Chicago bars to the amusement of men interested in his mother. Then, as a 5-year-old, the boy traveled by himself on a train to Minneapolis, where he met and stayed with his aunt and uncle, who provided love and stability, and introduced him to the wonders of nature. Then, his mother came and took him away, to the Philippine Islands.

Gary Paulsen writes this memoir in the third person, describing numerous traumatic episodes during the boy's childhood and adolescence. At 13, the boy plans to run away from the home where rats in the basement would beg for pieces of his jellied toast, and from the school where he cannot fit in and where his outside troubles make study impossible. But he stays, because he has found a safe place—the library—and a safe person—the librarian. "The library was how and where and when he came to learn things" (p. 276). The librarian gives him a library card, and he reads books and talks with her. And he writes for her.

There's more to the memoir, including information about the boy's years in the army, but it is the stories relating to the library that readers can directly connect to Gary Paulsen becoming the prolific writer of the now classic *Hatchet* and more than 200 other books, many with nature themes. (Interestingly, Paulsen chooses not to talk about his life as a writer of children's literature here; there is no Author's Note at the end.) He mentions his "Eighty glorious years absolutely packed with life" (p. 357). Readers can study his literary oeuvre as well as interviews, speeches, and other resources to fill in details of the years after the boy becomes the man. The exploration will be well worth it.

*Sullivan, M., & Blaschko, P. (2022). *The Good Life Method: Reasoning through the Big Questions of Happiness, Faith, and Meaning*. New York: Penguin Press.

"Socrates is always up for a conversation, no matter the hour" (p. 262). The professors who authored this book encourage readers who are looking for answers to life's big questions to turn to the ancient Greek philosophers. They aim to demonstrate how Plato, Aristotle, and others are relevant to the issues we face today and can help us both formulate and meet goals.

Sullivan and Blaschko invite readers to ask questions such as the following:

How should I allocate my money and time?....
How do I balance learning, working, family, friendships?....
Where do I stand on politics and community life?....
What will I worship, and why?
What will I do when the people I love suffer and die?
Why am I confident that all of this will be meaningful in the end?

Then they show how several philosophers navigated those questions and guided others in the search for what is right, good, and beautiful. The five chapters of the first part focus on desiring the truth, living generously, taking responsibility, integrity in terms of work, and loving attentively. Readers who wish can move on to the second part of the book, "God and the Good Life," to explore matters of faith, religion, and spirituality. The book is designed to be interactive, calling for response at intervals within the book. New Adults may feel supported on their paths knowing the companions traveling with them have the wisdom of centuries.

*Whitney, D. (Ed.). (2021). *You Don't Have to Be Everything: Poems for Girls Becoming Themselves*. Illus. González, C., Mockford, K., & Singleton, S. New York: Workman Publishing.

You'll recall the text set in Chapter 4 that included books with *becoming* in their titles. The theme continues here. The editor explains that when she envisioned an anthology of poems for young people, she looked for the voices she wished she had as a youth. "Strong voices, lonely voices, angry, elated, or curious ones. Voices from the LGBTQ+ community, turning their experiences into song" (p. 2). She groups poems thematically so that readers can choose to explore the feeling they need or want or are experiencing at a particular time, whether that be rage, loneliness, shame, attitude, sadness, longing, seeking, or belonging. The artwork invites readers to immerse themselves through different modalities. Readers (not just girls) may well read the descriptions of the poets at the end, and decide to pursue more texts by the poets who touched them here.

Sample Course Outline and Syllabus for a Course on New Adult Literature

There are so many ways a course on NA literature could be designed and organized. It will look different depending on the setting, the students, and the instructor's purposes. I taught it as a course for college freshmen during their first semester. Each time it evolved, based on what I learned from student feedback and on current events that affected us during our semester. The following outline is adapted from the latest iteration of the course. I hope you can take what is helpful, and then add, delete, reorganize, choose a different emphasis, select books that are relevant to your students, and make the course your own!

EDU 198: "New Adult" Literature: Exploring Books about Early Adulthood

Course Description and Overview

Description:

Where can readers who loved Young Adult literature as teens turn for pleasure reading as they leave adolescence behind? "New Adult" literature targets an audience ranging from about 17 to 25 years old. We'll meet characters negotiating academic and social aspects of college life; exploring intellectual passions and careers; forging new relationships; accepting challenges; and constructing a future. We'll read biographical texts and memoirs focusing on the early years of famous people, as well as informational texts about approaching the age of "twenty-something."

Overview:

A major part of this class will involve reading NA books (about a dozen) and participating in book discussions. Sometimes we will all read the same text and meet in one group. At other times, you will choose books from a selection I offer, and meet in smaller groups with other people who read the same book.

It is essential that you keep up with the reading and keep a reader's notebook/online conversation journal. I do not want you to summarize the book in order to prove you read it. Rather, you will examine your thinking as the stories progress, both about the literature itself and about your own reading processes. I will respond to your responses, so we will truly be in conversation.

In place of quizzes, you will respond to some writing and thinking prompts I will regularly provide during our class time. These will be easy to answer if you have read the books and will encourage creativity.

Three areas we will work on developing and enhancing throughout the semester are critical thinking, collaboration, and creativity. The texts will be thought-provoking and will lead naturally to discussion; listening to opinions and reactions different from your own; and sometimes decisions about changing your mind or your actions. There will be multiple opportunities for exploring ideas and responding to literature in personal and innovative ways, such as through artwork, fanfiction, and media production.

This course is intended to be an integral part of your acclimation to college life. You will discover places on campus (e.g., the university library) and off-campus (e.g., our town's independent bookstore) where reading and collaborative response to text are central to their missions. And you will become a part of a large and lively literary landscape.

Course Objectives

As a result of taking this course, you will be able to:

1. Define "New Adult literature" and explain several characteristics of the category.
2. Engage with literature targeted at readers in their late teens and early 20s, and respond in a free, thoughtful manner.
3. Engage with literature by diverse authors, and with texts dealing with social justice and issues related to diversity.
4. Be aware of your own reading processes and ways of responding to literature, and be able to explain those to others.
5. Discuss literature in a book club setting, and listen to other readers as they offer responses to texts and talk about themselves in relation to reading.
6. Respond creatively to literature by producing artwork; writing fanfiction or poetry; or using technology to produce media such as book trailers or video book-talking sites.
7. Participate in campus and community activities that relate to the topics we are exploring in our course.
8. Demonstrate increased reading stamina over the course of the semester.
9. Reflect on your growth and changes in reading over the course of the semester, and set clear goals for future reading development, for academic purposes, and for pleasure and personal satisfaction.

Required Texts and Materials

This is a literature-based course, so you will be responsible for reading about a dozen trade books. Some we will read as a class. At other times, I will offer options relating to certain themes, and you will choose which book you will read. Some books will be available for purchase in the college bookstore. Others you will be able to obtain through our college library or a public library. You can download library books through apps such as Libby, OverDrive, or Hoopla. At times, I will have copies available for borrowing. I will let you know which books will be due two to three weeks ahead, so that you will have time to find the books you elect to read.

I will put articles and other resources on our online learning site.

Course Outline, Assignments, and Evaluation

1. Ongoing online reading conversation journals (Reader's Notebook), and regular posting in our online Discussion Forums: 50%
2. Attendance and participation: 20%
3. In-class writing and thinking prompts: 10%
4. Exploring and engaging in campus activities and community activities, with reflections about your experiences, perhaps connecting them to themes in our course: 10%
5. Final paper: Synthesis, application, evaluation, and new goals related to pleasure reading and academic success: 10%

Important Policies and Notes

Attendance is mandatory, because your contributions are needed and much of your learning and growth will come from your interaction with your peers. This is an action-based course, and you will be expected to come to class prepared, and to participate. Plan on coming to every class. If you should *have* to miss a class, please let me know in advance if possible, and we will create a synchronous or asynchronous alternative.

Field Trips: You will be asked to explore places on campus (including the lake, the nature center, and the library; and off-campus (the independent bookstore, and nearby historic sites).

Weekly Schedule with Readings and Assignment Due Dates (**Subject to Change, with Notice**)

(NOTE: I will supply author names and bibliographic information for the required and suggested titles in class.)

Week One: **August 24**: Introduction. Book Trailer for *Fangirl*. Louise Rosenblatt and transactional theory. Metacognition. Introductions, including your favorite book or genre. International Dot Day activity. Begin literary autobiography. (Drafts will be shared and discussed on August 31.)

Homework for August 26: *Fangirl*, Chapters 1–9. Read and respond.

Homework for Next Week: Read *Fangirl* Chapters 10–27 for Tuesday; finish *Fangirl* for Thursday. Submit reading autobiography by September 2.

Week Two: **August 31, September 2**: Discuss *Fangirl* chapters. Be ready for a writing and thinking prompt (quiz replacement). Follow up with introductions and samples from *Carry On* and *Wayward Son*. Speeches, etc. Look back at the paths we took to get to college. Investigate peritext and epitext of *Fangirl*.

Homework for next week: Read and respond to *We Are Okay* for Thursday. Post your response online.

Week Three: **September 9**. Book circle, plus exploration of mental health resources, and other NA books dealing with mental health issues, including anxiety, depression, grief, and other social-emotional learning (SEL) issues in college.

Homework for Next Week: Read and respond to *Love from A to Z* for Tuesday. Post on International Dot Day online Discussion Forum by September 15.

Week Four: **September 14**. Happy International Dot Day! Discussion of *Love from A to Z*. Check out National Book Award Longlist in mid-September. Introduction of the theme of love/romance.

Homework for Next Week: Read a book about paths to/preparing for college: Choices include *The Impossible Knife of Memory; Sigh, Gone; Charming as a Verb; Piper Perish; Time of our Lives*. 2/3 by Tuesday, finish by Thursday.

Week Five: September 21, 23. Literature circles about ending high school/college prep selections.

Homework for Next Week: Focus on careers, identity, service, and finding meaning in work. Read a book from among the following *Wine Girl, Becoming Maria, More Myself: A Journey, Sylvie, With the Fire on High*. Alternative: find a NA novel or an informational trade book relating to a career or other life/work path you are interested in pursuing after high school or college.

Week Six: September 28, 30. Career theme Book circles.

Homework for Next Week: Prepare for Indigenous People's Day: *Braiding Sweetgrass; Firekeeper's Daughter; There, There; The Round House; Apple: Skin to the Core; Indigenous History of the U.S.* (2/3 for Tuesday, finish for Thursday).

Week Seven: **October 5, 7**. Book Circles; explore environmental, ethical, and disciplinary issues. Explore American Indians in Children's Literature website.

Homework for Next Week: Read a Romance-themed book. Choices include *We Contain Multitudes; Juliet Takes a Breath; A Queer History of the U.S., Last Night at the Telegraph Club; Felix Ever After.*

Week Eight: October 12, 14. Happy Ada Lovelace Day! Book Circles on Romance. Explore author speeches, etc.

NOTE: I am purposely leaving the next few weeks' texts and activities **tentative** or undecided. By the middle of the semester, I will know you better; and, with your input, I can determine what texts will be most relevant, meaningful, and helpful to you.

Homework for Next Week: Social Justice / Activism Theme. Options may include *White Rose, We Will Not Be Silent, The Boy who Dared, March Book 3, The Boys who Challenged Hitler. The Lightning Dreamer: Cuba's Greatest Abolitionist. The Plot to Kill Hitler/Faithful Spy. Kamala Harris: Rooted in Justice, Stamped: Racism, Anti-racism, and You.*

Week Nine: October 19, 21. Nonfiction. The activism theme continued. Perform *Undefeated*, by Kwame Alexander and Kadir Nelson.

Homework for Next Week: Biographies (some fictionalized) and memoirs in verse. Choose from among *Shout* (Laurie Halse Anderson), *Soaring Earth, Brown Girl Dreaming, Loving vs. Virginia*, and *With a Star in my Hands.*

Week Ten: October 26, 28. Lives told in poetry.

Homework for Next Week: Memoirs and Biographies in graphic novel format: Possible options will include *Primates; Feynman; March/Run; Nellie Bly; Flawed; Dancing at the Pity Party; They Called Us Enemy; Gender Queer.*

Week Eleven: November 2, 4. Biographies: Life in pictures.

Homework for Next Week: NA Historical Fiction: Select from the following: *Blood Water Paint, Copper Sun, Butterfly Yellow.*

Week Twelve: November 9, 11. History through literature featuring New Adults.

Homework for Next Week: Theme: Caring for our Environment. Choices include *The Book of Hope, The Story of More, Earth Squad, and How to Change Everything.* Work on final synthesis and reflection.

Week Thirteen: November 16, 18. Our beautiful world! How will we make it better?

November 23: We will not meet today, but you can use the time to visit the independent bookstore downtown and/or a local historic site or museum if you haven't already. Report on your visits to community places due November 30.

Homework for the Final Week: Whole class read: *Far from the Tree*, by Robin Benway. Finish final paper or project.

Week 14: November 30, December 2. Share and celebrate our success as readers. Book talks for pleasure reading over semester break.

....

Guidelines for Final Assignment: Synthesis, application, evaluation, and new goals related to pleasure reading and academic success.

- Plan on three to five pages, depending on how you space and configure margins.
- Start now. It is not a good idea to wait for the night before it is due to begin. If you jot down key ideas or an outline soon, the ideas will be incubating over the holidays. Give yourself a deadline for a draft—maybe right before Thanksgiving, or right after. You might talk with family members or friends at home, and find that you are developing and deepening your thoughts and you will have new things to add to your draft.
- Think about who your audience will be. I will be reading it, but I don't have to be the main audience you wish to address. You could write to yourself (either your present self, or the self you were as a high school senior, with your initial college goals in mind); you could write to your parents or guardians, or a younger sibling. You could write to your EDU 198 classmates.
- Use all your previous writing for this course as data to analyze. It might surprise you to look over what you were writing in September. The answers to the prompts and your responses to the books will give you information about yourself as a reader.
- You can ask yourself questions: How would I describe myself as a reader? Am I a different reader than I was in high school? How am I reading in my other classes? What did each book teach me? What did some characters teach me?
- Reflect on your academic, social, and/or personal growth over the semester. Were there surprises waiting for you in the dorm, in classrooms, and in natural surroundings? Do you know yourself better than you did in August? Is your world larger?

- Look forward. How will your new knowledge or skills or identity influence the path ahead? What goals (or New Year's Resolutions) will you set? What changes will you put into place to assure those goals will be met? What role, if any, will pleasure reading play in your life during the semester break, or over a longer period? What genres or authors do you want to pursue? What would you like to read that relates to the field of study (major) you are pursuing?
- You do not have to answer all these questions, and you can craft your paper any way you want. You have a lot of freedom. But it is an academic paper, so you should revise, edit, and proofread. Ask someone else to proofread, also. This would be a great opportunity to work with someone in the Writing Center. (You might be a part of the center as a tutor in the future.) The Writing Center is not a place for remedial writing. Tutors there deal with substantive issues in all kinds and levels of writing.

Conclusion

After reading the previous seven chapters, do you have a list of books that you hope to read in the near future? I hope that list is long, and that it continues to grow. I can't think of a better way to conclude than by offering two final book talks, one fiction and one nonfiction, that are about the power and pleasure of reading and books. So here is my parting gift.

Adams, S.N. (2021). *The Reading List*. New York: William Morrow.

Two of our characters sit firmly in the NA range. Aleisha, nearing the end of high school and hoping to be a lawyer someday, has taken a summer job in a quiet branch library. Her brother Aiden, in his mid-20s, has stopped his studies to take care of his mother, an artist who is housebound and mostly in bed due to what seems to be severe depression and anxiety. Aiden and Aleisha work opposite shifts so that their mother is never alone. It is exhausting, difficult, and painful for all of them.

Then there is Mukesh, who is also suffering. His beloved wife Naina was taken from him by cancer a couple of years ago. He searches for ways to stay connected and close to her, to listen for her, and to let her know how much he misses her. He finds comfort in reading the book he finds under their bed, *The Time Traveler's Wife* (2014). His three daughters are worried about him. His granddaughter Priya, who is an avid reader like Naina was but Mukesh is *not*, is a mystery to him.

Enter the Reading List. It falls out of a book at the library, and Aleisha, not being a reader herself, recommends the titles to Mukesh, one at a time in the order they appear. As the two of them read and communicate, they form not only an unintended book club, but a friendship. The books help each of them navigate tough situations and deep feelings. Unbeknownst to them, other people are finding the same list and getting satisfaction and wisdom from the novels.

When tragedy occurs, Aleisha blames herself; she has spent the summer caring about fictional characters, "... living other people's lives" (p. 319) while ignoring warning signs from the real people who depended on her! It is Mukesh who helps her get beyond this. "Please try to remember that books aren't always an escape; sometimes books teach us things. They *show* us the world; they don't hide it" (p. 319). The events in this story demonstrate this wisdom in concrete ways.

I invite you to pick up *The Reading List* to find out which eight titles were able to work their magic as various characters brought themselves to the stories and made them their own. You can also read the author's list of ten books that affected her thinking about people, writing, and the world. She explains,

> These books found me at just the right time in my life. I remember the characters as though they were friends, sometimes even family, I can remember exactly where I was and how I felt when I turned that final page. They've stayed with me ever since.
>
> (p. 369)

Aleisha and Mukesh would understand.

Writing and Thinking Prompts

Choose Option A or B:

A. Can you think of books that have affected you, by comforting you, giving you pleasure, increasing your understanding of people or the world, or changing the way you think and choose to act? Can you think of books that you believe would help specific people you know to benefit in certain ways? Reflect on these books, and/ or make a list of books that you might offer others, or leave in the back of some library books to be found by future readers.

B. Perhaps you are more like Mukesh and Aleisha were at the beginning, not really understanding what others saw in reading, wondering why people would choose to spend their time with characters who are no more than words on a page, invented by authors' imaginations. Ask some readers you know to talk with you about how books have changed them and what books they would recommend to others. Then make a list of books you've heard or read about that you might like to try. May the right books find you at the right time!

Kakutani, M. (2020). *Ex Libris: 100+ Books to Read and Reread*. New York: Clarkson Potter.

Let's assume that the books talked about in the previous chapters, along with others you recommend, have worked their magic, and the New Adults you work with now love reading for pleasure and want more suggestions for books they can both enjoy and learn from. They want classics; they want contemporary; they want all genres; they want diverse authors and characters. *Ex Libris* will keep them occupied for a long time. The author dedicates her collection of book musings "For Readers and Writers Everywhere." There are two- to three-page essays on books by or about Muhammad Ali and Abraham Lincoln; and selected texts by Joan Didion, Oliver Sacks, Toni Morrison, Barack Obama, Salman Rushdie, Dr. Seuss, and Vladimir Nabokov. Sometimes her essays bring together different books on particular topics or issues, such as work and vocations; democracy and tyranny; 9/11 and the War on Terror. There are plenty of discussions of single books, including Madeleine L'Engle's *A Wrinkle in Time*, Gabriel García Marquéz's *One Hundred Years of Solitude*, Tommy Orange's *There, There*, and Trevor Noah's *Born a Crime*. I've just given you a taste of the variety of treasures within these pages.

Kakutani wonders why we love books so much, and then answers her own question by describing books as tiny time machines:

> that can transport us back to the past to learn the lessons of history, and forward to idealized or dystopian futures. Books can transport us to distant parts of the globe... They give us the stories of men and women we will never meet in person, illuminate the discoveries made by great minds.... introduce us to

beliefs, ideas, and literatures different from our own. And they can whisk us off to fictional realms like Oz and Middle-earth, Narnia and Wonderland, and the place where Max becomes king of the wild things.

(p. 14)

Are we all on board?

Final Words of Farewell

Jane Goodall opened this chapter. I think she would be happy to let Greta Thunberg close our chapter, as well as our book. (I use the plural pronoun because now that you have interacted with the book, it belongs to you, too.) Let's all take Greta's words to heart: "We Are the Change, and Change is Coming" (2019, p. 100).

References

Goodall, J., & Abrams, D., with Hudson, G. (2021). *The book of hope: A survival guide for trying times*. New York: Celadon Books.

King. A.S., and the Book Love Foundation. *Gracie's list*. Retrieved from https://www.booklovefoundation.org/_files/ugd/f8eddb_306553e662ca4093aa7489a3083084a2.pdf.

Thunberg, G. (2019). *No one is too small to make a difference*. New York: Penguin.

Literature Cited

Green, J. (2012). *The fault in our stars*. New York: Dutton Books.

Green, J. (2008). *Paper towns*. New York: Dutton Books.

Montgomery, S. (2012). *Temple Grandin: How the girl who loved cows embraced autism and changed the world*. Boston. MA: Houghton Mifflin.

Niffeneggar, A. (2014). *The time traveler's wife*. New York: Scribner.

Index

For Product Safety Concerns and Information please contact our EU
representative GPSR@taylorandfrancis.com
Taylor & Francis Verlag GmbH, Kaufingerstraße 24, 80331 München, Germany